MURDER AND DESIRE IN ORANGE BEACH

TAMI RYAN &
JIM CAVANAUGH

We dedicate this book to all those who have suffered from violent crime and to all those Law Enforcement Professionals who protect us from it.

We also acknowledge all who love the beaches and oceans of the world and strive to make those places peaceful and safe places to enjoy.

TABLE OF CONTENTS

MURDER AND
DESIRE IN
ORANGE BEACH

ACKNOWLEDGEMENTS

Copyright © 2024 LM Authors
Tami Ryan and Jim Cavanaugh
Cover design by pro_ebooks
Front cover picture by Tami Ryan & Jim Cavanaugh
First edition

Edited by Emily Lisa from Fiverr who did an excellent professional edit.
We would also like to thank Debbie Thom for her proofreading the manuscript.

NOTICE

1

PROLOGUE

As she opened the door and stepped out onto the balcony, the rifle shot cracked, and the sound was masked by the fireworks finale. It slammed the woman back through the sliding glass door. Her life fizzled out as if it was part of the show. A second before, she was on the balcony crying since her lover failed to show up. The killer had waited for a few hours. Across the water secreted in a boat. The killer had carefully planned the murder and had watched the woman's condo before. It was the small tourist city of Orange Beach, Alabama. Not a common place for violent death. It is an inexpressibly idyllic beach community where even the police cars had a motto written on the side: "Protecting Paradise."

The killer had carefully sighted the Remington .308 caliber bolt action rifle through a Vortex scope with deadly patience. The killer cleverly used the cover of the fireworks show to mask the rifle's report. The distance was about 200 yards, and the victim was on the balcony overlooking the Perdido Pass. Because the shot would have an upward trajectory, the killer had fashioned a perch inside the boat, facing the stern. The killer was sitting on the floor inside the boat's cabin with the barrel of the rifle elevated, pointing out the cabin door. The killer wore eye and ear protection as the rifle shot inside the cabin would be extremely loud. The killer had to adjust to the slow movement of the boat. Standing and shooting from a solid surface was easy. Shooting from even a gently swaying boat was another matter.

The water here was shallow and still. The bow was nestled against the sandy beach of a tiny island called Bird Island. This gave the boat the needed stability to take a long shot. The first projectile exited the barrel at more than 3000 feet per second and spun like a flying drill bit, narrowly missing the woman. At that millisecond, she heard something fly past her ear. By the time she could think *What was that?* The second .308 caliber round was already inbound and struck her right in the X-ring, as shooters say, directly into her heart. Whatever sins the woman committed did not deserve this type of ending. Inside the boat, the killer's veins ran full of ice water, a creature devoid of any feeling this was just a task. At the moment, the community's attention was focused on the fireworks show. Small boats filled the Perdido Pass, anchored to watch the festivities. Once the killer's goal was achieved, the rifle was carefully packed into a case. The rifle stand was dismantled in less than a minute. The killer removed their shooting gloves and eye and ear protection. All packed up carefully in a metal box. The killer took off a set of coveralls and placed them in the metal box as well. The killer jumped out of the boat, pushed the bow off the sandy beach, and climbed back in by the stern ladder. The anchor was then pulled up. The lone figure, wet from the waist down, started the engine and slowly headed out into the Gulf of Mexico. Once clear of the beach, the killer went straight out for three nautical miles. The gulf was pitch black. Only the lights from the high-rise condos on the beach and a distant vessel were visible. The killer stopped the boat and let the engine idle. The long rifle in the case was then dropped overboard. The heavy metal box was then wrestled onto the starboard gunwale and pushed over the side. They both disappeared into the black depths. The killer then turned around and headed back to shore.

The killer had been scoping out the intended target for days. Watching the comings and goings through a pair of binoculars. Watching the marina for the perfect spot to anchor. After all, there would be a record number of boats there to watch the fireworks. This had worked well to the killer's advantage. Noise from the fireworks display, people screaming and cheering. Lent itself for the perfect setting and now the slender cord of life was snapped.

For the killer's target, it had been a long day. It has been several long days, to be exact. Things at work were crazy busy. So many issues and meetings. Trying to keep everyone focused and on the same page. She did not want to go to work today being it is the 4th of July, but she had a few ends to tie up and wanted them off her plate for the rest of the weekend. She planned on celebrating and not thinking about work at all. She was excited for the long weekend. Time to relax, breathe, and forget about work. She had a late date, watching fireworks from her balcony that overlooked the marina. It was the perfect view. Above the crowd, she could watch all the boats jockey for a spot to watch the fireworks. Her date would not be arriving until about 7:00 p.m., so she had plenty of time to relax and get ready. She kicks off her shoes and pours a glass of wine. She turns on some music, settles in on the couch, and relaxes. She starts thinking about the evening and how spectacular it is going to be. She had gotten a light pink teddy and matching panties that she was anxious to wear tonight. She was going to pull out all the stops. She wanted this relationship to go to the next level. It had stalled and her lover was holding back, not wanting to make any sort of commitment. She cannot figure out why. Tonight, will be the deciding factor. They have been seeing each other for years. Well, more like sleeping with each other for years. At first, she was OK with it, thinking he would come around, but he hasn't. She is tired of being just a sex buddy and nothing more. She wants more, and tonight, the gangster in her will give him an offer she hopes he cannot refuse. *We will be a couple or no more casual sex,* she tells herself. However that played out, she was ready for it. She finished her wine and headed for the shower. She had laid her new teddy out on the bed. Thoughts of answering the door wearing nothing but this skimpy teddy sent tingles through her body. She was already getting aroused at the thought of his expression when she opened the door. She is going to keep that arousal going. Hopefully, when he sees her, he will be instantly excited and waste no time. He will be able to tell that she has been thinking about him and waiting for him to be inside her. All this thinking about making love has caused her to take matters into her own hands. She jumps into the shower, leans against the side, and lets her fantasy begin. It did not take long, that is for sure. Later tonight, when they are making love, her willingness will be out of control. This one is just for relaxation. Finishing up her shower, wearing just the lightest of makeup, and putting on her teddy and panties, she looks at herself in the mirror. She is a beautiful girl. Gorgeous, perky breasts with a well-tanned, slender body. She pours herself another glass of wine. Her lover should be here any moment. She is excited and concerned at the same time. The sex is going to be amazing, but the conversation about being a couple might not go so well. An hour passes and he still has not arrived. It's the 4th of July and he's probably stuck in traffic. Another hour passes and still a no-show. She is no longer worried. She is angry. How could he do this to her? He has stood her up before but tonight he told her things were going to be amazing. Why had he lied to her again? Why was she putting up with this disrespect? Because she was in love with him. Love makes you do stupid things. Well, I guess this decides whether or not they will be a couple. His not showing up just shows her how much he does not care about her or her feelings. Decision made. She starts to weep for herself and the time she has put into getting this man to love her. She pours the last of the wine into her glass and decides to go out to her balcony and watch the last of the fireworks. Teddy and all. She doesn't care who sees her.

It had been a clear, beautiful summer night with a Thunder moon. It was a great night for fireworks and a perfect night for murder.

2

RANDI REYNOLDS

A FEW YEARS EARLIER.

It's a beautiful, sunny, warm summer day in Orange Beach, Alabama. Randi is sitting on her front porch enjoying the sunshine. She loves this time of day. Early morning before the sun gets too hot. She loves her house. She has it decorated with a very modern design. A lot of black and white. Glass and metal. Her artwork is mostly black and white and grays, but now and then, a picture with a brilliant splash of color hits you like a train. Her décor is where her color comes from. It's the warm colors of the coast, pale greens, blues, subdued orange, and yellow. The colors are limited, so they stand out. She loves the simplicity of life. Her home is not overdone with larger-than-life pictures and giant furniture that is too big for the space. Looking at her place is like looking at a design magazine.

As she sits enjoying her Latte', she thinks about how she got here. Her hard work, her upper midwestern work ethic, the ups and downs, and the pitfalls. Being a real estate agent is not easy. It's very competitive and, at times, can be as cold-hearted as a hooker to a john. Some real estate agents would sell their mother for a dime. Randi figured out very quickly which circles to run in. She figured out where the rich and influential people hung out. Little by little, she was accepted into that circle, and slowly and methodically, she was able to be the real estate agent to many very wealthy people. It did not come easy or overnight. A lot of hard work and a lot of schmoozing, which she didn't care for, but knew she had to do it to get ahead. Fortunately for her, no more schmoozing. Only five years after her move from Pensacola, she has a beautiful house in Orange Beach that is fully paid for, and she runs with the upper crust of Coastal Alabama. It's a far cry from the small farm town in Wisconsin. She grew up about 30 miles west of the Capital of Madison, Wisconsin. Known as the Dairy State and true to form, Randi had grown up on a dairy farm. The Reynolds had a large family farm, and everybody was involved in the operation. Randi's parents, Bill and Diane had four boys and two girls. Up at the crack of dawn to do chores before school, after-school activities (if you were involved) then home, chores, dinner, schoolwork. The whole scenario repeated itself day after day. There were no breaks on the weekends. Everybody knew their role and they performed their duties like clockwork. Her mom took care of the house. A lot of times Randi and her sister helped with getting meals ready. A family of eight and five hungry men meant a lot of food. Randi's mom was an excellent cook and ran the house like a Sergeant. A wonderful loving Sergeant, of course. Randi did her part but knew from a noticeably young age that she would not be following in the family's footsteps and stay on the farm. She had no interest in being a farmer's wife. She had bigger plans and wanted to get out of Wisconsin. It's not that she didn't love her small town: Wisconsin winters could be brutal, and you still had to do chores. You dressed appropriately and out the door you went. Randi had a magnificent home life and an amazing group of friends. She had fun in high school. Basketball games, football, prom, homecoming. Summer nights on the lake with friends and bonfires. Still, for as much as her loving family supported her and her fun teen years, Randi was determined to leave the cold and go someplace where it was warm most of the time. When Randi graduated, she said a tearful goodbye to her close friends and family and headed south. She had spent her senior year looking, discovering, and researching exactly where she wanted to go. No place that was too big or too touristy. After months of planning she settled on Pensacola, Florida. She had applied online to several companies for a job. She didn't care what company it was: she just wanted a job to go to when she got there. She was able to get an administrative job at a real estate agency. She had saved some money and her parents had opened investment accounts for their children, so Randi had a nice chunk of change to make her move to Pensacola easier. Her mother rode to Pensacola with her to make sure she made it safe and helped Randi look for an apartment. Her new boss let her know which neighborhoods to stay away from. Every city has them, and when you move to a new place, you have no idea what those neighborhoods are. She found a great apartment not far from the beach. It was a small one-bedroom in a fairly new building, and she loved the location. Her mom stayed for about a week, helping her get settled, and then flew back to Wisconsin. With tears in her eyes, she says goodbye to her mom. She is not afraid to admit it, but she is nervous. Being 18 years old in a city she knows nothing about and being this far away from her family was a little scary. But she was determined to make a successful life in Pensacola. Whatever that entailed. She found out she loved the real estate business. At times, it could get very hectic. People with lots of money coming to buy fancy top-floor condos and houses on the Gulf Coast. Large bougie homes on stilts dotted the coastline. She was a quick learner, and only after two years at the agency, she did study and earned her real estate license. She was well-liked at work, and they made every effort to help her be successful. After all, if she was successful then her company was successful. A win-win situation. Randi's life in Pensacola had run its course and she was looking for new territory. But after she had been there for 12 years, she wanted something new. She wanted to stay where it was warm and decided to move to Orange Beach, Alabama. She knew the real estate business was starting to boom there and she wanted to be a part of that. She had become successful in Pensacola and several of her high-end clients gave her some people to contact to help her get her foot in the door in Orange Beach. That didn't mean any of these people rolled out the red carpet, but it did help her make new contacts. She still had to work hard and prove herself but after 12 years in the real estate business, she was well-versed on how all that worked. She had to be out constantly. Be where the wealthy were. Eat at the finest places. She was not afraid to introduce herself to anybody. It comes with the nature of the job, so it didn't bother her to sit at the bar by herself and strike up a conversation with anybody. You never know who is looking to buy a house on the beach. She made friends easily and in short order, she had several friends that she hung out with.

She dated a little bit in Pensacola, but her main focus was success, so she never really got too involved with anyone. She wasn't ready. She wanted to go out and have fun. She had only been in her 20's. She did not want to be tied down. She moved to Orange Beach when she was 30 and wanted to be as successful, if not more. Unlike her friends, who had gotten married and had children, Randi was not about that at all. She had no interest in having children. It's not that she didn't like children. They just didn't fit into the life she wanted. She wanted to be on top. She wanted to be wealthy, and she made no bones about that. She was going to do everything she could to get to that level and no one was going to change her mind.

3

JOSH MYERS

Detective Lieutenant Josh Myers has been with the Orange Beach, Alabama Police Department for 18 years, working his way up the ranks. He had done more than his share of traffic stops, DUIs, and arguing with drunks, which never turned out well at all. Domestic issues, robberies, car accidents. He had seen it all. Being a Detective Lieutenant showed him a completely different life. A lot of investigative work. Since his divorce 15 years ago he has thrown himself into his job. The marriage ended amicably, and he remains friendly with his ex-wife. They were unable to have children and Josh believes that played a huge part in the divorce.

Josh grew up in Orange Beach, and he loved the beach. When he was younger, his parents, three brothers, and his sister were at the beach all the time. They were like fish, but their dad always taught them to respect the water. He was adamant about that. If red or purple flags were flying, they were not allowed into the water. They had seen too many drownings due to rip currents. His dad never wavered on the rules of the water. Besides that, they always had a great time. Picnic lunch, large umbrellas to take time out in the sun. Normally by the end of the day, the family was ultimately worn out. As kids, they slept well after long days in the sun and having fun. It was a magical time for Josh, and he looks back on it fondly. His parents are both now deceased. His siblings are scattered across the country, but they try to get together every year in Orange Beach. Josh loves having them there and they sit around and laugh, reminisce, and have several cocktails. Josh grew up in a great tight-knit family and feels blessed every day for the strong work ethic and family pride his parents instilled in him. When he graduated high school, he joined the army. He became a Military Police Officer and an MP. He was highly trained and had been stationed in Clarksville, Tennessee at Fort Campbell, Kentucky. Home of the 101st Airborne Division.

Josh developed a logical mind. He could think and put different pieces of complicated matters together. His strongest trait was leadership. He did not believe that he had to come up with all the answers. He assembled a team, and together, that team came up with the answers to solve a case. Josh encouraged this vibrant process inside the Orange Beach Detective Bureau. However, even larger than that, he utilized his colleagues across law enforcement in the same vein. Josh had learned in the military that strong teamwork was required to be successful. That teamwork went out on the far flanks of any investigation. Josh was able to sit at the helm of an investigation and steer the investigative shop from the ideas, data, and insight of his crew. As a result, he was a very successful Chief of Detectives for the city of Orange Beach.

4

DOCTOR CAMPBELL

Doctor Campbell was a very well-known and respected businessman. He was fair and honest in his business. His integrity was extremely important to him. His parents had always taught him that his integrity was one of the most important things a man can hold on to. He tried extremely hard to do just that. He looked up to his dad, Johnson Roy Campbell. He tried to follow in his dad's footsteps as far as being above board. His dad bought and sold properties. He purchased poor, run-down nasty homes that you wouldn't want to set a foot in. He would buy them from the city, fix them, and re-sell them. He didn't cheap out on the materials, but he didn't buy high-end either. Johnson was smart in what materials to buy, who to buy them from, and who gave him good deals. The houses he bought and fixed up were always done properly. If he hired a new contractor and found out they did shoddy work, he would fire them immediately. Needless to say, everyone knew Johnson Campbell and respected him. You knew if you got a job working on one of his houses, that would propel your business to the next level. Doctor got his start in the property business by working for and with his dad. He learned from the bottom up. He would go with his dad to job sites when he was just a little boy. He would watch his dad as he made sure everything was done properly. His dad never yelled at anyone. He didn't ever seem to get mad. He just told it like it was. His father made it clear what he wanted and how he wanted it done, and if the guys working on the house could not provide that, he would find someone else.

Doctor learned a lot and when he wanted to start his own Land Development Company, his dad was right there to help him get started. His company has been quite successful and has been for years. He was lucky to have his parents alive to see him succeed. Doctor wasn't as lucky in the romance department. He married his college sweetheart Amanda, and they had two daughters, Abigail and Courtney. The marriage fell apart when Courtney was 10. He married his second wife, Candace, at 33 and had a son, Beau, and a daughter, Jamie. That marriage fell apart when Doctor was 50 because he was never home. He believes both marriages fell apart due to his constant work to build the business. The stress on the marriages was just too much, but he finally realized that he was to blame for both failures. To Doctor, his marriages were like the Jimmy Buffet song "Margaritaville." The singer laments that "there is a woman to blame." At first, "it's nobody's fault." Then "it could be my fault," but in the end, "It's my own damn fault."

He put all his time and effort into his business and had very little time for his family. Three of his kids are grown. His youngest daughter has just graduated from college and lives with her mother. Doctor has provided for all his children quite well and he has a good relationship with both ex-wives. Since then, his business has surpassed everything he had hoped for and he now knows he must take time off, relax and have fun.

Doctor lives in a penthouse in one of the tallest buildings in Orange Beach. 10,000 square feet. Five bedrooms, five and a half bathrooms, media room, two huge balconies. One off the living room and the other off the master bedroom. He has everything there that is needed when his children come to stay with him, which is quite often. He has a great relationship with his kids, and he always puts them first when they are visiting. Doctor's penthouse is done in bright beach colors. A lot of sand color, light browns, creams, seafoam green, and pale yellow. The bedrooms are done with very regal furniture. Tall four poster beds, seating areas, and large windows that overlook the coast or the marina. Depending on which side of the penthouse you were on. Each bedroom had its own bathroom and a large-screen TV. Each bedroom was its private oasis. The master bedroom was exquisite. It had a massive king bed with the same grand regal furniture. Oversized chairs, and walk-in closets large enough to accommodate a department store. The master bathroom had two separate his and hers sink areas that could be closed off if needed. It had a massive walk-in shower and a soaking tub large enough to accommodate two people comfortably and romantically. Doctor has only owned the penthouse for a few years. He moved to Orange Beach about 5 years ago. Other than his kids, nobody has been to his penthouse. That was on purpose. He didn't want anyone to get any idea that he was a sugar daddy. He was far from it. He wanted any woman he dated to like him for him and not his money. When he lived in Mobile everyone knew who he was, and the women came out of the woodwork to try and latch onto him. Since he's been in

Orange Beach, nobody knew who he was. Slowly, people are figuring it out. But he keeps a low profile just the same. Both patios are equipped with remote screening that can be lowered in case of intense heat or if it's buggy outside. It's also dark enough that IF he were to ever entertain at his house, they could be on the patio without being seen by anyone. So, if he decided to sit naked on his patio having drinks or just having sex, nobody would see. He liked it that way.

Doctor never once considered bringing any woman to his penthouse. He did not want the hassle. When you have the amount of money Doctor has, it's a bitter pill to swallow when you realize the gold diggers come out of the woodwork. Outsiders trying to get a foot in the door or shallow women trying to get into his inner circle. He could see those women coming from a mile away like a Mack truck that lost its brakes. Those women never succeeded. He would sometimes amuse himself and see how far they would go. He was never surprised at any of their tactics. No matter where you live. Mobile or Orange Beach. No, he would wine and dine women and get them to take him to their place. It made life a lot easier. No mix-up with women leaving behind baubles for another woman to find or women showing up at his place unannounced. He liked his privacy and especially didn't want any uninvited guests showing up when his kids were there. If, and that's a big IF, any woman came along that he felt worthy to bring to his penthouse, she would be one hell of a woman that's for sure. He understands that is a major douchey attitude to have, but honestly, he didn't care. He's not shutting the door on having a serious relationship: he's just not found the right woman YET.

5

LAUREN SCAVONE

Lauren Scavone was a bright, bubbly, fun girl. She is a tiny little thing. Maybe 5'3", and if she weighed more than 100 pounds, it wasn't by much. She had an abundance of natural dark brown curly hair. She learned a long time ago that trying to tame her mane was pointless so she embraced her locks and let them do as they will. She wore her hair long so she could at least put it up in a ponytail if needed. She had a great sense of humor. Always laughing and she made friends wherever she went. She was outgoing and she truly never met a stranger. She made sure anyone and everyone she met had a good time. She never felt like she was better than anyone. Her parents taught her that.

"Being genuine and kind gets you farther than anything else." Her dad would always say. When you saw Lauren, you couldn't help but like her. She always greeted you with a hug and a smile. She was popular in high school. She made good grades. She wasn't going

to be Valedictorian, but she did her best and worked hard in her classes. She wasn't particularly athletic, but she did like being on the football and basketball cheer team. She was always there to cheer on and support her friends who were great athletes in their own right. Lauren had to work if she wanted to spend money. Even though her family was well off, she was not handed everything she wanted. If she wanted something extra, she had to work for it. Her father would tell her, *"If you never had to work for anything, you would not respect the things you got. However, if you worked for it and paid for it yourself, you valued those items more."*

Lauren was born and raised in Mobile Alabama. Mobile is a city and the county seat of Mobile County, Alabama. The population within the city limits was about 187,041. It is the fourth-most-populous city in Alabama, after Huntsville, Birmingham, and Montgomery. The Port of Mobile has always played a key role in the economic health of the city, beginning with the settlement as an important trading center between the French colonists and Native Americans, down to its current role as the 12th-largest port in the United States. Lauren's family was successful. Her dad Charles was a physician with The University of South Alabama Medical Center, which has 346 beds. Its roots go back to 1830 with the old city-owned Mobile City Hospital that was associated with the medical school. It is designated as Mobile's only level 1 trauma center. It is also a regional burn center.

Lauren's mom, Yvonne, was a stay-at-home mom. She was on lots of committees, she played golf regularly and did a lot of volunteer work. You know the basic stuff you do as a doctor's wife. Lauren had a brother who was three years older. Jeremy was an amazing athlete. He got a scholarship to play football at Auburn and was quite successful both on and off the field. He majored in

Architecture Design and Construction. He had his own successful business. He is married with two beautiful daughters. Lauren's family was an all-American family. Everybody was extremely close. Sunday dinners at her parents. Lots of Saturday's spent at football games watching Jeremy play. Lauren was not as outgoing as her brother. She didn't want all the glitz of Auburn so she opted to go to the University of Mobile in their Business program. She did quite well and when she graduated, she got jobs working for smaller businesses. She wanted to get hooked up with more high-end businesses. After several years of getting her feet wet and building a reputation for being a consummate professional, she finally landed a job for a very wealthy developer by the name of Doctor Campbell. He was not an actual Doctor. His real name was Doctor. His Company is **D Campbell Land Development LLC.** Her timing was perfect. As she interviewed for the job the previous Executive Assistant had resigned and moved. Doctor thought she would be a great fit and she was hired immediately. Lauren knew nothing about the art of Land Development, but she dived in up to her fingertips and got to work figuring things out. It was a little overwhelming at first but Doctor was very patient with her and gave her room to grow and figure things out. As she got more comfortable with her position, Doctor left her alone to do her job. She was smart, came from a good family, and was determined to be successful. Doctor knew Lauren's parents. They ran in the same circles so Doctor was aware of Lauren's background. Lauren had always found Doctor to be very handsome. He was about 50, 5'10" salt and pepper hair. He was a workout fanatic and was at the gym frequently. If he missed a day, it was rare. He wore clothes perfectly tailored to show off his muscular physique. Women would do a double-take when they saw him coming. He seemed very

aware and absorbed the admiration like a sponge. Lauren thought
he could be a little arrogant but he typically kept that for people
he didn't know well. Doctor worked hard to get where he was and
because of that, he was very careful who he let in his life and in
his business. He demanded complete loyalty. He worked hard and
he never demanded his employees do anything he was not willing
or capable of doing himself. He was someone who made himself
known. Maybe he worked a little too much. Since he was no longer
married, Doctor decided to branch out his business and head over
to Orange Beach, Alabama. Of course, he asked Lauren to go
with him and after two years of working for Doctor, she jumped
at the chance. She loved Mobile but new surroundings would be a
fun adventure. It didn't take long for Doctor's business to take off.
When they first got to Orange Beach, it took a lot of hours to get
the business set up. Some of the employees who worked in Mobile
didn't want to make the move so Lauren was tasked with finding
new employees. It was daunting, as Doctor wanted his business
up and running immediately. Initially, it was long days with lots
of hours. Lots of employee applications, interviews, second
interviews, and the list goes on. You can't open a business until you
have the right employees in place. Doctor was part of every single
interview. It was his business and he wanted to make sure 100%
that the people he hired were the best at what they did and the best
for his company. Ultimately, Doctor made the final decision on who
was hired. That was just fine with Lauren. She didn't want to end
up looking like a fool for hiring the wrong person. Lauren didn't
mind the workload and long hours as she was well paid. Doctor
got her a place that he paid for as part of her salary. Lauren was
loving the move to Orange Beach. New adventures are always fun.
She met new people and made new friends. She had developed

a crush. A big-time crush that she thought about constantly. The one thing she wanted was for her crush to feel the same way about her. She wasn't sure if he did. She hadn't said anything. She tried to keep her feelings from bubbling over like boiling spaghetti sauce splattering all over the stovetop. She has to figure out how to let him know without scaring him. That's extremely hard to do and so whenever they are together, she downplays the interaction but when she gets home the fantasies take over and cloud her brain. She plays them over and over. *Showering together, a slow sensual shower. Each other taking the time to soap up the other. Softly caressing their bodies with the luxurious bubbles. Washing each other's hair. Drying each other when done. He whisks her off to the bedroom. She massages him with oil, helping him relax after a long day. The massage just intensifies the sexual charge they both feel. She stops, he lays her on her back, and he starts kissing her, slowly and deliberately working his way down her body. Caressing every inch. He gently opens her legs and effortlessly slides in. Lauren has her legs wrapped around his waist. Slowly and lovingly, they move together in a rhythmical fashion that brings them both sexual satisfaction. Each of them moans in their ecstasy until it's over. He slowly rolls off her, wraps her in his arm and they fall asleep.*

Lauren thinks, *'I need to figure out how to make this happen in real life. I need to get a plan because this fantasy drives me crazy every time."*

6

CHELSEA HIGGINS

Chelsea grew up in a wealthy family. Her dad was Walter Higgins, III. The Higgins family's wealth came from the Aerospace Industry tied to the Redstone Arsenal in Huntsville. They owned 1000 acres in northern Alabama. Their home was a huge 8000-square-foot log cabin. Well, obviously, not a cabin, but the Higgins family referred to it that way. A massive porch on the back of the house with huge wooden rockers that overlooked the property. The entire back of the house was full of windows. When you drove up to the house it had the look of a cabin and was very impressive. You got a stab of immense admiration for this amazing property and view when you stepped out onto the back deck. Two massive fireplaces seemed to take over. The interior was a very modern country and mountain resort style. It had exposed beams in the living room and the fireplace stones went to the ceiling. A huge trophy buck was mounted above one of the fireplaces. The house would have fit perfectly in Wyoming or Colorado. But here it was in Northern Alabama. Quite an unusual home for this area. The Higgins were not shy with their money, but in the same vein, Walter Higgins III was extremely generous in his giving. Especially to children and veterans. Walter was always very patriotic and he felt if you were brave enough to fight and possibly die for your country, you were to be respected. Walter made sure any veteran that was in need, was going to get help. The same with children. They are our future and Walter wanted to make sure that no child was in need. Chelsea was the older of two daughters. Meredith was five years younger. Chelsea was doted on for the first five years of her life. She got everything she wanted. Her mother, Genevieve, spoiled her terribly. Walter tried to tell her that if she kept that up, Chelsea would grow up to be a lazy, spoiled, entitled woman. Walter was always trying to teach his family the value of money. Earn your keep. Make your way in society. Genevieve ignored it completely. Five years later when Meredith came along, Chelsea was having none of it. She had become an all-out brat. Walter showed Genevieve exactly what she had produced, but Genevieve refused to see it. The tantrums turned into a rebellious preteen and finally into an out-of-control teenager. This had put a tremendous strain on Higgins' marriage. Walter wants his daughters to be kind productive grown-ups. Genevieve wanted her daughters to think they were better than everyone else. Since that was how Genevieve saw herself. She wanted her daughters to be considered the elite in Huntsville, Alabama. Eventually, the Higgins' marriage fell apart when Chelsea was a senior in high school. Genevieve got a large settlement in the divorce. Walter was happy to be rid of her. Of course, now that she was single and able to go out to party and pursue other men, she felt her young daughters would just be in the way. No man wants to raise someone else's kids and she was willing to leave them behind. Chelsea was devastated that her mother would leave her. This caused Chelsea to lash out even more.

Walter told Chelsea that things would be different and that she would no longer be freely handed whatever she wanted. Walter loved both his daughters. He was trying to right the wrong his ex-wife had done to Chelsea. He felt none of this was Chelsea's fault. She was a child and was brought up to think everything should be handed to her. It was a hard road for Walter to travel but he was bound and determined to get her straightened out. Meredith, on the other hand, was never spoiled like Chelsea. Genevieve just didn't have the same love for Meredith as she did for Chelsea. Meredith's personality was the polar opposite of Chelsea's. She was truly a kind human being. She did well in school and she was well-liked. A beautiful, tall, slender brunette with blue eyes, she had no shortage of boys to go out with. She dated a little in high school but her main focus was to work in the family business. If that meant starting at the bottom and working her way up, then so be it. She knew she was not about to graduate from high school and be the Vice President of a company. No, she knew she had to learn the business and know it completely before she could achieve an important position. Chelsea, on the other hand, wanted no part of that. She wanted to do as she pleased and expected to be handed money on a whim. Chelsea was pretty in her own right, shorter than Meredith, with dark hair, and green eyes. Being five years older than Meredith, they were not in high school at the same time. Chelsea didn't have the same effect on people as Meredith. Chelsea was just plain, downright arrogant in high school. She walked through the halls like she was the queen of the school. She had a few uppity friends who thought they were better than everybody else, but that was it. She and her little group of snotty, bossy, girls stayed to themselves. When Meredith got to high school a lot of teachers wondered if she would be just like Chelsea and braced themselves for what was to come. To their enjoyment, she was the exact opposite and was very respectful to all the teachers. Once out of high school, Chelsea decided she was not going to college. She had no desire.

Walter told Chelsea, "If you refuse to go to college, then you will have to get a job working in the family business. If you don't, then I guess you won't have any money. You have to earn your keep. Make your way in life."

Chelsea had no choice but to go to work. She was paid well for what little she did, so she did what she had to do to fly under the radar. Her rebellious ways got her in trouble on several occasions. She had been pulled over a few times for driving too fast. The first thing she would say was, "Do you know who I am? Do you know who my family is?"

The officers always did. They acted like they had no idea who she was and she always got a ticket. The whole time they had to listen to her rant and rave and scream about "who she is." In the end, it never worked and she didn't care. She was going to do what she wanted. As hard as Walter tried, he just could not get Chelsea to understand that she could not continue to treat people with disdain. There was this huge disconnect between them and no matter what he did or said, Chelsea just didn't get it. Or didn't want to get it? She would hang out in the not-so-great part of town. The edge of trashy. She liked the rebel, I don't give a shit, attitude that part of town oozed out. She ended up meeting and dating a criminal drug runner, mostly to irritate her father. You know, bad boy image. Not a care in the world. The do whatever he wants kind of guy, just like Chelsea. He was a petty criminal. He used Chelsea for her money and she used him to give her family a bad name.

At the age of 22, she went behind her father's back and secretly married. She quickly realizes that this is a bad idea. After one year of marriage, this guy is convicted and sent to prison. Chelsea has no choice but to slink back home with her tail between her legs. Walters tells her she has to get a divorce and return to being a Higgins, and she would have to, again, go back to work for the family business and make her way. They have a guest house on the property that is about 3500 square feet and Chelsea is allowed to move into that. Meredith is not happy that her dad has given in to Chelsea again. Meredith sees through her poor pitiful me attitude. Walter is trying so hard to fix the damage Genevieve has done that Meredith just keeps her mouth shut. She knows that one day, the light bulb will go on, and her dad will finally see he's wasting his time. Chelsea manages to talk her dad into giving her a monthly stipend. She doesn't know anything about the business. She never paid any attention to it and she will have to take the time to learn. Until she does, she will need money to get by. Her dad agrees on a $10K monthly "allowance." Chelsea is stunned. $10K a month, is her dad serious? $10K is a pittance. No matter how she tries to work it, her dad stands his ground. Chelsea quickly figures out that if she wants family money, she will have to toe the line. She gets to live in the guest house. $10K monthly and barely working at the family business, not so bad, all things considered.

Walter encouraged her to go outside the family business. Get involved in the city. Go see who and what needs help to better herself and the people around her. She was able to get elected to the city council, mainly because of the Higgins name. She figured it would be easy to get her out of the family's work. Since she felt she was better than most, she used her new position to flaunt her name and run with the upper crust of Huntsville. She did just enough to stay out of hot water with her dad. Chelsea still did what she wanted when she wanted, but she learned to keep a low profile.

With a thousand acres, there was a lot of property to hunt on. They had ATVs and trail cameras to show where the best hunting was. Chelsea would have friends over, and they would ride the ATVs all over the property. After her mother left, Chelsea, her dad, and Meredith did a lot of hunting and fishing together. Walter trying to get his girls on the same page as far as the family goes. Meredith would often ask her dad.

Meredith: "Why are you trying so hard to get me and Chelsea to be closer? Chelsea is downright mean to me, and I want nothing to do with her."

Meredith understood what her father wanted but she assured him that was never going to happen. Meredith: "Just let us be two separate people and acknowledge we are never going to be friends."

Walter begrudgingly agreed. He has always gravitated more towards Meredith as she was more like him. Chelsea was like the prodigal child. Walter always hoped she would see the light, miraculously change her attitude, and discover what a wonderful family she had. Meredith knew that would never happen and hoped her dad would see it as well.

The untimely death of Walter was a crushing shock to Huntsville. An accident that left the family and the entire community in ruins. Walter Higgins III was worth 150 million dollars. With his constant generosity, his funeral was attended by thousands of people. His business alone had 800 employees. Walter was a well-respected, well-liked man and it showed at his funeral. It was a beautiful sunny fall day. Not a cloud in the sky. Light jacket weather and people came from all over to pay their respects to Walter Higgins. There were so many people that sheriff's deputies had to direct traffic. The outpouring of respect for Walter sent chills up Meredith and Chelsea's spines. They knew their father was adamant about helping people, but they had no idea how many lives he had touched. It was indeed humbling. When the funeral procession made its way to the cemetery, the line of cars was endless. People who didn't or couldn't go to the funeral lined the streets on both sides to pay their respects. Walter Higgins had truly touched the lives of many and they were all better for having known him. In an extremely morbid way, Chelsea found all the attention exhilarating and was flitting about talking to everyone, trying to make it all about her.

Meredith: "Chelsea, if you do not stop right now, I will pound you into a pulp!"

Chelsea: "I have no idea what you are talking about."

Meredith: "Stop making this about you. This is about Dad. These people are paying their respects. STOP with all the theatrics. Stop it right now or I swear I will pound the crap out of you!" Chelsea GLARED at Meredith. Meredith stared back and didn't say a word.

When all was said and done, Walter's attorney, Stanley Price, called Chelsea and Meredith in for the reading of the will. Walter had set up trust funds for the charities he wanted to continue to support. He had left several million in those trust accounts. The girls were not surprised since he had always talked about doing that. After all, they had enough money that they weren't worried about how much money he put in the trusts. Plus, the family business would continue to thrive and would always fund the charity trusts so they wouldn't run out of money. When it came to Chelsea and Meredith. The will was short and to the point. The remaining one hundred million is to be settled.

The will reads in part: "To my daughter Meredith, in your ability and willingness to dive into the family business and give 100% by working your way up to CEO, you will be given 90% of the family wealth. You will also be given the 1000-acre homestead."

Chelsea stands up so quickly that she knocks her chair over. "What the Hell! No way. No freaking way!"

Stanley: "Sit down, Chelsea!" Chelsea picks up her chair and sits back down, sulking the entire time.

"To my daughter Chelsea, it's time for you to wake up. You are given 10% of the family wealth and the beach house on Ono Island in Orange Beach. You now need to make your way in life. Since you've barely done anything with your life at this point, this is my last-ditch effort to get you to get her life together."

Chelsea is livid: "If you think for one minute I am going to accept this outcome, you are sadly mistaken," she says. She is not going down without a fight.

She looks straight at Meredith and says: "I will get the best attorney and fight this. See you in court, little sister!"

Stanley looks straight at Chelsea and says, "Your dad's will is airtight. Any fight in court would not change the outcome, and it would just cost you attorney's fees and court costs. If you are smart, you will accept what you have been given and figure out life going forward."

Chelsea grabs her purse and stomps out of the office. As Meredith and Stanley get outside his office, they see Chelsea speeding away in anger. Meredith looks at Stanley. "Well, that went better than I expected. Do you think she is mad?" Stanley just looks at Meredith and they exchange a wry smile.

Since Meredith had gotten the property, she refused to allow Chelsea to stay and live in the guest house. Meredith viewed Chelsea as a lazy mooch who had no respect for their dad, the business, or their family in general. Since Chelsea was given the house on Ono Island, Meredith told Chelsea she had to vacate the property immediately.

So, having been booted from the property, Chelsea packed her stuff, got in her fancy silver Porsche Carrera, and headed out for the five-hour drive to Orange Beach Alabama. *Good riddance Huntsville*, she thought. *Time to get out of here and start something new.* Chelsea believed she would never return to Huntsville and she was OK with that.

7

SHOVELHEAD DEMPSEY

Nothing ever went right for Mike "Shovelhead" Dempsey: even when it was going right, it quickly sent him down a greased chute to the proverbial septic tank. Shovelhead just couldn't escape himself: he was a loser with a capital L, but he never thought of himself that way. He always thought he was just one step away from having everything in his life fall into place, but getting shot to the moon in a big rubber band would have been a more likely scenario.

Shovelhead was having one of his typical days. It was pouring rain on the coast: he was stuck in his living room with a busted head on his Harley Davidson motorcycle. It was usually his fault. Shovelhead had been dragging the bike late on weekend nights with some of his other outlaw buddies when he blew the head. With some help from the guys, they were able to get the Harley up on a trailer and get it back to his house, push it up a ramp and get it inside the living room. The living room was where Shovelhead had to work on his bike. Because in this hovel he did not have a garage. The place was falling apart at the seams. It stank of old sweat and stale beer. Shovelhead picked up odd jobs when he could work at the construction site. He sold some meth to make money. He also sold some stolen motorcycle parts when he could get his hands on some. He would take them to swap meets and flea markets to try and make a few bucks. His existence was a subsistence. If it weren't for his bike club and his few friends in it, he probably wouldn't even get by.

Shovelhead had been in and out of the joint since he was a teenager. Having done five years, a nickel, he would say, for an aggravated assault when he shot another biker during a run in Daytona. *The scumbag deserved it,* Shovelhead thought. He was messing with one of the brother's girls. So out behind the bar, Shovelhead pulled a 9mm Beretta and shot that rival biker in the shoulder. He tried to get away, but the place was quickly swarmed by Daytona Beach PD Officers who were able to nab Shovelhead pretty quickly. He still had his pistol on him. Even the girl he stood up for testified against him in court. He was lucky to get off with only five years, mainly because the other guy had pulled a knife. Although Shovelhead's self-defense claim didn't work, it probably helped reduce his sentence to five years.

He's had other trouble with the law along the way. He had been busted for dealing meth, he was caught for having stolen motorcycle parts, and there was that fight in a bar in Biloxi, Mississippi, that landed him 90 days. It was just the way Shovelhead's life went. He traveled from one disaster to the next, trying to eek by in between. He was good at fixing Harleys: he had a lifetime doing it. He could not keep a steady job because he was unreliable. He would get drunk and high and not show up for work. So, he picked up some local repairs on the side, and he worked on the bikes his fellow outlaw bikers had, and now he was trying to get the head on his bike repaired. Even when you can do the work yourself to save a lot of money, Harley Davidson parts are not cheap. You have got to have the right parts, gaskets, and seals to make it run right. If you cheap out on something, it's eventually going to break down on you again. So, Shovelhead had the parts strewn about the living room. He was diligently working on getting his bike back on the road when he saw a message on his phone. The message was from Highside. One of his biker buddies from inside the joint had been doing a longer stretch for a murder rap. Highside was out now and lived in Florida. Shovelhead had not seen or talked to him in years. The brothers always talked in slang and code when they were talking about any criminal activity. They were smart enough and had been inside and outside the joint enough dealing with feds and detectives that they had to be careful what they said and how they said it. But still, they needed to communicate, or they would never get the jobs done. Although the message was cryptic, Shovelhead knew something was up. The message said, "Shovelhead, I need to meet with you. I have a big construction job. There's big pay in it. Meet me at the Barrel Tavern in Orange Beach next Wednesday at 7:00 p.m. Come alone, Highside."

Shovelhead knew the Barrel Tavern. He had been there many times. It was old and had been there for years. A lot of the brothers knew it and hung out there. Some might call it a dive bar, but the food was great, the beer was cold and you could get in a dark corner and talk quietly. Nobody paid any attention to you in there. There would be a few tourists but mostly locals. He damn sure needed the money, so he texted back to Highside, "See you there, old man."

Shovelhead went back to work on his Harley engine, he knew it probably would not be ready by Wednesday. So, he would just have to take his old pickup over. But that was OK. It would be less conspicuous anyway. He knew what Highside had in store, it was going to be something unique. Probably wanted him to run a load of dope somewhere. Other times Shovelhead might have turned that down if he thought the risk was too great. But right now, he was pretty desperate for the money. He started thinking about what the job could be and how much he was going to get paid. He thought. *I just have to get a big hit right now to get me by.*

Wednesday night came and Shovelhead slipped out his backdoor and into his old pickup truck. He had a thick beard, and he wore a ball cap pulled low over his forehead. Wearing just a pair of blue jeans and an old work shirt. He looked like everybody else from Mobile, Alabama, at that time of the afternoon. He fired up the pickup and headed out to the bridge across Mobile Bay. The sun was getting low in the sky behind Shovelhead as he cruised across the bridge. A flock of Pelicans on his right side almost keeping pace with his truck. *They rarely flap their wings*, he thought: what a life: they *just float, just above the water. Like a silent glider. Amazing creatures. I wish my life was like a pelican*, Shovelhead thought. *Seems they have it fairly well.* The sun glistened off the bay as Shovelhead made it to the other side of Mobile Bay and kept east on I10. He hit the exit for the Baldwin Beach Expressway, right at the Buc-ee's gas station. Shovelhead pulled into Buc-ee's, filled up, and went inside to use the restroom. He grabbed a hot cup of coffee on the way out. He got back in his truck and headed down the Beach Express toward Orange Beach, Alabama.

Shovelhead came over the toll bridge on the Beach Express into Orange Beach and turned left at the foot of the bridge towards his destination. He passed two Orange Beach police radio cars on the road, and he thought, this town is always crawling with cops and they don't mess around. I just got to get in and out of here as quietly as I can. I do not want any trouble. Shovelhead drove straight on Canal Road until he reached the Barrel Tavern, where he pulled into the unpaved sandy parking lot and parked under a shade tree. Shovelhead went inside: there were only a few people there: he spotted a table in the corner, went over, and sat down. A cute blonde waitress came over, she had a big smile on her face. *Probably wanting a tip already,* thought Shovelhead.

8

MAYORAL RACE

Chelsea had been in Orange Beach for about four years. She had been running in the upper crust that is Orange Beach. People are aware of who Chelsea Higgins is. Her dad, Walter, is well known throughout Alabama as quite a philanthropist. He didn't squander his money. If any organization asked for money, you could be sure that Walter was going to do his due diligence to make sure these "charities" were on the up and up. He had no problem saying no if needed. Eventually, shady companies knew better than to ask Walter for money. That, in turn, made Walter's giving a lot easier. Bougie people in Orange Beach wanted to cozy up to Chelsea because of her background. They were familiar with the death of her dad but had no clue that she only received 10% of the family wealth. Chelsea certainly did not want anyone to know, so she kept that very close to the vest. She was exaggerating some of her adventures and lifestyle since moving to Orange Beach. The locals called it OBA. After a few years, several friends encouraged her to run for Mayor. These included City Councilwoman Becki Hoover, District Attorney Meg Knox, School Board President Nancy Cotton, and Judge Beverly Robson. These high-powered women got together once a month for drinks, dinner, and a great time. They laughingly refer to themselves as "The Wonder Women."

Becki: "Chelsea, have you ever thought about running for Mayor?"

Beverly: "That's a great idea!"

Meg: "You would win, hands down."

Nancy: "You have the support of all of us. Besides, having a woman as the mayor would enhance the power of the women sitting here."

Chelsea: "I don't know the first thing about being a mayor. I have no clue how to run a city."

Becki: "Didn't you tell us you were on the city council in Huntsville?"

Chelsea: 'Yeah, but that was years ago."

Meg: "Well, things haven't changed much. I think you should go for it. We'll give you all our support."

Beverly: "With all of us behind you, you will surely win. Let's get started on your strategy."

The women got busy and helped Chelsea build her mayoral race campaign. Chelsea hit the ground running. She had money to run a strong campaign, but she didn't need much. The upper crust with whom she ran was more than willing to give her their vote. When all was said and done Chelsea won hands down and was the new Mayor of Orange Beach. Chelsea felt like she was finally getting back on top. She thinks, *Oh, the doors this would open. These people all want to be around me. They all want to work with me. I can get closer to the people who control things.* Chelsea was in her glory and her element. She always believed she should sit in the seat of the mighty. Her excessive hubris outweighed her talent. Her mother taught her that. A few years on a mudslide to nowhere and now she was climbing back. Chelsea Higgins was going to be the darling of Orange Beach. She took to being mayor like a bear to a dumpster. She was in her element. Flitting around like a beauty queen. She had several interviews after her mayoral win. Talking to all the news channels. Having a press conference in front of her office. Reporters shouting at her all wanting to make sure she answered their questions. Cameras from every local TV station and newspaper lined the sidewalk behind the reporters. Mayor Higgins was addressing all questions and how she was going to take Orange Beach into the future. Improvements the community has been asking for and a lot of normal stuff a new mayor needs to tackle. One of the questions was the proposed sale of a 100-acre property to D Campbell Land Development. The community was concerned about the traffic flow, the number of houses, and how the development was going to look. Would it cause school enrollment issues? Cause too much traffic? Stress the Utilities? All the basic community issues.

Chelsea: "I can understand your concerns about the new development. Since the sale was approved before I became mayor, I do plan on having a long conversation with D Campbell and getting deep into these issues, I, myself, want to see the plans. I don't believe our previous mayor would agree to anything that was not up to par for this great city. But I want to make sure myself. Now I have to get to work. Thank you for all your questions, and hopefully, I have put your mind at ease."

Chelsea turned and walked up to her office. Listening to all the cameras taking pictures. She had a big smile on her face. Yes, this was her calling. This is what she is supposed to be doing. Being in the limelight. Everyone listened intently to every word she was saying. She had no idea what she was doing, but she sure wasn't going to let on. Beverly, Meg, Nancy, and Becki had her back and they would help her out and give her advice and direction. After all, a strong woman leader base would set Orange Beach apart.

As she approaches the front door of her office building, Chelsea turns around, puts on a big smile, and waves to anyone still standing in front of the building. When she arrives at her new office, her friends are waiting for her. They start clapping when she walks in and cheers with champagne all around.

Chelsea: "I was so nervous out there. All those questions coming at me like bullets."

Beverly: "You did great. We watched the press conference from in here."

Meg: "You didn't look nervous at all. You answered the questions quickly and without hesitation."

Nancy: "You looked impeccable."

Becki: "When do you plan on getting together with D Campbell? Because now that you put it out there, you have to get it done."

Chelsea picks up her phone and calls her assistant. "Maria, Please Get D Campbell's office on the phone. I want to set up a meeting to discuss the new land purchase."

Maria: "Sure." With that, Maria dials D Campbell Land Development.

Receptionist: "Good Morning D Campbell Land Development. How may I direct your call."

Maria: "D Campbell, please."

Receptionist: "Who may I say is calling?"

Maria: "Mayor Higgins's office."

Receptionist: "One moment, please."

After a couple of minutes, someone picks up the phone.

Lauren: "Good Morning, this is Lauren, Doctor Campbell's executive assistant. How may I help you?"

Maria: "Mayor Higgins would like to set up a meeting with Mr. Campbell. She wants to go over the new land purchase and take a look at how it's going to be done."

Lauren: "Mr. Campbell is in a meeting at this time. Let me get with him and I will get back to you as soon as I can."

Maria: "Thank you, I appreciate it." With that, Maria gets back on the phone and lets Mayor Higgins know that she is expecting a call back about the meeting.

Chelsea: "When they call back, let them know that I will be leaving Wednesday for the mayor's conference in Birmingham. I'll be back Sunday and want this meeting on Monday morning. I have a busy schedule, and that is the only time I can meet. Make sure you make it clear to them that I want this meeting immediately upon returning." Maria made a face to herself: "I will be sure to pass that along."

Maria is well aware of how Chelsea Higgins is. She has seen these types of women come and go. She is not a fan at all but hey, she needs a job so she will be as sweet as she can be. She knows how to gush the proper amount to fly under the radar. Plus, she gets to listen to all the gossip and get the inside scoop on what's happening or is going to happen.

Within the hour, Lauren calls the mayor's office. She is connected with Maria.

Lauren: "Maria it's Lauren at D Campbell Land Development. Doctor would love to meet with the mayor. He said he would clear his calendar for any time she would like."

Maria was very surprised: "That is great, the mayor would like to meet first thing Monday morning. She would like to come to your office. She wants to meet the man and visit the company that made such a large bold purchase."

Chelsea and her friends spend the next few hours in her office chatting, laughing, drinking, and filling Chelsea in on all the things she needs to be aware of, to examine, and how to address any issues that might come up. But, above all, always be approachable. The previous mayor, Henry Shillings, was horrible at personal interactions with anyone. If someone had a question for him, he would clam up and refuse to answer. It's like his sphincter would clamp up so hard, it pulled his lips shut and it affected his ability to say anything. That is the biggest issue that lost him the reelection.

Chelsea spent the next two days in meetings and meeting people. Maria Fletcher had been in the mayor's office for years, so she and Chelsea spent some time together. This allowed Maria to show her the ropes and give her some guidance on how things worked. Chelsea was nice enough to sit and listen, but in actuality, she was going to do things the way she wanted. If she stepped on toes, she could not care less. She would be sweet about it, feigning naivety being a first-time mayor. She would be forgiven for not knowing the routine. Give her some time, let her get used to the new position, and don't push too hard. Give her the room she needs to get things in order. Chelsea would use all this newfound knowledge to her advantage.

Shortly after becoming mayor, she had personally met Detective Lieutenant Josh Myers. She was aware of who he was but had not had the privilege of meeting him prior. When he walked into her office, she could sense the strong sexuality he exuded. He didn't have to try: it was all natural. The way he walked, the way he looked you straight in the eye when he talked to you. That was unsettling. Beautiful brown eyes just looking straight at you. He never wavered in his look. It was almost like he was looking to see if he could see some sort of secret you were hiding, and Chelsea was hiding a lot.

Chelsea: "Good Morning, Lieutenant Myers. I hope your day is going well so far."

Josh: "Good Morning Mayor, Higgins. My day is going well. Thank you for asking."

Chelsea: "It's good to meet you and I hope our working relationship is going to be a smooth one."

Josh: "Well, I don't know why it wouldn't. Is there anything particular you wanted to discuss this morning?"

Chelsea: "Just the basics, since I am now the mayor, what I would like is to be informed of everything that is going on."

Josh: "Normally briefings for the mayor are done by the Chief of Police. Unless the chief directs me personally to do it."

Chelsea: "I know you are the chief of all the investigations and I would rather get any information directly from you. I will talk to the chief to have you brief me as needed."

Josh: "Of course, if the chief directs me to do so, I will. I hope you understand that I cannot go around the chain of command. If there isn't anything else you need from me, I have to get to work. It was very nice meeting you, Mayor Higgins."

Josh gets up and extends his hand to shake hers. Chelsea doesn't say anything. She stands up, shakes Josh's hand and he walks out of her office.

Chelsea is sexually charged by this no-nonsense, take-charge personality. He didn't bow to any pressure put on him. Said his peace and excused himself. Yeah, Chelsea is going to get to know

Detective Lieutenant Josh Myers. He has lit a fire in her that she has never felt.

As Josh leaves the mayor's office, he thinks. *"This woman sure is bold. Give her a briefing on all activities. I can already tell this could turn into a nightmare. I am not looking forward to this at all."* As he walks to his car, he huffs and puffs on what a waste of time that was. Oh well, he'll keep his head low, do his job, and try to stay out of the sight of Mayor Higgins. But, she is extremely attractive and unattached. And since Josh is no longer attached to anyone, he decided not to close the door on Chelsea Higgins and her demand. He will sit quietly and see what develops.

9

THE MAYOR'S CONFERENCE

Shortly after Chelsea became mayor, there was a Mayor's convention for all Alabama mayors in Birmingham. Three days of meetings and conferences. This was especially great for all the new mayors in Alabama. Chelsea was very excited to go and find out how other mayors run their cities and get some great tips since she was new.

Chelsea expected an escort since she was the mayor and Lieutenant Josh Myers was just the yummy escort she wanted.

Chelsea: "Maria, can you get me the Police Chief on the phone?"

Maria: "Sure."

Maria gets the chief on the phone and connects Chelsea to the call.

Chelsea: "Good Morning Chief. How are you?"

Chief: "I am just fine, Mayor. What can I do for you?"

Chelsea: "Well, I have the yearly mayor's convention in Birmingham coming up and I would like a security escort. You know, being the mayor and everything."

Chief: "I'm sure I can arrange that for you."

Chelsea: "Yes, well, I want Lieutenant Josh Myers to escort me."

Chief: "I am sure any of our other officers are qualified enough to provide a security escort for you."

Chelsea: "That may be true, but I would rather have Josh Myers. I want someone very experienced. You never know what could happen. I'm sure you can spare Lieutenant Myers for a few days."

Chief: "Of course, if that is what you want. I will get in touch with Lieutenant and let him know."

Chelsea: "Thank you, Chief."

The Chief calls Josh into his office.

Josh: "Good Morning Chief. What's up?"

Chief: "It's a great day, Josh: you are getting an all-expenses paid trip to Birmingham."

Josh: "Birmingham? I'm not so sure I'm that lucky. What are you talking about?"

Chief: "Mayor Higgins has the yearly mayor's convention in Birmingham next week and she has insisted that you be her escort."

Josh: "Come on, Chief, stop clowning around."

Chief: "I assure you I am not. Clear your calendar and change any plans you might have had. You can pick up Mayor Higgins first thing Wednesday morning. It's going to be great!"

Josh stares at the Chief, lets out a loud sigh, and leaves the office. The Chief smiles to himself as Josh walks out.

Bright and early Wednesday morning, Josh is in front of Mayor Higgins's house, waiting to take her to Birmingham. *She is prompt, I'll give her that.* Josh thinks as he gets out of the car. He helps her with her bag. They both get in the car and are on their way. *Great, a five-hour trip with someone I barely know. Oh well, I guess I'll make the best of it.* Josh thinks.

The trip ended up not being too bad. They got to know each other on a personal level. Josh likes to keep his personal life private, so he gives out just enough info to keep Chelsea satisfied. Chelsea, on the other hand, was a fountain of information. She told Josh about her family and their prominence in Huntsville. All the good things her family did for others. Chelsea made it known that she felt she was a little better than everyone else. Josh just listened and occasionally let out an "Oh really?" or a "Wow, that is great."

When they got to the hotel and Josh got to his room, he flopped on the bed wishing he was any place but here. He had things to do in Orange Beach and being gone for three days is going to drive him crazy. An hour later there is a knock on his door. Josh gets up and answers it. It's Chelsea.

Josh: "Hello, Mayor. Can I help you with something?"

Chelsea: "Yes, you can. There is a cocktail hour going on, and I want you to go with me. I'm new to this, and I don't want to go alone. It is embarrassing. I do not know anyone, so it would be nice to have someone to talk to."

Josh silently gritted his teeth: "Of course Mayor, whatever you need from me. Just give me a minute to change my shirt. You are more than welcome to come in if you would like." Chelsea enters Josh's room and takes a seat on one of the chairs. Josh grabs a shirt and heads to the bathroom to change. Five minutes later, he is ready, and they head to the cocktail hour. Josh knew several of the mayors from other law enforcement conferences, and he was quick to introduce them to Chelsea, hoping she would glom onto them so he could go back to his room. He was exhausted and just wanted to sleep. After a couple of hours and a few drinks, Josh was able to slip away. Chelsea had gotten herself in with several mayors and they were having a great time. Chelsea would never miss him. Josh heads back to his room with his drink in hand. He wanted a nightcap to sip. Josh jumps in a nice hot shower. It felt good after a long day. He slips on a pair of lounge pants and towel dries his hair. He goes and stretches out on the bed and turns on the TV. He closes his eyes and sips his drink. Happy to be alone and relaxed. After about 30 minutes there is a knock on his door. *Now what!? I can't catch a break. Whoever it is, please just go away!*

The knocking continues. Josh gets up and answers the door shirtless. Standing at the door is none other than Mayor Higgins. She has changed her clothes. Josh stares at her. He cannot take his eyes off her. He only sees Mayor Higgins in professional settings. Here she is, standing at his door wearing this beautiful cobalt blue floor-length lounge dress. Spaghetti straps, deep V down to her waist. The side of the dress has a slit that goes up to her hipbone. Chelsea Higgins is an incredibly sexy woman. She has a bottle of whiskey in her hand.

Chelsea: "Are you just going to stand there or are you going to invite me in?"

Josh cannot say anything. His brain has turned to mush. All he can do is stand aside and let Chelsea come in. Chelsea goes and gets a glass. She pours herself some whiskey and tops off Josh's glass. Josh takes a long, hard swallow. Chelsea sips hers. Josh finally finds his voice.

Josh stared intently, trying extremely hard to hide his erection: "Uh, Mayor. Umm yeah. What? What can I do for you?"

Chelsea takes Josh's glass, turns, and puts it on the table along with hers. She walks back over to Josh and starts running her hands up and down his bare chest. *What a magnificent creature! This man knows how to keep in shape!* She thinks. Chelsea slowly moves her hand down his chest and finds his erection. She has just confirmed what she was hoping. As Chelsea continues to lightly caress Josh she starts kissing him. Ever so lightly, softly. Nothing aggressive. That would spoil everything. It didn't take long for Josh to reciprocate. He wraps his arms around Chelsea and kisses her back. He slides the straps of her dress off her shoulders. She pulls her arms out of the straps and Josh can pull the top of her dress down to her waist. Her breasts are magnificent. He puts one arm around Chelsea's waist and cups one of her breasts with the other hand. Her nipples are slightly swollen and hard. Josh leans down, and with his tongue, he gently swirls her nipples. First one and then the other. Chelsea moans lightly. Josh runs his hand up the slit in Chelsea's dress and, to his delight, finds she is not wearing panties. Chelsea parts her legs slightly and Josh can get his hands between her legs. Chelsea has continued to lightly caress Josh at the same time. Josh slowly and carefully inserts his finger. Chelsea is ready. He can tell.

Chelsea pulls at Josh's bottoms. Josh helps her. She motions for Josh to sit on the bed. As Josh starts to sit down, Chelsea is on her knees in front of him, between his legs. Her breasts are still bare. She moves in and puts her mouth on Josh. Josh's arousal could not get any harder or stronger. He lets out a low, throaty groan. All Josh can think about is *Oh man, this woman. Lord help me, this woman knows what she is doing!*

Josh doesn't think he can take any more. Chelsea suddenly stops and stands up. She pulls her dress off to reveal the rest of her amazing body. She straddles Josh as he is still seated at the edge of the bed. She climbs on top and Josh is inside her. She is ready. The friction with Josh's pelvic bone is enough to send Chelsea over the edge. As Chelsea is exploding, she bucks her hips back and forth, holding on for dear life. Josh is doing everything he can to hold off. Once Chelsea has slowed down, Josh flips her over on the bed. She is now face down. Josh grabs her hips and pulls her up on all fours. Josh gets on his knees and enters her from behind. Holding on to Chelsea's hips, he pounds himself into her until he explodes. Chelsea, gripping the sheets with one hand, puts her hand between her legs and brings herself to a second orgasm. Josh collapses on the bed. Chelsea is lying on her stomach. Both panting and out of breath. A thousand thoughts go through Josh's head. *What the hell was I thinking? This is going to open a whole can of worms. This could cause me a lot of trouble. You just made a stupid mistake.* Between that thought and his intense amazing orgasm. He is torn. He will just have to see how this turns out.

Only after about five minutes does Chelsea get up off the bed, put on her dress, and leave. She does not say anything to Josh—not one word. Josh just lays on the bed in disbelief, recovering from the encounter. Twenty minutes later, he gets up off the bed and goes and takes another shower. When he's done, he climbs into bed and is immediately asleep.

When Chelsea gets back to her room, she does the same thing. Takes a nice hot shower and crawls into bed. She runs the scenario with Josh over and over in her head. It was so freaking hot and sexy that she works herself into a frenzy. Fortunately, she always carries a vibrator with her. She takes it out of the case. It does not take long and she is aroused again.

She finally falls asleep. Too much to drink and completely sexually satisfied.

For the rest of the conference, Josh tries to keep a low profile and stay out of Chelsea's way. They sat next to each other at the final dinner Saturday night. They headed back to Orange Beach bright and early Sunday morning. Neither one said anything about the encounter.

When they got back to Orange Beach, Josh dropped Chelsea at her house: before she got out of his car, she said, "Josh, you do not need to worry about anything. This is between you and me and I will never say anything about what happened. I trust you to do the same."

Josh: "Don't worry, mayor. This goes no further than you and I."

Chelsea: "Thank you, Josh. Business as usual."

Josh: "Yes, ma'am." *Let's hope so!* He thinks.

10

IS IT THE BEGINNING OF SOMETHING REAL?

On a beautiful summer evening in August, Randi had gone to a beach party with friends. There was a whole cornucopia of people there from every lifestyle you could think of. She is sitting on a comfy couch with friends laughing and having a great time. She happens to look up and staring at her is this very handsome man. He appears to be somewhat older than her. She is caught in his gaze. She tries to look away, but his piercing stare has caught her off guard. There is something about him that stirs inside her. He smiles and lifts his glass to cheer her. She timidly smiles back and lifts her glass in a silent cheer. They continue to make eye contact and he waves her over. Randi excuses herself and heads over to this handsome sexy man. Her legs are a little wobbly at the thought of getting close to this gorgeous creature. He introduces himself as

Josh Myers. Randi introduces herself as well. She always must tell people that she is Randi with an i, not a y.

Josh: "Nice to meet you, Randi, with an i. Are you new to the Orange Beach area? I would never have forgotten such a beautiful face had we met before."

Randi: "We have not met before. I have been here for about five years. I moved over from Pensacola."

Josh: "Pensacola isn't much of a move. Are you originally from there?"

Randi: "No, I'm originally from Wisconsin. I moved to Pensacola right after high school. I was there for 12 years, and I wanted a change of scenery while wanting to stay by the water. I am a real estate agent and Orange Beach seems to be an up-and-coming place where people want to be."

Josh: "Yes, people sure want to be in Orange Beach. The summers are crazy busy with vacationers, which keeps my department busy. Wisconsin, huh? I have never been, but I am a huge football fan, and I love watching the Green Bay Packers play."

Randi: "Yes, in Wisconsin, you live and breathe The Packers and the Wisconsin Badgers. It's in your DNA. Have you ever been to a Packer game?"

Josh: "No, it's on my bucket list."

Randi: "You won't be disappointed. However, you might not want to go in December. The weather can be brutal, but true Packer and Badger fans will always be there no matter the weather."

Josh: "That's a hardy group, for sure. How is the real estate business going?"

Randi: "Pretty good actually. I specialize in more high-end properties, including homes and properties for developers. There is big money in selling property to developers. I am just getting my foot in the door with that."

Josh: "I bet that you have to be tenacious in that work environment."

Randi: "Well, if you want to get ahead in this business, you cannot put your feet up and wait for success to come knocking. You have to get out there and make it happen. I've been in real estate for quite a while, so I am familiar with all the ins and outs. Tell me about you, Josh Myers."

Josh: "I am a Lieutenant on the Orange Beach Police. I run the Detective Bureau."

Randi: "Well, that is interesting, kind of sexy, too."

Josh laughed, "Not sure about the sexy part, but I love my career."

Randi: "So how did you get into all that, Inspector Clouseau?"

Josh smiled: "Oh, a realtor and a standup comic, nice combination."

Randi: "Just keeping the local detective on his toes you know. But how did you get into police work?"

Josh: "I'm originally from Orange Beach, joined the military out of high school. I was stationed at Fort Campbell, Kentucky. I became an MP Officer. I married my high school sweetheart but unfortunately, that didn't last. It ended about 15 years ago. We were unable to have kids and it took its toll. We ended on good terms. I liked being an MP and after the military, I decided to become a cop full-time. I applied to Orange Beach, P.D. They hired me and sent me to the police academy. I worked in patrol and made detective. Then sergeant and now Detective Lieutenant."

Randi: "Why did you leave the military?"

Josh: "My wife didn't want to do all the moving around that is required when you're in the military, so I decided to give it up."

Randi: "Have you dated much since your divorce?"

Josh: "Some. But my job keeps me busy and after 11 years of marriage, I just wanted my personal life to lay low and go slow. I have dated a little but nothing serious. How about you?"

Randi: "Same here. Building a successful business takes a lot of time. I've dated a little, but nothing serious."

Josh: "Well, Randi, would you like to go to dinner sometime?"

Randi hesitates. Her stomach in knots, she finally says, "Yes, I would like that." She hands Josh her business card, turns, and goes back to her friends.

Josh watches her walk away and sees how sexy she is. She is tall and slender. Her breasts look magnificent under her pale yellow summer dress. Her hair is a two-toned blonde color that comes just to her collarbone. Done professionally, but the color suits her. Green eyes that stand out against her blonde hair. He likes this Randi with an i and he is anxious to get to know her better. She robustly carries herself. Not bold and bossy, but tall and classy.

11

DEVELOPING ROMANCE

About two weeks after the meeting, Josh calls Randi and makes a date for dinner.

Randi: "Good Morning, this is Randi."

Josh: "Good Morning Randi, it's Josh Myers. How's it going today?"

Randi: "It's going great. I've had several showings in the last few days, and things have been crazy busy."

Josh: "I was wondering if you'd like to go to dinner tomorrow night? I hope it's not too last minute."

Randi: "Not last minute at all. I would love to go to dinner. Will you be picking me up or shall I meet you?"

Josh: "If it's ok, I will pick you up. How about 7:00 pm?"

Randi responds: "Seven is perfect. I will text you my address. See you then." Randi is excited and intrigued by Josh. He's handsome, tall and very fit. He is an upstanding person in the community. She would be interested in getting to know him better to see what he's about. She thought about what to wear. Something sexy to get his attention and hopefully blow him away.

Josh picks her up promptly at 7:00 p.m. Randi is impressed. She opens her front door and Josh is again taken aback by how beautiful she is. She is wearing a bright fuchsia, tight-fitting dress. It is very simple and plain in the front. When she turned around, the back of the dress had a narrow piece of material across the top that was embellished with sequin flowers of every color. The rest of the dress was opened down to the small of her back with five thin straps that went from the sequined band and crisscrossed to the side of the dress. It hugged her curves beautifully. Since the back was so sparkly, Randi wore a simple pair of diamond earrings. She certainly knew how to dress: she didn't overdress, and she outdressed a lot of women. She typically doesn't wear anything flamboyant or over the top, just great clothes that are put together perfectly. But tonight was different. She wanted to make an impression.

Her make-up is not overdone. She does not wear any heavy foundation. Her complexion is fair with some freckles, and she likes the more natural look.

Josh was speechless. He could not help but stand there and stare at her. Josh is not a suit-and-tie type of guy. A dress shirt, jeans, and cowboy boots are his all-American style.

Randi smiles: "Um, Josh? Are you ready to go?"

Josh: "Oh, sorry, you look stunning. I hope I am not too underdressed for you."

Randi: "Why, thank you, sir, and you are dressed perfectly."

Josh takes her hand, leads her to his car, opens the door, and helps her in. What a gentleman he is. That is exceedingly rare

these days and she takes note of that. Josh gets in and starts the car.
When it comes to life, Bobby Darin's "Beyond the Sea' is playing.
Randi starts singing.

"Somewhere beyond the sea,

She's there watching for me,

If I could fly like birds on high,

Then straight to her arms, I'd go sailing."

Josh sits and stares at her.

Josh: "I am impressed. That is one of my favorite songs. I'm
surprised you know the words."

Randi: "My mom is a huge Bobby Darin fan. She had his music
playing all the time. I do love that song." From then on, whenever
Josh picked Randi up, that song was playing, and they would hold
hands and sing along until it was done.

He takes her to Zeke's restaurant in the Marina. They have
a small wait for their table, so they sit outside, have a drink, and
watch all the excessively big and expensive boats come and go.
They engaged in small talk. It was only about a 15-minute drive
to the restaurant. The evening wasn't too hot. There was a nice
breeze so sitting outside having a drink wasn't uncomfortable.
They discussed their chosen careers, their background, and their
previous lives. About thirty minutes later, they are shown to their
table and Josh orders a bottle of wine. Josh loved hearing Randi
talk about Wisconsin. It seemed like a world away. Josh talked
about his time in the Military. He loves his job in Orange Beach.
He wants Orange Beach to be a community that you trust will
always be safe. He is not a dick to anyone. He could tamp down
an escalating situation quickly. Everyone knew him, and everyone
genuinely liked him. They knew that no matter what was going
on, Josh Myers was going to be fair, and if he felt you needed help,

he was going to make sure you got it. Randi can't help but stare at Josh. He is tall and ruggedly handsome. She estimates he stands about 6' 1". He is tanned, and he has light brown hair. His eyes are a beautiful dark brown. In Wisconsin, they refer to these as "cow eyes," which is 100% a compliment. When he smiles, his whole face changes shape. Josh Myers had two completely different faces. He has his professional detective face and his non-work face. That face and eyes soften when he smiles. Perfect white teeth that are enhanced by his tanned skin. He has the beginnings of crow's feet around his eyes. His work face is handsome, but his non-work face is downright gorgeous. Randi tries to keep him smiling so she can look at and admire him. Josh finds Randi intriguing. She certainly is her own person. Her personality is exceptionally large but not overbearing. Some large personalities are loud and obnoxious, but Randi's is on the outgoing, fun, nice-to-everybody side. Suddenly, out of nowhere, Randi puts her hand on Josh's knee. He is not expecting it. He looks straight at her, and she smiles but doesn't move her hand. Josh waits a minute or two and puts his hand on top of Randi's and gives it a light squeeze. She doesn't move it and they spend the rest of their date holding hands under the table. After all, prying eyes can be dangerous. After dinner, they head to The Gulf. A huge bar restaurant located on Perdido Pass that can serve 1100 people. The summer wind blows gently from the west heralding new beginnings.

There are two small bars, but the rest of the place is all picnic tables, comfy couches, and comfy chairs. It has seven huge umbrellas to cut the daytime sun. They have two different windows that you can go up to and order your food and drink and they bring it to your table. They find two soft easy chairs close to the water. There are strings of small lights all over the place. When it's dark, the lights give the atmosphere a soft glow as the rollers rumble on the nearby jetty. Josh gets them a drink and they continue talking about life. Josh finds the chemistry overwhelming. It's been a long time since he was in any sort of relationship. Nobody he ever met had galvanized his feelings and hammered his heart like Randi. She wasn't needy, she appeared to have no baggage from a past relationship. She has no kids to contend with. She just has this fun-loving personality, not a care in the world. Josh finds this refreshing. She has been easy to be with. He finds himself very relaxed around her and feels like he's known her forever. He relishes this feeling. There's no rub, no burr under your saddle.

Randi decides she likes Josh Myers. *He's easy, "easy like Sunday Morning,"* she thinks as she hums the Lionel Ritchie tune to herself. He seems to always be aware of his surroundings. When they were at Zeke's and again at The Gulf, he positioned himself so he could see everything that was going on. He was very good at being very attentive to her and also keeping an eye on the surroundings. It was as if he could watch the fish fry with one eye while watching the cat with the other. It made her feel safe for sure. The evening is filled with laughing and lightly holding hands. It was a fun, light time for both. Josh likes Randi and wants to see her again. When the night finally ends, Josh takes Randi home and walks her to her door. He wants to make sure she gets inside safely. They stand there for a moment. Randi reaches out and gives Josh a hug pressing against him very tightly. Josh is aroused by the softness of her breasts. He leans down and kisses her. She accepts it happily. Their kiss is extremely soft and sensual. It's loving and romantic. They stand at Randi's door, embracing and kissing for what seemed like forever. When they finally break from their embrace and say goodnight, both Josh and Randi are taken by how electric their kiss is. Josh makes his way back to his car and is not surprised he is extremely aroused. He sits for a couple of minutes, waiting for it to subside, but his continued thoughts of Randi make it impossible. He is finally able to make his way home. Randi gets inside her house and is struck by how her insides feel. She has not had feelings like this for anyone in a long time, if ever. She always kept men at a distance to not interfere with her goals. Josh has awakened something inside of her that she is not used to. The sexual want she has for him has knocked her from her moorings, setting her adrift. Somehow, she has to get back on course. As she gets ready for bed, she begins to imagine what it would be like to make love to Josh Myers. Having his tanned, strong, lean body on top of hers, touching her in ways and places that have been asleep for a long time.

12
IMPACT OF LOVE

Josh and Randi have been getting much closer since they first met. Josh can't stop thinking about her and he gets together with her every chance he can. His job is not 9 to 5 and sometimes he is out all-night investigating things that ruin vacations. The crimes that occur in big cities occur in Orange Beach as well, just not with the same frequency. Whether it's domestic violence, robbery, burglary, aggravated assault during a drunken bar fight, tourists being robbed or ripped off, or even boat thefts. Crimes are hidden behind the tourists and the scenic beauty. He's always working on something. His least favorite place to go is The Barrel. It's your standard low-rent bar. Nothing fancy, just burgers and fries. The beer is cold, and surprisingly, the burgers and fries are great. But that's about the nicest thing he can say. The people that run the place are honest and hardworking and Josh knows them. It's not that it's a bad place: it's the clientele that sometimes gives it a bad name. If Josh were looking for a sketchy person, the first place he would check is The Barrel. Most of the time, that's where he'll find them. He never had any issues going into The Barrel. The patrons know him. Know he's there for a good reason and they typically leave him alone. Now, will they help him find a particular person? Point that person out? Nope, they keep their heads down, look at their beer, and leave Josh to find who he is looking for on his own. Josh was ok with that and it kept the bar fights to a minimum.

He dealt with lots of police action there when he was in uniform, and now, as Detective Lieutenant, it is not much different.

Sometimes when his shift ends late, he'll text Randi to see if she is still up. She usually is and tells him to come over.

Josh always goes. He can't stand being away from her. She is on his mind all the time. He doesn't know what has come over him. He has never felt this way about anybody. Not even his ex-wife.

Randi, on the other hand, knows how Josh feels about her. She wishes she felt the same way, but she doesn't. She doesn't want a serious relationship. Not now, anyway. She has too many other things she wants to do and having a significant other gets in the way. For Randi, Josh takes up her lonely time, her bored time. They have fun together, and right now, she wants to have as much fun as she can. She is careful not to get too attached and certainly keeps her emotions in check. She does not want to give Josh the impression she is in love with him. Because she's not.

Josh always wants to make sure Randi is having a good time. Dinners, walks on the beach, rides in the country. Josh will pick an out-of-the-way place and book a romantic weekend away from all the stress of both their jobs. Never a hotel. It's a cabin in the woods, a bungalow close to the water. It's a high-rise condo that overlooks the city. He always finds the best restaurant and gets the best out-of-the-way table. It's as if the world disappears. Josh can't get enough and Randi uses Josh to fill her time. Plus, the sex is freaking amazing and who doesn't love that. Randi often has some guilt about all the things Josh does for her. Using him to fill her time. She has her own money and could easily pay for all the things they do together, so it's not about money. It's the emotional damage she could be causing Josh in the long run. She convinces herself that Josh is a big boy and knows what he's getting into. He should know not to get carried away until they have an actual sit-down conversation about where this is heading. If they did, he would realize that she is not interested in a permanent relationship. Since he had never broached the subject, Randi had just decided to keep her mouth shut and enjoy how life is going right now. She'll cross the relationship bridge when she comes to it. Until then, she will continue to slide down the banister laughing.

One night after a late shift, Josh texts Randi to find that she is up. Josh heads over to Randi's. He's only about 10 minutes away. Randi opens her front door and is immediately swept up off her feet. She is wearing a white satin camisole that comes just to her waist and a matching pair of satin shorts. The shorts have tiny pink flowers that go up the side seams. They are so short that her bottom peeks out just enough to cause a commotion. Josh picks her up, holds her tight, and kisses her so softly and deeply. Josh is never aggressive. Always gentle, kind, and loving, but tonight, he comes at Randi like a velvet freight train.

Randi: "Well, that was one amazing kiss. Have you been thinking about that all day?"

Josh: "Every second of every day I don't get to see you."

Randi: "How about a beer?"

Josh:" Absolutely."

Josh grabs a beer and gets Randi a glass of wine. They head out to her back porch. It's a beautiful evening. The moon is full and the sky is so clear you can see every star. They sit together on an outdoor cushioned couch. Josh wraps his arm around Randi and kisses her strongly but gently. Randi responds. It has been a few days since they have seen each other and Josh can hardly contain himself. After a few moments, Randi stands up and straddles Josh. Facing each other, she can kiss him madly and deeply. Once she straddles him, Randi can feel him pressing against her. Josh has been aroused since he walked in the door. They continue kissing deeply. Randi stops and pulls her top up over her head. She's not wearing a bra. Her breasts are full, round, and perfect. Josh takes off his shirt. Randi's soft breasts against Josh's naked chest cause Josh to groan with excitement. Still straddling Josh, Randi stops, grabs Josh's beer, and hands it to him. She grabs her glass of wine and they toast the day.

Randi: "How was work today? Catch any bad guys?"

Josh laughs: "Another stellar day in OBA, which is fine with me. The great thing about Orange Beach is that there is just enough crime to keep you busy, but nothing crazy like daily murders. How about you? Did you sell lots of houses today?"

Randi: "I closed one today. I love selling these high-end houses. The uber-rich clientele you get to meet opens a lot of doors."

Josh: "Seems like that is a main goal of yours. Opening doors to the top. Good for you. You should go for what you want and get as many doors opened as possible."

Randi: "Thank you, Josh. I appreciate that you can see my ambition and my goals and don't make fun of them."

Josh: "I would never do that to someone who is trying so hard to succeed. That is determination and stamina. I appreciate that about you." Josh takes Randi's glass of wine and puts it on the table. He puts his beer down as well.

Josh: "Now, where were we?" He lifts Randi to her knees as she continues to straddle him. Her nipples are even with his mouth. He starts caressing them, swirling his tongue around one and then the other. Holding Randi with his hands on her bottom. Holding her close. Randi is holding onto the back of the chair. The sensation is driving her crazy. Josh slowly lowers Randi back onto his lap. Her breasts pressed against his chest. With Josh's hands still around her buttocks, he slides his hands inside her satin shorts. No panties! Josh is over the edge. His hands caress her buttocks ever so lightly. So lightly, it gives Randi the shivers. Neither one can stand it any longer. Randi gets up off Josh and removes her shorts. Josh stands up and removes his jeans and his briefs. Josh sits back down. Randi, with her back facing Josh, sits down on top of Josh. She inserts Josh inside and with her hands on his knees, she moves ever so slowly, a rhymical movement. Josh can stand no more.

Josh: "I can't hold on any longer. Let's go, baby. Go with me!"

With that statement, Josh and Randi cry out at the same time, their bodies shivering and shuddering until they are finished. When they both finally recover, Josh puts his arms around her waist and holds her tight. Man, he loves this woman. His feelings for her are like none he's ever had. After a few minutes, Randi slowly lifts herself off Josh.

Randi: "Do you want to go in and take a shower?"

Josh: "Are you going to join me?"

Randi: "Of course, silly."

They both get up and jump into the shower. It doesn't take long before their arousal for each other starts again. The soft soapy caressing of each other's bodies drives them back to where they were an hour ago. Shower done, dried off, and into bed. Josh rolls over and lays on top of Randi. She put her arms around his neck, and they kissed longingly, hungry for each other. Josh takes his leg and slides Randi's legs apart. He lifts her body slightly and slides inside with ease. Randi takes her long, smooth, tan legs and wraps them around Josh's waist. Slowly and with purpose, Josh makes love to Randi again. They cum again at the same time. The second time is so strong and explosive. His movements are so forceful that Randi must hang on. Randi loves this hard strong action. As she starts to orgasm, she arches her back with her legs still wrapped around Josh's waist. She lifts her hips over and over, feeling Josh deep inside her. When they finally finish, exhausted, Josh climbs off Randi, wraps her in his arms and they fall asleep, satisfied.

Josh thinks as he slowly falls asleep. *"I want this woman for myself. I have kept these feelings close to the vest. Randi hasn't shown her hand or let me know with any certainty if she wants the same. We have not had that conversation yet, So I'll continue to pursue her. Give her everything I have, and hopefully, she'll ask for a commitment. When she does, I will ask her to marry me.* Not telling Randi exactly how he feels will turn out to be a devastating mistake.

13

BUSINESS AS UNUSUAL

D Campbell Land Development, LLC., has done well for the past twenty years. Doctor Campbell has worked his way around Alabama, buying up large pieces of land and transforming them into beautiful subdivisions. Doctor Campbell was no fly-by-night developer. He was known as a straight shooter in land development. He did not cut corners. He did not do shady behind closed-door business. He knew that eventually everything would come out and he revered and cherished his name and reputation. It also made it a lot easier to buy large pieces of property when the property owner, the city, mayor, legislators, and commissioners knew your reputation and your background for integrity. Doctor had found a piece of property for sale. One hundred acres across from the beach. Not on the beach but across the main Perdido Beach Boulevard. You were only a two-minute drive to the nearest beach parking. He wanted the subdivision to be reasonably priced.

Houses not squished together. A gorgeous pool with modern changing room bathrooms. He always liked putting a small green space in each of his developments. They didn't have to be large. Just a great place for kids to play, have family picnics or just get out and run around. Doctor was meeting with all legal entities of the city. Since he knew exactly what was needed for officials to make critical decisions. There had been several meetings already and as always, he was completely prepared. He had his land development checklist from the Professional American Land Title Association (ALTA), and he had the survey done and ready. It was perfect. Lauren had done a thorough job in getting things put together. She had obtained everything from the landowner who was willing to sign an option agreement.

He had the low areas checked for slopes, floodplains, wetlands, water elements, high points, and ridgelines. Unsightly views, natural or man-made bodies of water, wildlife, soils and rock, steep slopes, and plant communities, even government constraints. He knew all about the local attitudes toward new developments. He always challenged his team and posed the question, what is the future vision for this area? He made sure that they developed a comprehensive plan because 40-50 years from now, he wanted his development to still be a shining star for Orange Beach. He obtained all the relevant codes and ordinances (subdivision, zoning, energy, building.) He initiated a study regarding threatened and endangered species.

Other requirements included gathering thorough documentation to prove financial capacity, subdivision sketch plan, final subdivision plan, Planning Commission Approval, permitting, and fees. He had the subdivision costs worksheet. Engineering and survey reports are all done and ready for viewing. He had already completed soil tests and the removal of hazardous materials, estimates for landscaping, paving-sidewalks-driveways, and plans for a park dedication. The estimated retail value of finished lots and the construction sequence were also done. Everything had been approved by the city.

Doctor was meeting with Randi Reynolds. She is the real estate agent for the seller. Doctor was prepped and prepared for this meeting, but it was just a formality. He wanted the property, and the seller was ready. It now came down to numbers. Doctor never borrowed money for these purchases. His company had strong assets and he was very wealthy. He would pay cash and buy it outright. He typically got a better deal with an all-cash offer. His meeting with Randi is scheduled for 10:00 am.

Randi was ready and had done her homework for her meeting with Doctor Campbell. She has never met him personally but is aware of who he is and his reputation. She had seen him out and about several times, and from what she could tell, he seemed like a fun, outgoing guy. She is ecstatic that she is the selling agent on this piece of property. She met the landowner a couple of years ago and knew she was interested in selling but was unwilling to pull the trigger at that time. Randi was kind and subtle. The owner, Debbie Thompson, was older. She has two daughters and six grandchildren. She wanted to make sure they were taken care of but without the hassle of land ownership. After two years, Debbie was ready to sell, and the constant contact Randi kept with her made it easy for Debbie to have Randi handle the sale. Randi did her due diligence in the background of the property and the value. She was going to make sure that D Campbell Land Development, LLC was not going to try and swindle an older woman. Doctor Campbell didn't roll that way. He also knew the value and was not out to screw anyone. Just hoping for a small break since it's an all-cash offer. The land was valued at $22,000,000.00. Depending on how the negotiations go, he was ok with that amount.

Randi arrives a little before 10:00 a.m. Lauren meets her in the lobby.

Lauren: "Good Morning, Ms. Reynolds. It's good to meet you. I am Lauren Scavone, Doctor Campbell's Executive Assistant. Can I get you anything? Water, coffee, juice?"

Randi: "Good Morning Lauren, nice to meet you as well. I would love some coffee."

Lauren: "Absolutely, if you would like to follow me, I will take you to the conference room: there are pastries as well, and I will get the fresh coffee. Doctor will be with you in a moment."

Lauren escorts Randi to a conference room. It's stunning. Decorated beautifully but not overdone.

A large table for spreading out all sorts of paperwork and a lounge sitting area where you can leisurely discuss business over coffee or a drink. Very well thought out to not intimidate anyone. Lauren shows up with a fresh pot of coffee, followed by Doctor. He and Randi exchange introductions. They stand and stare at each other for a couple of minutes. Lauren is still in the conference room, watching the interaction. It's somewhat of an uncomfortable silence. Lauren does not like the lust-filled look they are giving each other. She is aware of what is going on. Like the Eagles' song, "You can't hide your lying eyes." She breaks the silence.

Lauren: "Um, Ms. Reynolds, can I pour you some coffee?"

Randi doesn't hear Lauren for a few seconds. "Oh, I'm sorry, excuse me, of course, that would be great."

Lauren: "Doctor, would you like some coffee as well?"

Doctor: "Sure, Lauren, that would be great." But he never takes his eyes off Randi.

Lauren is discombobulated inside. She doesn't like seeing the bedroom eyes between Doctor and Ms. Reynolds. Lauren knows that her relationship with Doctor isn't solidified in stone. She continues to hope that he will see the light and make her his main female focus. She's been working on that for a couple of years and treads lightly when it comes to affairs of the heart. She doesn't force herself, make demands, or throw hissy fits if he's out without her. She wants to be his only and trying to navigate that has proven to be an uphill battle. Now this beautiful woman walks in the door, and he can't take his eyes off her. *This sucks! This woman is gorgeous and older than I am. I can't hold a candle to that if Doctor makes a move.* Lauren thinks sadly.

She tries her best to be professional. She again breaks the silence and tells everyone to take a seat. Lauren always sits in on these meetings with Doctor and takes notes in case there is anyone she would need to reach out to. But today Doctor tells Lauren she isn't needed in this particular meeting since things are already pretty much done. Just the signing of the documents. Lauren stands there for a couple of seconds, not knowing how to react. Randi and Lauren look at each other and they both understand what is going on. Randi just smiles. Lauren turns on her heels and leaves the conference room. As she heads out, Lauren can barely contain her tears. She goes into the bathroom and cries silently for a couple of minutes. She composes herself and goes back to her office.

Doctor reaches out his hand: "Ms. Reynolds, it's so nice to finally meet you though I feel like I've seen you before. So much of our conversation has been over the phone. It's good to finally put a beautiful face with a voice and a name."

Randi smiles: "Thank you, Doctor. That is truly kind of you to say. I've seen you out before, so maybe subconsciously, you saw me in a crowd. Please, call me Randi."

Doctor: "Well, Randi, I will always tell a beautiful woman that she is beautiful. I find nothing wrong in pointing out the obvious. Some women get very touchy with a compliment. I hope I haven't offended you."

Randi: "On the contrary, I certainly enjoy all compliments that come my way. Keeps me humble." Doctor just looks at Randi and she starts laughing. Doctor shares the laugh. They take a seat at the table and get started. As they are passing the paperwork back and forth to look at it, Doctor decides that it would be much easier to be on the same side of the table. He gets up and walks around the table and takes a seat next to Randi. They continue to look over the paperwork. Doctor is sitting so close to Randi it feels like he is sitting on her lap. But she is not moving. She is smiling inside as she takes in this flirting with full force. Doctor is very handsome, fit, smart, well-spoken, and exudes confidence like nobody she has known before. Randi feels the excitement inside start to build. Her nipples start to get hard and she can start to feel the tingle work its way down her body. Doctor can immediately sense the change in Randi's aura. Something has shifted. He can feel her sexual vibration. Doctor and Randi both feel the attraction. As they sit so close and continue to talk business, their bodies are touching, and Randi becomes a little off her center. Now she can't concentrate on business.

After a couple of minutes, Doctor says laughing: "Randi, Randi, are you ok? Are you still with me?"

Randi: "Oh my gosh, I am so sorry. That was rude. Running all these numbers and the amount of paperwork I need to take back to Ms. Thompson to sign, I lost my train of thought." She wonders if that excuse worked.

Doctor: "Totally understandable: it's a lot of I's to dot and T's to cross. But we will get through it. When we finish, would you like to go get some lunch to celebrate?"

Randi: "Yes, of course. I would love to celebrate this transaction. I'm not going to lie, it's the biggest one I've been involved in, so this truly makes my day!"

Two hours later when they finished up, Doctor tells Lauren that he and Randi are going to lunch and he's not sure what time he will be back.

Lauren: "OK, thanks for letting me know. Ms. Reynolds, congratulations on the sale and it is very nice meeting you."

Randi: 'Thank you, Lauren, yes, it's a big day for me for sure. It's nice meeting you too. I hope you have a great rest of your day."

Doctor and Randi head out of the building together. Doctor with his hand on the small of Randi's back. As Lauren watches from her office window, she is hoping they will take two separate cars but is deflated when they both get into Doctor's Land Rover and drive off.

Lauren turns from the window. She goes and shuts and locks the door and weeps silently after what she just witnessed. Doctor is not even close to being hers. He made no bones about his attraction to Randi Reynolds. He wasn't embarrassed or concerned with Lauren standing right there. It's like she wasn't even in the room. Lauren wonders if Doctor views her as nothing more than friends with benefits, sex buddies for a few years now. What does she do? She loves this man. Genuinely loves this man and he has no second thoughts about her at all. She is going to have to bring this up and talk to him about it. She needs to know where she stands. If she is a fuck buddy, she is selling herself short. She needs to know how Doctor feels about her and then she will have to decide.

This is probably the beginning of the end. Lauren thinks as she continues to cry.

14

OFFICE LIAISONS

D Campbell Land Development has been in Orange Beach for almost three years now. To Lauren, the last three years have been amazing. She has a great job, an amazing, beautiful home, and a gorgeous single boss. What more could a girl ask for? She didn't have much of a social life, but she didn't care. Her goal was Doctor Campbell and she never wavered. Doctor made it clear to her that the harder she worked the better compensated she would be. To prove that, Doctor bought her a fully furnished home as part of her wage package. Nothing extravagant, but a nice little two-bedroom 2 1/5 bath place in an upscale building. Now it was another late-night getting documents ready for a deal.

Doctor: "Lauren, why don't you go home? Go out, go have some fun. Call your friends and go hang out."

Lauren giggled: "I would if I had any. I haven't had the time to go out and make any."

Doctor: "Lauren, you have to get a social life here. You can't spend every waking moment working."

Lauren: "I don't mind. We are trying to get the business up and running. Eventually, it will slow down and then I'll get a social life."

Doctor: "Well, see that you do. I don't want you to burn out and quit. You are too important to me and this business. I don't want to lose you. You're an amazing Executive Assistant."

The time after hours that they spent together was sexually exciting for Lauren so she didn't care about a social life. Doctor was handsome and unattached. Lauren has developed a huge crush on him. She knew he still saw her as a kid because he'd known her since she was a kid. But still, she could not help herself. She is, after all, in her 30's and a full-grown woman. Doctor is handsome and funny. An honest businessman and loyal to his employees. She had been attracted to him since she was a teenager. Being this close to him for hours on end had ignited a deep inner hunger that gnawed at her soul. She is aware that she is significantly younger than him and she is sure she goes unnoticed in the romantic arena that belongs to Doctor Campbell. She did her best to get noticed. She dressed professionally but maybe a little on the sexy side. She would stand a little too close and lean over his shoulder to look at his computer. Nothing aggressive but just enough to, hopefully, get him to notice her. If he has, he's not letting on.

Doctor has been around hundreds of women, and he is very aware of the antic's women use to try and get closer to him and it bored him. But he has finally noticed Lauren as a woman. He knows her family. They have their wealth and Lauren grew up in that wealthy enclave, so Doctor knows she's not after his money. Since he knows her parents, at times, it feels a little lecherous to be thinking of her sexually, but Lauren is 34, and they are both adults. Doctor decides that he will take Lauren up on her seductive charms and attempts. He plans to rid some sexual tension along the way and see what develops.

Lauren had not dated anyone since she moved to Orange Beach. She went out on a couple of dates but nothing as a steady diet. She was just super busy getting Doctor's company up and running. When things settled down, she was determined to branch out and find some friends to hang out with but right now, her goal was Doctor Campbell. One step at a time. It has been long nights for several weeks and things are finally coming together.

One night when they were working late figuring out logistics, they had ordered dinner to be delivered since it was going to be another late night. Lauren and Doctor had stopped for a little while to have dinner along with some wine, taking a little bit to refresh and release the stressors of getting a business up and running. They talked over dinner about business, how they were progressing, the path they wanted to take, and the new hires. Typical stuff.

Lauren had gotten up and taken their empty plates to the trash. When she was coming back to finish her wine, Doctor lightly grabbed her, pulled her onto his lap, and started kissing her, just a light-loving kiss. Lauren is momentarily caught off guard. She can't believe this is happening. She's been trying for months. She always figured he thought that she was too young. She assumed he still saw her as little Lauren Scavone. He stops and looks at her. She doesn't say anything. Just stares at him for several seconds and returns the kiss. She is paralyzed with desire. Her body is frozen but her thoughts race inside her. She is instantly so sexually aroused she is having trouble containing herself. Doctor lifts Lauren off his lap, takes her hand, and leads her to the couch in his office. He lays her down on the couch, climbs on top of her, and kisses her passionately. Lauren has been so hot for this man that she kisses him back with the same burning hot haste. Since Lauren is wearing a dress, Doctor has easy access to her. He slides his hand under her dress and pulls at her panties. She helps him get them off. He has his hands between her legs. He is very aware and gentle. This is not some excessive groping sexual encounter. This is more like they have been waiting, and the buildup has been out of control. As Doctor has his hands between her legs, he can feel how wet she is. He very slowly inserts his finger. Lauren arches her back and takes a deep breath. As Doctor continues, Lauren reaches out for him through his pants. He stands up and pulls Lauren up off the couch. He pulls her dress up over her head. She takes off her bra. Doctor sheds his clothes. He lays Lauren back down on the couch. Lauren's mind is racing. Her breathing has become very shallow. It's almost like she is afraid to breathe as she might break the spell. As he grabs her, they both stop breathing for a couple of seconds. Lauren wraps her legs around his waist as he fills her. Doctor slides his hands under Lauren's hips and slowly and rhythmically lifts her up and down. Lauren gets in the rhythm. She feels it in her entire body. She starts to let loose. Her rhythm gets faster. She starts to let out a soft low groan. Doctor can tell she is ready. They are both so sexually whipped up to action that when Lauren lets loose and starts to shutter, that's all Doctor needs. Doctor grabs onto Lauren with all his might while he explodes inside her. Their white-hot fever seems to last forever. They don't move, waiting for the moment to cool down. After they both recover, Doctor kisses Lauren, lifts himself off her, and helps her up off the couch. Lauren goes to his private bathroom, cleans up, and gets dressed. Doctor gets redressed as well. Back to work and nothing more is said about the incident. Lauren doesn't know what to do. The situation is a little awkward at this particular moment. She needs to recover, regroup, and see what happens. Needless to say, that encounter was amazing!!!

Lauren and Doctor started having sex regularly after that. She would do her thing: he would do his. When he was hot and bothered, no matter what time it was, Lauren was always ready. When he'd go to her place, she would answer the door in the skimpiest, sexiest nighties he had ever seen. They didn't stay on for long. He would swoop her off her feet and head straight to the bedroom and they were at it like teenagers. He would go on dates with other women to be seen out and to get his name out there. Ultimately, when these women would figure out who he was, they were working overtime to get on the inside. It never worked and he made sure he never had sex with these women. It only complicated things. No, he had Lauren. He doesn't know if she ever went out on dates or even had a boyfriend. If she did, she never mentioned it. If she had a boyfriend, it never stopped them from having sex. She was willing every single time he called. Sometimes, he felt bad as he suspected she had stronger feelings for him, but that conversation never came up. He has never told her he loves her, never took her out on a date. They worked together, so they saw each other all day long. They would have lunch together in his office and occasionally, they would lock the door and go at it on his couch. She loved to have him sit at the conference table, crawl under the table, and take him. One time when that was happening, Jerry Lunde, the accountant, knocked on the door.

Without thinking, Doctor said, "Come in."

Lauren stops what she's doing and is as quiet as a mouse. Doctor had papers in front of him as though he was working.

Jerry: "Hey, boss, can I talk to you?"

Doctor: "Sure, Jerry: what's going on? Is everything ok?"

Jerry: "Yes, I just wanted to drop off the numbers for the Wild Cove project. The numbers look great. We are coming in way under budget on this one. I was wondering if we could go through this right now if you're not busy."

As Doctor is trying to keep his composure, Lauren is still under the table, trying to be as quiet as a mouse. To barely move. Her breathing is so shallow you can't even hear it.

Doctor: "Uhm, oh, sorry, Jerry, I've got to hop on a conference call in a couple of minutes. Can we go over this tomorrow morning?"

Jerry: Oh sure, no problem. How about 10:00 am?'

Doctor: "10:00 am is perfect. Please close the door on your way out."

Just as Jerry closes the door, Doctor's orgasm explodes. He stiffens his legs and they tremble uncontrollably.

Lauren slowly crawls out from under the table, smiles, and walks out of the conference room leaving Doctor with his pants down around his ankles.

15

A MAN IN DEMAND

Doctor Campbell opens the passenger door for Randi. He helps her get in and then shuts the door. Randi quickly checks her lipstick while Doctor walks around to the back of the vehicle. She buckles her belt as Doctor opens the driver's door of his car. He climbs in and they head to lunch.

Lauren is watching from her office window, watching Doctor help Randi into his car. From her vantage point, he looks giddy. He has a pep in his step, as if one's stagnant blood has been set in motion.

Doctor: "Any particular place you would like to go for lunch?"

Randi: "I am a fan of Cobalt or do you have something else in mind?"

Doctor: "Cobalt it is." As he heads towards the restaurant, they chat about the business deal. About what it is going to mean to the community. He tells Randi when he wants to get started and how long he thinks the development will take.

First, they make a quick stop at Randi's office, and she takes all the paperwork inside and asks her assistant to look over everything. Randi is pretty positive that it's all correct but a second set of eyes always helps. She jumps back in the car and off they go to lunch.

Once they get to the Cobalt, Doctor asks for a private table far in the corner, away from the crowd. The restaurant is super busy today, people cutting out of work early because it's Friday. It feels like the whole world wants the work week to be over. Doctor wanted to have a conversation with Randi without having to holler over the noise. They are seated towards the back of the restaurant at a corner table but are still able to look at the water and the boats traversing Perdido Pass. Of course, they both know a lot of people and are smiling and waving and saying hello to everyone they know.

Doctor pulls the chair out for Randi and he sits next to her. Their knees are touching under the table. Neither one moves. Doctor can feel something from Randi. Something he has not felt for anyone in a long time. Randi feels it too. She is nervous. The vibration between them is, without a doubt, magnetic. This is something she has never thought about having in her life. She likes her freedom, not having to answer to anyone. Not having to worry about anyone. But this magnetic pull she feels is electrifying, even intoxicating. *What is happening? This is so crazy. I have never felt anything like this before. Not even with Josh. But man, oh man, I like it!* She thinks. She decides to let loose, go with the flow, and see what happens and where this is going to go. She will keep her guard up and try not to get caught up in all this intensity. That might be harder than she thinks.

Doctor wastes no time in getting to know Randi. He asks her what seems like 1000 questions about her upbringing and background. One right after another, non-stop. Randi starts to giggle and tells him to slow down. Doctor orders a bottle of red wine and they toast the property sale. They order lunch, sip wine, and fill each other in on their perspective backgrounds. Legs still touching. If, for any reason, Randi moved her leg, Doctor was quick to reestablish the connection. This did not go unnoticed by Randi. She found it intriguing. She knew who Doctor Campbell was. Pretty much everyone did. She had seen him out at various places, usually with a bunch of people. Sometimes, she would see Lauren with him, and she thought Lauren was his girlfriend. But when she saw her today and realized that she was his assistant, that just made Doctor fair game. There was one thing Randi was good at…. "the game." She played it multiple times to get what she wanted. She was never mean about it, she just knew exactly how to play it, to get what she wanted and hopefully get out without anyone knowing they had been played. Doctor was different. There was electricity in the air between them. They both felt it and they knew each other did as well. When lunch finally arrived, they ate and talked and discussed business. Both hope and agree to do multiple business dealings together soon. Randi was ecstatic about that. What a windfall it would be to work with Doctor Campbell regularly. She is instantly bubbling over with excitement at the prospect of this new adventure. A second bottle of wine was ordered and their lunch continued for a few more hours. The longer they sat there, the closer their bodies got. Every once in a while, Doctor would lightly graze Randi's knee. Randi would return the touch lightly and put her hand on his thigh for just a second. Doctor decides to take a chance and let his hand slowly slide up Randi's leg just to gauge her reaction. When she didn't flinch, he decided to move his hand a little farther up under her dress. He would inch up a little bit at a time to see how far he could get before she stopped him. She would give him a light smile: he would wait patiently, and finally, his hand would go up a little farther. Randi doesn't move his hand, enjoying the light touch on the inside of her thigh. Doctor continues his journey up her leg and finally reaches the very top where her legs come together. As his hand gets there, Doctor is excited and surprised at the same time. All the while Randi sips her wine and continues to discuss business as if nothing is going on. *How can she manage to keep her cool with everything going on under this table?* Doctor thinks to himself. He takes his fingers and very lightly caresses through her silky panties. Randi doesn't move for a few seconds, looks Doctor directly in the eyes, and lightly pulls Doctor's hand away. She squeezes his hand and places it back close to her knee. They just look at each other, not saying anything. They raise their glass to a silent cheer. *Yes, they will be lovers.* Doctor thinks to himself.

They finish their second bottle of wine and head out. Doctor takes Randi back to his office so she can get her car. Before she gets out, Doctor reaches over, pulls Randi to him and they kiss. An electric, sultry, longing kiss in the parking lot of his business. Doctor reaches under Randi's dress and runs his hands up her thigh. She opens her legs slightly. Doctor leans in and continues to kiss her deeply. Randi returns the kiss with such intensity that it sets her blood dancing like lightning across the night sky. They continue to kiss for a couple more minutes with Doctor's hand massaging Randi's thigh. When they part and start to readjust their clothes. They both look up and there stands Lauren directly in front of Doctor's car. Lauren had been standing there for several minutes watching the entire escapade. They both look up and are horrified that Doctor's assistant caught them in the car. Randi looks at Doctor and then again at Lauren. Lauren had tears running down her cheeks. *Wait, what? This is not making sense,* thinks Randi. *Why would Lauren be crying because her boss is trotting the hot with me? Oh, wait,* she thinks, *Doctor and Lauren must be lovers!*

Lauren, staring intently, finally breaks her gaze turns, and walks to her car. She gets in her car and doesn't move. She leans her head on the steering wheel and sobs. Secretly hoping that Doctor will come and see if she is ok. He doesn't. As she sits for several minutes crying, she is emotionally drained. She reaches into her purse and gets out her make-up wipes, she wipes her face and any make-up that happened to run or smear. Taking a deep breath, she starts her car and puts it in reverse. Lauren is hit with the realization that her relationship with Doctor is nothing and will not go anywhere. Dreams crushed: her soul ripped to shreds, she heads home distraught and a lot wiser.

Randi: "Doctor, would you like to explain something to me."

Doctor: "Explain what?"

Randi: "First, why is your assistant watching us, and second why is she crying?"

Doctor just sits there looking at Randi, not saying anything.

Randi: "Doctor, are you screwing your assistant?" Doctor doesn't respond.

Randi asks again. "Doctor? Are you screwing your assistant?!"

Finally, Doctor says: "Yes, I am screwing my assistant. But I am not in love with her, she is not my girlfriend, we have sex. We don't make love we have sex."

Randi: "Doctor, the look on Lauren's face right now and her reaction is not from someone who is friends with benefits."

Doctor: "Randi, there is nothing between Lauren and me. We started this arrangement when we first got here. New to Orange Beach, not knowing anyone, and getting the business off the ground did not allow us to meet anyone socially. When you spend long hours together eventually you do get horny. It was convenient. I used her, and she used me. We have never had a conversation about being a couple. I've never even taken her out on a proper date. Anytime we have been out together in public it was for business purposes only. I have never made any noise about us being together. This whole afternoon with you was dynamite and the most exciting thing that I have experienced in a long time. Don't worry about any of this at all. We are adults and are free to do what we want. Lauren is free to go out with whomever she wants and she can screw whomever she wants. I don't ask and I don't care."

Randi: "When I would see the two of you out and about, I thought she was your girlfriend. But when I met her today and saw that she is your assistant, it all came together and made sense to me. If I had the slightest notion that you were sleeping with her, I would have had second thoughts about doing this. I feel bad for her. The look on her face was pure soul-destroying. She is clearly in love with you. I think you should set the record straight. I don't want any altercation if we happen to be out and so is Lauren. Please clear the air with her."

Doctor: "I will, don't worry about that."

Randi: "So, that being said, do you want to get together later tonight?"

Doctor: "Absolutely. I've got a couple of things to finish up and then I'll head over. I will set Lauren straight."

Randi: "Give me a couple of hours. I need to stop by my office and see how my assistant is doing with the paperwork. Then I want to go home and shower and change."

Doctor: "Perfect, see you then."

As Randi gets out of Doctor's car, her brain is working and swirling about breaking her date with Josh. *Well, I am working on a deal with Doctor, so this is a work dinner.* She thinks. *Josh will understand.* She jumps in her car, pulls out her phone, and calls Josh to break their date. She has bigger fish to fry and Doctor Campbell is a whale.

16

HOW MURDER BEGINS

Waitress smiling: "How are you today? What can I get for you to drink?"

Shovelhead: "Miller draft and make it cold."

Waitress: "Our beers are always cold here, honey: you don't have to worry about that."

Shovelhead: "I'm not worried sweetie, just in need of a beer."

The waitress smiled, turned around, and, in a couple of minutes, came back with a cold draft beer and set it down in front of Shovelhead.

Waitress: "You should have been here about an hour ago. You missed all the excitement."

Shovelhead: "Really, what happened?"

Waitress: "Well, there were a few construction workers in here having some beers. Two other fellas came in and sat down and ordered a Bud Light. The construction guys started giving them a hard time. The next thing you know they're all fighting."

Shovelhead laughing: "That would have been fun to watch."

Waitress: "Yeah, it was quite a scene. We just got it all cleaned up right before you came in. We called the police, and Orange Beach PD came in and locked up all six of them—the four construction workers and the two other guys. They hauled them all off. Orange Beach PD does not mess around."

Shovelhead: "Was any of them hurt bad?"

Waitress: "No, mostly a bunch of punches and kicks. Didn't see any real bad injuries. Some blood, for sure. You know how it is."

Shovelhead: "I sure do. I like those better myself than the shooting and stabbing ones. Those always take so much out of you."

Waitress: "I know what you mean. Do you want to order something to eat?"

Shovelhead: "No I'm just waiting on a friend. When he comes, we might order something."

Waitress: "OK, I'll keep an eye out for you."

Shovelhead: "Thanks, sweetie." The waitress turns around and gets back to her job.

In a few minutes, Highside walked into the bar. He was an imposing man. He stood about 6'5" with grey hair around his temples, he had a rugged face and a slim body. Shovelhead knew he was a mean cat. Highside had been a leader in the biker gang before he was sent off on the murder rap years ago. But he stayed in the gang, even in the joint, everybody respected him. When he got back out, he was still a full-fledged riding member and head of their Tampa Chapter. Highside got his moniker when he was a young outlaw after having a bad wreck on a motorcycle that's called a "high side." It's when the motorcycle's rear wheel takes off and starts to travel around the side towards the front wheel, usually going around a curve. The back wheel goes out from under the bike and starts to spin around. After that wreck, he kept the name. Shovelhead's nickname was not as exciting. He had owned a Harley Shovelhead motorcycle. It was a type of engine that Harley had manufactured for a while. It was very popular with the bikers and very famous at its time. He had owned one of those and rode it when he first got into the outlaw club and so that became his nickname. But here they were, two brothers in the same outlaw club, two brothers who had spent time in the joint together, two brothers who had similar lives, violent, criminal, always scratching to get by. Two losers who believed themselves to be one of nature's rare gifts. They embodied the proverb "He that is full of himself is empty."

Highside looked around and spotted Shovelhead in the corner of the room. A little wave of his hand and he walked slowly over. They shook hands, touched shoulders, and greeted each other.

Highside: "Shovelhead, you old dog, you look like shit."

Shovelhead responded: "Thanks man, that means a lot coming from you." They both laughed.

Highside: "Do you know when the last time we saw each other was?"

Shovelhead: "Gosh darn, it's had to have been seven, eight years ago. Just before I was getting out"

Highside: "Yeah, that's about right. You seem to be OK. How's everything been going?"

Shovelhead: "Well, OK. You know I ride all the time. Cracked the head on my Harley and I'm trying to repair that. It's my fault for dragging it."

Highside chuckles: "Well, you can take the Harley out of the boy but you can't take the boy out of the Harley." They both laugh.

Shovelhead: "What have you been up to Highside? You sure spent a lot of time inside."

Highside: "Well, you know I've had my ups and downs. I'm back running the Tampa Chapter again. You know we are doing pretty good. I bartend some, we do a lot of runs. We make a lot of money for the club. You know how it is."

Shovelhead: "Yes, I do. Just be careful. You don't want to wind up back in the joint."

Highside: "Yeah, I know, but shit, we gotta do what we gotta do Shovelhead. We ain't like the rest of the people. We are the 1% you know."

Shovelhead: "I know it, baby. I've known it all the time."

Just then the cute blonde waitress returns to their table. She looked at Highside.

Waitress: "What are you having handsome?"

Highside: "You got any IPA back there baby?"

Waitress: "I sure do."

Highside: "Bring me one of them, a hamburger, and some fries."

Waitress: "You got it Darlin', anything on the burger?"

Highside: "Grilled onions."

Waitress to Shovelhead: "Ok, how about you, you want anything to eat?"

Shovelhead: "Yeah, I'll have a burger, too, with cheese, lettuce, tomato, and French fries."

Waitress: "You got it." She turns around and heads to the kitchen to put in their order and get Highside his beer. She returns with a cold IPA and leaves the men to their conversation.

Highside: "OK, let's talk business. I got a job for you. It pays ten grand plus five grand for expenses."

Shovelhead: "Ok, I'm listening."

Highside: "I learned a long time ago that doing these things costs money too. I don't want those costs to cut into your profit."

Shovelhead: "I appreciate that."

Highside: "This way, whatever gear you need you can pay cash and not leave a trail. Also, you won't be calling me for money for this and that."

Shovelhead: "Got it."

Highside: "We meet here today once. Once more when the job is done. That's it."

Shovelhead: "Alright, so give me something good to go on— something I can get to work on. I don't like it, but I need the cash. But since it's you, well, there are a lot of guys I would just walk away from. But you and me, we're tight. We're brothers. I know you're good for the money, and I know you won't stab me in the back, so let's have it."

Highside glances around the bar. Nobody is paying attention to either of them. The waitress has gone to the kitchen, the bartender is talking to some woman at the bar, trying to chat her up. But everybody is far enough away not to hear them or pay attention to what they are saying. Highside reaches into his pocket, pulls out a picture, and slides it across the table to Shovelhead.

Highside: "This is who I want you to whack. The address is on the back: it's here in Orange Beach, just off the beach road. She's the only one who lives in the house."

Shovelhead: "Wow, gorgeous, you fucking her?"

Highside: "No, I ain't fucking her! I ain't never been with her. It's business, Shovel, it ain't love, it's business."

Shovelhead: "Alright, I got it. Well, it doesn't matter anyway. I don't care about that. I just know I can get it done, and I can get it done easily. She's pretty good-looking in this picture, though. How old is she?"

Highside: "She's in her late 30s, I guess, somewhere around 37 or 38. She's a local. Her hours are very sporadic and all over the place. But if you can scope out her car and pick the right time, you'll be able to see when she's home."

Shovelhead: "Yeah, I can do that easy enough, I know that area pretty well. A lot of cars around, tourists and everything. A lot of people moving. It won't be hard to drive by that and get a look. What kind of car does she drive?"

Highside: "It's a 2022 green Mustang Convertible. You can't miss it. It sticks out. You'll know when she's home for sure with that car out front. It's her only vehicle so she'll be easy to track. I got the inside info on her. I know what she's about."

Shovelhead: "Any special way you want me to do this Highside? I mean is there any particular method you require? You aren't going to give me that crap like make it look like an accident, are you? Cause those are tough sometimes."

Highside says: "Nah, I don't care anything about it looking like an accident. You can make it look like whatever you want. I don't give a shit. Just as long as when you are done, she's deader than your old man's dick. That's all that matters to me."

Shovelhead: "Alright, I can take care of this no problem. I can use any technique or method I want, is that right?"

Highside: "Yeah, I don't care what you do or where. You have to figure that out. Run her over, burn her up, stab her, shoot her, bash her head in, blow her to bits. I don't care, drown her if you want. Just make sure she's dead and she ain't coming back."

Shovelhead: "OK, Highside. I can take care of that. Is there a particular time you want this done?"

Highside: "Well, I would like to have it done in the next 30 days. I know you need some time to make a plan, cruise by her place a couple of times. Get the lay of the land. Try and figure out her schedule as much as you can and get things together. If you can't do it within 30 days, call me and let me know. When you call me, you know, talk construction."

Shovelhead: "Yeah, for sure. I got it. Let me see what I can do."

Highside then reached into his pocket, pulled out an envelope, handed it to Shovelhead, and said. "Don't open it here. There are seventy-five hundred-dollar bills in there. I'll give you the other seventy-five hundred when the job is done and we'll meet back here afterwards. Same way, come alone, we'll meet on a Wednesday after you've done the job. Just give me a little lead time to get up here from Tampa. I'll be driving. I don't want to fly. I don't want any record at any airport, so you just give me a little time, a couple of days' notice. I'll meet you here on the Wednesday following the completion of the job."

Shovelhead: "OK, that sounds good High."

Highside: "I want this done without ANY contact between us, whatsoever. You got all the information you need. I added that extra five grand for expenses, you keep the change. You know what I want. I don't need a whole lot of questions back and forth and you know any extra contact can be dangerous."

Shovelhead: "I got it High. You won't hear from me until it's all done."

Highside: "Alright brother, after this blows over, give it a few months, and when everything cools down. I want you to come down to Tampa and spend some time with me. Maybe we can ride a little bit. You know, cruise somewhere. Head over to Daytona and have some fun. How does that sound?"

Shovelhead: "I would like that High. Sounds great. I haven't been down that way in a while and I need to get back there."

The waitress returns with their meals. The burgers are everything people say they are—hot, juicy, and delicious. The guys devour their lunches in silence and have another beer.

Highside: "You slip out of here Shovel. I'll pay the bill and you just head on back to Mobile. I'll talk to you soon."

Shovelhead stands up and takes the last swig of his beer and walks out of the Barrel Tavern.

Highside takes a few more bites of his hamburger, finishes his beer, and waves the waitress over.

Waitress: "Where did your friend go?"

Highside: "He's already gone. Just give me the ticket. I'll take care of the tab and take care of you too."

Waitress: "Thanks Baby. Are you new in town? I ain't never seen you in here before."

Highside: "Really, I've been here before. I guess I just have that face that is easy to forget."

Waitress: "Yeah, I guess so. Alright, here's your bill."

Highside reaches into his wallet, pulls out a bunch of $20 bills, pays the bill, and gives the waitress a hefty 30% tip

Waitress surprised: "Wow, thank you so much. I appreciate. It's hard enough to get a decent tip in this place."

Highside: "Yeah, I know what that's like sometimes: good luck, baby."

Highside gets up and walks outside. He gets in his brand-new Audi convertible and heads out of Orange Beach, back to I10, and back towards Tampa.

Shovelhead heads back to mobile. *The next time I'm in Orange Beach, there will be one less voter*, he thinks. One less woman, one less human. He almost feels bad for her, but he needs the money, and life has never treated him right, so it's her bad luck. He cruises down I10 with the radio blasting.

17

JOSH AND THE GUYS

Randi sits in her car in Doctor's parking lot and calls Josh.

Josh: "Hey you sexy thing. I was just thinking about you. So far, it's been a slow, normal day, and I will be done by 4:00. I cannot wait to see you! I have been looking forward to this all week."

Randi: "I am so sorry Josh: I have to break our date."

Josh: "Why, what's going on?"

Randi lying: "I am trying to close the huge 100-acre property sale to D Campbell Land Development. It's a huge payout for me. We have things about 95% done. I have to go back to Ms. Thompson and clear a few things up and then get back with D Campbell Land Development and get things signed. This is too important not to get finished tonight. I hope you understand."

Josh: "Of course I understand. I'm extremely disappointed but I would not stand in the way of your business. Maybe we can reschedule for tomorrow night."

Randi: "Of course, if all goes well tonight then yes, we can get together tomorrow night. Thank you so much for understanding."
Josh: "Of course. Good Luck and keep me posted."

Randi hangs up the phone with a little bit of guilt. Josh is a great guy, but she doesn't have her appetite whetted for him like she does for Doctor: he is the flavor she craves. Like Doctor and Lauren, she is not beholden to Josh. They haven't talked about their future. She has told him she loves him but she is not IN love with him. Why should she feel guilty? Because Josh is a stand-up guy. But she can't dwell on that right now. She has to go home and get ready for a night out with Doctor!

Josh is crushed. Tonight was the night he was going to tell Randi he was in love with her. He had a special romantic dinner away from prying eyes. He had it all arranged. He has been planning this for weeks. Now this! Well, he can't be mad. It's business. It's Randi's livelihood and he would never get in the way of that. Especially since it's such a huge opportunity. He will just re-group and postponing for 24 hours is no big deal. He'll just have to wonder about it for one more day. He is so stressed as to how she will handle it. Will she be shocked, surprised, excited? All these things ran through Josh's head and he has been mentally preparing for each scenario.

Oh well, it's Friday night, so he called a couple of buddies and told them plans had changed and if they wanted to go get dinner and drinks. They all agreed on Big Mike's Steak House at 6:00 pm. Josh went home, got ready, and headed out to meet friends. Big Mike's was packed as usual. They don't take reservations but the wait is usually not that long. Josh and his three closest friends, Larry Wright, Kevin Murphy, and Steve Dawson, order drinks and wait for their table. Larry is a friend from high school and is now an

Assistant Chief of the Orange Beach Fire Department. Kevin is a state trooper and Lieutenant of the Alabama Marine Patrol. Steve is a former partner and is now a sergeant in the Orange Beach Police Patrol Division. They sat outside, waiting for their table, talking and laughing. Having a great time. They waited for about thirty minutes until their table was ready. Big Mike's Steak House has been in Orange Beach it seems like, forever. Great steaks at a great price. The restaurant is very rustic, with wood-paneled walls and metal corrugated ceilings. It has a horseshoe-shaped bar. Two different seating areas. The guy's got a table in the back corner next to the wooden American Flag that hung proudly on the wall. Of course, they all ordered steak and baked potato. Finally, Josh lets the guys know his plans.

Josh: "Well guys, I've got something to tell you."

Kevin: "Yeah, What's on your mind? You get a promotion?"

Larry: "Promotion? Wow, that would be awesome."

Steve: "Maybe end up being Police Chief?"

Josh: "I wish that were the case. But no, I'm not getting promoted—not that I know of anyway."

Steve: "Spill it, man. What's going on?"

Josh: "I've decided to ask Randi to marry me!"

They were shocked and sat silent. Josh hasn't said much about his relationship with Randi. He always keeps his personal life very close to the vest. Which is why they are all surprised.

Kevin thinks. *Josh must love this girl to lay it all out like this.*

Larry: "No way, are you serious?"

Steve: "Are you sure about this? How long have you been seeing each other, a year 18 months at the most."

Josh: "I am dead serious. I don't mess around with things like this. Since my divorce, I have kept women at bay emotionally and for very good reasons. But Randi, man, she just got to me. Got to my soul, my heart, my mind, my cravings!"

Kevin: "Does she know how you feel about her? Have you told her you are in love with her or have you just told her you love her? Those are two completely different feelings."

Josh: "I have told her I love her, yes. However, I have not told her I am IN love with her—not yet. I want to say all that when I ask her to marry me."

Steve: "Has she told you that she loves you or that she is madly in love with you?"

Josh: "She has told me she loves me. But, like me, she keeps her emotions and feelings close as well. I truly think neither one of us wants to get hurt. But when I pop the question, I want there to be a full-on dialogue on where we are, where we are going, and where we WANT to go.

Larry: "Don't you think you should have already had that conversation? Since you haven't, she might not react how you think or want. Maybe instead of asking her to marry you, why don't you tell her you are in love with her and want a future together? Try that and see her reaction first before you go full tilt and ask her to marry you. When do you plan on asking her?"

Kevin: "I agree with Larry. Tell her you are in love with her. Have that conversation first man."

Josh: "Well, I was going to ask her tonight but she got this huge land deal that she is working on that will be a significant windfall for her. She's finishing up the agreement with D Campbell Land Development tonight. The sooner the papers get signed, the relief that it's all done will set in. Then we can celebrate. I think this will work out better since we will have two things to celebrate."

Kevin: "Congratulations, man. I'm happy for you. I sure hope you'll be celebrating. Randi is a beautiful, fun, and personable woman. You two seem to be perfect for each other."

Larry and Steve in unison: "Here, here." As they all lift their glasses.

Steve: "Here's to a wonderful, happy, amazing future."

Josh is so happy that his friends are happy for him. Sometimes you don't see what your friends see. But they've all met Randi and they like her. It's time to finish dinner and go celebrate his news.

The guys pay their tab and head across the street to Luna's restaurant for more drinks. They walk in the door: the place is pretty busy. Typical for a Friday. They find a place at the bar and order drinks. Talking, laughing, telling jokes. Larry heads to the bathroom. As they are relaxing with their drinks, Steve looks over and sees Randi in the corner with some dude. Steve pokes Kevin and shows him what he sees. Kevin raises his eyebrows in surprise. Before either one could say anything, Josh noticed it as well. He doesn't say anything at first. Larry comes back from the bathroom and senses something is not right.

Larry: "Hey, what's going on? What happened to the party?"

Kevin points to the corner of the room.

Larry: "What the Fuck!"

Josh: "Guys, calm down: I'm sure there is an explanation."

Josh heads over to the table. Randi sees him coming but before she can say anything to Doctor, Josh is at the table.

Josh: "Hey Randi!"

Randi stands up and Josh plants a kiss on her. Doctor is taken aback by this and so is Randi. The public display of affection has always been low-key with them. They agreed on that. *What is Josh doing?* Randi is not happy about this.

Randi: "Hey Josh, what are you doing here?"

Josh: "Oh, me and the guys got together last minute when you canceled our date."

Josh introduces himself to the man at the table.

Josh putting his hand out: "Hi, I'm Josh Myers."

Doctor stands up and says, "Nice to meet you, Josh. I am Doctor Campbell. I own D Campbell Land Development. Randi and I are finishing up our land purchase paperwork. Her client accepted my offer and we decided to get a drink to celebrate the transaction. You look familiar to me: do we know each other?"

Josh: "I am a Detective Lieutenant for the Orange Beach Police Department, I'm sure you've seen me around."

Doctor: "You are probably correct. It's very nice to meet you."

Josh: "You as well." Turning to Randi, "Congratulations on the sale. I know it's been a long process. I can't imagine how excited you must be. I'll let you get back to celebrating the good news and Randi, I'll see you tomorrow night."

Josh turns and leaves heads back to his friends and takes his place at the bar.

Larry: "Well, dufus, what was that all about?"

Josh: "That is Doctor Campbell of D Campbell Land Development. That's who bought the 100 acres from Randi's client. They are celebrating the sale agreement. It's a huge payout for Randi. I'm excited for her."

Steve: "Doesn't it bother you that she is sitting in the corner with this guy?"

Josh: "No, should it? It's busy and loud in here, If you want to have a business conversation, sometimes you need that privacy. I'm not worried."

Steve: "As close as they are sitting and as cozy as that, it doesn't look like business to me."

Larry: "Well, if that's business it's the oldest business."

Kevin: "If she's in that business, you don't want none of her business."

Josh: "Come on guys, the bottom line is. It's none of your business!"

Kevin: "Really, look at that guy. Plus, I've heard of him and he's worth a fortune."

Josh: "Guys like that are usually players and don't like to get bogged down with just one woman. Besides, Randi makes her own money, and since she is the only realtor to work with both sides, on the sale of this property, she will make about $1,000,000.00. Like I said, I'm not worried. Let her have her celebration tonight. She and I will have our special celebration tomorrow night."

The guys looked at him like he had a kink in the brain, but if he's not worried, they will mind their business.

Randi and Doctor watch Josh head back to the bar. Randi was embarrassed by what just happened. Doctor is also surprised since Randi has made no mention of having a boyfriend.

Doctor: 'Um, do you want to explain what just happened?"

Randi: "Yes, I can explain."

Doctor: "Because I just witnessed a man coming over and kissing you very intently and familiar."

Randi fidgeted, "Yes, I can explain. Josh Myers and I have been seeing each other. Nothing serious. He's a great guy, but I am not interested in him romantically. We go out on dates, we hang out, and yes, we have sex—just like you and Lauren. The big difference between me and you is that Lauren is madly in love with you. I am not madly in love with Josh. There is nothing romantic between us."

Doctor: "Are you sure? Cause that was no casual kiss. Do you think Josh is madly in love with you?"

Randi: "Well, he's told me that he loves me, and I have told him I love him. But he does not rock my world. Yes, Josh and I had a date tonight. Yes, you and I had business to take care of. If I was in love with Josh, nothing would have happened between us today, and I would be out with him, not you."

Doctor: "Well, I don't want to have any trouble with the local Detective Constabulary."

Randi: "Yes, I agree. We are having dinner tomorrow night and I will reaffirm with him that he and I are friends with benefits."

They went back to their discussion about business, keeping an eye on Josh and the guys. After about 30 minutes, Josh and the guys got up to leave. Josh came back over to their table.

Josh: "We are headed out, Doctor. It was great meeting you. You did well having Randi as your realtor. She is the best. Enjoy the rest of your evening. Again, Randi, congratulations on the sale."

18

THE ONE YOU LOVE
FINDS ANOTHER

Josh turns and leaves, catching up with his friends and they head out to another bar. They end up at the Gulf, a cool restaurant on the west side of the Perdido Pass. This is where Josh met Randi and this is where he plans on proposing.

Larry: "Listen, Josh, you are one of my best friends. I can't let you go without telling you how I feel about this whole dinner Randi was having. They just looked too cozy, too familiar."

Kevin: "Dude, I agree with Larry, We were watching you walk over and when Randi saw you, we could see just a slight "oh shit" on her face."

Josh: "Come on, you guys. This is the conversation you want to have right now?"

Steve: "Josh, you are a great friend. A stand-up guy. We don't want to see you get hurt. You haven't been seeing her that long. A marriage proposal after less than two years is shocking, especially for you."

Josh: "Like I said, she has gotten into my soul. She feels different to me than other women I've dated. To me, she is everything I could ask for. I know this is unusual for me but in my heart, I know it's right. I hope you guys understand."

The guys just stand there all staring at Josh. They don't like it. They are very wary of the situation. But when someone is determined to marry someone. They put blinders on. They all hope Josh sees things before it's too late.

Randi and Doctor watch the guys leave. As the guys reach the door, Doctor puts his hand between Randi's thighs and slides it up to her panties. Randi slightly opens her legs and lets Doctor caress her between her legs. All the while trying to keep her composure. She is so horny at this moment she's afraid she'll come right here in the restaurant. She lets Doctor caress her for a couple of minutes longer and moves his hand. Randi takes a deep breath. Doctor smiles at her knowing exactly what she is going through. He cannot wait to get her into bed. Caressing her body from head to toe. Touching every inch. Tasting every inch. All these thoughts are giving him an enormous erection. Unless he calms down, he'll never get out of the restaurant unnoticed. Talking business can crush an erection in record time. So, back to paperwork, numbers, dates, timelines. The rest of the "business dinner" went very well. Randi and Doctor both agree that they need to have conversations with Lauren and Josh first. They both were ready to get out of there and move on to more romantic things.

Doctor takes Randi back to her house. Josh is sitting in his car just down the block. The conversations he had with his friends caused him to take a step back. He didn't want to wait until tomorrow night to see Randi. He wanted to see her tonight. He figured her meeting wouldn't last that long so he decided to go by her house and wait. When he sees Doctor's car pull up, he figures Randi will just hop out and go inside her house. As Josh opens his door to meet her on her porch, he sees Doctor get out and walk her to her door. What he sees next knocks the wind out of him.

Josh watches as Doctor walks Randi to the door and kisses her longingly and lovingly.

Doctor: "Do you have any idea how horny I am right now? I can barely walk."

Randi: "I know exactly how you feel. I'm struggling to control myself. It'll only be a couple of days. It will be worth the wait."

As Doctor and Randi stand on her front porch, Josh feels like someone just took a bat to his chest. This can't be right. This can't be happening. Josh simply cannot wrap his head around what he is seeing. He stands by his car frozen in shock. He can barely breathe.

Doctor wants to take her inside and make love to her right now. But they agreed to have the conversations first. After several minutes, Randi opens her front door and slips inside. She leans against the front door being lifted to the stars. She tingles with emotion: this guy is heavenly. The whole evening with Doctor has raised a whirlwind within her. She tries to shake it but she can't. She is invigorated and stressed at the same time. Having the conversation with Josh will not be easy. As Randi turns to lock her front door, she hears a knock. She smiles and pulls the front door open.

Randi: "Ok, Doctor, we agreed to wait until...."

There stands Josh, just looking at Randi. He isn't saying anything, just standing there. Randi is rocked on her heels at what Josh heard.

Randi: "Josh, what, why, what are you doing here? How did you know I was home?"

Josh: "I didn't want to wait until tomorrow to see you, so I drove by to see if you were home from your "business meeting." I guess the guys were right. This was more than a business meeting."

Randi: 'The guys? What are you talking about?"

Josh: "The guys told me something didn't look right. They had their suspicions. I told them no: you are all wrong. Randi wouldn't do that to me. I love her and she loves me. What is going on?"

Randi just stands there.

Josh: "Randi, what is going on? Can you at least be honest with me?"

Randi: "I'm sorry Josh. I wanted to have this conversation with you and was going to have it tomorrow night. I care about you, but you just don't touch my soul that deeply. I love being around you, we have fun together, and the sex is amazing."

Josh: "You love me, love being around me, we have fun together and the sex is amazing. Sounds like a pretty awesome relationship to me."

Randi: "It would be for someone else. See, Josh, I don't have that clap of thunder for you. I don't get that feeling in my stomach, and I don't miss you when you're away. I'm sorry. I thought you felt the same way. We're just friends with benefits. I'm okay with that. I thought you were too."

Josh: "Friends with benefits. Fuck buddies! That's how you think of our relationship? Fuck buddies."

Randi: "Josh, why are you so upset about this? We never had any conversation about being monogamous. Ever. What am I missing?"

Josh completely deflated: "You are right. We never had that conversation out loud. It's my fault that I assumed it wasn't needed. It's my fault for falling in love with you without saying anything. It's my fault for thinking that you were going to be in my life forever. It's my fault that I assumed you felt the same way. To think you would want to marry me."

Randi: "Marry you? Where did that come from?"

Josh: "Never mind. It doesn't matter anymore anyway."

Randi: "Josh, what are you talking about? Getting married? Do you want to marry me?!"

Josh: "Well, not anymore. Goodbye, Randi."

Josh turns, walks out the door, and heads back to his truck. Holding onto the ring in his pocket so tight it left marks in his palm. He takes the ring out and looks at it. Puts it back in his pocket and heads home, grubbing along and feeling so low he could walk under a dachshund.

Randi just stands at the door. She watches Josh pull away from the curb and disappear down the street. *What have I done?* She thinks. *Has Josh been that invested? How could I have missed that?* She closes the door and tries to think about what just happened. *Josh mentioned marriage. We have never discussed marriage, not once. I don't even know where that came from.* Randi sits on the couch and tries to put the pieces together. Josh had become so intoxicated by her that his brain was scrambled, and he was now living in a fog of the mulligrubs. She has never made any noise about getting married. She never even brought it up. It's not something she wants. Not now, anyway. Maybe not ever. She thinks back on their time together and is trying to remember if they even had that conversation. Even if they did, Josh didn't get the memo. *It's not my fault that he got caught up. He should have said something earlier. Let me know his intentions. Don't just spring on me getting married. No, this is all on Josh. I am not going to feel guilty about what just happened.* She continues to think to herself. *Then why do I feel like shit right now?* She wonders.

19

LOVE CAN'T FIND A WAY

Doctor leaves Randi's house. Gets back in his car and has to adjust himself so he can drive. What an incredible night. Randi Reynolds is one of the sexiest women he's ever met. The way she looks, her dress, her vibe. She exudes a sexual prowess that he's never experienced. The sexual tension between them is out of bounds. His hand between her legs, running his hand up to her panties under the table at the restaurant, was such a turn-on that he was having a hard time controlling himself. He knows this woman will be a sexual dynamo and he wants every part of her sexuality.

As he leaves, he decides he needs to take care of business with Lauren and get it out of the way. He doesn't want to let it fester over the weekend. He heads to Laurens condo. He knows she'll be up after what she witnessed today in the parking lot.

Lauren leaves work and decides she needs to go out and be social. She doesn't want to sit at home with her thoughts. She makes a quick trip home and changes her clothes. Something sexy to get some attention. She gets an Uber and heads out. She starts at the Coastal, then to the Gulf, and finally ends up at Flora-Bama. The place is packed. Tourist season and Flora-Bama is a tourist destination. She runs into a couple of female friends and hangs out with them for a while.

Emily: Hey Lauren, how the heck are you? We haven't seen you in days. What's going on with you?"

Lindsey: "Work still crazy busy?"

Lauren: "Yes, but it's finally settling down. I decided I needed to get out more. Work will always be there. This place is packed. But, looking around there are a lot of cute guys in here."

Emily: "What's the guy's name who has a crush on you? The tall, cute guy who always wears cowboy boots?"

Lauren: "That's August. Yeah, he's super-hot. I haven't seen him in a while."

Lindsey: "Well, look over your left shoulder."

Lauren turns to look, and there stands August staring at her. He smiles at her. Lauren smiles back. She turns to Emily and Lindsey.

Lauren: "See you guys later!" She makes a bee-line to August. Emily and Lindsey smile and decide to go dance.

Lauren makes her way over to August. They give each other a huge hug. It's loud inside and you have to yell to hear each other.

August: "Do you want to go outside so we don't have to yell at each other?"

Lauren: "Absolutely." They make their way outside. It's a beautiful warm summer night.

August: "I thought you fell off the face of the earth. What's been going on?"

Lauren: "Work, work, and more work. But no more. I am going to slow down. Work will always be there and there is no sense in killing myself."

August: "You need to go out and have some fun. We all do. You have to experience life and all that it has. Like you said, work will always be there. The fun, not so much. I want to take you out sometime. Would you be up for that?"

Lauren: "Absolutely, I would love that. Let's go back inside and have a drink."

They head back inside Flora-Bama and have a few more drinks and lots of dancing. After about two hours, Lauren kisses August.

Lauren: "This was a lot of fun. I am going to head home. It's been a long day. I'll talk to you soon." August walks Lauren to her Uber and says goodnight.

An hour after Lauren gets home, Doctor lets himself into Lauren's building and heads to the elevator. He pushes the button for Lauren's floor. He gets to her door and knocks a few times and Lauren finally opens the door. She had been drinking and she looked disheveled. Well, it is late. She was probably in bed. She opens the door and there stands Doctor in the doorway. She just stares at him and she finally stands aside and lets Doctor come in. She is wearing a skimpy powder blue teddy with matching panties. Her breasts are firm and perky and you can see them through the teddy.

She just stands there looking at him.

Lauren: "What do you want? Why Doctor?"

Doctor: "What do you mean why?"

Lauren: "Why would you do this to me?"

Doctor: "Do what? Listen, Lauren, we are not in a relationship. We never have been. You are my executive assistant. You do an amazing job. As part of your salary, you have this beautiful place and we fuck. That's what we do. We fuck. We have never had any conversation about being together. You should have understood that from the beginning."

Lauren: "I was hoping that over the past few years, you would see how good I would be for you. I have made myself available for you every single time you call. I opened my heart and my legs to you whenever you wanted. I've done every sexual thing we could think of at any time. Doesn't that mean anything? I have been hoping you would fall in love with me."

Doctor: "Lauren, all that means is you like to have sex. You like the excitement of possibly getting caught. That doesn't mean we are in love with each other. Look, Lauren, you are a beautiful woman but I am not and will not ever be in love with you. I have never promised you anything and I have been clear about that."

Lauren, looking beaten down, rushes to Doctor and wraps her arms around him, hugging him tightly. Doctor just stands there waiting for her to settle down so they can get this resolved. He's not sure how since she's been drinking. She reaches down and grabs the erection he still has for Randi. Doctor doesn't move. Lauren starts to undo Doctor's pants. First, his belt, then the zipper. She reaches her hand inside and starts to caress him. Lauren drops to her knees, releases him, and puts him in her mouth. Doctor is standing inside the door watching Lauren give him a blowjob. He is so horny from being with Randi and this visual is taking him over the edge. Doctor pulls Lauren up, pulls her teddy up over her head, and tosses it on the counter. He slides her panties off and tosses them as well. He lifts Lauren onto the counter and slides her to the very edge. Doctor inserts himself inside Lauren. She is holding on as he voraciously moves in and out. After a few minutes, Doctor picks Lauren up off the counter and takes her to her bedroom. Lauren is already naked. Doctor steps out of his pants but doesn't bother to take off his shirt. He goes back to what he was doing.

He stops, lifts Lauren up turns her over. Tells her to get on her hands and knees. Doctor enters her from behind, holding onto her hips for leverage. As he is positioned to take her from behind, Lauren puts her hand between her legs and brings herself to life. As her body reacts and starts to pump. It's enough to make Doctor let go at the same time. He lets out a moan so loud he's afraid the neighbors would hear. He continues to pump as his arousal starts to subside. Exhausted, he climbs off Lauren and lays on the bed. Lauren, herself exhausted from her explosive orgasm, curls up next to him. Doctor lays there for a few minutes. He gets up and starts to get dressed.

Lauren: "Where are you going?"

Doctor: "I have to go."

Lauren: "Oh, are you going to go fuck her after you fucked me?"

Doctor just stared at Lauren: "See you at work Monday."

Doctor leaves, leaving Lauren crushed. Her thoughts slide down on a toboggan of unhappiness. She can't believe any of this is happening. She always thought in the back of her mind that Doctor was screwing other women. She pushed that to the side not wanting to think it was true. But what she saw today confirmed her worst fears. She is nothing more to Doctor Campbell than his executive assistant and F-buddy. Lauren got up, changed the sheets on her bed, and went to take a shower. She never expected Doctor to show up. When she saw Doctor standing there, she couldn't control herself. She just did what she automatically does when he's around. Opens her legs. She is not looking forward to Monday.

20

LOVE IS COMPLICATED

Josh slowly drives back to his place. His mind is a NASCAR raceway. The speed and sound are confusing him. His thoughts are a scrambled mess. He is trying to hold it together but he's losing his grip. *How could I have gotten this so wrong,* he thinks. *How did I not see the red flags?*

Looking back, all the signs were there, screaming at him every time they got together. He just didn't see them. He was so wrapped up in Randi Reynolds that he was like a squirrel dodging traffic on an L.A. freeway.

He put everything he had into this, his heart and soul. He didn't want to push her too hard, so he kept his composure and kept his feelings close to the vest, waiting for the right time to let her know. His thoughts consumed him. Should I have done it sooner? Should I have laid it all out on the line months ago? If I had, would things have been different? Maybe not, *but I would have known before I found myself wallowing in this Serbonian Bog.*

Being a Detective Lieutenant, you have to keep your emotions in check. He is a professional and when doing your job, you have to look at things from a distance. You don't get involved emotionally. You don't take one side over the other. You look at everything with a neutral point of view. But in real life, Josh isn't that way. He's romantic, he's affectionate, loving, caring, and very thoughtful. He has two completely different personalities. He has his work persona and his personal persona. He keeps his personal persona for home and with family. If he is off duty and out in public, he has to have somewhat of his work personality up front. But at home, behind closed doors, he is a dynamo in the romance department. He took all the energy that he had to keep under wraps during his shift and poured it out when he was with Randi. He gave her every inch of his being. Randi took it, but it always seemed to Josh to be a little aloof in her response, above the clouds maybe. Josh figured she was waiting for the right time. Making sure he was as genuine as he appeared. Hoping she was opening up to his love and accepting it wholeheartedly.

His friends saw something tonight he didn't. Maybe he did and didn't want to admit it. *Otherwise, why would he go to Randi's house and park a half block away? Was he subconsciously second-guessing? Wanting to prove the guys wrong? Catching Randi in a lie?*
He doesn't know. He's just utterly crushed. Josh gets back to his place, goes inside, and turns on one small light. Just enough to make out his living room. He goes to the liquor cabinet and takes out a bottle of bourbon. He gets a small glass, sits on the couch, and goes over, again, what just happened. He leans his head back on the couch, takes a sip of bourbon, and starts to weep.

The weeping turns into crying and eventually an all-out guttural beastly moan that causes his whole body to cramp up. He is crushed. He is sobbing like a baby. He doesn't care. The old story that men aren't supposed to cry has always been a myth. To "buck up" and be a man is lost on him. He never bought into that. He is deeply emotional and sensitive and this is crushing his soul. He continues to sip bourbon and cry. His soul has been sucked dry. It's now a vacuum and his mind is trapped in a swirling web of uncertainty. All the plans he had made up in his head had disappeared like a magician's nasty trick. The life he imagined he was going to have with Randi was gone. The children he thought they would have, gone. He takes the engagement ring out of his pocket and stares at it. Almost like it's going to say something to comfort him. To tell him she was never worth it. *He's better off.* He thought. But his heart feels different. He carefully places the ring back in the box and sets it on the coffee table. He is exhausted but at the same time, he cannot help himself and goes back to pacing his house like a caged lion. Back and forth for hours, all the while sipping bourbon. Always crying. After hours of this and with the bourbon gone, Josh slowly makes his way to bed. He is worn out. He has no tears left. He has no energy left to cry. He strips down, crawls into bed, and thinks about all the lovemaking he and Randi had done in this very bed. All the raw animal sex they had in this house. The hours of laughing, talking, making love. The one thing that hits him at this exact moment is Randi never once asked about their future. She never brought it up. She never asked where this relationship was going. He hadn't noticed. He was just so enamored by her that he missed it.

Lying there with all this running through his head and thinking about the last several months. His mind wanders back to their lovemaking. He thinks about Randi's naked body on top of his. Her perfect breasts, the way he fit inside her perfectly. The way they fit together. It's all running through his head over and over. Eventually, he falls asleep. He is so exhausted that he sleeps until 10:00 am. He is woken up by his phone ringing. It's Kevin.

Kevin: "Good Morning, stud. Are you all ready for tonight? Do you need us to come over and give you a pep talk?"

Josh: "What are you talking about?"

Kevin: "The proposal dummy, have you forgotten already that you are proposing or did you change your mind?"

Josh hesitates: "I changed my mind. I'm not proposing."

Kevin: "So you came to your senses?"

Josh: "No, Kevin, it's over."

Kevin: "What do you mean it's over?"

Josh: "Me and Randi, it's over."

Kevin: "What, no. What the hell happened?"

Josh: "It's a long story."

Kevin: "I'll call the guys and we'll be right over. I'll grab breakfast."

Josh: "Kevin, I'm not in the mood right now."

Kevin: "Of course you're not. But that's when you need people around you the most. We'll be there in 30 minutes. Get up, take a shower, and get the coffee brewing."

Kevin hangs up, and Josh lies there for a few minutes, his head pounding from too much bourbon. He gets up, takes some aspirin, goes to the kitchen, and starts the coffee. He heads back to the bedroom, throws the covers up over the pillows, and heads in to take a shower.

Thirty minutes later, on the dot, Kevin, Larry, and Steve show up at Josh's door. They have enough food to feed an army. Josh lets them in, and they immediately head to the table and spread out the feast. Josh grabs cups for coffee, and the guys help themselves.

They all sit around the table, chowing down and drinking copious amounts of coffee. Josh ended up making three pots before all was said and done. The conversation revolved around small talk. Baseball, surfing, beach parties, and crimes that Josh is involved with at this moment. There were jokes, laughing, retelling stories about stupid stuff they had done. Purposeful small talk. Intentional. Four guys sitting around shooting the shit, having breakfast. Trying to get Josh in a better place this morning. Let him know that his friends will always have his back. Nobody brought up what happened. They want Josh to bring it up. If he does, they will listen and talk about it. If he doesn't, they won't press him for details. After breakfast was done and everybody had their fill to eat, there was a short awkward silence at the table. They guys just look at Josh.

Josh: "Ok, y'all have been great to do this for me. Not asking questions. Not bombarding me the second you walked in the door. But I know you are all dying inside wanting to know what happened."

Larry: "We damn sure are. But we aren't going to press the issue."

Steve: "We know you'll tell us when you are ready. We just wanted to come over and let you know we got your back."

Josh begins to tell them everything that happened last night. They guys didn't interrupt. They didn't ask questions. They just sat and listened to him. You could tell by the look on his face and the sound of his voice that he was crushed. The guys know how deeply Josh feels about things. They would make jokes about how sensitive he is. But not now. Today was different. Josh's heart thumped at his ribs between each little lost hope and they could see it. They could feel it. For as long as they have known Josh, they have never seen him like this.

After filling the guys in on what happened. Josh now becomes angry. Rightfully so. He's angry at the lie. The breaking of their date. Randi lying about her relationship with Doctor. Lying that it was only business. Not being truthful with him about where she stands. Seeing her kissing another man. Josh thinks back on the last year and a half. How many other guys has she been with? There have been weekends when Josh was busy working. Was she out fucking other men? He would call her when he finished work. Sometimes it would be 1:00 am and she was happy to have him come over. Was she out fucking some other guy and then fucking him later that night. All of these thoughts rolled out like an avalanche. The guys would only sit there and take it all in. After what seemed like an eternity, Josh was done. Exhausted again for having to relive the whole thing.

Larry: "We are all so sorry about this. We knew you loved her but didn't know to what extent. We understand how crushing this is to you. You need time to heal."

Kevin: "Dude, this sucks balls. I don't know what to say right now. This isn't right what's happened."

Steve: "Josh, could you take off and get out of town or just take a few days off and lay low to get your head straight?"

Josh: "No, I can't do that right now. I am going to be just fine. Talking it out and having you guys listen to me rant helps to make things clearer. I am not going to sit in a pot of pity soup. I'll grieve for a couple of weeks and then I'll put it away. It's all I can do at this point. Thanks, guys, for coming over and listening. Thanks for breakfast. I know you all have other shit to do, so get out of here. I'll be just fine."

They all share a laugh and the guy's head out. As they are walking out the door, Larry turns to Josh, "One thing before we go. That guy Doctor is a real dickhead and he's not half the man you are."

Josh: "Thanks, guys."

They made plans for that night to go out and get Josh's mind off of what was going on. Someplace different without the usual suspects showing up. As the guys head out the door and down the sidewalk, Josh closes the front door. He is tired and emotionally exhausted. He cleans up the mess from breakfast. He goes out on his patio. It's a beautiful, clear, sunny day. *A great day for the beach.* He thinks. Again, he goes over in his head what is happening and can't help himself and starts to cry all over again. Silently, but cries for what seems like hours. To him, it's like a death in the family. A death in his family. He told the guys he would grieve for a couple of weeks, but that was a lie. It'll be months. He is secretly hoping that Randi will come to her senses and come back. Recognize the mistake she has made. He will give her time to figure it out. When she does come back, he will welcome her back with open arms. It's all he has to hold onto at this point.

21

LOVE HURTS BUT LIFE CONTINUES

This has been a rough week for Lauren. After last weekend seeing Doctor and Randi making out in his car. Doctor came to her condo, telling her he was not and would never be in love with her. In her drunken stupor, she thought if she got him sexually aroused and ended up in bed, he would have a change of heart. He just screwed her, put his clothes on and left. But she needed this job. It paid well and she was good at it. She is going to have to learn how to navigate the workplace with this new revelation. Doctor came in Monday morning like nothing had happened. He hadn't a care in the world. He appeared to not be concerned with Lauren's predicament. He had her order lunch and called her into his office to talk about it. As they sat and had lunch, Doctor laid it all out on the line. About their relationship, his feelings, her feelings. He likes their working relationship. She is an amazing assistant and he didn't want to lose her. Would she be able to continue this working relationship after everything that has happened? Lauren agreed that she would put this behind her and concentrate on her job. They finished lunch and as Lauren was cleaning up Doctor came over to her and hugged her. As she is hugging him back, he slides his hand up her skirt. Pulls at her panties just enough to get his hand inside. Lauren widens her stance and Doctor inserts his finger. Lauren catches her breath and allows Doctor to do what he wants. He brings her to the brink and she holds on so she doesn't fall. Doctor doesn't move until she finishes. Once Lauren recovers, Doctor removes his hand and looks her in the eyes. He doesn't say anything. He turns around and goes back to his desk, leaving Lauren to clear their lunch dishes.

As Lauren walks out of Doctor's office, her mind is twisted. *What is she doing?* She thinks. *She just stood there and let Doctor do what he wanted. He knew he could bring her to orgasm with his hand. He's done it over and over. She couldn't move. It felt so great having him hold her in one arm while he brought her to ecstasy with the other. I can't keep doing this. I can't let him use me anymore.* As these thoughts run through her head, all she can think about is Doctor and how much she loves him. Is she going to be able to stop this, knowing how he feels about her? She thinks. *I better get my shit together and get some courage and strength to say no if…no when this happens again.* Lauren heads to the lady's room and cleans herself up.

The rest of the week went without any issues. Doctor was busy getting things in place for the new development and he had a meeting with the Mayor on Monday morning. Lauren made sure that everything was in order. Monday morning, promptly at 10:00 am, Chelsea Higgins walks into the main lobby of D Campbell Land Development. The receptionist greeted her and let Lauren know the mayor was there.

Lauren comes down to the lobby and greets Mayor Higgins. She saw this woman and immediately knew that this was the kind of female Doctor Campbell gravitated towards.

Lauren: "Good Morning Mayor, Higgins. How are you this morning?"

Chelsea: "I am doing great, thank you. Does Mr. Campbell have all the paperwork and plans ready and out so we can go over them?"

Lauren: "Everything is all ready to go. If you'd like to come with me."

As they took the elevator to the 6th floor, Lauren showed Chelsea to the conference room. She showed her that there was fresh coffee and pastries if she was interested and that Mr. Campbell would be right in.

After leaving the conference room, Lauren thought, *Well, before today, she only had Randi to contend with, but now, she knows Doctor will eventually make a move on the mayor. Why not? Get in good with the mayor and you can get lots of things going your way.* Lauren is feeling more and more dejected as the day goes on. Time to get out and start meeting people. Meaning MEN!!

Chelsea pours herself a coffee and takes a small pastry as she waits. Thinking D Campbell would be sort of arrogant and keep her waiting to prove a point. But she was wrong. She had just taken a sip of her coffee and Doctor Campbell walked into the conference room.

Wow, what a handsome man. He could knock the wind out of any woman. Chelsea thought as she stood there and stared at him.

Doctor: "Good Morning, Mayor Higgins. It's great to meet you. Congratulations on your win. Mayor Shillings didn't do much for the city. I'm sure you will be able to turn that around. I see you have some coffee. Is there anything else I can get you before we begin?"

This is one attractive woman. I wouldn't mind getting my hands on that. Thinks Doctor.

Chelsea: "No, thank you. This is plenty. I do have a busy day. Could we possibly get started?"

Doctor: "Yes, of course. Please take a seat. If you don't mind, I'd like to sit on the same side as we go over the documents. It's a little difficult to explain while looking at the documents upside down. Of course, if that makes you uncomfortable, I can have my assistant Lauren come in and sit in on the meeting."

Chelsea: "That is not a problem at all. There is no need to take your assistant away from her duties. I'm sure you will be professional."

Doctor: "Alright then, let's get started." Doctor takes a seat next to Chelsea and starts to give her the overall view of his plans. He showed her all the prior work he had done to make sure the development met the environmental guidelines, the city guidelines, and what was expected. He wanted the name of this new development to stand out as part of the Orange Beach persona.

As they are going over the paperwork, Chelsea is enthralled with the cologne that Doctor is wearing. Doctor glances at Chelsea, notices something immediately and pretends he is unaware. As the meeting goes on Chelsea quietly sniffs a few more times. Each time getting a little bolder.

Doctor: "Excuse me, mayor. I don't mean to be rude, but are you OK?"

Chelsea: "I am so sorry. I can't help but notice the cologne you are wearing. I have never smelled anything like that before. What is it called?"

Doctor: "It's from Roja: it's called Enigma."

Chelsea smiling: "Well, you should wear that all the time. Women would be all over you!"

Chelsea returns to the documents, thumbs through them silently for a few moments, and says, "Congratulations on your land purchase. I believe it will be great for Orange Beach."

Doctor: "Well, Mayor, I am happy that you approve of this project."

Chelsea: "Doctor, you can call me Chelsea. I want people to know that I am approachable and willing to listen. You have done a great job on this. This is going to be a great addition to the city." Chelsea puts her hand on top of Doctor's. Doctor grabs her hand and squeezes it in return. Chelsea turns and looks Doctor straight in the eyes.

Chelsea: "Doctor, maybe sometime we could go get dinner and a drink to discuss this a little more. I'd like to hear your total vision on this project."

Doctor: "Well, if you're not busy tonight, that would be great. Unless you have other plans of course."

Chelsea: " I have no plans at all, but tonight would be great. Why don't you come by my office at about 6:00 p.m.? We can have a drink there and figure out where we want to go to dinner."

Doctor: "That sounds perfect. Six it is." They both stand, shake hands and they walk to the elevator. Doctor rides with Chelsea down to the lobby. He escorts her to the door. They shake hands again and Chelsea heads out.

22

KILLER WITH A PLAN

Shovelhead was manic. He had gotten the job from Highside two days ago and he knew the days were ticking away. He had to get over to Orange Beach and scout out this job and he still wasn't finished fixing his bike. He picked up some odd jobs fixing motorcycles in the past week and now he had a break in the action. He needed to cruise over to Orange Beach and see if he could get a look at the address and, hopefully, the woman he was supposed to have a blood-stained date with. Shovelhead had lived a life of crime, but he wasn't some kind of serial killer. He shot that biker in the bar in Daytona Beach and did the nickel on it. But he never murdered anyone. He has been in some nasty bar fights and even fights with other bikers. He wasn't against wielding a motorcycle chain in somebody's face if they did him wrong. He was a violent cat for sure, but this job was on another level. He couldn't afford to make a mistake on this one. With his prior criminal record, if he got caught on this, it was his last chance. As the politicians say, it's the economy stupid, and that's what was driving Shovelhead. The economy and it sucked. He needed the cash and it was fifteen grand. He needed this money to get moving and get things together in his life.

So, he jumped in his old pick-up truck, it was about 9:00 a.m. It was a warm and sunny morning on the coast of Alabama. He turned on a country music station and headed out across Mobile Bay. Down to the Beach Express and down to Orange Beach. The place was filled with tourists, the season was in full swing. Orange Beach was directly adjacent to the Florida panhandle and that whole section of the coast was known as The Redneck Riviera. People from the southern states, Tennessee, Georgia, Alabama, Mississippi, Louisiana, and Texas were all frequent visitors to this coastal paradise. As a consequence, the main drag in Orange Beach was often full of pick-up trucks because it was probably the most common vehicle in the south. So, Shovelhead's pick-up, even though it was a little older, would go unnoticed on Perdido Beach Boulevard. Nobody would give it a second glance as it was cruising around. The town was full of them. Shovelhead had the address with him and he was going to cruise by that first to see if the target's car was in the driveway. It was 10:00 a.m. and she might be at work. Highside had told him that she had sporadic hours. There is no telling when she might be there. He also had the address of the office where she worked. If she wasn't home, he was going to drive by the office and check that out as well. Shovelhead cruised down Perdido Beach Boulevard, past the high-rise condominiums on his left that faced the beautiful beaches of the gulf. The sun was on his left shoulder. His thoughts turned to how exactly he was going to finish this job. He hadn't settled on a method yet: he wanted to get a look at the locations and, hopefully, the victim first.

He passed a restaurant called Live Bait and at the next restaurant called Doc's Steaks and Seafood, he took a right into a neighborhood known as Summer Wind. Shovelhead slowly cruised into the neighborhood. There were a few construction workers in one corner building some new houses. The houses were close together and very beachy looking. Some were on pilings to keep them above the water and where a car could be parked underneath. Others were on a straight foundation. Shovelhead rolled past the address: it wasn't far from the swimming pool, and there were no cars in the driveway. He did another loop around the neighborhood and saw there were two ways in and out. He could go in by Doc's but you could also go around back and snake through the parking lot of Live Bait and get out that way. That could be a big help. Go in one way and out the other. He also looked for any cameras on any of the poles and didn't see any. He did notice that a lot of the houses had ring doorbells on them and that was something he would have to contend with if he was going to commit the murder here. He did not see the green Mustang convertible he was told the woman-owned. He rolled around just once and left. Shovelhead was a suspicious-looking guy who didn't want to be noticed. He made his way back to the main road and took a right to drive down past the office where "his best girl" (as he called her) worked. After all, what other girl did he have worth fifteen grand? It wasn't long before he spotted the office and parked right in front was the green Mustang. *Bingo*, he thought, *I'm going to be able to get a look at her.* He drove past the office, did a turnaround in the four-lane, and pulled into a parking lot of a condo complex that was across the street. He parked his truck and waited. He was lucky. A lot of these complexes have security gates and some even have a gate attendant. But this one did not. There were a few cars in the parking lot and plenty of people moving around during the tourist season. Workmen and tourists coming and going, lots of different people starting their day and he could blend easily. Shovelhead positioned himself perfectly to see across the street and waited like a gator in the nearby marsh.

Randi was getting the paperwork ready for her new client. She had the perfect house picked out. Susan Knight was new to the area and wanted a place near the water. She knew she couldn't afford a place on the water but as close as she could get. She got a ton of money in a divorce settlement and her dream was to have a house someplace warm and by the water. The front door to the realty office opens and Susan walks in.

Randi: "Good Morning, Susan. How are you this morning? Well, I have found the perfect place for you. I think you are going to love it!"

Susan: "Good Morning, Randi: I could barely sleep last night. I know you have done your due diligence and this house will be great for me."

Randi: "Well, let's stop wasting time and get going: I have all the paperwork ready, just in case. We'll both go in my car. It's not very far from here. It'll take maybe fifteen minutes."

Susan: " Okay, sure. I can't wait to ride in your Mustang. It's a beautiful car."

Shovelhead had been there about twenty-five minutes when the front door of the office opened, and two women walked out. He instantly recognized the object of his affection. She was tall and thin, with blonde hair. From where Shovelhead sat, she looked like one sexy piece of tail. There was another woman with her. She was much shorter, with brown hair just past her collar.

They both got into the green Mustang, backed out, and headed west toward Gulf Shores. The city of Orange Beach ends at the Gulf Shores State Park. The park is just a few miles of dunes, with a park pavilion with hiking and biking trails. There was a large lake across from the beach for fishing, bird watching, and picnicking. The beautiful dune beaches draw tourists during the summer season. On the other side of the park is the City of Gulf Shores, Alabama. Another small enclave that advertises itself as a small town with a big beach. After that, it's Mobile Bay where huge shipping goes into the shipyard and commerce of Mobile. Shovelhead knew she wasn't going to go too far. He just had to make sure he could see the car and put his eyes on her to make sure he had the right person. Shovelhead pulled out of the parking lot and followed her at a distance until she turned right onto Highway 59, the main artery of Gulf Shores. She continued a few miles north, turned into a neighborhood, and pulled up to a house. Shovelhead was able to drive by and get a good look at the two women as they got out of the car. He drove by and got a glimpse of his target and that's all he needed. No sense pressing his luck any further today as he did not want to get noticed. He just wanted to get a feel for her and the car. Both women went inside the house. Shovelhead drove down a few blocks and turned around, and this time, when he came back, he got a good look at the license plate. Memorized it pulled over a block away and wrote down the Alabama tag number.

23

BUSINESS BECOMES PLEASURE

Doctor and Randi have been spending much of their free time together. Doctor will charter a boat and they will spend all day out enjoying the gulf, the sun, and each other. Their boat days always end up in bed. Making love to the gentle sway of the boat is very relaxing and exciting. Doctor always makes sure the trip is perfect. He will hire a chef to make whatever Randi desires, along with a fully stocked bar. Randi wants for nothing on these trips and she is over the moon excited that her days now involve hanging out with the upper crust. She has been striving for this her entire adult life. Doctor Campbell is uber-wealthy, successful, sexy, handsome, and generous and she is going to absorb all that he has to offer for as long as it lasts. She is getting used to the finer things in life and being Mrs. Randi Campbell has a nice ring to it. It's a 100% about-face from her attitude of not wanting to be married. But Doctor can open doors and take her to places she has only dreamed about.

Doctor loves making plans for him and Randi. He loves to surprise her with every adventure. Randi is appreciative and loves every one of their outings. If she hadn't, she would have been an amazing actress. Doctor would do anything for Randi. His feelings for her have grown exponentially and he wanted to see if that would continue. They hadn't talked about marriage and he had no plans at this moment, but the thought does keep running through his head. He just loved being with her. She is fun, funny a little sassy, and sexy as hell. Their outings always ended up in bed. He loved the charter boats the best. On one such charter, after a while in the sun, having drinks and an amazing meal, they retired to the bedroom for a while. Randi doesn't say anything while she takes off her tiny bikini. As they both stand naked, she guides him to the spot she wants to be caressed. He obliges. Randi closes her eyes and enjoys the massage for several seconds.

She is ready and he's afraid he won't be able to keep his composure. Doctor lays Randi down on the bed and kisses her deeply. Randi reaches over and takes Doctor in her hand. She starts to rub and caress him ever so gently. This goes on for several minutes. Finally, Randi pulls back and looks at Doctor. She's at the edge. Doctor gently climbs on top of her, eases her legs apart, and slowly and teasingly inserts himself. She lifts her hips a couple of times and she is there. She gives out a light moan and presses Doctor against her as her orgasm pulses. He follows her lead and lets her finish. Towards the end, Doctor finishes himself with such intensity he swears his whole body cramps up. They relax and recover for a while. They get dressed and head back up top to enjoy the rest of the charter. As the sun starts to set, the chef prepares an amazing dinner with champagne, and they enjoy the end of the day as the sun sets beyond the horizon.

Doctor has decided to surprise Randi with a trip to Europe. *He's thinking more toward the Christmas season so he has a few months to prepare. It's going to be an amazing trip. He knows Randi will love every second. He can't wait to surprise her. It's going to be epic.* He thinks.

24

BUSINESS AT THE OFFICE

Doctor shows up at Chelsea's office promptly at 6:00 p.m. Maria is just leaving. Before she heads out, she shows Doctor to Chelsea's office. As Maria shuts the door behind Doctor, she can't help but think. *Whoa! What a gorgeous man. I wonder if he is available?* she giggles to herself. She knows that Doctor wouldn't look at her twice. But she can dream. As she heads out the door, she wonders what those two have planned for this evening.

Chelsea: "Well, you're right on time. I like that. It shows you respect for my time. Come in and sit down. I have beer, wine, and bourbon. What is your choice?"

Doctor: "I'll have bourbon and branch."

Chelsea: "Coming right up." She hands Doctor his drink and pours herself a glass of red wine. "How was the rest of your day?" Is there anything else you need from me to get your project moving forward?"

Doctor: "I don't think so, I've had all the proper meetings with all the committees that I needed to speak to. Seems like every committee had to go over every single detail. It was exhausting repeating myself over and over. That's not to say I won't need your help in the future in case there are any glitches."

Chelsea: "Of course, I would be happy to intervene in any way I can. So, let's talk about this project. I know you are sick of talking about it, but just give me the cliff notes. Start date, estimated completion date, etc."

As they sit and have their drinks, Doctor fills Chelsea in on all the details. He's got the contractors lined up. It might take sixty days to coordinate their schedules and they should be ready to go. They continue with small talk, families, backgrounds, and past life experiences. Doctor likes Chelsea. She seems easy to get along with on a personal level. It could be completely different on a mayoral level. He'll just have to wait and see. He's learned to view from a distance how people are but you have to figure out quickly who they are, and he excelled at that. They had a second drink and enjoyed each other's company before they headed out to dinner.

Doctor: "I have my private driver, Max, outside. I have the perfect place for dinner. The Voyager Restaurant at the Perdido Beach Resort."

Chelsea: "Wow, that place is fabulous. Let's go. Did you make reservations?"

Doctor: "Don't worry, I always have a table there."

They get there at 7:00 p.m. and are ushered in immediately to the best table with a view of the pool and the gulf. Several people on their way out said hello and congratulated Chelsea on her win. When their dinner came most people had the grace enough to leave them alone so they could eat in peace.

Chelsea: "You still smell good."

Doctor: "Thanks, Enigma is my favorite."

Chelsea: "I've never heard of Roja, but their colognes are to die for."

Doctor: "Yes, I found them several years ago. They are from London and they have quite a few to pick from. I've tried them all. I probably have all of them in my closet. It's the only brand I wear. It continues to get noticed regularly. I'm glad you like it."

Chelsea smiling: "It's very enchanting. Like you can't get enough."

Doctor smiling back: "Why thank you, Chelsea. You are very observant."

Chelsea: "Speaking of observant, I love that watch you're wearing. It's very unusual and not a Rolex. I thought very successful men only wear Rolex."

Doctor: "Rolex is a great watch and the world's best-known luxury watch. I have a full watch collection and I don't own one Rolex."

Chelsea: "Really, why not? It's not like you can't afford it."

Doctor: "I guess I'm just not a herd animal. A lot of wealthy men wear them. In my opinion, they are just seeking status. My watches cost as much or more than a Rolex and the movements are as fine and intricate as a Rolex but most people won't recognize them."

Chelsea: "OK, what is the name of these ultimate watches?"

Doctor: "Patek Phillippe, Zenith, A. Lange and Sohn. Glashutte original and many others. The one I'm wearing now is a Glashutte original 70's chronograph."

Chelsea: "Well, I love the deep blue dial and the square face. It's extremely unusual."

Dr.: "Thank you, you are very perspicacious. They are rare to see in the wild."

Chelsea: "Well, and an expansive vocabulary too. That word is new to me."

Doctor laughed: "Yes, well, it just means someone keen and observant, someone who notices everything."

Chelsea: "Well I do admit I am guilty of that." As they both laugh. There seemed to be a spark between them. They both felt it. A sexual prowess that Chelsea found exhilarating.

I wonder if she's thinking what I am. I wonder if she's got the same feeling I am having right now. Doctor asks himself.

Doctor: "Chelsea, have you ever been married?"

Chelsea, not wanting to divulge the horrible marriage she had in her younger years, kept it short.

Chelsea: "Married for a very short time in my early 20's. Stupid love that didn't last. No kids. How about you?"

Doctor: "Married twice. Two kids by each wife. My youngest just graduated from college, so they are all pretty much grown and doing their own thing. I have a good relationship with my ex's and a great relationship with my kids. I have rooms in my penthouse that are there for them when they come and visit. Which they do quite often."

Chelsea: "Penthouse?"

Doctor: "Yes, the title penthouse makes you think it's to die for, but the name makes it sound a little more bougie than it is. It's on the top floor of the building. It has a great view of the Gulf and the marina. It's the best of both worlds."

Chelsea: "It sounds enchanting. I live on Ono Island. My family has had a house there for years. When my dad died, I wanted to get out of Huntsville. The house was left to me, so I decided to leave Huntsville and make a fresh start. So far, it's been great. I've made some great new friends. Shockingly being elected mayor! I mean, when my friends talked me into running, I laughed about it. I thought, why not? It'll give me something to do. Not in my wildest dreams did I think I would win. Now I have tons of mayoral duties that I have no clue about. It's a little overwhelming."

Doctor: "You seem very intelligent. I'm positive you will catch on pretty quickly. If you ever need any advice on how to handle people, just let me know. I've spent my life handling people."

Chelsea: "Thank you, Doctor, I appreciate that."

Since it was a beautiful summer night, after dinner, they took a ride to The Coastal and got a seat outside. They ordered drinks, listened to the sound of the gulf, and enjoyed each other's company.

Chelsea wonders: *Can I get this man into bed? He's gorgeous, tall, well-built, and smells heavenly. I will have to play this cool. Being the new mayor, I am getting recognized all the time. I hadn't thought of that. Oh well, this will be a challenge to see if I can pull it off.*

Doctor thinks: *The new mayor could be good for me. I never do any shady business dealings, but there could be a time when I will certainly need her help. A close relationship would help that. Besides she's pretty, available, sexy, and funny. Getting her into bed could be an adventure. It feels like she is thinking the same thing. Well, let's see what happens.* "Neither one is ready to leave. No reason to. It's a beautiful night. Neither one has anyone at home waiting for them. They don't have other plans later on so they enjoy the evening. A table opened up in the far corner of the outside patio, so they moved to have a little more privacy. Not that they were discussing nuclear secrets. They just wanted to have a conversation without anyone listening in. They continued to talk and laugh and get a little closer. Doctor squeezes her hand lightly. Chelsea put her hand on his leg. Rubs it a couple of times and let go. She doesn't want prying eyes to see anything. Neither is married, but she doesn't want the citizens of Orange Beach to get the wrong idea, thinking that D Campbell Land Development is going to get special treatment. The Land Development portion won't but Doctor Campbell is going to be getting a lot of special treatment if she has anything to do about it.

When they are finally ready to leave, they head back to Chelsea's office.

Doctor: "Let's have a nightcap. I'll have Max wait outside. How does that sound?"

Chelsea: "That sounds perfect." They head back to the mayor's office. Doctor hadn't noticed before what a great office it was. Very homey. Something you would expect from a female mayor. He laughs to himself. *Her office is like a mullet. Business on one side of the office and a relaxed, quiet, cozy area on the other side.* There was an overstuffed couch with tables on either end. Two chairs, also overstuffed, sat side by side that faced the couch with a coffee table in between. There were lamps on the side tables that gave the room a soft romantic glow this time of the evening. With everyone gone, there would be nobody barging in. Chelsea got them each a nightcap. Doctor a bourbon and branch and her a glass of red wine. They settled on the couch and cheered their future business relationship. It didn't take long for things to change dramatically. Chelsea puts her glass of wine on the coffee table. She takes Doctor's bourbon and puts it down as well. She turns to him and starts kissing him. She has caught Doctor off guard since he was contemplating making the first move. Oh well, it doesn't matter at this point. Doctor readily kisses her back. He pulls her tight to him as they continue to kiss. Chelsea's skirt has worked its way up far enough that Doctor can put his hands on her backside without a fight from her clothing. His caresses go from her backside to her thigh. Her skin is like silk, they pause for a minute and Doctor starts to unbutton her blouse.

Chelsea helps him. When her blouse is completely unbuttoned, she takes it off and drops it on the floor. She instantly stops and looks at Doctor.

Chelsea: "Wait one second, I better lock the door."

Doctor: "This time of night, Why?"

Chelsea: "Cleaning people."

She gets up and locks the door for safety. Goes back and decides to sit on Doctor's lap.

Chelsea: "Now, where were we?"

25

I SPY

Maria is on her way home from dinner with friends and has to drive past the office. As she goes by, she notices Chelsea's car and Doctor's driver are still in the parking lot. Strange, they couldn't possibly be discussing the land deal this time of night. Maria's curiosity gets the best of her. She pulls in and lets herself into the building. Wanting to be quiet so as to not scare anyone. She gets to Chelsea's office and tries the door. *It's locked. Interesting*, she thinks. She puts her ear to the door and listens. She doesn't hear anything but waits a few more minutes. Suddenly she hears some sort of movement from behind the door. She waits a few minutes longer and decides to get out her office keys and looks for the one that opens Chelsea's office door. She very quietly slides the key into the lock.

Doctor unhooks Chelsea's bra and lets it fall in front of him. Her breasts are magical and her nipples are hard with anticipation. He leans in and starts to give each nipple some attention. Very softly and sensually. Chelsea moans as Doctor continues with her nipples. With one hand still on her backside, he slowly finds his way into her panties. Chelsea gets up and takes Doctor's hand to stand up. After he stands up Chelsea helps him out of his pants. She has him sit back down as she moves the coffee table out of the way. She takes off her skirt and panties. Now completely naked, she gets on her knees and proceeds to fellate him. The visual is mind-blowing to Doctor. *No better place for a woman to be is with her head between your legs!"* He thinks. He puts his head back on the couch and enjoys it.

At that moment they hear someone at the door! They stop and listen quietly not making a sound. Cleaning people probably. They quietly wait for them to leave both thinking. *Good thing the door was locked!*

After a few minutes and they hear nothing, they get back to what they were doing. Small interruption, but that didn't quash their arousal for each other. Chelsea is back on her knees as Doctor continues to enjoy. When Chelsea stops and stands up, Doctor takes her over to her desk and leans her over. He spreads her legs and enters her from behind. He reaches around and grabs one of her breasts as he takes her from behind. Chelsea still has her stilettos on and it makes her a perfect height for Doctor to slide in. Chelsea, with her hand between her legs, is about to let go. As they both start to come, they both let out a muffled moan of ecstasy. Breathing hard, continuing to moan softly. As they finish their orgasms and start to recover. Neither one moves. Doctor is still inside Chelsea as she is leaning over the desk. Neither one of them heard the key in the lock or noticed that Maria had cracked the door just enough to watch the action. Maria doesn't move. She stands there and watches the entire thing. She didn't realize she was a voyeur but she couldn't help herself. *Oh, Man!* she thinks. When

Doctor and Chelsea are both done and stand there recovering, Maria backs away slowly and quietly closes the door. She leaves undetected with a huge smile on her face. As Maria drives away from the office, she watches the video she had just taken on her phone of the mayor doing a little *bow-chicka-bow-wow* on her desk. *These could come in very handy!"* Maria smiles to herself.

26

BOLD CHELSEA

Chelsea had decided that Doctor Campbell was going to be her husband. Come flood waters or the fires of hell. Whatever she had to do to make that happen, she was going to do. Of course, she had to be crafty in her approach. Her position led her to give Doctor special privileges. Completely under the table and unnoticed by others. Nothing big or elaborate, but just enough to keep him hooked. Any committee meeting where he needed her backing, she was going to do just that. Chelsea has developed an arrogant attitude as of late. Mayoral attitude. Since she always thought she was better than everybody else, it didn't take long for that to spill over to her mayor title. She had gotten pretty savvy about how to get around things, get things done her way, and get what she wanted with just enough finesse to fly under the radar. She and Doctor have talked about several other projects he had in mind and properties he was hoping to buy, so they were always getting together to strategize. Having those meetings in the privacy of Chelsea's office helped. They didn't want Orange Beach to see them together regularly. The citizens might not like the mayor and the biggest land developer constantly meeting. Makes for bad press. So, her office was much better suited. Besides, the extracurricular activity was amazing. There was never a meeting where they didn't end up naked. They worked the room. Her couch, the chairs, her desk (which was her favorite) desk chair, the floor, the coffee table. You name it, they had sex on it. Truth be told, they had more sex than they talked about business. She knew the way to a man's heart was not through his stomach. No, it's through his pants. She was determined to get Doctor so hooked on her sexual prowess that he would come begging. Chelsea had gotten to the point where she would just show up at Doctor's office unannounced. She would walk right through, ignoring everyone on her way to the sixth floor. Eventually, when this happened, the front desk girl would immediately call Lauren and let her know the "witch" was headed up. At first, Lauren was cordial, kind, and accommodating. But after several times, she had enough and was going to call Chelsea out. She could give two shits and a case of toilet paper that Chelsea was the mayor. She was rude, condescending, and snooty.

Brenda from the front desk called Lauren: "Hey, Lauren, the mayor just flew by me on her broom. She's on her way up."

Lauren: "Geez, Louis, AGAIN. What the hell is wrong with her? She is the rudest person I have ever met."

Front Desk: "Girl, you are preaching to the choir. You have fun with that."

Lauren: "Gee, thanks!"

The elevator door opens and Chelsea floats out on her way to Doctor's office.

Lauren: "Excuse me, mayor?"

Chelsea, irritated: "Yes, Lauren, what is it?"

Lauren: "I don't mean to be rude, but you just cannot continue to show up here unannounced."

Chelsea: "Well, my dear, I think you are being rude. Not once has Doctor ever told me I had to have an appointment. Until he does, you don't need to worry your little head about it. Do we understand each other?"

Lauren: "Oh, I understand."

Chelsea turns on her heels and heads to Doctor's office. Lauren typically gives Doctor a heads-up that she is coming but she decided to keep her mouth shut this time. Randi is in Doctor's office. *Let's see how this encounter will turn out!* Lauren smiles to herself and heads to the break room.

Without knocking, Chelsea bursts into Doctor's office startling both Doctor and Randi. They were sitting at the conference table discussing new properties. Of course, Doctor's hand is in between Randi's legs. Randi decided to come to their meeting panty-less. Makes the meetings so much more enjoyable. Chelsea is startled to see someone else in the office. Doctor carefully and slowly removes his hand from between Randi's legs.

Doctor: "Mayor Higgins, did we have a meeting this morning?"

Chelsea stopped and looked Randi up and down with a light look of disdain: "Hi Doctor. I'm sorry, who's this?"

Randi extended her hand: "Hello, Mayor, Randi Reynolds. I'm Doctor's real estate agent. We are working on some new properties that hopefully will come up for sale soon."

Doctor stands up and shakes hands with the mayor as well. "It's good to see you again mayor. Is there something I can help you with? Do you need something from me for any upcoming meeting?"

Chelsea, still startled: "Actually, yes, there is an upcoming board meeting to discuss some new projects." She lies.

Doctor: "Ok, well I am busy at the moment. Stop by Lauren's desk and let her know when a good time will be for you and I will make sure I clear my calendar."

Chelsea seething: "Oh, of course. I am so sorry to interrupt. It's nice meeting you, Randi. Do you have a business card? You never know. I might need some property."

Randi dug in her briefcase: "Of course, here you go. Just let me know when the time is right and I'll come up with something perfect."

Chelsea says her goodbyes and leaves Doctor's office, closing the door behind her. As she heads to Lauren's office to "make an appointment," she notices a snarky grin on Lauren's face. *Little bitch* she thinks.

Chelsea: "Tell Doctor that I will be available later this afternoon to go over an upcoming board meeting. He can meet me at my office at 4:00 p.m."

Lauren, still smiling, "I'll give him the message, but he may be all tied up with, ahh, Randi."

Chelsea stomps out of Lauren's office.

Lauren immediately calls down to the front desk, "Brenda, take cover. The wicked witch of OBA is on her way and she is spitting fire from her eyes."

Front Desk: "Oh, I hear her coming. Clicking those stilettos like someone typing a hundred words a second." Lauren and Brenda both giggle. Brenda smiles as Chelsea walks past her without a glance. As she gets past the front desk, Brenda sticks her tongue out.

Randi to Doctor: "Whoa, does she always just storm in here whenever she wants?"

Doctor: "Yes. Usually, Lauren gives me a heads-up that she's here. I'm not sure why she didn't warn me this time."

Randi: "She could have been in the restroom. Even if Lauren was gone from her desk, it's pretty bold to just walk into someone's office unannounced."

Doctor: "Tell me about it. I have to remember to lock my office door. Especially when you are here. That could have been embarrassing, to say the least. My hand between your legs, you with no panties. Oh, I'm back to getting worked up. Now, where were we?"

Randi gets up and locks the door. She turns to Doctor and he is smiling. No more interruptions. Doctor stands up and heads towards Randi. He lifts her skirt to her waist. He gets on his knees and takes Randi right there as she leans against the door. As her knees start to buckle, she has to grab the door jam. Doctor finishes, stands up, and holds on to Randi so she doesn't fall. When she recovers, they head over to the couch so she can sit down. The thought of Chelsea busting through the door, catching them in this position, makes Doctor very turned on. Within minutes Doctor is on top of Randi. He slides her legs open and slides in. Randi wraps her legs around his waist and Doctor finishes what they started. With their meeting "done," they clean up and talk for a few minutes. Randi says goodbye and heads towards the door. She stops at Lauren's office.

Randi: "Hey Lauren, did you know Chelsea was here?"

Lauren: "What do you mean here."

Randi: "Well she just barged into Doctor's office like she owns the place."

Lauren: "Yeah, she does that all the time. I didn't know she was here. She must have rolled through when I was in the break room."

Randi: "Yes, Doctor said you always give him a heads up when she's here. Wow, she's pretty bold."

Lauren: "You have no idea."

Randi: "Good to see you, Lauren. Have a great rest of your day."

Lauren: "You too."

Lauren sits back in her chair, deflated. She was hoping that Chelsea would have caught them in flagrante delicto. Lauren knows what they do behind closed doors. She and Doctor used to do the same thing. All the time. One of these times, they won't be so lucky, and the mayor will walk in on some pretty spicy stuff. *Doctor would probably ask her to join them.* She thinks with disgust.

Doctor comes out of his office.

Doctor: "Lauren, how come you didn't let me know the tornado was here?"

Lauren: "Because I didn't know she was here. I was in the breakroom for about fifteen minutes. Maybe you should tell her she needs to make an appointment."

Doctor: "Well, it would be great if she did, but I need her on my side on some of these upcoming projects, and I don't want to rock the boat."

Lauren snarky: "She could have caught you rocking Randi's boat."

Doctor: "Don't be crass, Lauren. You're better than that." He turns and walks back into his office. Lauren sits at her desk with a huge smile. Doctor is getting himself into some hot water. He better be careful because he has one dipstick and too many purring engines.

27

BLACKMAIL SMELLS SO SWEET

Maria gets to work bright and early on Monday morning. Mayor Higgins doesn't get to the office until about 10:00 a.m. She is out schmoozing and meeting the important people of Orange Beach. When she finally arrives and decompresses from all the running around, Maria asks if she can speak to her.

Maria: "Mayor Higgins, would it be possible to talk to you for a few minutes?"

Chelsea: "Why of course Maria, come in and sit down. What's on your mind? Before we start, I do want to thank you for all the help you have given me in getting settled. I don't think I could have done it without you."

Maria hesitates: "Thank you so much, mayor. First off, can we talk about John? He is always coming into the office sick. He's sick today. Walking around sniffling, moaning, and groaning. Eventually, he will get someone else sick. Can you please speak to him about NOT being here when he's sick?"

Chelsea: Of course, Maria, I know exactly what you are discussing. It drives me crazy as well. I will talk to him and clarify that he is not to be here if he is sick."

Maria: "Thank you so much. Secondly, I want to talk to you about my salary. The cost of living has gotten so bad and it's starting to become a struggle financially."

Chelsea: "I'm sorry to hear that, Maria, but I just cannot give you a raise right now. Maybe soon when I can get my head wrapped around my duties."

Maria: "What do you mean "soon?" Like two months, six months, a year?"

Chelsea: "I just don't know, Maria. I cannot promise any exact time frame."

Maria: "That's unfortunate, for sure. But I think I have a solution."

Chelsea: "OK, let's talk about it."

Maria takes out her phone and hands it to Chelsea.

Chelsea: "What's this?"

Maria: "Push play."

Chelsea hits the play button. Her mouth drops open as she watches the video of her and Doctor on her desk. She is at a loss for words. Her mind has gone numb. What the Hell!

Chelsea: "What the hell do you think you're doing? You ungrateful little bitch! What do you think this is going to get you!?"

Maria: "Look, I don't get paid enough for this position. You just said you were not going to give me a raise. My family is in Sarasota Florida. I'd like to go back home. Until I find a job there my funds are stretched to the limit."

Chelsea: "So you're going to blackmail me?!"

Maria: "That's a pretty harsh word, blackmail. I look at it more like securing my future."

Chelsea seething: "Securing your future?! Ok, spill. What exactly do you want Maria? Give me a number."

Maria: "I want $250,000.00."

Chelsea: "Excuse me?! A quarter of a million dollars? Are you crazy?"

Maria: "The big question is, what's it worth to you? All I want is to go back home. This will help me. I'll even give you my phone so you can delete the video once I get my money. I'll go to Florida, and you'll never see me again. This is not something I am going to use over and over. This is a one-time deal so I can have a stable future."

Chelsea, trying to wrap her head around what has just happened: "Well it's not like I have that kind of money in my purse. It'll take me a couple of days."

Maria: "I understand."

Chelsea: "I can have it Wednesday. We'll take care of it then. Maria, you better not back door me on this."

Maria: "You have my word. I just want to get out of Orange Beach."

Chelsea can barely contain herself. Her first reaction is to jump over her desk and go after Maria. It's taking every inch of composure to keep from doing that. Maria leaves Chelsea's office and closes the door behind her. When she gets back to her desk, she has a huge smile. Finally, she can get back to Florida and be near her family and not worry about her future.

Chelsea feels like a rabid dog inside. *What the Hell is Maria thinking? Why is she trying to ruin her? That little bitch. If she thinks she will get away with this, she is sadly mistaken. This is going to take a careful strategic plan: I need to think this through.* Chelsea muses.

28

BLACKMAILERS LAMENT

Tuesday after work Chelsea calls Maria into her office to discuss business.

Maria: "Are you having second thoughts?"

Chelsea: "No, no, absolutely not. I just want to talk about this and make sure we are on the same page. I have contacted my banker and I will have the money tomorrow night as promised. In return, you have to give me your phone. I get to be the one to delete the video so I know it's gone. It's a lot of money I'm giving you, so I will hold you to your word that you will not come back around and ask for more."

Maria: "You have my word. This is a one-time deal."

Chelsea: "Well, I can certainly understand you wanting to be close to your family, and yes, that does take money. Let's have a drink to solidify this transaction."

Chelsea goes to her liquor cabinet and pours two drinks. She hesitates for a minute, turns around, and hands Maria her drink. *I typically don't drink hard liquor, but since Chelsea has agreed to the payment, I don't want to be rude and not accept the drink.* Maria thinks, smiling inside.

Chelsea: "I do have one favor."

Maria: "What's that?"

Chelsea: "Before you leave, would you be so kind as to help me find a replacement for you?"

Maria: "Of course." Maria thinks. *This was a lot easier than I thought it would be. Chelsea wants to make sure this video disappears. As long as she pays me, it will.*

Chelsea and Maria talk about Maria's replacement, moving to Florida. A lot of small talk. Chelsea mostly just sits and listens.

As they finish their drinks, Maria starts to feel unstable. Chelsea notices but ignores it.

Maria: "Thank you for the drink and for understanding my circumstances. I should probably get home."

Chelsea: "Of course, I will walk you out."

As they get to Maria's car, she gets a little off-kilter. Chelsea helps her into her car.

Chelsea: "Maria, are you ok to drive home? You seem a little unstable."

Maria: "No, I'm fine. It's been a long day."

Chelsea: "Let me hold your purse while you get buckled in."

Maria is having a little trouble getting her belt buckled but she finally manages. Chelsea hands Maria her purse.

Chelsea: "Maria, are you sure you're ok? I can call you an Uber."

Maria: "No, that won't be necessary. I'll see you in the morning."

Maria backs up and heads out of the parking lot. As Chelsea watches Maria drive away, she takes Maria's phone out of her pocket and stares at it. *Blackmail me, you little bitch.* Chelsea thinks, *Not in your wildest dreams.*

Chelsea goes back into her office and decides to watch the video again. As she was watching, she didn't realize how hot the whole thing was. She runs the scenario through her head, sips her drink, and smiles. *Yes, this could come in handy for me. I might need it in the future. There might be something I want and this might be just the ticket to get it!* Chelsea thinks. She goes over and opens her safe. She is smart enough to know she had better turn off the phone. She holds the power button for a few seconds, throws Maria's phone in the safe, and shuts the door. Chelsea thinks, *Now, what are you going to do, Maria? Go back to Florida with your tail between your legs.*

29

BEST LAID PLANS OF LOSERS

Shovelhead was going to be thorough and make sure he got the right woman for Highside. *This girl is pretty cute*, he thought. *She was smokin' hot.* If he had met her in a bar, he'd probably be trying to hit on her for sure. She would probably not even give him a second look. Highside could pick her up for sure. *He was one hell of a lady's man.* Shovelhead hadn't gotten close to her, but he could tell by the way she carried herself that she was a real classy lady. Now he knew her house, he knew her car, and he got a couple of glimpses of her. He knows where her office is. Things were starting to come together. He pulled into a fast-food market, went in, grabbed a six-pack of Pabst Blue Ribbon. He got back in his truck, cracked one, and took a long guzzle. He headed back to Mobile. *Now is where the planning had to come together.* Shovelhead thought to himself. *How am I going to whack this woman? I can get her dead but the main thing is to keep from getting caught. I have to do it quick and easy. Cops are crawling all over*

Orange Beach and Gulf Shores. In a city like Mobile, where it's more crowded, it is easier to slip away. This place is tough. Not as many roads and I have to get the timing just right to make a quick exit. *What's fast?* He thought. *I gotta do it fast. I don't have time to be fighting with her. She is pretty tall, if she puts up any resistance, it's not going to be pretty. I could stab her, try to cut her throat, but I'll get blood all over me, and if I get stopped, I'm toast. No, that's not going to work. It's got to be clean. In and out.* He thought about drowning her, but he realized he didn't have the money or equipment to make that work. *I could make contact with her phone. That just made more chances to get caught. She could always be with another person in public and all that will make things too complicated. Running her over with my truck is a possibility but that just means there could be a ton of evidence on the truck. Trying to get out of Orange Beach with a banged-up truck would be tough, especially if there was blood on the bumper. No, that's not a good idea, and this time of year, there would be a strong possibility of a lot of witnesses. Hard to run somebody over without anyone seeing it. Which means I'd have to get her in an isolated spot.* He thought about poisoning her, but he had no idea how that would work. *I'd probably end up poisoning myself. I'd have to get close enough to try and get it in her food.* That idea, too, was way too complicated. *Plus, I'd had no idea where I would even get any. No, that's not a good idea. I could strangle her, but then I'm back to the fight and resistance aspect. She could be clawing at my face, ripping my clothes, screaming, hollering, fighting like a crazy bitch to get away. Someone would be bound to hear that and come and see what is going on. Then I'd be toast, locked up again.*

Well, the only and best scenario is that I would just have to shoot her. That's it, it was the fastest, easiest, and cleanest way to do it. I'd just have to pick the place where it would all go down. Her home, her office, in a vacant house, or somewhere in between. I still had to figure out the logistics of all that. So, he finally settled on shooting her down like a rabid dog. He took another swig of beer and just then passed an Alabama state trooper parked on the side of I10, *I put that beer down just in time.* He laughed. Shovelhead didn't give a shit. Even if the trooper had pulled him over, he was going to do what he wanted to do and that was just the way it was going to be. As he headed back to Mobile, he felt like he had a successful reconnaissance of his upcoming job. He saw the target at two different locations, he made her vehicle, he got her tag number, and has settled on his method for murder. It was Wednesday night, so there was a church meeting at the outlaw clubhouse tonight. Church was the slang the bikers used for their weekly Wednesday night meetings. They would all gather, drink beer, and hang out. Talk Harley's and make connections. If you needed some Meth, that was the time to get it. If you needed something done, that was the time to arrange it. If you needed a Harley part, that's where you'd hit one of the brothers up. If you needed some girls, they showed up later, after the church meeting. Shovelhead had murder on his mind and planned on thinking more about it on his way to church. He rolled up to church in his truck, wishing he had his Harley finished, but that was going to take him another week. He carried in a case of Pabst Blue Ribbon, nodding and smiling at the guys already there. He stuck it in the refrigerator behind the bar, grabbed one walked over to the pool table, and grabbed a cue. He started in on a game of pool with Drew "Nasty" Johnson. one of his biker brothers. Johnson got that nickname because he always exuded a multiplicity of odors that assailed one's nostrils. He reeked of every nauseating scent that a person had ever experienced. Even a shower didn't help. It was built into his pores. Shovelhead wondered if Nasty had ever even taken a shower. If he had, it was hard to tell. Others said he got the name from raping an ugly woman during a bike run at Sturgis.

Some of the other brothers said that woman was so nasty that no one in their right mind would lay a glove on her. Either way, he earned the moniker. Nasty was extremely nasty, and he wasn't very good at pool either. Maybe all that dirt and sweat clouded his eyes. Shovelhead just racked up the wins, one after the other. Shovelhead was a really good pool player. As the saying goes, "It was the sign of a misspent youth." Too many hours in beer joints and pool halls and that made Shovelhead damn good with a pool stick. After a few minutes, Iron Mike Sneed came over and sat on one of the bar stools next to the pool table, drinking a long neck. He waved to Shovelhead. Shovelhead ran the table and finished up the game with Nasty. While Nasty was re-racking for the next game, Shovelhead slid over to Iron Mike.

Shovelhead: "Hey, How's it hanging, Iron?"

Iron: "OK, Shovelhead, how's that repair coming on your wheel?"

Shovelhead: "I should have it finished this week. I'm anxious to get that head on the bike. I wanna get it sealed up and those gaskets right. I don't want no more problems with that head."

Iron: "I hear ya man. That's a great motor. I love seeing you ride it."

Shovelhead: "Yeah, it makes me feel good when I get on that thing. I love going down the beach road on it. It makes me feel alive."

Iron Mike got his nickname because he was always packing at least one gun and sometimes two. He was an excellent shot because he had been in the military. He was a dead eye and he knew it. Under his outlaw vest, he always had a .45 pistol with an exotic handle and a fancy derringer in his boot. He loved to show off his iron and everybody knew that whatever happened, Iron Mike would be packing some heat. Shovelhead knew Iron Mike was the perfect guy to ask. He sits a little closer to Mike.

Shovelhead: "Mike, I need something fast and cold that won't tie back to me. It's gotta finish the job quickly and be reliable. You know where I might be able to get ahold of something like that?" Iron pulled out his phone and hit his contact button.

Iron: "You ready for the number? I'm not going to send it to you. You gotta type it in yourself."

Shovelhead: "Ok." Iron Mike verbally read off the number.

Iron: "His name is Press and he'll get you whatever you want. He's cool, he's cold even. He won't ask no questions and he ain't cheap. But he can deliver whatever you want. If you need some advice, just tell him what you need and he'll know. Just a little advice for you, Shovelhead: Just ask for a meet-up. Don't mention anything over the phone. That's how he does business. In a parking lot somewhere or on the side of a back road. It's better that way. Try to keep everything distant, you know. The cops or the feds can track everything on your phone. Just be smart, but he's the guy who can help you out."

Shovelhead: " I got it, Iron. Thanks a lot. Do you want to shoot a game of pool? It looks like Nasty has had enough."

Iron: "Yeah, I'll take you on Shovelhead. What do you wanna bet?"

Shovelhead: "How about your old lady? She's kinda cute."

Iron: "Man, you're not as good as you shoot pool. You're gonna have to drop the price a little bit."

Shovelhead: "Alright, we'll do it for a round of beers to start with. Maybe I could work my way up to her." They both laugh.

Shovelhead spends a leisurely night drinking and laughing with his brothers. After the church meeting was over a few bikers' old ladies and groupies showed up and joined in on the party. Shovelhead talks to Michelle, one of the biker groupies who was an on-and-off stripper at one of the local clubs. She needs to get her car fixed to get back and forth to work. Shovelhead agrees to fix it for the small price of a blowjob. Shovelhead gets up off the bar stool and he and Michelle head out back behind the bar. Shovelhead drops his pants: Michelle gets on her knees and holds up her end of the bargain. It's been a while for Shovelhead so it didn't take long. After they were done, they headed back inside for another beer. Michelle isn't a bad girl: she is young and hot. She's just really messed up. Too much meth and too many rotten guys, but she hangs around the club and gets swapped around from man to man to do whatever they want. That's why they let her hang around. She goes on some of the runs with the guys but it's always on the back of a different motorcycle. Nobody is down on her, she's down on her luck just like a lot of them are. She's just part of the fabric of the scenery of the club. Shovelhead will keep his word. He'll fix her car next week. The one thing he's best at is turning a wrench. It's about 1:00 am when he leaves the clubhouse and heads back home. After all those beers and a blowjob, he conks out almost immediately when his head it's the pillow. *More murder planning tomorrow* he thinks as he falls off to sleep.

30

TOOLS OF THE TRADE

Shovelhead slept so hard that even one hundred Harley's revving up in his driveway wouldn't wake him. He didn't move an inch. He didn't even roll over. He was tired from the eyeballs down. Now he was up early with a cup of coffee, back in the living room, determined to finish up his bike and get the engine head repaired so he could get back on the road. God, he missed riding that bike. He was going to spend the next two days putting it together, no matter how late he had to stay up. He had a few beers in the refrigerator, but he would set his shoulder to the wheel and finish this. He sat down on a milk crate next to his bike, got out his wrenches, and started to work. Working on his motorcycle was always relaxing to Shovelhead. He was comfortable with wrenches and steel. He worked slowly and meticulously. He didn't rush the job. Stripping bolts and screwing up gaskets would just make it worse. He knew motorcycle engines, and of course, he loved Harley Davidson's. If he couldn't be riding one, he wanted to be working on one. But now it's time to get this finished. He worked steadily for four hours, getting all the parts right, getting the gasket set, and getting that head back on the engine. He had to disconnect a lot of things to get in there and he was putting all those parts back. He decided to take a break and have a cup of coffee. He sat down on his rotten, nasty, oil-stained couch and his thoughts turned to his upcoming job for Highside. *What was he going to do with all that money?* He thinks. *Fifteen grand!* He had already gotten seventy-five hundred that he had hidden in a hole in the wall behind the headboard. He hasn't touched it yet. It is a lot of money at one time for Shovelhead, as he thinks to himself. *This time I'm not gonna just blow it like before. No, no casinos this time, no girls, no crazy runs. I am gonna use this money smart. I just have to figure out how to do that.* He continues to think. *I better stop thinking about how to spend it and think about how to earn it. I need to call the contact Iron Mike gave me to move this thing along.*

Shovelhead picked up his phone and dialed the number Iron Mike gave him. A man answered the phone and said, "Press."

Shovelhead: "Press, this is a friend of Iron Mike's from the club."

Press: "Ok, how can I help you?"

Shovelhead: "They call me Shovelhead. I live in Mobile. We need to meet in person so we can talk. I have some questions for you, too."

Press: "OK, when do you want to do it?"

Shovelhead: "I'm available anytime, you just tell me when."

Press replies, "I'm over in Tallahassee right now, but I'll be in Pensacola the day after tomorrow. You wanna meet over that way somewhere?"

Shovelhead: "Yeah, that'll work. You got a place we could meet?"

Press responds, "There's an ice cream shop out on Navarre Beach. Just beachgoers and tourists, so nobody will pay us any mind. Just meet me at the ice cream shop in Navarre the day after tomorrow and we can talk business all you want. Just come alone!"

Shovelhead: "I'll be there. I'll be riding my bike."

Shovelhead knew he had to finish the bike because he wanted to ride it over to Navarre Beach, which was about 90 miles due east of Mobile on I10, or he could drop down and take the beach road. Either way, it'll be a chance for a nice ride and do some business as well. *I could make a full day of it.* He thinks. *I'll leave here early, slip over to Orange Beach, and see if my best girl is home first thing in the morning. That way, I can pick the right time. From there I can shoot over to Navarre Beach to meet Press. Yeah, that'll be a full day. I gotta make sure I do this right.* Shovelhead got up, tossed his coffee in the sink, and went back to wrenching his Harley. He continues to think about how he's gonna spend that fifteen grand.

The next day, about 4:00 p.m., Shovelhead had finished the bike. It looked good. He threw his makeshift ramp out the door and rolled the bike out to the front yard. He hopped on it and fired it up. It roared to life. *It's feeling good.* Thought Shovelhead. *I'm gonna take a quick spin and see how she does.* He pulled out onto the street and snaked out of the neighborhood until he got out on the big four lane. Once he did, he gave that bike some gas and it took off. *It's feeling smooth now.* Thinks Shovelhead. *Yep, thing is gonna ride me forever!* Shovelhead was enjoying the wind in his face and his hair. The sound of his Harley. At this moment, not a care in the world. He's gonna have a lot of money in his pocket soon. He feels like, finally, everything is going his way. Shovelhead thinks. *While I'm out, I might as well go get something to eat.* He takes his bike down to the local Hooters. He went in and found a place at the bar. He ordered a beer and some wings and watched all the pretty girls serve the customers.

The next morning, Shovelhead was up early. He left his house at 6:00 a.m. and cruised over to Orange Beach, which took him the better part of an hour. Nobody was moving much this time of the day. The tourists weren't up yet and the sun wasn't quite up high enough for the beachgoers. It was a pretty quiet ride to get through town. He took a right at Doc's Steaks and Seafood restaurant back into the Summer Wind neighborhood where his "best" girl lived. *It's pretty nice back here!* He thought. *Too bad she's not gonna be around much longer to enjoy it. Just wanna do one cruise by her house to see if her car's there. If it is, I'm going to leave and wait on the highway to see what time she comes out.* It was a little after 7:00 a.m. when he cruised through the neighborhood. There sat the green Mustang convertible parked right in front of her house. Shovelhead rolled slowly through the section of smart pastel beach houses so he wouldn't garner any attention. He drove back out to the Perdido Beach Boulevard, turned right, and found him a spot just in front of Pete's Ice Cream which wasn't open at this time of the day. Sitting at Pete's, he had an easy view of the road and all the cars going by. He'd for sure see the Mustang go by when she was on her way to work. He was prepared to wait: he didn't have to be in Navarre Beach until noon. He had plenty of time. The last time he saw her, she was at her office around 10:00 a.m., so he believes that's pretty much near the time she gets to the office. He knows that she has a sporadic schedule sometimes, but he had to take a chance to see if he could catch another glimpse of her. Shovelhead sat patiently, just watching the traffic and enjoying the cool morning air. About 9:30 a.m., he saw the Mustang cruise down Perdido Beach Boulevard. He looked at his watch and noted the time. *Ok*, he thought. *I got your schedule now. I know about when you leave, where you go. That's all I needed to find out.*

Shovelhead got back on his Harley, pulled out of Pete's ice cream, and turned back west towards Gulf Shores. He drove into Gulf Shores and went to the Sunliner Diner. He pulled up, went in, and ordered him a big breakfast of ham and eggs and biscuits. The service was fast and Shovelhead was out of the diner in about 30 minutes. Back on his Harley, he got on the beach road and made his way along the 50-mile trip to Navarre Beach. He had plenty of time to make it there for his noon meeting with Press.

Shovelhead enjoyed his ride along the beach road. He had a little stop-and-go traffic through Pensacola but still had about 15 minutes to spare when he rolled into Navarre Beach. He pulled up in front of the ice cream shop, stopped and waited. At straight up noon, a blue BMW with one male driving pulled up next to Shovelhead. A well-dressed young man got out, walked over, and said. "You Shovelhead?"

Shovelhead replied, "Yes."

Press responds, "I'm Press: good to meet you, brother."

Shovelhead: "Same here. Iron Mike says you are solid and anything I need you could provide."

Press: "Iron Mike's a good guy. We've known each other for a long time and yeah, I can get you what you need. No dope though. I don't mess with that stuff."

Shovelhead: "I understand, Press: I ain't looking for that."

Press: "All right, what exactly are you looking for?"

Shovelhead: "Well, I need some advice from you. I gotta take somebody out quick and I'm only gonna have a few seconds to do it. I wanna get away nice and clean, and nothing that comes back to me."

Press: "You wanna be up close and personal or far away?"

Shovelhead: "It looks like I'm gonna have to be real up close. Ain't no chance for distance."

Press: "Are we talking three to five feet away?"

Shovelhead: "Yes, just like you and I are standing here talking."

Press: "How about noise? Does it matter, do you care?"

Shovelhead: "Well, it would be better if it was quiet but I know that's not always possible."

Press: "Well, you'd be surprised what I can do, Shovelhead, but quiet costs money too. But I could probably help you out. You want fast, close, quiet, and nothing back to you."

Shovelhead: "That's right. That's exactly what I want."

Press: "I got just the rig for you. But it's gonna cost you three grand and that's a bargain price cause you know Iron Mike. Otherwise, it would be thirty-five hundred. But Mike deals with me and sends me business so I try to treat his brothers right."

Shovelhead: "OK, can you tell me how it works?"

Press: "Don't worry about it. When I deliver it, I'll show you exactly how it works. It'll be simple and easy."

Shovelhead: "OK, that's just what I want. Simple and easy. When will you have it?"

Press: "Give me a week, I got some other business. I gotta be in Biloxi for a big trade and I've got to get your special thing set up. So, let's meet back here next Thursday. Same time. We'll sit in my car, I'll have what you need, and I'll show you how to use it. Bring cash."

Shovelhead: "We'll do. I'll see you next Thursday. Thanks, Press."

Shovelhead walked over to his Harley, hopped on, and fired it up. He cruised slowly out of the parking lot, got on the road, and headed out of town. Press sat in his car for a while, checking his phone for messages. *It looks like it's gonna be another busy week.* He thought. *But heck, the money is rolling in, so it's all good.*

As Shovelhead rolled back down the beach road, all of his plans ran through his mind. *Three grand, damn.* He was upset about that. He thinks. *It takes money to make money, I guess. But that would have cut into my profit. There's no way around it. I can't do the job without the right tools and it ain't worth getting caught. Highside is a damned good dude since he thought of adding on five grand for expenses. I have some more stuff to get to.* he thought. *Still, it's twelve grand clear right now and I got some money upfront to buy what I need. One more meeting with Press and get the tool, and the following week, I'll get the job done. Highside said he wanted it done within 30 days so that will still be within the window. There will be no more reconnaissance of his best girl. No twice was enough.*

One time with his pick-up truck and one time with his bike so he should be ok on that. When he does the job, he won't be carrying his cell phone. He knew the feds could track it. So, he'd leave that in Mobile. It'll be a good alibi if anything ever comes up. "I was home" he would say. "Go ahead and check my phone." But now, it's back to Mobile.

31

WHERE ART THOU?

Bright and early Wednesday morning the mayor's staff shows up at their usual time. Administrative assistants, file clerks, mail clerks, and accountants all stream in and head to their respective desks. Even John seems to be in good health today. Everyone is there except Maria. Oh well, sometimes traffic can be heavy. It's not the first time anyone has been late due to traffic. Nobody thinks much about it. Chelsea gets to the office at her typical 10:00 a.m. time. Maria is not at her desk. *Interesting.* Chelsea thinks. She goes into her office and calls the administrative assistant Ruth.

Ruth picked up her phone. "Good Morning, Mayor: how can I help you?"

Chelsea: "Have you or anyone else heard from Maria?"

Ruth: "No ma'am. We thought she might be late due to a traffic issue but she should have been here by now."

Chelsea: "Can you please give her a call?"

Ruth: "Right away."

Within a few minutes, Ruth is back on the phone with Chelsea. "I'm sorry, mayor. She doesn't answer her phone."

Chelsea: "Well, please keep trying."

Ruth: "Yes ma'am." Ruth continued throughout the day to contact Maria with no luck. Five o'clock came and Ruth headed out the door along with everyone else. Never getting ahold of her. Thursday morning rolls around and there is still no sight of Maria. Chelsea appears to be getting worried and has Ruth call Detective Lieutenant Josh Myers.

Josh: "Detective Lieutenant Myers, how can I help you?"

Ruth: "Good Morning, Detective Myers. This is Ruth Murphy from Mayor Higgins's office. The mayor wanted me to call you. Her administrative assistant, Maria Fletcher, has not shown up for work the last two days and doesn't answer her phone. Would it be possible for someone to do a welfare check?"

Lt. Myers: "Yes, of course. Just give me her full name and home address, and I will have patrol do it right away."

Two hours later Orange Beach patrol contacts Josh and lets him know that they are unable to make contact with Maria Fletcher. Her car was not at her home, and she didn't answer the door. They got in touch with her landlord and he let them in her apartment. She was nowhere to be found. No sign of a struggle. They did not see her purse, phone, or car keys. Everything else looked in place. A very tidy apartment. At this point, all they can do is put her car and plate number on a BOLO and contact her next of kin to make further attempts to locate her and if necessary, file a missing person's report.

32

GODZILLA VS KING KONG

Friday is finally here, and Lauren is anxious to get out of work. She has plans with friends and is also going to meet up with August later. She's been spending more time with August. He takes up space in her brain to keep her from thinking too much about how messed up her life has gotten. The time she used to spend with Doctor has decreased substantially. Doctor still shows up at her place but not as often. Yes, she still lets him in and yes, she still has sex with him. Even though she knows he's sleeping with Randi and is 99% sure he's also sleeping with the mayor. When he shows up, Lauren lies to herself, *if he's here, he's not totally 100% interested in Randi or Chelsea. So, there's still a chance.* Lauren goes home, changes her clothes from work to fun, and Ubers to Big Beach Brewery in Gulf Shores to meet her friends. They sit outside in Adirondack chairs under the night sky and listen to the band. The band tonight is great. Sometimes at the brewery, it's hit or miss with the music but tonight it was fabulous.

After a few drinks and dancing they Uber over to the Coastal. It's such a great place to hang out on a warm summer night. They get a table by the boardwalk, order some drinks, and have a good time. As they are telling stories and laughing, Lauren looks up and sees Mayor Higgins sitting at the bar. Looking at her phone, she appears to be alone. Lauren, having already had just enough liquid courage, decides to go say hi to the mayor. She excuses herself, stands up, and heads over to where the mayor is sitting. There's an empty chair and Lauren plops herself down.

Lauren: "Hello Mayor Higgins. How are you doing?"

Chelsea stared: "Oh, hello Lauren. I'm fine. Are you here alone?"

Lauren: "No, I'm with a few friends. We have a table by the boardwalk. I saw you sitting here so I thought I would come over and say hello."

Chelsea: "Thank you, Lauren: I am waiting for someone, so if there isn't anything else."

Lauren: "There is just one thing. I don't like you. I find you to be a conceited bitch who wallows in self-admiration. You strut around like a preening peacock. I hate to destroy your illusion, but you are nothing more than a used-up urinal cake at the highway rest stop. I don't care that you are the mayor. I know that you and Doctor are sleeping, scratch that, having sex. Just so you know, he's having sex with Randi Reynolds, AND Doctor and I have been having sex for a few years now. So, if you think you're something special. You ain't. You and Doctor want to use each other to get ahead. Hey, knock yourself out. In business, you gotta do what you gotta do. But if you think that Doctor Campbell is going to drop everything for you. You got another thing coming. If I ever have any chance to do it, you're going down like a fat kid on a seesaw."

Lauren stands up to leave. "Mayor, I enjoyed our little chat. You have a great rest of your evening." Lauren returns to her friends.

Chelsea watches her walk back to their table. *Little girl, you have no idea who the hell you are messing with. You better watch your back. You could find yourself unemployed.* Chelsea tried to contain her anger. *So, Doctor is sleeping with Randi and Lauren! This throws a monkey wrench into my plan for being Mrs. Campbell. Child's play.* Chelsea smiles internally.

Chelsea's friends show up. Becki, Beverly, Meg, and Nancy all show up together. They get a table and get started. It's "Wonder Women" night and what a night it will be. The other people out having dinner and drinks know this particular group of women is extremely powerful. Except for Chelsea, they truly are very nice and accommodating to the people of Orange Beach. But, sometimes looks can be deceiving. As the women have drinks and dinner Chelsea can't help but continue to look over at Lauren. Getting madder and madder with each glance.

Meg: "Hey Chelsea, something got your eye?"

Chelsea: "What are you talking about?"

Meg: "Well, your mind seems to be wandering and your attention is someplace else."

Chelsea: "Sorry, the group of girls at the table over there. I couldn't tell right away but the one girl in the yellow dress, that's Doctor's assistant."

Beverly: "Speaking of Doctor, how's that going? You and him have gotten pretty tight. Any extracurricular activity you'd like to spill?" The four women turn to Chelsea with bated breath.

Chelsea looks at the women for a couple of seconds. She doesn't say a word but gives them a wink. They all cheer, laugh, and give a toast to future activity. Chelsea sits and ponders her next moves. *Yes, I've got more than one move to make. I thought I was home free in being Doctor's main squeeze but apparently, there is still competition. Oh well, minor glitch.* She smiles to herself. She gets back to the party.

Lauren is now having a better time thinking. *Sticking it to Chelsea was the best thing ever. Man, that felt great. Letting her know that she isn't the only fish in Doctor's pond.* She stands and says goodbye to her friends. Lauren: "Hey, I got to bounce. I'm meeting August."

Her friends shout and cheer. Lauren smiles and winks. As she heads out, she looks at Chelsea and she smiles and waves. Chelsea watches her leave and has a militant spark flash in her eyes, not acknowledging the wave.

33

PAINFUL SIDE OF MURDER

It was the morning of the 5th of July. Lieutenant Myers was up early as usual. It was a Saturday and Lieutenant Myers had the day off, if a police lieutenant is ever off. At least he would go through the motion of being off. It was always hard to shut off his mind from everything that was always going on at the department. Running a squad of half a dozen detectives in this beach tourist city was a great job but it never really slowed down. Josh's phone rang, it was 911 dispatch.

Josh answers, "Lieutenant Myers."

Dispatch: "Lieutenant, patrol Sergeant wants you to report to a building at Perdido Pass. They've got a body there inside one of the condos that they say is a homicide."

Josh: "OK, I'll gather up some detectives and head over. Text me the address."

Dispatch: "Yes sir, right away."

Josh: "Thank you, I'm heading out."

Josh strapped on his gun and gathered up his badge and wallet. He texted two of his detectives that he would be needing them at the condos at Perdido Pass for a reported homicide. Dispatch will send them the address. Josh walked out to his police cruiser, a black, unmarked SUV. He got in and headed down to the beach highway. Lieutenant Myers lived on the bay side of Orange Beach where there is a large residential community full of boaters and water enthusiasts and lots of natives to the town. From his place to Perdido Pass would take him about ten minutes. Down canal road, towards Perdido Beach Boulevard where he would make a left to get to the pass. It's an idyllic place. A swooping bridge connects the island at Orange Beach and Gulf Shores, Alabama, to Florida's Perdido Key. But the other side of the bridge is still Alabama for a few miles. Both sides of the bridge are in the city of Orange Beach. Josh looked at his phone while driving and saw the address of the reported homicide. It is a nice, upscale building right on the water near the pass. As he drove in, he saw the Orange Beach radio cars and the patrolmen out front. It was early and it was quiet. At least for the next hour or two. It was summertime and these condos would be full of owners and renters down to enjoy the gulf sunshine. It was peak tourist season in Orange Beach. At the beginning of July, people were here for fun and murder only rolled in on storm clouds for a beach holiday. They weren't here to share the shade of their umbrellas with violent crime. Josh knew that the city leaders did not want to hear about too much crime in their section of paradise. They preferred clear blue skies, gentle waves, white sands, and ice cream socials. This is what brought in the green tourist dollars. Josh met a patrolman who was standing outside in front of the condo building.

Josh: "Good Morning Joe."

Joe: "Good Morning, Lieutenant."

Josh: "Where are we at?"

Joe: "Straight ahead, Lieutenant. On the seventh floor, go left off the elevator, and you'll see the guys up there. The sergeant is up there waiting for you."

Josh: "I've got a couple of my detectives on their way. Send them up as well when they get here."

Joe: "Will do, sir."

Josh walked across the lobby. It was a beautiful building. All pastel colors, Beachy decorations of seashells, pelicans, and fish that don't let you forget you are at the coast. Josh jumped on the elevator and hit seven on his way to the specter of death. As the elevator doors opened Josh took a left down the hallway. *Life is downstairs* he thought. *Death is upstairs.* Let's see what's going on with this homicide and what caused it. He met the sergeant in the hallway, he pointed at the door down the hallway facing the bay.

Josh: "What have you got sergeant?"

Sergeant: "We got a white female, shot through the chest. She is in her nightclothes. She is lying right in the doorway off the balcony. It's a pretty bloody mess in there. We didn't see any weapons. Didn't see anybody else. We took her pulse: we had a paramedic check her. She's been dead a while."

Josh: "Do you have a name?"

Sergeant: "Her name is Lauren Scavone. White female, she's 34. She works for a local land development company called D Campbell Land Development. She was supposed to meet some friends for breakfast, but she didn't show up. They called her phone and all it did was ring. When they couldn't get an answer after repeated tries, they drove over to her condo and started knocking on the door. When they still didn't get a response, they found the building manager and he had the maintenance guy come up with a spare key for a welfare check. They opened the door and peeked in. When they saw her body, they immediately rushed in to see if she was ok. When they quickly determined that she was dead they walked out, closed the door, and called us. We dialed the victim's phone number. The phone is on the counter."

Josh: "OK Sergeant, do you have all their names? The super's name?"

Sergeant: 'Yes sir, we have all that".

Josh: "Do you know if they messed up the crime scene?"

Sergeant: "They were in there. How much they touched I have no idea at this point."

Josh: " Ok, Sergeant. I'll have one of my detectives interview all of them. We will collect all their shoes. We will have to get their fingerprints in case we might have to eliminate anything that was touched."

Sergeant: "Yes, sir."

Josh: "Did you call for a forensics team?"

Sergeant: "I did, sir. As soon as we asked for you, we made a call to forensics. One other thing sir, the patrol lieutenant, he's on his way. He said he got a call from the chief saying the mayor heard about an apparent murder victim found at the condo. The only way she could know this quickly is she must be monitoring our frequency."

Josh: "Well, there isn't anything she can do about it right now."

Sergeant: "The chief said she's been on his butt about it. Worrying about the tourist industry."

Josh: "We are all worried about the tourist industry. But right now, I'm more worried about people getting murdered. I was supposed to go to the beach today and work on my tan."

Sergeant: "I don't think you're going to get much of a tan today."
Josh: "You got that right. Thanks, Sergeant."

Josh waited for his two detectives to arrive. When they got there, they stood in the hallway and discussed what they had. He directed one of the detectives to interview Lauren's friends who found her. Make sure they collect all their shoes and ask them if they will agree to be fingerprinted since they entered the crime scene. They might have accidentally touched something and left their print. Interview everyone about their whereabouts leading up to the discovery of the body. Also to determine next of kin location so we can set up notification right away.

Josh to the other detective, "Let's call the crew in: we've got a whole lot of interviews to do in this building alone. Did anyone hear anything? See anything or anyone?"

Sergeant: "It looks like a bullet wound but that is yet to be determined."

Josh: "As soon as forensics arrives, we'll be able to take a quick look."

The forensics team arrives, and they, along with Josh and one of the detectives, put on booties, white suits, and gloves and carefully enter the crime scene. Lieutenant Myers stood to the side as the photographs were taken of every inch of the location. Especially the position of the body and the fact that the sliding glass door was open. The female was on her back, her feet just barely on the edge of the threshold of the sliding glass door. She had on a small teddy: she had long, dark, curly hair. She was trim and in shape. A tiny little thing. The carpet underneath her was covered in blood. There was a small hole in the front of her chest. Dead center in the middle of her heart. There was some blood at that point, but Josh knew it was probably a through shot since the blood on the carpet was extremely large. Josh thinks the victim was standing facing the balcony door when she was shot. Since it was a through shot, he turned and looked behind her to the wall in the living room. There he saw two bullet holes. One is slightly higher than the other by about two feet. Directly into the wall. He pointed that out to the forensics team.

Josh: "Guys, looks like two bullet holes here. Get photos and see if you can dig them out."

Forensics: "Yes, sir."

Within a few minutes, the medical examiner and her team arrived and greeted Lieutenant Myers.

Josh: "Hello Doc."

Doctor Terri O'Leary: "Hello, Josh."

Josh: "Sorry to get you out here on a Saturday morning."

Doctor O'Leary: "That's no problem, Josh, part of the job."

Josh: "Tell me about it. Our life of crime."

Doctor O'Leary: "That's exactly it. It looks like your weekend is ruined, Lieutenant. Brief me up, what does it look like?

Josh: "A scientific wild ass mess is what it looks like. Female, 34. Her name is Lauren Scavone. She lived here alone. From what we can determine, she worked for a local land development company and some friends found her this morning. We didn't get any calls regarding shots being heard last night or this morning. Looking at the wall, it looks like two shots. But I guess nobody heard anything. We'll have to see if we can determine a time of death."

O'Leary: "Let me get a quick look at her. We can do a cursory exam and turn her over once forensics is done with all the pictures."

The forensics team told Josh and the doctor that they were through with their general crime scene photos. O'Leary asked them if they could stay for a little bit longer and take a few pictures as she directed. O'Leary and Josh stepped over to where the body lay on the floor inside the patio door.

Doctor pulled down the top of the teddy Ms. Scavone was wearing so they could see the wound directly in the center of her chest.

Josh: "That looks like a perfect shot. Dead in the X ring. Do you see any tattooing, Doc?"

O'Leary: "No, none evident at the wound, the killer was not close. Someone knows how to use a gun. Whatever gun it was."

She then takes Ms. Scavone's face in her right hand and opens her jaw. She took a flashlight out and looked inside her mouth. She opened her eyes and looked at each one. She moved her hair. She looked around her face and neck, carefully examining her neck area. She asked the forensic crime scene photographer to take a photo while she held her mouth open. Took photographs of her eyes, around her neck, and her head. She then looked at her lower torso, pulled up the bottom of her teddy, and looked for any wounds in her abdomen area. She didn't see any in her pelvis area. Her panties were still on. She looked at her legs, all the way down to her feet. Ms. Scavone was wearing a pair of slippers. O'Leary carefully examined her feet and then asked Josh to help her turn the body over.

O'Leary: "Quite a bit of lividity here. She's been dead for several hours. This did not just happen."

Josh: "I can see that."

As they turned Lauren's body over, they could see a gaping wound in the center of her back about the size of a small fist.

O'Leary: "That is a big wound. Probably a rifle, a handgun isn't going to make that kind of wound."

Josh: "I believe you are right. There is some velocity behind that. Punched her right out."

O'Leary: "That is the reason for all the blood underneath her on the carpet."

As Doctor O'Leary examined the back of Ms. Scavone from her head down to her feet. Checking the backs of her arms, her legs, her feet, her buttocks, her back. She saw no other wounds or bruises. She could see no contusions: she could see no marks on the back of her neck. No garrot or knife wounds. There were no apparent signs of a struggle. She turned the body back over and said to her assistant.

O'Leary: "Will you please bring in the body bag so we can take her out."

The examiner's assistants came in and put Lauren in the body bag to move her.

Josh: "I know you haven't done a complete examination doc, but do you have any idea about the time of death?"

O'Leary: "It's pretty hard to pinpoint exactly at this time, but I would say about 12 hours ago maybe. You've got to give and take a little bit."

Josh: "I understand. You are saying roughly 9:00 p.m. last night?"

O'Leary: "That is a rather good guess. If I had to say right now, sometime between 7-11:00 p.m. I might be able to tighten up that timeline once I get her back to the morgue, do a more thorough exam take some measurements and samples, and get a good look at everything."

Josh: "OK Doc. I understand it's never an exact answer on a preliminary exam. I appreciate it as it gives us something to work with until we know for sure."

O'Leary: "I will call you Josh just as soon as I get through with the exam. Probably be sometime tomorrow, but I will try and start on it today."

Josh: "Thanks again. I appreciate you trying to get this done quickly. I know your plate is full and it is the weekend. It will help us out to get the information as soon as possible. We don't have these kinds of murders in Orange Beach, so we want to get this figured out as soon as possible."

O'Leary: "I understand. You're going to have a lot of political pressure to solve this. Good luck to you and don't forget to get some rest yourself."

Josh: "You too, doc. Remember, your life is crime."

O'Leary: "Crime and death. Had I known this as a kid, I would have become a lawyer."

Josh stepped out on the balcony with one of his detectives. They looked out at the beautiful scene of Perdido Pass. One of the most idyllic spots in all of the United States. Crystal clear blue/green water. Little sandy islands dot the bay. Marinas in every direction. Pleasure crafts moving about. Jet skis are starting to move out into the bay and out into the Gulf of Mexico, which is just a couple of minutes under the bridge. It is such a beautiful spot, and yet you have this violent murder. It looks like it happened last night which was during the Fourth of July celebration. Josh turned from the balcony and looked into the condo. Was someone there standing in front of Lauren Scavone on the balcony and shot her point-blank range with a rifle? He didn't notice any tattooing around the wound. Tattooing is the marks from a close-end gunshot to the human body. If the gunshot is within just a few inches or a foot from the body, the gunpowder exiting the barrel along with the projectile will leave black marks around the wound. Medical examiners can see that and determine sometimes how close the firearm was to the body. As you get further away, that distance is erased as to how close the gun was to the body. If someone had been in the condo with Ms. Scavone and remarkably close to her, there would be evidence of tattooing. Josh didn't see any of that. The shots in the wall behind her were a little bit elevated. When he looked at Lauren's positioning. She was a petite woman. He turned and looked back down toward the bay.

Josh to his detectives: "Maybe the shot came from down by the bay?"

Detective: "What? You think we got a frogman killer, it's all water. It would be pretty hard to shoot a gun while treading water?"

Josh: "I understand that, but I'm just trying to look at these angles. Could it have been someone on the island? On a boat? It is just a strange set of facts here. There is no evidence that another person was in the condo other than Ms. Scavone. There is no sign of a struggle, no bloody footprints, no tattooing on the wound, there is no evidence that anyone else was here. Yet she is dead and right inside the balcony door. The holes in the wall look like an upward trajectory shot.

Detective: "Well, forensics took all those measurements of the height of the bullets in the wall, and of course, we will have the height of Ms. Scavone from Doctor, and then we can have the crime scene team draw out that exact trajectory for us."

Josh: "Maybe we'll be able to tell from that. I want them to lay a string from those two bullet holes from where they think it would go through Ms. Scavone's chest and tie it right off here on this balcony railing. I want to see how high it is compared to the balcony railing. Maybe we can look down that string and possibly see where this was. We got two bullet holes. We don't have two reference points for one of them, but we do have two reference points for the one that killed Ms. Scavone. Make sure forensics gets on that immediately. Keep this condo locked up as a crime scene until we can get that information and get those strings tied up, along with some photographs. It's going to help with our analysis in this."

Detective: "Yes sir, will do. I'll let forensics know exactly what you want done. We'll get it completed. I'll talk to the superintendent and make sure this is locked tight and we'll get a key as well. We will keep an officer here until you are totally through with the place."

Josh: "Sounds good. The family is certainly going to want to get in and gather up Ms. Scavone's belongings. See what you can find out about that. Have Sergeant Miller contact the family."

Detective: "Yes, Lieutenant, I will."

Josh: "I'll be meeting with them as well. Have someone bring them over to my office when they get here."

Detective: "Yes, sir, for sure."

Lieutenant Myers took out his phone and dialed the assistant chief of the Orange Beach Police.

He filled the chief in on what he had, all the information they had gathered, and where they stood at this moment.

The assistant chief: "Thank you, Josh, for the update. I would like you to work with the Orange Beach Public Information Officer to handle all of the press inquiries."

Josh: "I will certainly do that. I am heading back to my office now, and I will make sure that the PIO is briefed."

The assistant chief: "I will inform the chief of what is going on. He's already been called by the mayor so he will be happy to get any information to give her. I appreciate the quick update. I know you got lots to do."

Josh went outside and shook hands with the sergeant. Told them to hold the condo as a crime scene for a couple of days. He spoke to his detectives as he walked out the door that he was headed back to his office.

When he got back down to the first floor. He did a complete walk around the entire condo lobby. He went around the outside of the building. Looking up and down. He looked across the bay. Out towards the Perdido Bridge. Just looking in every direction. Taking it all in. It was a place Josh was remarkably familiar with before it was the scene of unspeakable violence. Murder changes everything. The place looks different now. It will forever hold the aura of violent death when he drives past it. Now he had to just let his brain gather information. Even information he didn't know he would be gathering. He learned to be an observant person in his military and police careers. To take it all in, to absorb and notice when it was required to do so. He looked, he walked, and he observed. He then walked back to his police cruiser and got in. He started the engine, put it in drive, and headed back to his office. It wasn't going to be the Saturday he thought he was going to have. It was going to be the day he took his first step along a journey seeking justice for Lauren Scavone.

34

SORROW IS HEAVY

When Josh got back to the office, he asked Sergeant Miller if Lauren Scavone's family had been notified of her death. Miller walks out the door: "We are headed out now. Mobile is so close that I want to give them the information in person."

Sergeant Miller has had to do this multiple times. She hated it. She hated giving families the ultimate horrible news. Watching them fall apart. Trying to figure out why. Why was their loved one targeted? What had their son, daughter, mother, and father done that was worth having them murdered? For Sergeant Miller to get through these encounters, she had to step back for a couple of minutes, and she would meditate and calm herself down to give the information to the family. Sergeant Miller gets in contact with the Police Chaplain and explains the situation. Within minutes they are both in Miller's car headed to Mobile.

A couple of hours later, Sergeant Miller and the Chaplain are standing on the Scavone porch. Sergeant Miller knocks loudly.

Yvonne Scavone answered the door: "Hello. Can I help you?"

Sergeant Miller: "Mrs. Scavone?"

Yvonne: "Yes, I am Yvonne Scavone, and you are?"

Sergeant Miller: "My name is Sergeant Miller of the Orange Beach Police Department and this is Chaplain Hodson. We are here regarding your daughter Lauren."

Yvonne: "Chaplain? Is something wrong? Has Lauren been in an accident? Is she hurt?"

Miller: "May we come in, Mrs. Scavone."

Yvonne: "Oh, of course. My manners." Yvonne steps aside and lets in Miller and the Chaplain.

Sergeant Miller: "I am so sorry to inform you, Mrs. Scavone, but your daughter Lauren is deceased."

Yvonne: "What? I don't understand. What did you just say?"

Miller: "Your daughter Lauren is deceased."

Just then Charles appears in the living room and Yvonne runs to Charles. He stares at Yvonne. The look on her face is utter horror. She is not speaking. Charles is confused as to what is going on.

Charles Scavone: "Hello, I'm Dr. Scavone and you are?"

Miller: "My name is Sergeant Miller and this is Chaplain Hodson. We are with the Orange Beach Police Department. I am here to inform you that your daughter Lauren is deceased."

Charles turns and stares at Yvonne who just stands in the middle of the living room. She is now shaking so badly that she can barely stand up. Charles walks over to Yvonne and carefully helps her sit down.

Charles: "Sergeant, Can you please tell me what the HELL is going on?"

Miller: "Your daughter was found this morning at her residence by several friends. She was supposed to meet them for breakfast and when she did not show up, they went looking for her. They found her deceased in her living room."

Charles: "Deceased? Deceased how?"

Miller hesitates: "I'm Sorry, Dr. Scavone. Your daughter was shot."

Charles: "Shot in her living room?"

Miller: "As far as we can tell, she was alone."

Charles: "Alone, this does not make any sense. If she was alone, how the hell did she get shot?"

Miller: "We believe she was shot from outside the residence. Initial investigation shows that she was probably standing on her balcony watching the fireworks and someone from a distance, probably on a boat, shot her."

Charles: "Lauren is the kindest, sweetest person there is. She has never met a stranger. She always makes sure everyone is welcome and has a good time. I cannot believe someone would deliberately go out of their way to kill my Lauren."

Miller: "We are trying to determine that exact thing. Dr. Scavone. Who killed your daughter and what is the motive? Do you know if she had a boyfriend? Was she serious about anyone? Maybe she was seeing a married man and got found out?"

Charles: "A married man? Please do not even go there and insult my daughter by accusing her of sleeping with a married man."

Miller: "Dr. Scavone, I am not accusing your daughter of doing anything. We are trying to find out who would want her dead. I know these are hard questions, but they must be asked."

Charles takes a deep breath: "We are not aware of any man in her life. She has never mentioned dating anyone seriously. We know she was putting in long hours helping Doctor Campbell get his business up and running. He might have the answer to that question. We have known Doctor Campbell for over twenty years. We were very excited when he hired Lauren to be his Executive Assistant. When he decided to move his business to Orange Beach, we were relieved to know that a family friend would be with Lauren and help her get settled. Lauren used to babysit for Doctor and his wife when she was in high school. We were comfortable in letting her go. Since they work so closely together, Doctor might know more about her social life and we do. Give me your contact information and I will call you when Yvonne and I get to Orange Beach. We will be leaving within the hour."

Miller: "Alright, again. I am so sorry about the loss of your daughter."

Charles shows Sergeant Miller and Chaplain Hodson to the door and goes over to Yvonne. Charles: "Honey, we must go to Orange Beach. I am going to call Jeremy right now and have him go with us."

Yvonne just stares at Charles. Tears start to roll down her face. She had been in such shock she hadn't heard one word Charles said. Charles carefully picks up Yvonne and hugs her tightly. She starts to sob uncontrollably. That turns into screams. Loud, throat-burning screams that probably could be heard for blocks. The two of them are sitting on the couch. Yvonne starts to fall apart and Charles tries to keep her from doing so. Charles wants nothing more than to just sit on the couch with his wife for hours. Hug her tightly until all this subsides. But they cannot. They must get to Orange Beach. Charles gives Yvonne something to calm her nerves and goes and calls Jeremy.

Jeremy: "Hey Dad. How's it going? Are you calling to set up a tee time?"

Charles: "No, Jeremy. I need you to get here immediately. We have to go to Orange Beach."

Jeremy: "Orange Beach?"

Charles: "It's Lauren."

Jeremy: "Oh, no, has she been in an accident?"

Charles: "She's dead, Jeremy. She's been murdered."

Jeremy: "Murdered? No, that's not right."

Charles: "Jeremy, I need you to come to Orange Beach with us. Get here as soon as you can. We must go now!"

Jeremy: "Ok, ok, I'm on my way."

Jeremy shows up about fifteen minutes later. Charles and Yvonne are ready to go. They immediately get in the car and make the hour-long trip. As soon as they get to Orange Beach, they head directly to the Police Department to find Sergeant Miller.

They spend an hour getting all the information they could get. They meet Lieutenant Josh Myers who is heading the investigation. Sergeant Miller takes them over to the morgue. Charles makes Yvonne stay in the car while he and Jeremy go inside. They are out in a matter of minutes and confirm to Yvonne that it is indeed Lauren. Charles gets in the car and holds Yvonne. Jeremy crawls in the backseat. He sits quietly, weeping, watching his parents struggle to cope with this horror show they have been thrown into. Seeing his parents distraught is more than Jeremy can take. He leaves the car and starts walking. Hands in his pockets, Jeremy just walks down the street. Gets to the corner and turns and goes back. He does this several times as his parents grapple with the loss of their only daughter. After the fourth or fifth time of walking to the corner and back, Jeremy goes back to his parents. He tells them to get in the back seat. Jeremy climbs into the driver's seat and they make their way back to Mobile. Jeremy and his wife make the arrangements to get Lauren's body back to Mobile. With Charles being a Doctor, he deals with death regularly. When it comes to your child, it is horrific and the tone is completely different.

Three days later, Lauren Scavone was laid to rest. The city of Mobile turned out. Everyone knew Lauren and her family. Shock over the murder of one of their own was horrible. Doctor Campbell closed Campbell Land Development and the entire company made the trip to pay their respects to Lauren and her family. Afterward, Doctor made his way to Charles Reynolds.

Doctor hugging Charles: "You have no idea how sorry I am about this. Lauren was my right-hand woman, and we worked a lot together—so much so that I had to force her to get out and get a social life. I had no clue that she was in danger. If something was going on, she never said anything to me. I loved that little girl!"

Charles: "Thank you, Doctor. We were confident that when she went to Orange Beach, she would be safe working for you. But life has a way of tricking you. Our precious daughter is gone, and as of now, we have no idea why."

Doctor: "I will keep on the Orange Beach Police to make sure they are working 24/7 to find out who did this."

Charles: "Thank you, Doctor. You are a true friend." Charles turns back to his family and they head back to their home. Charles thinks to himself. *A broken family. We will never be the same. Our lives are forever more damaged.*

35

LOVE LETTERS

Randi walks out of her house to go to work and finds a note under her windshield wiper. A threatening note. She immediately gets on the phone with Josh. They haven't seen each other or spoken since they broke up, but this is different, she is scared, and this is police work.

Josh recognizes the number: "Lieutenant Myers." Trying to keep his demeanor professional.

Randi: "Hi Josh, it's Randi."

Josh: "How can I help you?"

Randi is taken aback by how cold this feels. Well, she can't blame him.

Randi: "I found a threatening note under my windshield wiper this morning."

Josh: "How do you mean threatening?"

Randi: "I mean this note is scary. Can you please come over and take a look at it?"

Josh, his stomach tightening: "I'll be right over." It only takes him a few minutes to get to Randi's. As he pulls up, he sees Randi standing by her car. His breath catches in his throat, his heart seems to stop and his breathing becomes shallow. He is struggling to get out of his car. Randi looks freaking amazing, waiting for Josh to exit his vehicle. As Josh gets out, Randi runs over to him very shaken up. She throws her arms around his neck. *What the hell is going on? What is she doing?* Josh thinks. He carefully takes her arms from around his neck.

Josh: "Randi, where's the note?"

Randi: "It's under my windshield. It's face up so I could read it, but I didn't touch it."

Josh heads over to Randi's car and looks at the note: " Watch your back, *little girl: watch who you're running with. If you are not careful, you could get hurt. Change your ways.*"

Josh: "Randi, have you gotten anything else like this before?"

Randi: "There was one on the door of a house I was selling. It said, *"You better be careful."* I thought it had something to do with the house. Now with this one, I'm afraid they are related. I have no idea who would leave this. I haven't had a run-in with anybody that I know of. I haven't had angst with any of my clients. I'm scared, Josh." As she tries to wrap her arms around him again. Josh doesn't let her.

Josh: "OK, Randi, I know this is scary, but I need you to calm down. Let's stop and think. I need you to think hard about the last few weeks. Has anything out of the ordinary happened? Anything that you thought was minor?"

Randi: "Not that I can remember, Josh I am scared to death. How do you expect me to calmly stand here and go back through my head the last month."

Josh: "Look, Randi. I know it's scary, but please try to calm down and think. I am going to step over here and call patrol. I'll get a uniformed officer to make a report."

In a few minutes, an Orange Beach police SUV cruiser pulls up. The officer gets out. "Good morning, Lieutenant."

Josh: "Hey, Charlie, this is Ms. Randi Reynolds. There's a threatening note on her car. I want you to take a report. Then bag and tag and send it for latent prints. Then I want you to put Ms. Reynolds's house under special patrol under my authority and make it good. I want cruisers going by often and more often."

Charlie: "Yes, sir, We'll make it look like a new precinct."

Josh then takes a photograph with his phone of the note.

Josh: "Do you have any security cameras?"

Randi: No, not yet."

Josh: "OK, Randi, tell Charlie everything you told me. He'll write a report. We've got a special patrol put on your house. Please stay alert, and watch your surroundings. Any little thing let me know, even if you think it's minor. I've got other duties: Charlie will take it from here."

Randi: "Wait, you're not going to stay?"

Josh: "No, I've got other priorities."

Josh returns to his car and heads back to the police department. He looks in his rearview mirror and sees Randi standing there, looking dejected, watching him leave.

36

FLOWERS FOR A MURDER

When the seas are running a few feet high in the Gulf of Mexico, the winds whip the phosphoresce tops off of the foamy waves to give the soft look of white star dust. It's a deceiving phenomenon. Once in the water, swimmers can feel the strong pull of the undertow. Lifeguards warn of riptides and the Coast Guard is putting out warnings for mariners of choppy seas and strong winds in the gulf off Orange Beach. That won't stop the tourists with their brightly colored umbrellas, 55-gallon drums of sunblock, giant beach wagons, coolers of beer, and unruly children. They flock to the white sand to get a tan, cool off, and forget about their work-a-day world. Murder is not on the minds of the tourists at Orange Beach. Spotting a dolphin, maybe, or watching the pirate ship that is an attraction for families that cruise up and down the coast firing its air cannon every few minutes. The nearby U.S. Coast Guard helicopter training center in Mobile always provides two or three helicopters overhead for entertainment, flying up and down the coast. Speed boats full of tourists, sailboats, charter fishing boats, pleasure boats, and parasailing. It's a very active water sports area. Lifeguards will flip back and forth in the water on their jet skis and also patrol the beach in their 4-wheel drive ATVs. All of this atmosphere is light years away from violent murder. This tranquility and beauty are the softer side of life, but what's about to transpire in Orange Beach will burn in the eyes with bitterness. The gut-wrenching reality is that life can be taken in an instant because of the desires of someone else. Because of hatred, jealousy, or greed. A life can be snuffed out faster than a squabble of seagulls can fly away from a small child running down the beach. Sharks live in these gulf waters, sharks of every type. However, today Orange Beach is about to get hit with a land shark. A shark of the human species. A shark that can take a life as fast as a real one. A shark that shows no mercy and only kills with a defining purpose. For this shark, it wasn't hunger that drove it, it was greed.

Shovelhead has now gotten started on his task after he met with Press for the second time and obtained the tools required. He knew he couldn't take his vehicle or his cell phone with him. He obtained another vehicle for the murder. He was cruising over to Orange Beach and just crossing the bridge at the toll booth at the canal. He turned left to go east on the canal road. His thoughts raced with how all this was about to transpire. It was 8:15 a.m. and he'd be there in fifteen minutes. By his past two reconnaissance trips, he knew his baby would be home. His ten-thousand-dollar ticket was about to get cashed. He made a right turn off the canal road down toward the beach road. At the red light, he turned onto Perdido Beach Boulevard and slowly drove down past all the beach-front high-rise condominiums on the left-hand side and the shopping malls on the right. The day was breaking slowly and the traffic was light. Press' last words stuck in Shovelhead's mind as he drove the last few yards towards the residence.

Press: "Whoever it is, I hope they deserve it."

Shovelhead thinks, "We probably all deserve it."

Now that particular phrase by Press continues to run through his mind. *I hope whoever it is, they deserve it.*

Shovelhead passed the Live Bait restaurant and made a right turn at Doc's Steaks and Seafood. He drove back into the neighborhood behind the establishments. He cruised up to the residence, where he saw the target's car. There it was, by itself, in front of the house. She was home, *She had to be up,* he thought. He previously saw her go into her office at 9:15 a.m. It's almost 8:30 a.m., so this should be a perfect time. Shovelhead had secured a white van for the job. It had no permanent markings on it. He had put two magnetic signs on the sides of the van to complete his deception. He pulled the van sideways in front of the house so the sign could be seen by his target. He was wearing a white jumpsuit over his street clothes. He had a white baseball hat on with no markings. He wore sunglasses and he carried a large bouquet in his left hand. The pistol and rig that Press had supplied, he had in a holster on his right side. He made a slit with a knife through the white coveralls to generally hide the gun but still be easily accessible. He walked up to the porch with the flowers in his left hand halfway in front of his face, so if this was a ring doorbell camera, it wouldn't be able to identify him. He wore gloves and with his right hand, he rang the doorbell. He then reached inside the slit in his white coveralls and put his hand firmly on the pistol.

As she is finishing up getting ready for work, she hears her doorbell. Who would be here this early in the morning? She never meets clients at her home. She peeks through a blind and sees a florist van and a delivery man holding a huge bouquet. She smiles to herself. *What a thoughtful man. What a great surprise. He is always surprising me with something.* She wanted to give the delivery man a tip, so she got her wallet and quickly grabbed a ten-dollar bill. With the excitement of a surprise bouquet, she flings the door open wide.

Shovelhead waits for his target. He hears the doorknob click, and the door flings open. There stands this beautiful tall woman with a big smile on her face looking at the flowers. When Shovelhead finally saw her up close and personal, he took half a step back. This woman was stunningly beautiful. He couldn't tell from a distance exactly how striking she was. She looked like a movie star. He hesitated for just a couple of seconds. *This is the creature he is about to kill? Fuck it!* He thought. *A job is a job and I need the cash.* Just then, Shovelhead pulled out the pistol that Press had supplied him and did exactly what Press had instructed. He pulled the trigger and held it down. The gun let out a long burp of bullets that sounded like a commercial sewing machine, directly into the torso of the woman standing in the doorway. The force of the shots pushed her back inside the door, where she fell into a bloody mess. Her feet were blocking the open door as she fell backward. Shovelhead turned quickly and dropped the gun and the flowers in the bushes right off the porch while making his exit. He carefully went back and got in the van, pulled out slowly, and drove away. He didn't see anybody around. It was still early morning. He wasn't going to speed to draw attention to himself. He just wanted to make it to the beach road and head back out.

He planned to take a right on the beach boulevard and head down past the Gulf Shores State Park and into Gulf Shores. It was a more crowded tourist area, and once he got on the 59 highway, he could head back north, all the way up to I10 and then back into Mobile. He needed to get out of Orange Beach and away from the scene before anybody discovered the body. As he turned right outside of Doc's Seafood onto the beach boulevard, he had the window down in the van. He heard nothing. No sirens, and he didn't see any radio cars. Everything was quiet. *Well, so far so good.* He thought. *So far, the plan is working. Hopefully, nobody knows she is dead yet.* Within just four minutes, he was passing the Gulf Shores State Park, and in a few more minutes, he was in the heart of Gulf Shores, headed north. *Clean getaway.* He thought. *Haven't seen a cop or heard a siren and now I'm already in a different town.*

Shovelhead's thoughts turned to the money and how he was going to spend it. But then he snapped himself back to reality and thought, *It's not over yet. I've got to get back to Mobile, get rid of this van and these clothes, and burn them. There could be some minor blood splatter somewhere, I can't take a chance. I've got to focus on this right now.* Shovelhead pulled over once he was through Gulf Shores and in a rural area north of Foley. While still inside the van, he went to the back and took off the white jumpsuit. He put it in a trash bag in the back, where it was easily hidden. Took off the plain white hat and put that in the trash bag as well. He put on the cruddy baseball cap he normally wore. He popped out of the van like a Meerkat and took down the two magnetic signs. He then got back in the driver's seat and headed north to I10 and his trip back to Mobile. Once he was back home, he went to his backyard and threw the magnetic signs, the bag that had the coveralls, gloves, and hat in the 55-gallon drum in his yard. He threw in some pieces of wood and started a fire. He then went back and got in the van and drove the few miles to the rental place where he picked it up two days ago. He paid the bill in cash, went out, and called a biker buddy to come and pick him up at a tavern down the block.

Shovelhead: "Hey, Bennie, I need a ride home. Can you come and pick me up?"

Bennie: "Sure, but it'll be about 45 minutes."

Shovelhead: "OK, great."

When Shovelhead got home, he was feeling pretty good. He got rid of the clothes, He left the gun at the scene, and he got rid of the van. He got out of Orange Beach without hearing sirens of any kind. Everything was looking pretty good, as far as he could tell. He'd watch the news tonight in case there was any report of a murdered woman. He just had one big loose end to take care of. Once he was finished, he'd give Highside a call and tell him to meet him back at The Barrel bar next Wednesday to get the other seventy-five hundred dollars.

37

HOW JUSTICE BEGINS

A couple of residents in the Summer Wind neighborhood, Terry and Meg, decided to take a walk over to the pool that morning before the sun got too high. Meg wanted to go shopping that same afternoon and she was hoping to get a little bit of pool and sun time in early. She convinced Terry to walk over with her. They got their beach towels, and sunscreen, put on their bathing suits, and headed over to the pool. As they were walking by some of the other houses in the neighborhood, they saw one with its front door wide open and a person's feet sticking out.

Meg: "Terry, will you go over there and take a look? Something is wrong."

Terry was a big strong guy and wasn't afraid of anything.

Terry: "I'll go take a look: you stay here just in case."

As he rushes over to the house, he is met with a scene of absolute horror. A woman lay in the doorway and the floor was covered in blood. Her blouse was bright red from all the blood. She was dead. There wasn't a sound coming from inside the house. No movement of any kind. There was a green Mustang convertible in the driveway.

Terry calls back to Meg, "She's dead." He'd been around the block long enough to know that.

Terry yelled inside the house, "Is there anybody in there?" There was no answer. He reached into the pocket of his bathing suit and pulled out his cell phone. He dials 911.

911 Dispatcher: "Orange Beach Police Department, what is your emergency?"

Terry excitedly says, "It looks like someone has been murdered over here in the Summer Wind neighborhood. You better get some cops over here as soon as you can."

Dispatcher: "OK, we'll get somebody on the way. What is your name please."

Terry provided his name.

Dispatcher: "Can you stay on the line with me sir until we get an officer on the scene?"

Terry: "Yes, I can."

Dispatcher: "I have officers and paramedics on the way."

Terry sadly said, "I don't think you're going to need the paramedics."

Dispatcher: "Well, everybody is headed your way. Stand by."

Terry: "Yes, ma'am, I'll be here."

It wasn't even three minutes when the first Orange Beach Police cruiser came into the Summer Wind neighborhood. Terry was standing in the middle of the street and waved his hand at the officer as they came around the corner. Another car was behind him, and again another. Three radio cars. Terry talked to the first officer and pointed at the front door of the house. The officer drew his duty weapon. He walked up to the front door and stepped in. He saw the victim and the blood all over the floor. With another patrol officer right behind him, they went in and did a quick security sweep. The house was empty except for the victim. They went out as gingerly as they went in. Outside stood the patrol sergeant.

Sergeant: 'What have you got, guys?"

Patrol Officer: "Well, you can see she didn't stand a chance. There is nobody else in the house. Doesn't look like anything else was disturbed inside. But we just did a real quick sweep for other victims or anyone hiding in the house."

Sergeant: "OK, we'll have paramedics here in a matter of seconds and we'll have them take a quick look. I'll call the Detective Lieutenant and have him get some detectives over here fast."

The sergeant asked the first patrol officer, "Did you run the tag on that green Mustang?"

Patrol Officer: "Not yet, Sarge. We ran into the house first thing and did the safety sweep."

Sergeant: "OK, go ahead and run the tag and pull the registration and details so we get a name to see who this female is."

Patrol Officer: "OK, I'll do it right now."

The patrol officer went to his SUV to run the tag on the Mustang to confirm the victim and the address. Within two minutes, he waved the sergeant over to his SUV.

First Officer: "Here it is, sarge: the tag comes back to this address to a woman named Randi Reynolds, age 38. Here's her DL picture."

The officer shows the sergeant the picture on the laptop computer. The sergeant goes back up on the porch, looks down at the victim's face, which is partially covered in blood, and sees a wound, but he can tell it's the same woman. He goes back down to the patrol officer's SUV and says, "Wow, that is Randi Reynolds:

that's the girl that Lieutenant Josh Myers used to go out with. They just broke up a few months ago."

Patrol Officer: "So Lieutenant Myers knows her?"

Sergeant: "Yeah, he knows her. I've got to call him. Excuse me."

The sergeant walks out into the middle of the street, pulls out his cell phone, and calls Josh Myers.

Sergeant: "Josh, we just got called to a homicide. You need to meet me in the parking lot of Doc's Steaks and Seafood on the Perdido Beach Boulevard as quickly as you can."

Josh: "OK, Sarge, I'm on my way."

Within a few minutes, Lieutenant Myers arrives in his unmarked SUV at the parking lot of Doc's Steaks and Seafood. The restaurant is closed this early in the morning. The sergeant gets out of his car, walks over to where Josh pulled in and they start a conversation.

Josh getting out of his car, asks, "What have you got, sarge?"

Sergeant: "Josh, I need you to hold on tight because this is going to come as a shock to you."

Josh: "Sarge, what are you talking about?"

Sergeant: "Josh, we got a homicide back here in the Summer Wind neighborhood."

Josh: "OK, well, we can handle it."

Sergeant: "I know, but well, Josh, it's Randi."

Josh was shocked: "WHAT?"

Sergeant: "It's Randi."

Josh: "It's Randi? Randi Reynolds? My Randi is dead?!"

Sergeant: "She's dead, Josh. She's been murdered."

Josh: "Oh My God! I've gotta go see her. I've gotta go see right now!"

Sergeant: "Hold on a second, Josh. Calm down and let's think about this. You dated Randi. You broke up not too long ago. You know that's going to be an issue. We all know you are not involved in this, but it's all got to be done the right way."

Josh's legs start to buckle: "Yeah, you are right about that, but God, I can't believe this."

Sergeant: "Just hold on, let's call the Assistant Chief and the Chief. We'll need to make a plan because we want this done right."

Josh barely above a whisper, "Ok. Yeah, ok, ok, ok. But I've got to go see her. SARGE, I've got to go see her!"

Sergeant: "No, Josh, not yet. Let's call the Chief first and set up a meeting. We've got a little time, and we'll figure out a course of action."

Josh again, barely above a whisper, "ok."

Telephone calls are made to the Assistant Chief and the Chief of the Orange Beach Police Department. They arrive at the parking lot to talk to the sergeant and Josh about what is going on and how to handle the proceedings. The sergeant lays out the facts, and the Chief is very aware that Josh used to date the victim.

Chief: "Ok. Josh, you know this is going to be a tough one since you supervise all the detectives. How are we going to make this work? You're going to have to be scrutinized since you once dated the victim."

Josh: "Chief, I understand. I'll do it any way you want. I'll do everything you want, but I can't be cut out totally. It's still my beat, it's still my victim even if I had a personal relationship with her."

Chief: "OK, that is understandable. But this has got to be correctly. You can't take the case as the lead and well, we have to look at you too. I know we'll clear you. Let's start at the beginning. What time was the murder sarge?"

Sergeant: "Well, we got the call just about 8:40 a.m. Of course, we don't know what time the actual murder happened. We haven't had the medical examiner here yet. We haven't interviewed the witnesses. So, we don't know. It could have been first thing this morning or sometime last night. Right now, we don't have the answer."

Chief: "Alright, Josh, where were you last night?"

Josh: "I was home in bed, Chief. I got up this morning at my normal time, 6:00 a.m. Got dressed, had some coffee and was at the office by 7:30 a.m. I was at the detective bureau from 7:30 until I got the call from the Sergeant."

Chief: "That will be easy to check. Do you have any security cameras at your house, inside and out?"

Josh: "Oh yes, I have security cameras all over the place. Outside cameras, ring the doorbell. You can easily see me coming and going from anywhere around my house. You'll be able to establish that I was home."

Chief: "Alright, here's what we are going to do. I'm going to call the Baldwin County Sheriff and the Chief of Gulf Shores and I'm going to get two detectives. One from the county and one from Gulf Shores. They are going to come over and I'm going to let the Baldwin County Sheriff's Detectives spearhead this investigation. They will have to do some work to absolutely clear you as a suspect. We have to make sure that you were not in this area and also clear you of any motive. They will lead the investigation so that it can't be tainted. You will shadow them and work along with them and I will be directing them along with the Sheriff and the Chief of Gulf Shores. That will help us to make sure you're not pushing the investigation in any direction away from you. I will also call the D.A. and clear that with him. Do you understand, Josh?"

Josh: "Yes, sir."

Chief: "This is for your benefit, Josh: until we catch the killer, we don't want anybody saying that Detective Lieutenant Myers is involved in any way. By having the detectives from the other two departments taking the lead it'll be done without bias."

Within the hour, Baldwin County Sheriff's Detective Lieutenant Larry Hooper arrives, and a Detective Sergeant Henry Scott from the Gulf Shores Police Department shows up as well. They all shake hands, and the Chief of Police fills everybody in on what has taken place and gives them directions on how he wants the investigation to proceed.

Chief: "I am going to allow Josh to shadow you, but you guys are in charge of the case. Right, Josh?"

Josh: "Yes, sir. I also have another homicide I'm working on as we speak. Lauren Scavone was killed on the fourth of July. The best we can determine is she was killed by a sniper at the condos near the Perdido Pass"

Chief: "Is that related to this homicide Josh?"

Josh: "Well, sir, Lauren Scavone worked at D Campbell Land Development, and Randi Reynolds was dating Doctor Campbell, the CEO and owner of the company. So, they could be related. At this point, we just don't know."

Chief: "Well, all the more reason for you to stay very close to what's happened with this murder today. Everything could be connected and you've got the ticket on the other one. You keep the other one and you shadow these guys on this one. Got it, guys?"

Detectives in unison, "Yes, Sir."

The three detectives, the sergeant, and the two chiefs all go up to the scene a few blocks away. Forensic examiners have already arrived. The paramedics have finished up. Patrol has the road blocked off and is doing a neighborhood canvas for witnesses. One of the detectives working the forensics walks up to Josh Myers, holding a plastic bag.

Forensics Detective: "We've got something here, Lieutenant, you're gonna want to know about."

Josh: "What is it, Paul?"

Paul: "Well, this is a 9mm Glock pistol. It's got a silencer attached with an extended 30-round magazine and the magazine is empty."

Josh: "Any live rounds found at all?"

Paul: "No sir, thirty spent casings all over the porch."

Josh: "Ok."

Paul: "It's consistent with the wounds on the victim. She was shot at least 20-30 times. Most rounds hit her, but a few missed and were up in the wall near the ceiling behind her head. They were on an upward trajectory for sure. We lined those out and measured everything so we will have all that in our report, but the trajectory of the rounds inside the victim you will have to get from the M.E. of course."

Josh in shock: "Sure."

Paul: 'We recovered those 9mm rounds in the walls as well."

Josh quietly: "Good work Paul."

Paul: "Thanks, Lieutenant."

How is Josh going to break this to Randi's family?

38

THE ALLIES ASSEMBLE

Josh and the two detectives now assigned to the case looked into the envelope that the forensic officer was holding. They could see the semi-automatic pistol with the silencer threaded onto the barrel. They could also see the extra-long 30-round magazine sticking out from the bottom of the grip.

Josh commented, "That's some rig."

Detective Hooper: "It sure is. I haven't seen one like that around."

Gulf Shores Detective Sergeant Henry Scott: "That is some serious murder prep right there."

Josh: "I have to call my buddy at ATF in Mobile: with that silencer on there, we're going to need a little extra help. Plus, we need to trace this gun and try to find out all about it. Maybe we can get some answers."

Josh excuses himself and steps away from the others out in the middle of the street in front of the murder scene. He takes out his cell phone and calls Mike Conover, an old MP buddy of his from Fort Campbell, Kentucky. Mike is now a federal agent serving in the Bureau of Alcohol, Tobacco, Firearms and Explosives. He had been assigned to the Mobile, Alabama, office. Josh has known Mike for a long time and has always relied on him. They have worked a few cases together in Orange Beach, but Mike's territory was all of southern Alabama and there was a lot of crime and activity for him to cover in Mobile. He was a very busy guy, but he would drop everything in a minute to help Josh. Josh listens to the ringing on the other end of his phone.

Mike: "Josh, how are you, old man? Haven't heard from you in a while. Wild women, police, and the beach. Man, you've got it made."

Josh: "Well, there are some days I do, but I'm telling you Mike, this particular day is hitting me pretty hard."

Mike: "What happened old man?"

Josh: "I've got a murder on my hands down here and it's a girl I know."

Mike: "Well that doesn't sound good Josh. I'm sorry to hear that. My heart goes out to you. Anything I can do?"

Josh: "The chief has assigned two other detectives, one from Baldwin Co. and one from Gulf Shores PD as leads on the case. I'm just shadowing them, but we found at the scene a small Glock pistol with a silencer attached. It's quite a rig and I'm going to need your help in looking at it, analyzing it tracing it, and steering us in the right way to see if we can get any leads off it. We've got it now but of course, it's got to be run through the state lab or maybe your lab, depending on what you tell us. Do you think you could get over here? "

Mike: "I'm already on the way. I should be there in an hour. Just text me the address where you're at and I'll see you there. I just have one quick question. Why are there two different detectives leading this and not you? Why is the chief having you shadow? That makes no sense to me, knowing your career and professionalism."

Josh: "Uh, well, Mike, the victim is a woman that I was dating for about two years. We broke up recently. The chief wants to make sure the investigation is above reproach."

Mike: "Oh man, Josh, I had no idea. I am so sorry. How are you doing?"

Josh: "For now, I'm holding it all together, but I'm not sure how long that is going to last. Thanks, Mike, I'll send you the info. You're the best. See you soon."

Special Agent Mike Conover left the ATF Mobile office, got in his government vehicle, and headed to Orange Beach. Mike has been an ATF agent for twelve years. He started in Birmingham and ran the gritty streets up there where crime was rampant. He locked up a lot of people and recovered a lot of firearms and explosives trying to keep Alabama safe. After high school, with his father's urging, Mike chose the Army and wound up as an MP at Fort Campbell, Kentucky, serving with Josh Myers. They became fast friends and both loved law enforcement. Josh went back home to Orange Beach and he always told Mike how nice it was on the Alabama coast. When Mike was hired by the ATF, he was assigned to Birmingham, but after seven years, he got another opportunity to transfer down to the Mobile office. Mike jumped on it, having been a coastal boy himself in the Virginia area. He loved living near the water and the whole lifestyle that went with it. Mobile was a perfect fit for him. He and Josh had always remained friends and kept close contact and they helped each other out whenever they could. *Orange Beach is having quite the time.* He thought. *They just had a murder on the 4th of July and now this one. Pretty unusual in that small coastal city which is paradise under the sun. Crime was present there just like everywhere else. Certainly not the extreme violence they'd experienced lately. They have that routinely in Birmingham and Mobile but usually not in Orange Beach. Orange Beach and violent crime are as rare as a snowman on the beach. An automatic pistol with a silencer. I'll have to get a good look at it and see if we can help Josh and Orange Beach PD out.*

Back at the crime scene. The detectives huddled in the street about what their next move was. Forensics was still inside the residence, processing the scene. Patrol officers were conducting a neighborhood canvas and the detectives needed to come up with a strategic plan.

Detective Hooper: "We've got to notify the next of kin pretty quickly. Let's try to get some information on where her family is so we can give them a call."

Gulf Shores Detective Sergeant Henry Scott: "I'll take care of that. Let me get all of her history from the patrol officer and see what I can run down. I'll get with her employment office to see if anybody there could tell us anything. How big of a place is it, Josh? Do you know?"

Josh: "They have a fancy office right here in town. I'm not sure how many employees they have. But it's a pretty successful real estate company. I think the biggest interview we're going to have to conduct pretty quick is with the CEO of D Campbell Land Development."

Detective Hooper: "A Doctor runs a development company? Why do we need to interview him?"

Josh: "He's not a Doctor. His actual first name is Doctor. It's unusual, for sure. He has been dating Randi Reynolds as of late, plus his Executive Assistant was shot with a sniper rifle, and I'm pretty sure you all know about that."

Gulf Shores Detective Sergeant Henry Scott: "Yeah, yeah, of course."

Josh: "We haven't been able to get any solid leads on that. We don't have the murder weapon. This young woman was killed while she stood on her balcony right in the middle of the fireworks show that covered the sound of the shot, and man, it's been a dead end, and now Randi Reynolds is murdered. Both women have a tie to Doctor Campbell. She just did a big business land purchase for D Campbell Land Development which scored her quite a hefty profit. So, we've got to talk to him as soon as possible since two people who are very close to him have been violently murdered."

Detective Hooper: "Yes, well, hopefully he's got some good answers about that. Let's head over there right now and see if we can talk to him. Maybe a surprise interview would be better than making an appointment. There is going to be a shock in hearing about this, and if he's not involved, we want to get his initial reaction."

Gulf Shores Detective Sergeant Henry Scott: "Good idea."

Detective Hooper to the Gulf Shores Detective Sergeant Henry Scott: "You run down next of kin. Josh and I will go do the interview with this CEO fellow and see what we can get. Also, see if you can get a list of employees at the real estate office so we can get interviews set up with everybody who works there. You also talk to the family."

Josh: "No, Larry. I want to talk to the family. Just get me the contact info, and I will have my office contact the family. I want to do this myself."

Gulf Shores Detective Sergeant Henry Scott: "Ok, you got it."

TAMI RYAN & JIM CAVANAUGH

Josh tells the Patrol Sergeant: "I will send out five of my detectives to try and get all the video camera footage along the beach boulevard, all ring cameras in this neighborhood plus any from Doc's Seafood, Ruby Slipper on the corner. Even Live Bait and Wolf Bay. Try the condos across the street. One of these cameras has picked up the killer coming or going. We are going to have to start sifting through all that video. We've got to get started on that. The quicker we can get the videos locked in, the more time we can save."

Patrol Sergeant: "OK, Let me know if you need any of my gang to help on it."

Josh: "Thanks, Sarge."

Just as the detectives are about to leave, one of the forensics officers walks over from the scene.

Forensics Officer: "We're going to be wrapping this up in just a few minutes if you guys want to get a real good walk-through before we go."

Both Detectives: "Yeah, that'll be great. We'd like to do that once you guys are done."

Detective Hooper turns to Josh. "Josh, I don't think it's a good idea for you to go inside. You have been out of sorts since we got here. I think your brain is going a hundred miles a minute. From my perspective, you appear to be barely holding on. I know you are trying to keep it together professionally but it will do you no good to go up to the house. Having to step over Randi's body, it's going to be too much to handle. It would be for anyone." As Josh starts to protest Detective Hooper stops him. "I'm making an executive decision here Josh. You cannot go into the house. We'll take care of it."

Josh has no choice but to stay behind.

39

THE PAIN OF MURDER

Within a couple of minutes, the forensics officer waves them in and the two assigned detectives walk up, go inside the house, and do a complete walk-through. At this point, everything has been photographed, blood samples taken and every bit of evidence like fingerprints, hair, fibers, etc. have been collected. Everything that has been recovered has been listed on the report from forensics. The detectives didn't notice anything missing or moved inside the residence. They see Randi's personal belongings there. Nothing seems out of order. The only sign of violence in the house is in the immediate doorway, which is covered with the victim's blood.

The two detectives go back outside and the medical examiner has ordered that the body can now be moved since everything has been processed. Randi's body is loaded up on a gurney and is brought out. Josh asks the medical examiner if he can have a few minutes. Everyone steps away from the coroner's van and they give

Josh some privacy. Josh puts his hands on the body bag, puts his head down, and silently weeps. He stands there for several minutes and the reality of Randi being murdered hits him and his legs start to buckle. Detective Hooper runs over and grabs Josh to keep him from hitting the ground. They stand up, Josh straightens himself. He does his best to compose himself to continue.

Detective Hooper: "Look, Josh, we can handle the rest of the day. Maybe you should go home for a while and collect yourself. It's no reflection on you or how you handle your job. This is a shock to your system and you need to process what's going on."

Josh: "Thank you, but I'm okay. I need to be involved in every part of this investigation. When it's all done, I'll take some time to rest. Now, I want this killer caught."

The medical examiner puts Randi's body into the back of the coroner's van. The detectives talk to the medical examiner Doctor Terri O'Leary. As she is removing her rubber gloves, she looks at the detectives and says," Gentleman, this is a bad one."

All Josh can do is stand there and listen to the conversation. He was trying to concentrate on what was being said and trying to control his emotions. He's afraid if he opens his mouth to ask even one question he'll break down for good and he can't let that happen.

Detective Hooper: "Give us some hard facts doc."

O'Leary: "There isn't going to be a surprise on the cause of death. She was shot at least 25 times from what I can see."

Detective Hooper: "Twenty-five times? That's a whole lot of bullets."

O'Leary: "Yeah, I haven't seen many like this, if any. You usually get a few pumped into someone but twenty-five, that's crazy overkill. I'll be interested to see if I can get the trajectory nailed down. I didn't find any on the floor under her body that went through. Of course, they could very likely still be inside her body. There were a few in the wall and ceiling. Up behind the front door. It's just too hard to say, at this point, forensics can fill you in on those rounds and how exactly this transpired. Once I get her to the morgue, I'll be able to get a thorough examination of everything. I will try to give you a better feel when I'm done. She died pretty quick with all those wounds."

Detective Hooper: "OK doc, can you tell us anything, like when you think the time of death was? It will help us in our early interviews. I know you haven't done a complete exam yet."

O'Leary: "Yeah, I'd like to see if I can tighten that up but I can tell you that I think this is fresh. That body has only been there just a few hours. So, I'm not sure of the exact time right at this moment but I would say somewhere in the last four hours, maybe five."

Gulf Shores Detective Sergeant Henry Scott: "That puts it anywhere from daybreak until now."

O'Leary: "Yeah, probably about then."

Gulf Shores Detective Sergeant Henry Scott: "It may fit since people generally won't open their door to someone in the middle of the night. There doesn't seem to be any forced entry on the front door. There's no key in it. So, we can surmise it was opened from the inside. When the killer came up to the door, we can assume it was light enough for the victim to see who it was."

O'Leary: "Who found her?"

Detective Hooper: "Two neighbors, Terri and Meg who live down the street were walking to the pool about 8:40 a.m. They saw the door wide open. They looked over and noticed feet sticking out the doorway. Terri ran over to check and called 911 immediately."

O'Leary: "So nobody heard any shots?"

Gulf Shores Detective Sergeant Henry Scott: "Well the gun was found here at the scene and has an attached silencer."

O'Leary: "That explains that question. I don't envy you guys, looks like a tough one."

Detective Hooper: "Thanks a lot doc. We'll talk to you later."

O'Leary: "I'll have a report for you first thing in the morning. We can talk more then."

Josh steps away from the group, texts Mike Conover and says, "We've got to do an interview here right away on a key player in this case so when you get here just meet me at police headquarters. As soon as I clear this interview, I'll come over there and get with you and we can look over the gun."

Mike texts back: "Got it. I'll just grab a cup of coffee on the way. Ain't no problem."

The two detectives get into one car, and Josh gets into his car on the way to their initial interview. Josh starts his car, and instantly, Bobby Darin is singing. Tears start to roll down Josh's face as he quietly sings.

"Somewhere beyond the sea,

She's there watchin' for me,

If I could fly like birds on high,

Then straight to her arms, I'd go sailin'.

40

DEALING WITH LOSS

As Josh got back to his office, he contemplated who was going to notify Randi's parents about her murder. It's not something he ever did. He always assigned that task to one of his colleagues. But this was different. This was Randi. The woman he was madly in love with and wanted to marry. The thought runs through Josh's head. *I don't even know if Randi ever told her family about me. I wonder if she ever mentioned me at all in any conversation. How do I tell them I wanted to marry her if they never even heard of me? I will just have to wait and see how they react and if they mention if Randi ever talked about me.* Josh will have to deal with this when Randi's family gets to Orange Beach. Josh is dreading this call. He's been with other families when getting this kind of news. It is agonizing but this is something he wanted to do himself.

Josh walks into the Chief's office: "Good Morning Chief. How is your day so far?"

Chief: "Good Morning Josh. What is on your agenda today?"

Josh: "I have got to call Randi's family and let them know what's happened."

Chief: "Josh, do you think you should be the one to do that? With your history with Randi and how you feel about her, are you sure this is something you can do? Can you convey what has happened without getting emotional yourself?"

Josh: "Honestly Chief, I have no idea. But I want to be the one to tell Randi's family. I must be professional and sympathetic without getting caught up in their emotions. Can I do that? We will find out."

Chief: "Josh, I want you to call whatever local police department for that area and have them take the police chaplain to the Reynolds house. I want someone to be with the family. Have them give the Reynolds family the initial news and have the Reynolds call you. Then you can fill them in on what is going on. Good Luck."

As Josh leaves the office: "Thanks Chief, I'm going to need it."

Josh goes to his own office and closes the door. He has Sergeant Joyce Miller contact the local police department and get them on the phone.

Columbia County Sheriff John Land: "This is Sheriff Land."

Josh: "Good Morning, Sheriff, My name is Detective Lieutenant Josh Myers. I'm from the Orange Beach, Alabama, Police Department. We would like someone from your department to head over to Bill and Diane Reynolds' home to give them a death notice. If you could take your police Chaplain with you, that would be great. I want to fill the family in myself on what happened. I'll give you my contact info and if you would please give it to the family, I will talk to them directly. We want the Chaplain there in case.

Sheriff John Land: "OK, sure, we can do that. Who is the victim and how are they related?"

Josh: "The victim's name is Randi Reynolds and she is Bill and Diane's daughter."

Sheriff John Land: "I will handle it myself, Lieutenant."

Josh: "Thanks, Sheriff."

Josh sits back in his chair and waits for the impending phone call. He is trying to gather his thoughts and calm his nerves before he has to have a conversation with Randi's family.

The Columbia County Sheriff and the police Chaplain head out to the Reynolds farm. Diane Reynolds answers the door: "Good Morning, Sheriff. Can I help you? Is something wrong?" Just then, Diane's daughter Meghan comes to the front door.

Sheriff: "Good Morning. Is Mr. Reynolds home? We want to speak to you together, please."

Meghan: "He's in the barn. It'll take a minute for me to go get him." Meghan runs to the barn and gets her dad.

Bill rushes to the house: "Good Morning, Sheriff. What is this all about?"

Sheriff: "Can we have a seat." He introduces the police Chaplain.

Sheriff: "We have been asked by the Orange Beach, Alabama Police Department to come and give you a death notice for your daughter Randi."

Bill frantic: "What?!"

Diane: "Oh No! What's Happened?"

Sheriff: "We do not have the details. Detective Lieutenant Josh Myers wants to give you the details. Here is his number. Please call him immediately, and the Chaplain and I will stay here while he fills you in."

Meghan gets up and rushes out of the house. She heads to the barn to get two of her brothers and calls the other two who are in the field to get to the house immediately. It's about Randi. All four sons drop everything and rush to the house. As they walk in the door, Bill is on his cell and has it on speaker.

Josh: "Good Morning, Mr. & Mrs. Reynolds. Are you the parents of Randi Reynolds, who currently lives in Orange Beach?"

Bill: "We are."

Josh: "My name is Detective Lieutenant Josh Myers of the Orange Beach Police Department."

Diane: "What's happened?"

Josh's voice gets stuck in his throat. Hearing the anxiousness of Diane's voice has just set him back. Josh is struggling to get the words out.

Diane: "Lieutenant Myers? What has happened?!"

Josh: "Mrs. Reynolds, I'm calling to inform you that your daughter Randi has been murdered."

Bill: "What? What are you saying? What do you mean murdered? Someone went and killed my daughter?"

Josh: "Yes, Mr. Reynolds. I am sorry to have to tell you this."

Diane in a low guttural scream: "NO, NO NO, NOOOOO!!"

Meghan: "Murdered?"

As Diane slumps to the floor crying, Meaghan sits next to her and wraps her arms around her.

Bill: "What the hell happened? Who would do this? Do you know?"

Josh: "We do not have a suspect at this time or an answer as to why."

Their four sons are standing in the kitchen. They listen to their dad on the phone.

Bill: "Give your information and address to my son. Diane and I will be on the next flight to Orange Beach. I will call you when we arrive." Bill hands the phone to Greg.

Bill sinks to the floor next to Diane. He grabs her and pulls her into his chest. As Diane continues to sob, Bill starts to cry. Meghan, still on the floor next to her parents, is hugging them as tightly as possible. The entire family is in shock. This is such a tight-knit family that what affects one affects them all. The entire family is shredded. They are all in shock and tears. Hugging, crying, and trying to console each other. Diane is so distraught: that she cannot get up off the floor. Her legs won't work. She simply cannot get up. Vic calls the local doctor and explains what is going on. In this small town, Doctors are neighbors and the doctor rushes to the farm and tends to Diane. Bill and the boys finally get her up and into bed. The doctor gives her a sedative to help calm her down. Once they get Diane settled and calmed down, Meghan makes plane reservations for her entire family. She helps Bill pack for the trip. Meghan makes sure Diane's bag is packed and ready to go. Neighboring farmers heard what was happening and they all stepped up to take care of the farm and chores while the family was out of town.

Their flight is at 6:00 am the next morning. Two of the neighbors show up and take the entire family to the airport. It's a somber flight and the whole family is exhausted. The Reynolds siblings take over while in Orange Beach as their parents are in no shape to be front and center. They all get to Josh's office and Josh has the horrible task of giving them all the details.

Josh fills the family in on everything he has. Josh tells Randi's family that he knew Randi personally and that they were friends. They thanked him for his friendship with Randi and it was obvious that Randi had not told her family about him. Saddened and heartbroken, Josh continues to support and help Randi's family while they are in Orange Beach. Vic and Greg are given the task of identifying Randi's body. The family goes back to their hotel and makes plans on what to do next.

Meghan: "Dad, how do you want to proceed?"

Bill: "My mind is numb right now, Meghan: I suppose we will have Randi flown home."

Diane, still dazed and in shock, says just above a whisper, "No, Bill, I don't want to do that."

Bill: "What do you mean?"

Diane: "Randi never wanted to stay on the farm or in Wisconsin. She hated the cold. She left right out of high school for places warmer. She loves the beach, she loves the warm weather, she thrived down here. I do not want her to have to leave the place she loved. I want her to be where she is most happy."

Vic: "What are you suggesting, Mom?"

Diane: "I want to have Randi cremated. We can take some of her ashes home with us and put the rest of her ashes in the Gulf."

Bill: "I think that is a great idea, Diane. I will call Lieutenant Myers and see if he can help us arrange that."

Bill gets on the phone with Josh about their plans. Josh is more than happy to assist Randi's family. It took a couple of days to get everything done with the cremation. Getting a boat secured that would take the family out to the Gulf.

Bill: "Josh would you like to accompany us on the boat since you and Randi were friends? You have been so helpful to us."

Josh: "Thank you, Mr. Reynolds. I deeply appreciate the offer, but I do not want to intrude on your private family farewell to Randi. I will watch from the shore."

Josh takes Randi's family to the marina, where the boat will take them out to the gulf to spread Randi's ashes. They were able to get a Pastor to accompany them as well to say a prayer over Randi. Josh stands on the beach and watches the boat head out. He has a pair of binoculars so he can watch the spreading of Randi's ashes. Josh watches the family hold hands and bow their heads in prayer. Each family member takes a small amount of ashes and drops them in the Gulf. As Josh watches, he sees Diane buckle a little bit as Bill and one of her sons hold her up. Josh himself sits down on the beach. Puts the binoculars back in their case. He puts his head down and weeps silently. Crushed and devastated by the loss of Randi's family along with his own. Part of his sadness is that he could not keep Randi safe. Josh thinks to himself. *She came to me when she was getting threatening notes. I did my job professionally but kept my distance emotionally. Had I made a huge mistake? If I had put my pride aside and watched out for Randi a little closer, would she still be alive?* This causes Josh to cry harder. He will never know the answer to his question and that will haunt him for the rest of his life.

41

ALL ROADS LEAD TO DOCTOR

Doctor Campbell stands up and starts to pace across the room with both hands holding his head.

Doctor almost yelled, "I can't believe this. Lauren was murdered in July and now Randi. Something is going on here. You guys have got to do your job."

Detective Hooper: "We're trying to Mr. Campbell. Please come back over and sit down."

Doctor walks back over and sits down to face the detectives.

Detective Hooper: "Tell us your whereabouts from last night at 6:00 p.m."

Doctor: "Now, just hold on a minute. You don't think I had anything to do with this?"

Josh: "At this point, we don't know who is responsible. That's why we are here asking questions. I'm sure you understand."

Doctor: "Yes, yes, I've already been through this with Lauren. Ok, last night at 6:00 p.m. I was home getting ready for a dinner appointment with a contractor from one of my developments. He's the contractor that runs all the underground utilities. Electric, water, gas. He's got a big company and I always work with him. We were getting together to discuss the new neighborhood project."

Detective Hooper: "OK, what's his name? Do you have a phone number?"

Doctor: "His name is John Simpson and his company is out of Mobile."

Detective Hooper: "Alright, and what's that phone number?

Doctor: "My assistant will get it for you."

Detective Hooper: "OK, thank you. So, you were home getting ready for your dinner meeting with John Simpson?"

Doctor: "That's correct. Our dinner appointment was at 7:00 p.m. at the Voyager Restaurant in the Perdido Beach Resort. That's where I like to go to talk business. They always have a table ready for me in a quiet spot, so my meetings are not disturbed by a bunch of noise. We met there promptly at 7:00 p.m. and had dinner. We stayed and talked for quite a while until about 9:00 p.m. We said our goodbyes and left."

Detective Hooper: "You both arrived in separate vehicles?"

Doctor: "Yes, we did. We met at the restaurant and both left in our separate cars."

Detective Hooper: "Alright, where did you go after you left the restaurant."

Doctor: "I went home. It was 9:30 p.m. by the time I got home. I took a hot shower, put on some soft clothes, made myself a drink, and sat down to watch a little news, and I went to bed. It was a long busy day and I was exhausted. I was in bed about 11:00 p.m."

Detective Hooper: "Were you alone?"

Doctor: "I was alone."

Detective Hooper: "I assume you have security cameras and an alarm system at your home?"

Doctor: "Yes, There are extensive security cameras around the entire property. I live in a penthouse condo. There was a concierge who was at the door when I got home. You can check with him as to my arrival home. I didn't leave my place until this morning at 6:45 a.m."

Detective Hooper: "OK, what did you do at 6:45 a.m.?"

Doctor: "I came directly to my office, just like I do every workday."

Detective Hooper: "Was anybody already here when you got in?"

Doctor: "My assistant was here. You just met her. She's always here very early, and I am always here at 7:00 a.m. I always start my day early in this business. The early worm gets the drop on the bird."

Detective Hooper: "I understand. So, to confirm. You are at your office at 7:00 a.m. every day.?"

Doctor: "Yes, even this morning. I got here at 7:00 and have been here the whole time."

Detective Hooper: "Alright, Doctor, thank you very much for your time. We are going to talk to Mr. Simpson, check with the Voyager, and we'll talk to your concierge. We will look at all the security footage from your complex and the Perdido Beach Resort to confirm everything you've told us. I hope you understand, we have to check everything out you just told us so we can eliminate you as a suspect."

Doctor: "Of course, I completely understand. I don't have anything to hide from you guys. Please, find out who is doing this. Something has to happen. I'm worried about what's going on.

These two women were very close to me and now they both have been murdered. Do I need to get protection? Do I need to get a bodyguard?"

Detective Hooper: "Well, that is up to you, sir. It's certainly your right to do so. We don't have any leads that anyone is targeting you. If you are worried and want to feel safe, that decision will be up to you. Can you think of any reason someone would have to harm these two women? Would it be related to your business?"

Doctor: "I have no idea at all or suspect anyone who would want to murder those two women. Wait. I'm sorry. I, I, in the shock of the moment, almost forgot to tell you."

Detective Hooper: "Yes, go on."

Doctor: "About three weeks ago, my bookkeeper, Jerry Lunde, came to my office and told me that he suspected Lauren had been siphoning money from my accounts. He said she had taken several hundred thousand dollars and moved to a separate bank account."

Detective Hooper: "Did you verify this?"

Doctor: "I called my actuary and asked him to come in and go through all the books and do a complete and total audit of my finances to see if any money had been taken and if they could tell by whom."

Josh: "Has that process begun?"

Doctor: "Not yet. They are supposed to start on Monday. I have extensive holdings, and of course, if she had done that, she might have been able to hide it somewhere."

Detective Hooper: "I see."

Doctor: "The actuarial company has extensive resources. They will come in with two or three people and it would take about a week."

Detective Hooper: "I understand. Did you call Orange Beach P.D. and report that about Lauren stealing money?"

Doctor: "The bookkeeper said she did, but he didn't show me any data to back up his claim. So, my thought process was to see if it was true and if the actuary could prove it, I would let you know. If it wasn't true, I didn't want to drag Lauren's name through the mud after what happened. Since the audit will be starting this week, I want to wait for the results."

Detective Hooper: "Thank you, Mr. Campbell. We appreciate your cooperation and candor. This is not the time to hold back any information. If we are going to catch the person or persons who did this, we will need all information, no matter how insignificant you think it might be."

Detective Hooper: "Now, Mr. Campbell, were you in a romantic relationship with Randi?"

Doctor: Yes, our business turned to pleasure."

Detective Hooper: "Alright, Lieutenant Myers said that you also had a romantic relationship with Lauren Scavone."

Doctor: "I had a sexual relationship with Ms. Scavone. It was never romantic. Please keep all of this personal information private. I respect both of these women and they have families."

Detective Hooper: "Of course. Now, please tell us more about both of those relationships."

Doctor: "Lauren had been my Executive Assistant when I was located in Mobile. She moved here with me to get my business started. Through long work hours, we developed a sexual relationship. We weren't romantic. We were not a couple. We had sex for convenience. It was a mutual agreement. As far as Randi goes. We had a business deal that was profitable for both of us and well, we did develop feelings for each other. I realized lately I was falling madly in love with her. At this point, I am trying to hold everything together as far as Randi goes. It's getting harder to sit here calmly and discuss this with you without falling apart. I truly cared for Randi Reynolds. I wanted to be around her as much as I could. Now you're in my office telling me she's been murdered and immediately started asking questions about my whereabouts. You didn't even bother to give me a chance to absorb what you were telling me. I'm in shock. I'm having a hard time trying to figure out who would want to kill Randi. When we were out together, she was fun, friendly, and spoke to everyone. Laughed and joked with anyone. She was just an all-around nice genuine person. None of this makes sense to me at all."

Doctor sits at his desk, puts his head down, and starts to cry.

42

SEVENTH SON OF
THE SEVENTH SON

Suddenly and without notice Doctor lets out a blood-curdling scream. It took the Detectives by such surprise that it caused them both to jump. Doctor pounded the desk with both fists. Not being able to hold it in any longer. Doctor just kept pounding the desk and trying to contain his anger.

The detectives kept quiet and sat and waited for Doctor to calm down. After several minutes, Doctor was finally able to compose himself. He looks at the detectives.

Doctor: "I do think I need to talk to my attorney as well, and I need to think about getting some security. It seems like I'm caught up in this mess."

Detective Hooper: "We understand. Those are certainly all your rights. Here are our cards. Call any of us if anything changes."

Doctor: "Thank you, I will for sure."

Detective Hooper: Mr. Campbell, before we leave, I am curious about your first name. You are not a doctor?"

Doctor finally able to control his emotions: "No, I am not, nor was my father. I admit it is a rare and unusual name."

Detective Hooper: "I agree. I have never met anyone with that as a first name."

Doctor: "My father is the seventh son in his family. There are nine children in my family."

Detective Hooper: "Wow, nine children, that must have been a busy house."

Doctor: "Yes, it was great growing up. There were two girls and seven boys. I am the seventh son, a very rare occurrence."

Detective Hooper: "I see how that would be so."

Doctor: "Traditionally, in the old days and when tradition ruled, the seventh son of the seventh son was named Doctor. That was how other people knew you were the seventh son of the seventh son and you were supposed to have healing powers and to be lucky. People would travel great distances to be healed by the seventh son,"

Detective Hooper: "That is an incredible family history. I'm sure there probably aren't many men named Doctor."

They all shake hands and the detectives get up and walk out of Doctor's office. They got John Simpson's phone number from Doctor's new executive assistant and left the premises.

Once back in the car, Detective Hooper says to Josh. "Well, Josh, what do you think? Is he good for it? Do you think he's acting or is he a victim in this whole thing?"

Josh: "When we first told him about Randi's murder, the way his face looked. It sure looked like real shock."

Detective Hooper: "You've seen guys try to fake that before."

Josh: "I have. Guys can get pretty slick about how they react to things when they are prepared and know you are coming. Unless, of course, he had no idea we were coming, then the shock was real."

Detective Hooper: "It's suspicious. Two people he's very close to, both were involved with him sexually, one romantically, and one involved in his business, is murdered. His bookkeeper is throwing shade that his assistant might be stealing money. He has no proof of any embezzlement at this time. That could be a motive for murder. Greed."

Josh: "Yes, greed is always a good motive for murder. But if that's the case, why would he kill Randi? He was dating her. They just made a multimillion-dollar deal for a new development. It makes no sense to kill her."

Detective Hooper: "There is a lot we don't know about their relationship or their financial dealings. There could be a whole lot of things going on under the tent here that we haven't uncovered yet. As far as their relationship, were they a serious couple or just casually dating and having fun? Maybe we can glean some information once we get her phone. Once we talk to her fellow employees, friends and acquaintances, and her family, they might be able to give us more information about her relationship with Doctor Campbell. There's a lot to find out before we can get going."

Josh: "I know but with no gun found at Lauren's murder or any witnesses. It's like trying to pull a rabbit out of a hat, I can't even find the damn hat and it's been a tough slog. She was shot during the fireworks finale. That investigation has been nothing but a cold turkey. I have just not been able to get any decent lead in that case since it happened. It is as if she was killed by the creeping fingers of the night, a shadow, a specter. I have nothing to go on."

Detective Hooper: "With it being the 4th of July, no less. Maybe it was a patriotic shadow, Josh. Those are frustrating, but look, at least today we do have a gun."

Josh: "Well, that narrows it down. That's true about the gun and my buddy from ATF is about to meet us at police headquarters. Maybe we can get something started with that. Maybe we could get at least one lead. I'm hoping we might turn up an eyewitness in the neighborhood. Maybe something will come of that or one of the many security cameras will get something. Between the gun and those things, maybe we can move this thing ahead on this morning's killer."

Detective Hooper: "Let's hope so and always keep an open mind, they could be unrelated murders also."

Josh: "Or maybe it is a rare double murder committed by a rare Seventh Son."

Detective Hooper: "Then he would be unlucky instead of lucky because if so, we will catch him."

Josh: "I agree. By the way, I know it's complicated. Me knowing Randi and us dating for a while."

Detective Hooper replies: "You know, in small-town America, it's not unusual that police officers know or have been friends or acquaintances or are even related to victims. In big cities, it is easy to assign more detectives. But in small towns, it's hard to get away from all that. I think the Chief has done the right thing. He's split the pie just perfectly by putting me and the Gulf Shores Detective Sergeant Henry Scott on it. We'll make sure everything is done right, and that way, nobody can say you tainted the case. By you shadowing along, it'll allow us to keep a strong connection to

Lauren's murder as well. Maybe we can see if these two murders end up being connected in any way. It's an Orange Beach murder and it's your ticket. We're just here to make sure nobody can come back and say it wasn't done right."

Josh: "I know and I appreciate you guys coming in on it. It is the only way we can do it. The bottom line is to catch whoever is responsible. That's my focus right now."

Detective Hooper: "Absolutely, us too."

The two detectives roll into the Orange Beach headquarters along with Josh and head to the detective bureau. There sitting at Josh Myers' desk with his feet up on it drinking a cup of coffee is Josh's buddy from the ATF, Special Agent Mike Conover.

Conover getting up: "Josh, I am so fricking sorry about Randi. I know you must have loved her. I know it crushed you when you guys broke up and now this. I'm here for you, man. You look like shit. Are you sure you should be here? We three can handle this, you know."

Josh: "Thanks, Mike. I know you guys can handle it, but like I told the detectives, I have to be in on this. I want to make sure whoever murdered Randi is caught. It's going to be hard: I know. When it's all done, I'll take some time off."

Mike: "Well, you come to Mobile and you and I will hang out for several days. I got the time to take off as well. By the way, I also talked to the Special Agent in Charge, Tim Donnelly. He said to get you anything and anybody you need to get this solved."

Josh: "Thank you, Mike. Tell Mr. Donnelly thank you as well."

Josh introduces Mike to the other two detectives. They all shake hands, pat each other on the back and give each other a shoulder hug. They sit and get down to business. Josh picks up the phone, calls forensics, and says. "Bring that pistol in from the murder this morning in Summer Wind."

In a few minutes, the forensics officer walks in with a large brown paper bag marked with an evidence tag. He tells the lieutenant, the two detectives, and the ATF agent to all initial that they are in possession of the gun at the moment, and the officer says, "Do you want me to leave it with you and come back at a later time?"

Mike: "This will only take a few minutes. Maybe fifteen minutes if you want to just wait."

Officer: "I can."

Josh: "Just wait outside the squad room. Don't go anywhere. We'll get it right back to you once we look it over."

Office: "OK, thanks. By the way, I brought a bunch of rubber gloves for you guys if you plan on handling it."

Mike Conover reaches into his jacket pocket and says, "No worries, I always have them ready."

He pulls out a pair of rubber surgical gloves and snaps them on.

Mike: "I can check you for hemorrhoids, Josh, if you need it."

Josh laughs, 'No thanks, Mike. I prefer you examine the gun.' They all smile. Mike picks up the gun with his gloved hands and lays it on the desk.

43

GHOST GUN

Special Agent Mike Conover had seen a lot of firearms in his career. In ATF, guns, explosives, and arson crimes were routine business. Conover had also worked his share of violent murders with his federal colleagues and police agencies. He always respected their investigative responsibilities and knew that together, they were a solid team. Conover picked up the gun carefully with his gloved hands. The slide had been locked back with a zip tie. Standard procedure to make sure the gun is safe to handle before it is placed into evidence. There was no magazine inside the gun. Conover flipped it over and looked at it very carefully.

Conover: "What kind of pistol would you say this is Josh?"

Josh: "It looks like a pretty standard Glock to me. With that silencer attached, that is unusual."

Conover: "Right. It looks like a Glock, but it's not a Glock."

Josh: "What do you mean?"

Mike: "There are no markings on this gun. If it was made by Glock, it would be stamped with a serial number as required by Federal Law. It would have the manufacturer's markings on it. This gun has none of those things. What you have here, Josh, what we call officially in ATF, is a PMF."

Josh: "What? Now you're talking that Federal slang."

Mike: 'Yeah, I know. It's bureaucratic slang. It means Personally Manufactured Firearm. In effect, it's a ghost gun. That's what it's called on the street. A ghost gun."

Josh: "Well, it looks just like the real thing. How does that come about?"

Mike: "Well, it happens in many ways. Some guns can be 3-D printed, but many are manufactured from kits. I would say that this gun was made from a kit that was purchased. It has 80% of the gun already manufactured by someone. A buyer then orders the kit on the internet, except it is not a completed firearm. So, under Federal Law, technically, it does not meet the definition of a firearm. We just had some of those regulations changed to stop this, but it has always been an uphill battle because so many of these kits are on the street. This one look's like it was made from what we call an 80% kit. The receiver part of the gun still has to have some machining and drilling before it can function as a weapon."

Josh: "So what you are telling me is, the killer made the gun?"

Mike: "Well, maybe, but not necessarily. Someone else could have made the gun. He could have gotten it from someone who traffics these. That makes them untraceable. A lot of the street gangs. White supremacist gangs, militiamen. Any government zealots, crackpots, bikers, killers, you name it. They want these guns that cannot be traced. Here is an example of that."

Josh: "So he buys this kit on the internet, but it's just not a complete gun. How does he know how to make it exactly?"

Mike: "Well, he can also buy from the same seller or a different seller at a gun show the 80% frame and receive the instructions and template showing exactly where to drill, how to drill, and where to cut. How to fit the parts together. The whole process may take him two hours in a workshop, and he can come out with a completely functioning gun that has no markings, no serial numbers, and is completely untraceable. When I say completely, I mean by serial number. Sometimes, we can go back and match machining marks or tool marks from tool drills and dyes. Just depends on if we can get to the "factory" that is making these things. If a guy is putting out more than just one. Some people buy them to just make one. Some people buy them and sell them. We are always trying to stop and shut down the suppliers. The so-called factory may just be someone's dirty basement."

Josh: "Well, that does not help me much. I was hoping to get a good lead off a gun trace on this. No, you're telling me there isn't going to be a gun trace."

Mike: "Sorry about that, Josh. No, this is going to send it in a different direction. Let's look at the silencer."

Mike carefully unscrews the silencer looks it over carefully, examines it, and gets a flashlight to look through it.

Josh: "What do you see, Mike? Anything we can use?"

Mike: "This is not a commercially manufactured silencer either. Silencers in themselves are firearms under the National Firearms Act. They must be registered with ATF, just like a submachine gun. You can't just possess it. You cannot make it for yourself. It must be legally registered. This one has no serial number. Again, it cannot be legal, it's already automatically illegal and that carries a federal penalty. Just possession of this is a federal crime. It looks to be well made. It has a baffle system inside. I can see the washers. It has been stuffed with some sort of steel mesh to absorb the sound. It will deaden the sound quite a bit. It doesn't completely make the gun silent. It's not like Hollywood. Depending on the size of the cartridges used and how much powder is in it, it reduces the report significantly so that a person doesn't generally recognize it as a crack of a gunshot. The larger the cartridge, the harder it is to reduce the sound, so the silencer would have to be larger on a larger caliber weapon. This is a 9 mm pistol, so the silencer would be efficient on a gun like this. It would reduce the report significantly, probably to the sound of something like a screen door slamming. People would hear it if they were in proximity but not necessarily recognize it as a gunshot."

Josh: "That would coincide with where the body was found by two neighbors who were walking to the nearby pool. Nobody reported any gunshots last night or this morning. We thought that was unusual, until we found the silencer."

Mike: "Well, that is why the killers use it, so they can get away without being noticed. There is something else about this gun that is unique as well. This gun is fitted with a special switch that converts it into a submachine gun."

Josh: "A sub-machine gun?"

Mike: "See this little square box on the back of the receiver here? The slang for that is a Glock switch. Glock does not like ATF to call it that. So, we do not officially because they don't make it, they don't endorse it, they don't condone it, they operate within the law, but the street slang is Glock switch. It is this little mechanism that converts the pistol to fully automatic fire.

Josh: "Wow, this guy was prepared. He had a silencer and a switch to make it fully automatic."

Mike: "So when the killer held the trigger down, as long as he held the trigger down, it would empty the magazine."

Josh: "We found a 30-round magazine there and Randi was shot so many times that even the coroner couldn't believe it."

Mike: "If someone is in proximity to you and holds that trigger down, it's going to empty the full magazine right into you. You aren't going to survive something like that. It's too many wounds too fast. I know it's not much consolation, Josh, but when you're hit with a gun like this, death is going to be very quick."

Gulf Shores Detective Sergeant Henry Scott: "Well, at least we did get one break. The idiot dropped the gun."

Mike: "Well that is a possibility for sure, but I think he deliberately left the gun."

Josh: "Why would he do that?"

Mike: "We've seen this a lot with contract hits around the country. The killers don't want to leave the scene with the gun. If they are stopped by an officer or a deputy, it's proof positive they are the killer. It's too much attachment to the murder. That's why they use a ghost gun to start with. They don't want it to be traceable. They whack you and drop the gun at the scene. It has no traceable markings and no serial numbers. Even if you happen to catch someone ten blocks away, they don't have the weapon on them. I'd say he knew enough to drop the gun there. He knew you'd find it and he also knows it can't be traced to him or her."

Josh: "I get it. A machine gun, a ghost gun, a ghost silencer, and a killer who is a pro or at least a semi-pro who knows to drop the gun at the scene."

Mike: "That's the beginning of this mess Josh, I'm sorry to say."

Josh: "What's the next step, Mike? What do you recommend on the gun?"

Mike: "You can send it to the state lab, of course. They are first rate, and they can print it and swab for DNA, or if you'd like, I can take it to the ATF lab in Atlanta. They are experts in this. They will also do a DNA swab and latent fingerprints. Not only that, but they will also be able to take the mechanism apart very carefully and look for anything inside that might be a lead. They will dust for fingerprints in every little corner and then they will be able to write a report detailing how the gun was made, what kind of gun it is, and that it was modified to be a submachine gun that is illegal. A complete forensics workup on the gun for you. You can then let the state lab concentrate on all the other aspects of the murder. It sounds like their plate is full already with the crime scene you had this morning."

Josh: "The state lab is great, and they are there helping us out. I know they work with your lab, too, so let's do it that way. We can team up. You guys do the gun, the silencer, and all that goes with it. State lab will work on the forensics of the murder scene. State lab said some of the bullets had hit high above Randi in the back wall of her living room. They got some of those recovered so they could match them to the gun along with the ones recovered from Randi's body."

Mike: "That is kind of consistent with a machine pistol. If he held the trigger down with a 30-round mag, it would ride up. Ride up right through her chest, maybe up through her head and up above her head or above her shoulder and that's how they ended up in the wall or the ceiling. The most likely event is when she opened the door, he held the trigger down until the magazine was empty.

Most of the bullets would have hit her initially, but the last few would have missed as the gun rose."

Josh: "That is exactly what the crime scene looked like. Plenty of wounds inside her and a few behind her embedded in the wall. Mike, you've been a great help to get us started on this. Is there anything else that we need to do regarding the gun and the silencer?"

Mike: "We've got informants all over the coast down here from New Orleans to Tallahassee. I'll contact the Tampa division that runs Florida. We have an office in Pensacola and Tallahassee. I'll also get with the New Orleans division that is in Biloxi. We'll scour the coast to see what we can come up with, anything that is similar. Maybe we can get word on a supplier that we can talk to. We'll send the recovered bullet images and put them in the national integrated ballistics network. We call it NIBIN. That's at our forensics lab in Atlanta. That will tell us if any similar bullets were used in any other crime in the region. It's possible the gun was used before but I kind of doubt it since it was dropped at the scene. The killer would not have dropped it if it was previously used in another crime and they had been carrying it around with them. But it does happen that a lot of criminals use these guns more than once. We'll check the database just to make sure."

Josh: "Thanks, Mike. Let me know immediately if you pick up anything or find anything. In the meantime, we will be working this case hard."

Mike: "You got it, Josh. If we have anything you need, just let me know and I'll get it for you. Equipment, manpower, tools, anything at all. Agents to help with interviews to bolster you up with this investigation, you let me know. We'll get someone over here immediately. You've got these great detectives and more of your own, but sometimes, with a case this big, you can run out of manpower. This case does involve a federal crime. The illegal possession of a ghost gun and a silencer. Anything you need from us we'll team up and get it taken care of."

Josh: "Thanks, Mike. You are the best." Josh calls in the patrol officer who brought the gun up from the evidence locker.

Josh tells the officer, "Special Agent Mike Conover is going to take the gun and the silencer to the ATF forensic lab in Atlanta, and they are going to examine it for fingerprints and DNA and go through the whole inside. Please take him down to the evidence room and sign it out to him."

Mike Conover then places the firearms and silencer back in the evidence bag as the officer watches. They all re-initial the evidence tag and mark the back of the envelope with the current time.

As everyone says their goodbyes and leaves Josh Myers' office, he sits in his swivel desk chair and takes a deep breath. *"So much for the easy ones."* He thinks. *"First, a sniper with no trace and now, what looks like a pro hit, and both in Orange Beach. Paradise has a slimy underbelly, and it is his job to clean it up."*

44

A STAKE THROUGH HIS HEART

Lieutenant Myers was in the office early. Two days ago, Randi was murdered, and he has been working long hours. His team of detectives was trying to get any strong leads on the case, and they had another full day scheduled with lots of interviews still to do. They had lots of video footage from nearby cameras from businesses and homes that they had to go through, hoping to see something that would break it open. They had been examining all of Randi's history, and associates, examining her computers, her phone, and her timeline. Every possible avenue they could think of to try and make some headway, and of course, they had notified her family.

Lieutenant Myers' secretary, Jeannie, comes in and says, "Lieutenant, Sergeant Dawson from patrol is on the phone for you."

Josh: "O.K. Jeannie, Thanks." Lieutenant Myers picks up the phone. "Hey Steve, what can I do for patrol today?"

Sergeant Dawson: "I'm going to need your help."

Josh: "What have you got going on?"

Sergeant Dawson: "I'm down at the boat ramp at the end of Marina Boulevard. We got a car here with a body in the trunk. "

Josh: "Makes it hard to drive that way, doesn't it, Steve?"

Sergeant Dawson: "You got that right, Lieutenant. This one is a real mess. We arrived about 45 minutes ago. Started as a simple abandoned vehicle. You need to take a ride over."

Josh: "I'll be right over in a couple of minutes, and I'll bring a couple of guys with me."

Sergeant Dawson: "Thanks, Lieutenant."

Josh Myers went out to the squad room and gathered up two of his detectives.

Josh: "Come on, guys. We need to get over to the boat ramp at the end of Marina Boulevard. They've got a body."

Detective #1: "Another drowning?"

Josh: "Maybe, but if it is, he drowned in the trunk of a car."

Detective #1: "Bad spot for swimming."

Josh and the detectives arrived at the boat ramp and talked to Sergeant Steve Dawson. Back off near the water was a black BMW sedan sitting with the trunk open. The officers have blocked off the marina with yellow crime scene tape. The Orange Beach Marine Police's launch is at the end of the boat ramp. Ensuring that no boat traffic can come on or near the scene.

Sergeant Dawson: "Lieutenant, we got a call about an hour ago about a car being here at the marina. Some of the boaters were complaining that it was too near the boat launch and was interfering with the boat traffic. You can see it didn't completely block the launch ramp but it is close enough when multiple people are trying to maneuver around it. There was no one around. It's pretty deserted when boats are in the water. We went ahead and checked the tag: we got a name and phone number. We called the number, and we could hear it ringing in the trunk."

Josh: "What, you don't usually leave your phone in the trunk, Steve?"

Sergeant Dawson: "Not if I can help it, Josh, so that was my first clue that something wasn't right."

Josh: "I hate it when that happens. Go on."

Sergeant Dawson: "When we heard the phone ringing, we got the fire department over here and got them to pop the trunk, revealing a body. We checked for a pulse, but he's dead. Looks like he was shot in the head. So, we backed off and called you immediately, along with some more officers, to secure the scene. We put the marine patrol boat out as well."

Josh: "I see that, Steve. Great quick work securing the scene. Let's go over it and see what we have."

The Sergeant, Lieutenant Myers, and the two detectives walk over to the BMW and look in the trunk. Inside is a male, Caucasian, smartly dressed. Short-sleeved shirt, blue jeans. He lay on his left shoulder with his head towards the passenger side of the trunk with an obvious bullet wound in his right temple. Lying next to his head is a pistol.

Detective #2: "It could be suicide. There's the gun."

Josh: "It could be. What else do we got in here?"

They pull out their flashlights and start visually looking in the trunk to not disturb anything. In the back of the trunk, they see several pistol boxes.

Detective #1: "What have we got here, Lieutenant? Look at this: Smith and Wesson, Colt, Sig Saur, Glock. That's quite an assortment of handguns or at least boxes."

Josh: "We don't know if they are empty or not. Let's not touch them just yet until we get the body taken care of. What's this over here on the left side? Looks like some gun parts, magazines. Looks like this guy is a real gun aficionado with all this material."

Detective #1: "Here are some magazines. Guns and Ammo, Rifleman, Tricks of the trades, etc."

Josh: "I know just the guy to call. When somebody has all this going on. Let's get the lab guys over here. Get all the pictures taken, get everything dusted down, and get this body removed. Do you have the name of the victim?"

Sergeant Dawson: "Yes, sir. The car is registered to Preston Rodrigues so we think it's him. We pulled his driver's license photo from Florida and it looks just like him."

Josh: "Prepare to notify next of kin. Let me go over here and call the ATF."

Josh stepped away from the group and called Mike Conover in Mobile.

Mike answers the phone: "Orange Beach Police, we are normally lying on the beach. What can I help you with?"

Josh: "Man Mike, you never quit. You never seem to miss a chance to get me."

Mike: "You know how it is, Josh, some get to hang out on the beach, and some of us have to work."

Josh laughed: "I get it. I get it. Listen, I got another body over here in Orange Beach."

Conover: "Man, your beat is getting tough lately."

Josh: "I don't know what this is about, but we got a body in a car trunk at the end of Marina Boulevard. There's a pistol in the trunk. There's a bunch of gun boxes in the trunk as well."

Conover: "What kind of boxes?"

Josh: "Cardboard pistol boxes, like when you buy a new gun. We haven't touched them or looked in to see if they are empty or not. There are at least a dozen. There are all kinds of gun parts as well: magazines, holsters, firearms literature. Something is tied in here. This guy is a gun aficionado or something."

Conover: "I've got to go down to the Federal Courthouse and drop off some papers. Once I do that. I'll be on my way over. I should be over there in about 90 minutes. Does that sound OK?"

Josh: "Perfect. Thanks, Mike, I appreciate it. Sorry to bother you so soon."

Mike: "It's never a bother, you know that. I'll be there as soon as I can."

Josh and his detectives begin their investigation into the death of Preston Rodrigues. They locate his address in Florida. They sent one of the Orange Beach detectives to meet with the Pensacola Police to go to the house, look around, and also locate and notify the next of kin. Forensic crime scene examiners arrive and start photographing the car. Inside and out. The body in the trunk, every possible place where there could be any evidence. They secure some food wrappers that are on the front seat of the car. A fast-food drink container and a straw. They dust the inside passenger side for fingerprints and await the arrival of the medical examiner to move the body.

Crime scene processing takes a while. The experts have to arrive. Everything has to be done very methodically and carefully. After about an hour Doctor Terri O'Leary, the medical examiner, and her team pull up. They examine the body first, gently pick it up move it outside the car, and lay it on a stretcher on the ground where the medical examiner quickly examines the mouth, face, and body. Turns the body over to look for any additional wounds or blood. He tells the team to wrap it up, put it in a body bag, and walks over to Josh and his team, who are standing just off to the side.

Josh: "What have you got, Doc?"

O'Leary: "He is dead."

Josh: "I called you over here for that answer? We figured that out by ourselves."

O'Leary: "Yeah, but you're not trained. I had to go to school for years to make that determination."

Josh: "That's some great training you got."

O'Leary: "Well, that's why you call me. A bullet wound in the right temple. I didn't see any other markings on the body at all. Of course, he'll have to be stripped down to make that determination. I didn't see any blood anywhere else. No other gunshots are obvious. He's fully clothed as you can see. We did pull his wallet for you. Here you go."

Josh takes the wallet and hands it to one of his detectives and tells them.

Josh: "Check the wallet, photo the contents, bag it, and tag it."

O'Leary: "Who is he?"

Josh: "His name is Preston Rodrigues, and he lives in Pensacola."

O'Leary: "We saw all the gun stuff in the trunk. We were careful not to disturb any of that. The pistol is still lying next to where his head was."

Josh: "We wanted you guys to get your procedures done before we touched anything. We'll get in there now and secure all that stuff. Now that you're done, do you think it could have been a suicide?"

O'Leary: "It's hard to make that determination right now. The wound is in his right temple. The gun is there but he wasn't holding it. It's possible, was the trunk locked when the body was found?"

Josh: "Yes, initially it was called in as an abandoned car and patrol found it locked. They had to get the fire department here to pop it."

O'Leary: "He would have to have crawled into the trunk, closed and locked it, and then shoot himself in the head. It's certainly possible to do but we just need to examine him further to figure out if it is suicide. We will swab his hands for gunshot residue. That will be a big indicator for sure. Unfortunately, with all the gun boxes and paraphernalia in the trunk, it's possible he was shooting those all the time, and that will leave residue on his hands, and that won't give us much of an answer."

Josh: "Of course. I always get the complicated ones."

O'Leary: "That's why you're a Lieutenant."

Josh: "Sometimes I wish I was just a corporal."

O'Leary, walking to the van, "I know the feeling. Being in charge ain't what it used to be. I'll call you as soon as I find anything."

Josh: "Thanks Doc."

Josh turned to his colleagues: "At this point, we don't know if we got murder or suicide, but we have lots of work to do. Let's see if we can get any leads from witnesses on this road. Maybe someone saw his car go by and could have a time as to when that was. We don't even know when it got here. Wait a minute, guys, let me yell at the doctor before she goes. Doc, I forgot to ask you, what do you think about the time of death? Do you have a preliminary idea at all?"

O'Leary: "It's pretty fresh: I don't even see the rigor mortis set in. This guy hasn't been there for long. But I'll know more after a thorough examination of the body."

Josh: "Thanks, Doc."

O'Leary: You know, Josh, I've been coming to Orange Beach a lot lately. Normally it's just a drowning case or car wreck. What is going on over here? It's your third murder in the last couple of months. All shot."

Josh: "I know, we are big on waves here. Now it seems like we are big on crime waves as well. The mayor isn't happy. She's been jumping down my throat. She wants this stuff wrapped up. It hurts the tourist trade when you start getting things like this happening more than once. People want to go someplace where they can have fun and not worry."

O'Leary: "I hear that. It would be big news in Mobile if we had a third gunshot victim in a couple of months, let alone in Orange Beach."

Josh: "I'll let the public information and the chief handle all that stuff. I've got more than I can do already."

O'Leary: "I'll call you as soon as I have any news."

Josh: "Thanks doc. I'll be seeing you."

Josh walks back to where his detectives are standing and starts discussing the strategy for this case when a black SUV pulls into the parking lot and out pops Mike Conover.

Conover: "You had a body in that car?"

Josh: "Yes."

Conover: "Is it Preston Rodrigues?"

Josh: "Yeah, how did you know that?"

Conover laughed, "Cause I'm fed, and we know everything. No, this guy is one of the worst gun traffickers on the Gulf Coast. We've been tracking him for more than a year."

Josh: "That's why we called you, with all the gun boxes and firearm paraphernalia in the trunk."

Conover: "This guy is a real problem. He's cagey and hard to get to. We were able to make one good undercover buy from him, but we had more in the works. We had an undercover agent into him, but he's very careful."

Josh: "What do you know about him?"

Conover: "He mainly works the coast, back near the other side of Pensacola to New Orleans and he's tied in with a lot of thugs. He knows the criminal element pretty well. He's kind of a cut above, he's a little more polished. He drives this BMW. He's not a guy hanging around in bad neighborhoods. But he can supply those people with just about any gun they want. From what we can tell, he makes damn good money at it. He hits a lot of gun stores, purchasing guns and buys stolen guns. We know he is heavy into ghost guns."

Josh: "Ghost guns like the one we had with Randi's murder?"

Conover: "Exactly. This guy could be good for that type of gear for sure."

Josh: "How about the silencer and the machine gun thing?"

Conover: "The Glock switch? Yeah, he could supply that. He could get you the silencer and the switch. This guy can get it all as long as you got the cash. That's why we are trying to catch him but we've got to have the proof. The US Attorney wants to solve the case so we've been trying to get this guy shut down. Looks like somebody shut him down the hard way. Let's have a look."

They all walk over to the back of the trunk of the BMW. They see the pistol lying by the passenger side of the trunk. There are also numerous pistol boxes.

Josh: "We can inventory these now since we have the evidence tech right here. We've got you here Mike as well so let's go ahead and do an inventory and see what we got in these boxes."

Everybody puts on rubber gloves. The evidence technician starts pulling the boxes out one by one. About half of the boxes are empty, and the other half still have pistols in them.

Conover comments: "Those empty boxes, those guns are on the street somewhere just waiting on hurting someone. At least these others won't get a chance to. All this stuff, these empty magazines here, ammunition. This is all the stuff this Rodrigues would trade-in. He could pretty much get anything."

Josh: "Let's look at this gun lying here by where his head was."

Mike Conover picks up the gun with his surgical-gloved hands. Drops the magazine and lays it down. Works the slide and ejects a live round. Looks in the breach.

Conover: "Yes, this is a Sig Saur P239, 40 caliber semi-automatic pistol."

Josh: "Not a ghost gun?"

Conover: "No, this is a legally manufactured gun. Maybe it matches one of the empty boxes. We can check the serial numbers and see. Of course, we can trace this gun—where it was purchased, by whom, and/or if it's stolen."

Josh: "I don't understand why this guy has guns in gun boxes that he gets from gun shops?"

Conover: "What this guy does is, he finds a corrupt gun dealer. Just like any other profession, a small percentage of gun dealers, like a small percentage of priests, judges, politicians, doctors, and lawyers are criminals. There is always someone who will do something wrong, even in the police Josh. We've even got corrupt cops, right? One percent of any of those professions can wreak havoc on any community. Crooked gun dealers will sell the guns out the back door with no paperwork. They are dangerous because they can supply and buy many guns for a guy like Preston Rodrigues. The guns are off the books. They can be reported as lost or stolen. When they get audited, they can say they never got the shipment, they can log it out to a false name. There are many ways they can hide where the gun went if they are criminally motivated. What Preston would do is he would get them in on his scheme, especially someone who isn't doing so well with his business. Preston would promise them a lot of money, but they would have to go out the back door. He obtained some of his firearms that way. It is the black-market trade: the guns are not destined for sportsmen or legitimate gun owners"

Josh: "Yikes, that's not good."

Conover: "Other ways he does it, he could get a clerk in a gun store to steal brand new guns from the gun shop owner. Grab a half dozen pistols. The licensed dealer will think some random guy off the street stole them somehow and pilfered them. Broke in and took them. Either way, they are gone, and the crooked employee can sell them to Preston to make their way to the street. We also think he's got a guy in the UPS terminal stealing them as they are coming off the line."

Josh: "Oh man, this guy has some sources."

Conover: "He also has some kits. Ghost guns. We know he supplies silencers and submachine guns. This guy is the fuel on the fire of violent crime up and down the coast."

Josh: "So what you're saying is you're not going to miss him much?"

Conover: "Miss him, I'm gonna miss him like the fiery itch of gonorrhea. This guy was making sure that a lot of people were getting killed. All for money. He was nothing more than a vampire feeding off the blood of the ultimate victims."

Josh: "We've got a lot of work to do here. Trying to figure out who popped this guy. Do you think it could be related to Randi's murder with that ghost gun silencer machine gun switch?"

Conover: "There is no question that this guy could be the supplier. He's capable of supplying all that stuff and he's right here in your backyard."

Josh: "We need to keep our eyes open to see if there is a connection. What do you recommend here, Mike, from your end?"

Conover: "Look, this pistol here is just a standard Glock pistol. I've got the serial number off it and I'll put an urgent trace on it with the ATF National Fire Arms Tracing Center. It doesn't help for me to send this to the ATF lab. What you need to do is let your Alabama State Lab do the firearms identification examination on this gun to see if it's the weapon used on Preston. That's the first step. I'll trace the serial number, and you get with the state lab to check ballistics, and we'll take it from there. I've got a complete file on this guy. All kinds of questions I can probably answer as they come up and I'll bring it with me when I come back tomorrow, and we can go through it. Also, I have an undercover agent who's met with Rodrigues and made a gun buy. I think he bought five pistols from him. We can bring that agent over if you think that's important. Together we might be able to look at Rodrigues' background and try to figure out what happened."

Josh: "Thanks Mike, that is great. I have to talk to the medical examiner regarding this guy's death. Get the gun examined by the state lab and see what steps we should take going forward. I appreciate you coming over so quickly and thanks again for all your help."

Conover: "OK, Josh, I am going to write down the make, model, and serial number of every gun in the trunk. There are seven, all pistols. Also, I am going to do the same for all the empty boxes. I will trace those, too, and the missing ones I will put in ATF's database as suspected trafficked guns. Maybe, from all those traces, we can pull something together, I will get you the undercover agent's phone number he was using with Preston, and you can sort that out when you go through all of his phone calls. I will let you know when I get some information back."

Josh: "Thanks, Mike."

45

HARD FACTS DON'T LIE

Lieutenant Josh Myers called a strategy session for his investigators, including Detective Hooper, Gulf Shores Detective Sergeant Henry Scotts, and ATF Special Agent Mike Conover, in his office bright and early at 9:00 a.m. Josh wanted to go over what leads they had, what leads they needed to cover, and what assignments they could make. He also brought in the half dozen detectives he supervised in his bureau and the Lieutenant of the patrol division. They sat around a conference table and Lieutenant Myers began.

Josh: "Alright, gang, we've got to work together as a team. We have our colleagues here from the Sheriff's Department, the Gulf Shores Police Department, and ATF. We have to help them move this case forward and find out who killed Ms. Reynolds. Let's go over where we are so far. Ms. Reynolds was shot at her home at approximately 8:30 in the morning in the Summer Wind Community when she answered her door. She had 26 bullet wounds from her waist up to her face, with four bullets missing her and embedded in the wall at the edge of the ceiling behind her. She did not have a ring or door alarm system, so we don't have video of the assailant going up to the door. You guys were able to pull some video from Doc's Seafood Restaurant showing a few different vehicles pulling into the neighborhood at various times. We've been trying to check all those out. Some were construction workers for the new houses going up in the community so we have to sort through all the leads on that before we can settle in on any one particular vehicle. We did, of course, find the pistol and a bouquet at the scene. Mike Conover here can brief us on that status."

Conover: "Thanks Lieutenant. The pistol is a personally manufactured firearm which is normally called a ghost gun. We see those trafficked a lot in the criminal circles. It's made from what is called an 80% kit. It's then drilled and machined and fitted with the rest of the parts to make it a functional weapon. It has no serial number and no markings. It is a copy of a Glock 9 mm. It had an attached silencer that was illegally purchased and manufactured, also with no serial number or markings. It's known as a ghost silencer. No trace can be put on either one of those weapons. In addition, there was a switch attached to the rear of the pistol. In street slang, it's referred to as a Glock switch. It's a little device that makes the pistol function as a submachine gun. The pistol had a 30-round magazine. The magazine was empty. The ATF laboratory processed the weapon for DNA and fingerprints. They were able to lift a partial print and DNA from touch DNA or sweat DNA is what the lab told me on the pistol magazine that was inside the gun. The partial is not something they can run through the database, but if we do get a suspect, it can be something that can be compared to that suspect. The DNA is something we can work on. We do have a profile on that, so the lab is submitting it for matches in the DNA databases."

Josh: "Thanks, Mike. That is a big help. It would be great to get an immediate DNA match."

Mike: "Unfortunately, that usually only happens in the movies, for us only now and then. It would make our lives a whole lot easier if it did."

Josh: "O.K. Let's continue. We have the gun and the silencer left at the scene. You have heard that briefing. We don't have any video from the house. We do have a video from the restaurant at the corner, but it's not close. Just some distant shots of vehicles coming and going before the murder. We do have a bouquet that was dropped in the bushes as well. That is a substantial lead. We have sent detectives to go to all the florist shops from Pensacola to Foley and so far, we haven't turned up any leads or purchases that would lead us to any particular person or vehicle in this case."

Detective Asterino speaks up: "Lieutenant, you know, we were watching the vehicles from the video from the seafood restaurant coming and going to the neighborhood. A lot of construction work trucks. Hard to discern anything. One vehicle did have a sign on it that said Florist or it looked like it said Florist. We couldn't zoom in on it, but we are trying to get that video enhanced to see if there is a particular name for the florist shop. That has been ongoing and we are waiting on getting that enhancement back from the lab."

Josh: "When do you think that will be available?"

Asterino: "They said it should be in by tomorrow. We can look at a close-up of it. Maybe it will give us the name of a flower shop. That is going to be a better lead for us."

Josh: "Thank you, Asterino, stay on that."

Asterino: "Yes, sir."

Josh: "OK, is there any other information we've gleaned from interviewing the friends of Randi Reynolds, Sergeant Miller? Do you have anything else from that?"

Miller: "No sir, we've interviewed just about all of her friends and co-workers at the real estate office. We can't find anything or any reason why anyone would want to kill her. We can't find any evidence of her using narcotics. She's not involved in any gambling. We pulled her bank records. By all indications, she is a hard-working woman. A very successful realtor. She just did that big land sale with D Campbell Land Development. We know she was having a sexual relationship with Doctor Campbell."

Josh stressed about that last sentence: "Yes, that's right."

Miller: "We haven't found anything in that relationship that would lead to a reason for murder. There are no reports of him being abusive. There have been no calls to the police regarding any domestic issues. None of her co-workers reported anything suspicious about her appearance regarding bruises. Everyone we talked to said they got along great. A very cordial and friendly couple. Everything about their relationship seemed normal."

Josh: "Thank you, Sergeant. Maybe we have to expand that circle of interviews. Go back a few years in her life. Check out her background when she was living in Pensacola. Maybe there was a bitter break-up or a strained relationship with a co-worker there. There is something we don't know or haven't found yet. We've just got to kick every log over and see what crawls out."

Miller: "Yes, sir, we will get right on that and expand the territory."

Josh: "OK, stay on those leads and we will reconvene in a couple of days, and let's see where we are. Lieutenant Hooper, can you call the state lab and see if they can expedite and see if they can match that DNA with what the ATF lab in Atlanta found? Maybe we can speed that up a bit."

Hooper: "Sure, Josh, I'll get on that right away."

In a couple of days, Josh reconvenes with his investigative team.

Det. Asterino opens the meeting, "We've got the enhanced photographs back from the forensic lab of the video from Doc's Seafood about the white van with the florist sign. You can see the sign on the side of the vehicle as the van makes its turn into the Summer Wind neighborhood. It says florist and there is a bouquet."

As he says this, Det. Asterino passes photographs around to the investigative team sitting at the conference table. Everyone takes a look at the picture. There are no markings on the van, it doesn't have an address or phone number.

Asterino: "It's a good lead, but it doesn't take us in any particular direction. We don't have a place to go from here. Just a generic sign. We all know that it ties into the bouquet dropped at Ms. Reynolds's house, but there were no tags or markings on the flowers."

Mike Conover: "Josh, over the years, we've worked a lot of bombings with slight leads like this. Where bombers would travel to place the bombs, and they would have these elaborate disguises to escape detection. Just looking at this, that sign on the van could be painted on, but it looks like a magnetic sign, which is very common. There can't be that many sign companies along the Gulf Coast. There aren't thousands of them. There is a finite number and we should be able to cover those with all the agents and detectives we have collectively. If we could cover a swath from just East of Pensacola all the way west to Mobile. We should be able to cover all those sign shops in a week or two and see if anybody can remember or has any record of making a sign like that. We have the photographs. We can supply those to all the detective teams and agent teams and see what we can uncover."

Detective Hooper speaks up: "I think that is a good idea, Josh. I can get some sheriff's detectives: we've got your detectives. We could get some ATF agents. We can call Mobile and Pensacola PD's. We can get help from them as well. We can all spread out and start covering those sign shops. Maybe we will catch a break."

Josh: "Yes, I do think it's a good idea. Let's get that in motion and get everybody set out to do that. It's gonna take some time, so let's get started immediately."

A week later, Josh gets a call from Mike Conover, who is in Mobile at the ATF office.

Mike: "Josh, I have some good news for you. An ATF agent and a detective from Mobile Homicide contacted a sign shop. There were about eight shops in Mobile, and I believe this was number six. When they showed the photograph to the clerk at the store, he immediately remembered the guy and the sign."

Josh: "Go on."

Mike: "He said he thought it was unusual that anyone would purchase a sign that didn't have any business information on it—no name, no address, no phone number. He said he makes signs all day, every day. People want there to be clear contact information for anyone who sees it. This particular sign stood out for sure. He said the guy bought two magnetic signs and paid cash. There is no record of any credit card transaction."

Josh: "That's not much help. If he didn't use a credit card."

Mike: "We did pull the store video, and there he was, clear as day, picking up the signs and paying cash. He can be identifiable. Here's the good news. We then pulled the videotape from surveillance cameras outside the store and we got a pick-up truck with a clear view of the tag number as it was leaving the sign shop. We ran the tag and it came back registered to a Mobile resident who is an outlaw biker named Mike "Shovelhead" Dempsey."

Josh: "That is great work, Mike. We've finally got a name to work with."

Mike: "Yes, he's got a criminal record. He did some time in the joint in Florida, Raiford State Prison, for aggravated assault. He's also got some Meth arrests and stolen motorcycle parts. The usual outlaw biker stuff."

Josh: "That's great: anything else?"

Mike: "Mobile detectives who work on the biker side said he hasn't been in any trouble in the past few years. He has a couple of traffic tickets. They do see him when they get involved with other bikers. He frequents the outlaw clubhouse over there. We have his address. We want to do a drive-by and take some pictures for you. See if that pick-up truck that is registered to him is there, plus what else is over there."

Josh: "That's a good idea, Mike. Go ahead and get that started. Get those pictures. I'll get with the rest of the guys over here and do some other work and see what we get on this Dempsey character. Let's get back together tomorrow."

Mike: "Sounds good, Josh."

Josh reassembles his team that afternoon and fills them in on the lead from the sign shop in Mobile.

Josh: "This is a pretty good lead. Let's see what we can find out."

Detective Hooper: "Let's build on that name. Can we do something with that white van? He either owns it, he stole it, he borrowed it, or rented it. If he owns it, we'll find that out pretty easily. The only thing we could check on are rented ones. Why don't we make an effort on that, just like we did with the sign? Now we have a name we can go on, so it shouldn't be too hard to go to a U-Haul place or

Rent-All place that rents plain white vans and see if this Dempsey character rented a van. You have to have a driver's license to rent a vehicle and he might have thought he was far enough away from Mobile where it would never get back to him. If we could put him with the signs and the white van, that would be something."

Josh: "Good idea Larry. I think we should start on that immediately. Can we get that going today?"

Detective Hooper: "Yes, sir. We have his name and his driver's license photograph. Let's take everybody who was on the sign teams, redirect them to the rental places, and see if we can uncover a place where he might have rented the van."

It didn't take too long to find the U-Haul place where Mike Dempsey had rented a white van. Josh got a call the next morning from Sergeant Joyce Miller.

Miller: "Good Morning Josh. One of the team's working Mobile has found a U-Haul place where Dempsey had rented a white van. A Ford van two days before Randi Reynolds' murder. He then returned the van the same day as the murder."

Josh: "Alright, now we are making some progress. We've got this Shovelhead character with the sign and the white van. One break leads to two, two breaks lead to three, and three breaks lead to prison. This is going the way I like right now."

Josh went home that night, took off his shoes, sat on his couch, and turned on some blues music. Josh is a fan of the blues. He's loved it for a long time. The music was soothing to him. His grandparents always had it playing when they went to visit. He dearly loved his grandparents and listening to the blues always brings back fond memories of them. The most American music, his grandpa would call it. Josh loved the lyrics, the tunes, and the distinct notes. It was soothing to him. Heck, he even liked Christmas Blues. This music always seemed to calm the end of a hectic day. His friends couldn't understand. As he sat listening to the music with a glass of bourbon on the rocks. He started to think about why an outlaw motorcycle gang member would want to kill Randi. *Randi wasn't the type of woman who ran with bikers. She wasn't the type of woman who would even know any bikers. It was as far from her lifestyle as doing drugs. She was much more polished and upscale to even entertain the thought of knowing anyone like that.* Not that Josh had anything against the bikers. He thought they, themselves, had a very independent mindset. But it was the polar opposite of Randi's. A completely different way of living. He cannot understand why or how her path would cross with a biker. *We got some breaks today. We have a name we can work with.* He thought. He wanted to be careful of confirmation bias. Where you make things fit because you want them to fit. Not because they do.

He was always conscious of that. Leads and evidence dictated the direction he was going to go. He thought of the song by Paul Simon, "Call Me Al," where the lyrics describe hints and allegations, incidents and accidents, not conjecture, supposition, rumor or innuendos, just hard facts.

Josh's goal was to get everything right. He always worked from a foundation of facts that would lead him to the killer. He didn't want an innocent man. He didn't want to hang anybody, frame anybody, get the wrong guy, or even put the wrong guy in prison to close a case. He wasn't into that. Facts dictated what mattered. No matter what the pressure was, he gave everybody the benefit of the doubt until the facts said otherwise.

It was going to be a busy week. Josh thought. With this new breaking evidence in Randi's case. He got up early Monday to get into the office. *Who knows what will happen next,* he thought as he arrived at Police Headquarters.

46

CHOIR BOY

Lieutenant Myers looks up from his desk and Sergeant Joyce Miller and one of her detectives are standing in the doorway.

Miller: "We've got something for you, Lieutenant."

Josh: "Alright, Sergeant, come on in."

Sergeant Miller sits down. "I think it's something good you're going to like."

Josh: "I sure need that today. I need something on these murders to move us ahead."

Miller: "This may be it."

Josh: "O.K. Go ahead."

Miller: "Mike Conover and Mobile Homicide Detectives sent over the surveillance pictures they took when they did a drive-by of this guy Mike "Shovelhead" Dempsey's house in Mobile that lead from the sign shop."

Josh: "OK."

Miller: "Of course, he's the same guy that Asterino found renting the white van two days before the Reynolds murder. When they did the drive-by, there was the same pick-up truck that was at the sign shop, but there was also a Harley Davidson bike parked out in the front yard. It was very unique-looking."

Josh: "We knew he had a motorcycle. He's an outlaw biker."

Miller: "Exactly. But we extrapolated on that information and we went back to Doc's Seafood and went back two months of the stored videos. We've got a video of Dempsey a couple of weeks before the murder riding his bike past Doc's and turning into the Summer Wind neighborhood."

Josh: "You've got Dempsey on his motorcycle going into the neighborhood a few weeks prior?"

Miller: "Yes, sir. We thought it was a fairly good lead."

Josh: "That is going to help us for sure."

Miller: "But that's not the best of it, sir. We also pulled the cameras from the toll road bridge from the Foley Beach Express the night before we found Preston Rodrigues' body at the marina. One shows Shovelhead Dempsey clearly on his motorcycle that evening at about 8:00 p.m. We even got a clear picture of his tag. We've got him sitting on it crossing into Orange Beach."

Josh: "You are starting to make my day Sergeant. I'm starting to feel a lot better."

Miller: "It's my job, Lieutenant, to always make you feel better."

Josh: "I know that, Sergeant. I appreciate that. We've got Dempsey buying the sign. We've got him renting the van. We've got his pickup truck at the van rental. We've got him at the van rental. A video of him at the sign place along with his pick-up truck at the sign place. Now we've got his motorcycle coming into Ms. Reynolds's neighborhood. Of course, we have the white van that he rented coming to Orange Beach on the morning Ms. Reynolds was murdered. The driver is wearing a white hat and shirt."

Miller: "Shoot, I almost forgot. We've also got his pick-up truck on surveillance in Ms. Reynolds's neighborhood. That was a few weeks before his motorcycle was spotted there."

Josh: "Very good, so two different surveillance runs of Ms. Reynolds's neighborhood before the murder that include both of Dempsey's vehicles."

Miller: "Yes, sir, and now we have him coming into Orange Beach the night before Preston Rodrigues's body is found."

Josh: "Do we have anything that puts him right at the marina?"

Miller: "Not so far, sir. We do have detectives who are trying to pull surveillance at the marina to see if they can see anything or locate any witnesses. You know, it gets deserted in the evening."

Josh: "I understand." We are still waiting for the DNA match and the partial print on the magazine from Ms. Reynolds's murder weapon. But I think this is enough so we can move forward with a search warrant for Dempsey's house. Putting him in Orange Beach on the night of the murder is significant because we also have the contacts on Rodrigues's telephone, where he gets a call or two from Dempsey. Dempsey's phone subpoena is not back yet, but at least we have something on one end."

Miller: "Yes, sir."

Josh: "Thank you, Sergeant. Draw us up a search warrant for Dempsey's residence in Mobile. Put a team together. I'd like to hit it in the morning and have an interrogation plan ready if we can get him down to Mobile Homicide and interview him there rather than at his house. See what you can do, but I want to get a good search warrant and an interview."

Miller: "Yes, sir. What items do we need to seize in the search warrant?"

Josh: "Well, we can't ask for the gun or silencer. They were both dropped at the scene. But what we want is any clothing that was seen when Dempsey was coming across the toll bridge on the morning of Ms. Reynolds's murder. The white hat, the white shirt. If that could be recovered, there could be blood splatter. Also, the night he came across on the motorcycle probably to meet Rodrigues. We want any clothes that he might have been wearing on the motorcycle. Since you have a photograph of him at the toll bridge. Particularly describe what he was wearing."

Miller: "Yes, sir. It's typical outlaw biker garb. The denim vest that is pissed on all the time. That they never wash."

Josh laughed: "Yeah, those outlaw bikers never wash their colors. I want the vest, the shirt, the pants, boots, anything. In the murder of Preston, the killer was up close. That was a contact wound. The M.E. already ruled out suicide, so the killer was standing very close. There is going to be blood splatter on their clothes. We want those clothes because he could have been wearing the same clothes when he murdered Ms. Reynolds. That's about all we have right now. Shoes and clothing are what we are after most. Oh, and sunglasses too, these guys never wipe them off."

Miller: "OK, Lieutenant. I will get right on that. I will get a team together so we can hit that first thing in the morning."

Josh: "I'll talk to Mike Conover at ATF. I will also call the Lieutenant in Mobile Homicide so we can get this all squared with them."

Miller: "Great, thank you, Lieutenant. I will keep you posted."

Lieutenant Myers and his team, including ATF and Mobile Homicide Detectives, arrive at 7:00 a.m. at Mike Dempsey's residence in Mobile, Alabama. They executed the search warrant for evidence of a homicide in the cases of Randi Reynolds and Preston Rodrigues. The team enters and Dempsey is alone at the house. He's taken outside to be interrogated as agents and detectives sweep the house for the evidence described in the search warrant. Dempsey agrees to accompany the detectives down to the Mobile homicide office for an interview.

He's shaken up by the cops rousting him. He was put in an interrogation room and Josh Myers and Detective Larry Hooper sat down. Lieutenant Myers starts.

Josh: "Look, Shovelhead, I am not going to cut any corners with you. This is some serious shit. We are not going to play games. We are just going to tell you what we got."

Dempsey: "OK, but I haven't done anything. I'm clean. You got the wrong guy."

Josh: "If that's the case you got nothing to worry about, right? I'm only after the right guy. I use evidence to tell me who the right guy is."

Dempsey: "Yeah, but I don't: you got nothing on me. I don't know nothing about nothing. I don't know anything about no murders in Orange Beach. I don't go to Orange Beach. I haven't been to Orange Beach in ten years. I was there a long time ago, but I don't go over there anymore. I stay on my side of the Bay."

Josh: "Look Shovelhead, it isn't going to do you no good lying to us."

Dempsey: "I ain't lying. I ain't been there in years."

Lieutenant reaches into his briefcase and pulls out a photograph of Mike Dempsey on his motorcycle at the toll bridge crossing into Orange Beach the night before the body of Preston Rodrigues was discovered. He lays it on the table in front of Dempsey with a clear date stamp. Dempsey looks at the picture, he looks at Myers, back at the picture, and back at Myers.

Josh: "No matter how many times you look at the picture, Shovelhead, it isn't going to turn into somebody else. It's still going to be you. Here's the back view."

As he lays out another photograph with the tag number visible.

Dempsey: "OK, OK, so I was in Orange Beach. That ain't no crime. It ain't a crime to be in Orange Beach. What's the big deal? So, I forgot I went over there. People forget shit all the time. It ain't a crime to forget shit."

Josh: "Can they forget murder."

Dempsey: "Murder? I ain't murdered nobody."

Josh: "Can they forget two murders?"

Dempsey: "Two murders? I ain't murdered nobody. I keep telling you that. You got the wrong guy. You're just trying to pin this on me because I'm a biker."

Josh: "No, we're not. We are not trying to PIN anything on anybody. We are going to go through what we got, and maybe things will clear up for you, Shovelhead."

Dempsey: "OK, go ahead. Lay it on me. I ain't scared of nothing."

Josh: "Let's start with this. We've got a videotape of you buying the sign that says florist with flowers on it at a sign shop in Mobile a few weeks before Ms. Reynolds was murdered."

Shovelhead: "So, that ain't nothing."

Josh: "You better just listen to me, Shovelhead, before you answer. We've got a videotape of you driving your truck there and coming back to pick up the signs. We also have a videotape of you renting a white van at a rental place in Mobile two days before Ms. Reynolds' murder."

Dempsey: "The things you are talking about people do every day. Rent vans, order signs, go for a ride."

Josh: "Here's the best part. We have your DNA on a 30-round magazine from a ghost gun that is the murder weapon of Ms. Reynolds and a partial fingerprint that matches one Mike Dempsey from your prison record."

At that moment, Shovelhead hangs his head.

Josh: "We also have video of the van with the tag number that you rented, with you driving it, entering Orange Beach at 8:14 am on the morning of Ms. Reynolds' murder. Fifteen minutes before she was killed."

Shovelhead reaches up with his right hand and just holds his head and does not say anything.

Dempsey: "Just maybe you are trying to frame me."

Josh: "No, with all this evidence, we are not framing you."

Dempsey: "I don't know what to say."

Josh: "Well, Shovelhead, I am not quite finished. We also have a video tape from the Orange Beach toll plaza of you coming in on your motorcycle the night we believe Preston Rodrigues was murdered at the Orange Beach Marina."

Dempsey slouches down in his chair.

Josh: "That's why we are here this morning. We've got a search warrant for clothes that you were wearing when you were passing the toll plaza on the videotape. Your biker colors, your shirts, we're taking all that stuff from your house. That was such a close shot on Preston Rodrigues, I'm sure there is some of his blood splattered all over your colors. We're pretty sure it's going to match his DNA."

Dempsey slides down the chair even further.

Josh: "By the way, we also have phone records connecting you and Rodrigues where you exchanged several calls. We know he supplied you with the gun you used in the Reynolds murder, and we figure you probably killed him with one of his guns that he was going to sell you. We did find the murder weapon in the trunk of Rodrigues' car for his murder, but we have the blood splatter that is going to cement that case against you."

Dempsey continues to slouch in his chair and is not saying anything. He finally puts his head down on the table.

Josh: "Here's the bottom line. You've been in the joint already. We got you solid on two ice-cold-blooded murders. Solid, DNA, fingerprints, and videos. You are toast. You are not going to squeeze out of this. You know how it works. You would be lucky not to get the death penalty on either one of these. Ms. Reynolds was shot twenty-six times. What do you think a jury is going to think of when they see those pictures when they are told it was a submachine gun with a silencer? In the cold-blooded murder of Preston Rodrigues, the gun trafficker? Probably, you are trying to cover your tracks and kill a witness in your case. Either way, you are toast on both. They will be giving you a shot of nitrogen up at the state prison before long unless you decide you want to cooperate with us and tell us what the hell all of this is about. We know you have no ties to Ms. Reynolds: we want to know the rest of the story."

Dempsey lets out a sigh and sobs a little bit. "My life has been nothing more than a shit burger. I never got a good taste of nothing. Every time I tried to get ahead, I would get knocked back down harder than the time before. Yeah, I was in the joint. Aggravated assault, meth. I'm not that bad of a guy."

Josh: "Life's tough, wear a helmet. We got to play the hand we've been dealt. I know you weren't dealt an easy hand. But you have to deal with the reality of it. You have to look at the poker hand in front of you and deal with it. You can't be wishing you had a straight flush when you have a pair of deuces. You have to know your next move. You have to know when to fold. If you don't want to get the death penalty, you need to cough up the truth. That's the only way this is going to work. Tell us what's going on."

Dempsey starts sobbing and finally says, "You know, I can't believe I'm in this position. I can't believe I have to do this. I do not want to rat on any of my brothers."

Josh: "Your brothers? Do you have other guys involved with you?"

Dempsey: "Yes."

47

CONFEDERATES IN ARMS

Josh: "You might as well get it off your chest 'cause ain't none of them gonna help you now. The whole thing is laid straight out in front of you. It's all pounding you down in the dirt to nothing but a little nub. If there are other people involved, that could help you out. The District Attorney could maybe spare you the death penalty. Maybe give you a break. At least if you try to cooperate. Seems like you don't have a choice. You have got nothing else left. You think about whatever it is you got to do. The why and for who. Do you have a reason? You need to be straight with us."

Dempsey: "OK, OK, can I get a smoke? How about a Coke or something to drink? I'm dying over here."

Sheriff's Lieutenant: "I'll go grab it for him." He stands up, goes out the door, and returns a short time later with some cigarettes and a couple of cans of Coke. They all sit back in their chairs.

Josh: "Look, Shovelhead, just relax and tell us the truth. That's all you have to do. We will make sure the District Attorney knows we are taping it and that you fully cooperated. You can hear me say it right here on the tape. I want you to say it first. Say you want to cooperate with this investigation and want that cooperation to be considered in any sentencing you will get. The District Attorney and the Judge will hear the tape."

Dempsey sighs, lights a cigarette, takes a deep drag, and takes a long swig of a Coke.

Dempsey: "When I was in the joint in Florida. I was there with one of my brothers."

Josh: "You mean a biker brother?"

Shovelhead: 'Yes, a biker brother. There were several of them in there. One of them was Highside."

Josh: "Highside, What's his real name?"

Dempsey: "I'm not sure I can even tell you. All anyone ever called him was Highside. He's from Tampa. He is the head of the Tampa Chapter right now. He'll be easy to find, I'm sure. All the Feds down there probably know who he is. I hadn't seen Highside since I was in the joint. He was doing twenty-five on a murder wrap. He finally got out about three years ago. He called me back in early June saying he wanted to meet up, that he had a construction job."

Josh: "Construction job?"

Dempsey: "That's what we call it."

Josh: "All right, we'll check the phone records. Did you call him on your cell phone?"

Dempsey: "Sure did. He came up to Orange Beach and wanted to meet at the tavern over there on Canal Road called The Barrel."

Josh: "I am familiar with it. Seems like I've been there a thousand times."

Dempsey: "Highside said he had a job for me and he would pay me ten grand plus five grand for expenses. Ten grand is a lot of money. I had no steady work. I was in the middle of repairing the heads on my Hog and I needed the cash bad. I first thought it was going to be running some drugs up from Texas. You know, the usual shit. Maybe steal some motorcycles, steal parts, you know, been there, done that. It was cool. But this was something a lot more. He said he wanted a woman killed. He gave me her name and address and a picture. He said he needed it done in thirty days. He gave me half the money upfront. Seventy-five hundred bucks and the other half when I finished. I'm supposed to get it this week. Highside left everything up to me. All the details. How I was going to do it, where, when. It didn't matter to him at all. He didn't want to know anything. He didn't want me to call him at all until it was done and she was gone. He would then come up and pay me the other seventy-five hundred dollars."

Josh: "It's been a few weeks already. You just now getting the money?"

Dempsey: "Yeah, I was going to get it this week. Highside promised to give me five thousand for expenses, and I used some of that money to buy that rig I got from Press, who was a friend of a different biker buddy. Press would supply anything you needed."

Josh: "Preston Rodrigues?"

Dempsey: "Yeah, we called him Press. We met over at Navarre Beach and he got me that machine pistol and silencer and showed me how to operate it. Just hold the trigger back and you can empty the whole magazine. It had a 30-round mag in it. Hell, I never even practiced shooting the damn thing. He said, don't worry about it. If you're going to be that close to the victim, just hold the trigger down and they'll be dead. So, that's what I did and he was right."

Josh: "So you drove up to Ms. Reynolds' house in a white van with the florist sign on the sides, you had a bouquet and the pistol in your pocket?"

Dempsey: "I had the pistol in a holster on my belt. I cut a slit in the coveralls so I could get to it quick. When she opened the door, I wasn't expecting her to be that beautiful. I took a step back and thought for a second, what the hell was I doing? But, damn, I needed the money. So, I killed her as she was smiling at me for the flowers. She dropped like a rock. Man, that was a bloody mess. That gun was amazing, it was so damn quiet and so fast. Stitched her right up."

Josh is disgusted at the flip way Shovelhead is describing the murder of the love of his life. Josh grits his teeth, he is seething inside. He is struggling to maintain his composure. He wants nothing more than to fly across the table and beat the ever-loving shit out of Shovelhead Dempsey. Detective Hooper looks over at Josh and notices his demeanor. He knocks Josh on his knee under the table to tell him to calm down. Josh looks at the Detective. The Detective nods and Josh finally snaps back to the task at hand.

Josh: "Ok, you kill Ms. Reynolds, then what happens?"

Dempsey: "I got back in the white van and drove back down to the beach road, turned right to go to Gulf Shores. Didn't see any damn rollers around. I didn't hear any sirens, so I figured I was scott-free. I turned right on 59, and when I got north of Foley, I pulled over and took the signs off the van, took the coveralls off. Came back over to mobile and burned those clothes and the signs in a trash barrel behind my house."

Josh: "So you don't have any of those clothes in your house?"

Dempsey: "No, sir. The white coveralls and hat have all been burned up with the signs."

Josh: "OK, Did you call Highside?"

Dempsey: "I was going to call him today or tomorrow."

Josh: "Why did you wait?"

Dempsey: "I had a loose end I need to tie up."

Josh: 'What was that?"

Dempsey: "Preston Rodrigues."

Josh: "You wanted to make sure Press was out of the way?"

Dempsey: "Look, I thought I was scott-free on the Reynolds murder. This guy, Press, would always know I was the one who did it. You learn you can't trust anybody ever. I didn't want to go back to the joint. I waited a little while and then I called him up and told him I needed another rig. He agreed to meet me at the marina in Orange Beach and that's the night I went over to whack him. Stupidly, I took my motorcycle over to meet him.'

Josh just sits and stares at Shovelhead.

Dempsey: "It felt like a good plan. I was going to whack him with his gun. The gun he was going to sell me and that's what I did. We stood behind his car at the deserted marina. I asked him for an automatic pistol. He showed me a few. He grabbed one. I asked him how it loaded. He showed me. I asked him for a box of ammo. I asked him to put some in the magazine. He shows me how to load it and rack it. I said OK. He handed me the gun and when he turned around to reach in his truck again, I shot him in the right temple. I just pushed him forward and he went straight into the trunk. I dropped the gun in the trunk, threw his feet in, and slammed the trunk. I got on my hog and left. That was that. There was nobody around."

Josh: "You figured you were scott-free?"

Dempsey: "Yep."

Josh: "So you wore white coveralls when you killed Ms. Reynolds and burned the clothes up. But you wore your regular clothes to kill Preston Rodrigues. Now we are at your house and we got your colors. You know there is going to be DNA and blood all over that."

Dempsey: 'Yes, sir. That was the biggest mistake I made. I hate it, and I never should have done it that way.'

Josh: "It's too late for that now, Shovelhead. What did you think was going to happen next?"

Dempsey: "I wasn't counting on you dicks following me and finding out about me. I was going to collect that money and go have some fun."

Josh: "Where's the money now?"

Dempsey: "It's up in my bedroom behind the bed. I cut a hole in the drywall and stuck it in there."

Josh: "How much do you have left?"

Dempsey: "It's all still there, I ain't had time to spend any of it. Except for the money I spent on the gun, the van rental, the signs, and the flowers. There is probably four thousand in there. I was looking forward to the other half but now that ain't gonna happen."

At this point, the Sheriff's Detective steps out and calls the search team, alerting them to the location of the hidden money. He tells the search team to call the District Attorney, advise the Judge, and get an addendum to the original search warrant to add the money that wasn't described on the warrant, so they can get it legally seized. The Sheriff's Detective then comes back into the room and sits down.

Josh: "Alright, Shovelhead. Let's go back to Highside. When are you supposed to meet him?"

Dempsey: "All I have to do is give him a call with a few days' notice, and he'll head back to Orange Beach, meet me at The Barrel, and give me the other seventy-five hundred dollars. That's the deal."

Josh: "We are going to step over here into this other room and you are going to call him and set up the meeting."

Dempsey: "What? What do you mean? How am I gonna make and keep that appointment when you got me locked up?"

Josh: "We'll figure that out later. First, you are going to call and set up that meeting. Then we will tell you what we are going to have you do."

Dempsey: "Well, damn it!! I'll call him."

Josh: "You don't have a choice now, do you?"

In a few minutes, they take Shovelhead into another room with a telephone that is on a recorded line. Shovelhead calls Highside in Tampa and leaves a message. "Meet me at The Barrel next Wednesday at 7:00 p.m." Everything is set in motion.

Josh: "That was good work. Now, do you think you can get him to talk about it on the phone?"

Dempsey: "There ain't no way he's gonna talk about it on any phone. He probably won't even talk about it in person. He's just gonna show up, give me the money and leave. Probably tell me to keep my fucking mouth shut. You have no idea how hard this guy is. No way."

Josh: "Ok, I understand. We'll have to decide how we are going to handle that. We will tell the DA that you cooperated, Shovelhead. We are now going to take you back to lock-up."

Dempsey: "OK, can I keep them cigarettes?"

Josh: "Yeah, keep them. You're gonna need them."

48

A SLIPPERY CHARACTER

Josh asked his team of detectives to research the name that was provided by Mike "Shovelhead" Dempsey as the person who hired him to do the killing of Randi Reynolds. He asked them to pull all the records they could and come into his office to brief him.

Detective Sergeant Joyce Miller, two detectives from the squad, Detective Lieutenant Larry Hooper and Gulf Shores Detective Sergeant Henry Scott, all met in Josh's office.

Josh: "Alright Sergeant, can you give us a rundown on this Highside character?"

Joyce: "Yes Lieutenant. His name is Lennie "Highside" Manthe. He is a male Caucasian, and he is 54. He did a twenty-five-year stint in Raiford State Prison in Florida on a murder wrap. He killed another biker in Tampa.

Josh: "Well, another great citizen."

Joyce: "Oh, he's upstanding, alright. He had quite a record before he went inside. Aggravated assaults, dealing meth, stolen motorcycles. You know, the usual stuff. Bar fights. Then he went down on that murder rap."

Josh: "When did he get out?"

Joyce: "Three years ago."

Josh: "Where is he now?"

Joyce: "Right back where he started from. He's head of the Tampa Chapter of the Outlaw Club. I called Tampa PD detectives. They know him well. They said that the little club is running meth and stealing motorcycles. They never stop. They have trouble with them now and again and they keep their eyes open for this guy. He's kind of cagey."

Josh: "So he's not out front causing a lot of trouble? More like running his little crew from behind?"

Joyce: "That is exactly right. The detective said he runs a few girls at the local strip club, The Kitty Kat. He's always tending to them. They said he drives around town in a new sports car. He doesn't always dress like a biker. He can slip around in and out. He's like a chameleon. Tampa PD said it would be great if we had something on him. They'd love to pick him up for it. They said they just missed him last year. They had ATF agents working undercover on rival bike gangs across town and they thought they might get into him that way. It never panned out. They know where he's at. He's always by their clubhouse down there on the Dale Mabry Highway in Tampa."

Josh: "Thanks, Joyce. Look, guys, we got Shovelhead Dempsey nailed on these two murders. If that blood spatter comes back on the outlaw biker colors, he wears, we'll have him dead to rights for the Preston murder. We already have his DNA, a partial print, pictures, signs, videos, and now his statement on Randi's murder as well as Preston's murder. We've got solid information and facts. Now we've got info that Highside paid Shovelhead to get the job done. We don't know why. Why does this Highside biker in Tampa who did twenty-five years for a murder rap want to kill Randi Reynolds? It doesn't make any sense. There is something we are missing here and Shovelhead doesn't seem to have that answer. He was just paid to do it, and he did it, no questions asked. We've got to get something from Highside, he has more answers."

Detective Hooper: "Well, he is a career criminal, so he's going to be a hard nut to crack. What about putting a wire on Shovelhead when he is supposed to meet Highside to get the rest of his money? We could surveil him at The Barrel."

Josh: "I'd like it for the evidence for the case, but I don't like it for a guy that has killed two people. We're going to put him out in a tavern and have to be there surrounding him. Too many things could happen. He could run, try and grab an officer's gun. Shovelhead could say the wrong thing to Highside. Cause a disturbance. There are too many variables with that. I just don't want to go with that. Let's think of another way. Shovelhead said he would not talk to him about it anyway. He will just give him the money and leave."

Detective Hooper: "Based on what Shovelhead told us, he should be coming up with the seventy-five hundred dollars that he owes him. So, we get a search warrant for the seventy-five hundred and his vehicle. When he pulls into The Barrel, we stop him, we search the car, we find the money. That's the beginning. We bring him down to the station, which is just around the corner, and we interrogate him. See what we can get: try to get him to slip up. He might lawyer up, but at least we can give it a try. We'll have the money and that will be some proof."

Josh: "I agree with you, Larry. I think that is probably a better way to go. The undercover tape would be nice, but this guy doesn't even talk on the phone. It's doubtful he's going to say anything to Dempsey. He'll probably just hand him the money and walk away without saying a word. We probably wouldn't be any worse off. Let's just see if we can do that. Get the search warrant drawn up for his vehicle. Maybe Tampa PD can give us a little light surveillance on Wednesday to find out what he is driving. We can get the driving time and maybe they can tell us when he leaves the clubhouse or his place. That way we will know when we can expect him up here on Wednesday evening for the meet. We'll search his car, get the money, and bring him over to Orange Beach PD for an interview."

Detective Hooper: "Sounds good."

Josh: "One more thing Larry, before we leave. We are asking the DA for subpoenas for Highside's bank records, credit card records, and phone records, to see if we can match the call he made to Dempsey. See if he has purchased any big-ticket items. Any money movement with the fifteen thousand. Two separate seventy-five hundred transactions. Thank you, Joyce, as well."

The following day, surveillance was put in place. Tampa PD reports that Highside left his house on Wednesday morning at about 10:30 a.m. They watched him get on the interstate and leave town. It's about a seven-and-a-half-hour drive to Orange Beach. So, the team was prepared. They had the search warrant in hand. They took their positions around The Barrel Tavern around 6:00 p.m., Expecting Highside to roll in about 7:00 p.m.

Highside slowly pulled into The Barrel Tavern right on time in a crisp new Audi Sedan. He was spotted by the team and quickly surrounded. He was taken out of his car and his vehicle was searched. In the trunk, they found a small, zippered bank bag with a .380 Walther PPK pistol and seventy-five hundred dollars in hundred-dollar bills. The officers handcuffed Highside and put him in the back of an Orange Beach Police cruiser. They called a wrecker to tow the vehicle and took Highside to Orange Beach PD. Lieutenant Myers met with his team in the conference room. They set the strategy for the interview.

Josh: "Sergeant Miller, I want you to call Mike Conover over at ATF and tell him we found a .380 pistol on a convicted felon and we need his help on these murders. We don't know if we are going to have a charge on him today, so we'd like Mike to get a federal warrant for a felon-in-possession charge. At least we can turn him over to ATF if we can't get anything more on our case today."

Joyce: "Yes sir, we'll call him right away."

Josh turns to Larry: "This guy is going to be a tough nut to crack. Maybe we can get him to slip up on something. Let's see what we can get."

Detective Hooper: "I agree. Good job with Shovelhead Josh. Let's go ahead and talk to Highside. I'll be right there with you."

Josh: "Let's go!"

Highside was cocky, he was leaning back in his chair with both hands behind his head.

Highside: "Boy, you think you guys are slick grabbing me with that little pistol and some money? That's not my pistol anyway. I didn't even know that was in the trunk. You got nothing on me."

Josh: "Just hold your horses' hotshot. We know all about you."

Highside: "Man, oh man, you are a real detective. You discovered I was in prison? Whoa, Ho, Ho. Aren't you the prime smarty smart? I'm blown away, Inspector Clouseau. I'm not scared of you or this rinky-dink town you're in."

Detective Hooper: "OK, Highside, enough with the antics. We're on some serious business."

Highside: "OH, serious business? What happened in Orange Beach? Two seagulls jump a pelican. Maybe a tourist had their tires slashed. Pretty dangerous work you have, "Lieutenant.""

Josh: "That's right, we do a lot of beach stuff here, but what we want to talk to you about is different. Murder for hire."

Highside: "Hey, I ain't involved in no murder. No way, no how. I did my time on murder. I learned my lesson. I was re-hab-il-i-tated. I can spell that for you if you want. I got glowing reports from the prison Chaplain and all the screws down at Raiford. They all loved me. I don't do that stuff no more. Besides, I was framed on that murder job."

Josh: "We know you hired Shovelhead Dempsey to knock off Ms. Randi Reynolds."

Highside: "Shovelhead Dempsey, hmm, that name sounds familiar, but I don't reckon I've ever met the fella."

Josh: "Let me refresh your memory about Shovelhead. He's called your phone."

Highside: "Damn, a lot of people call my phone. I'm sure you know I'm head of the Tampa Chapter. They get my number and think it's a big deal to call the boss. You know how that goes. That doesn't mean I talked to him or that I even know him."

Josh: "We've got him calling your phone. We got a statement from him that says you offered him ten thousand dollars and an additional five thousand for expenses to kill a woman in Orange Beach named

Randi Reynolds. That you met him at The Barrel Tavern in early June and paid him half the money and that you were coming tonight to pay him the other half of seventy-five hundred dollars. Coincidentally, we just happened to find that exact amount in the trunk of your car. Would you like to explain that?"

Highside: "It don't need a whole lot of explanation. I carry a lot of money around. All the time. I don't trust no bank."

Josh: "Oh, is that right?"

Highside: "Yep. Banks are the most corrupt business there is. They are so shady I wouldn't trust them to pick up dog shit. I want to carry my own money. That way, I know exactly where it is at all times. Unfortunately, sometimes you just got to use a bank."

Josh: "Sometimes?"

Highside: "Yeah."

Josh: "Really, what bank do you use when you "have to"?"

Highside: "Why, that ain't none of your business. You don't need to worry about any of that. You got no business worrying about what I'm doing with my money. That seventy-five hundred dollars is my money. I was thinking about buying a boat trailer. I was coming around here and cruising around up by the marinas. Checking them out. Maybe I could make a deal with one of them. That's what I was thinking. Expanding my business opportunities. I figured I had a trailer then I could go and buy a boat to put on that trailer. A little speed boat. Charge people to take them out for a ride. Cause I am a speedy boat kinda guy."

Josh: "And the pistol that was in the bank bag with "your" money?"

Highside: "I don't know anything about that pistol or how it got in the bag. I went to the bank to get the money. They handed me the bag. Maybe the bank left it in there by mistake, but it doesn't have anything to do with me."

Josh: "Let's get back to Shovelhead Dempsey. You were at Raiford State Prison with him in Florida?"

Highside: "Heck, I was in there with a thousand guys. I can't remember all of them."

Josh: "Well, this guy you did time with that you say you don't know, is a member of your same outlaw biker club. He gave us a statement that you hired him to commit murder."

Highside pushes back from the table and stretches his arms above his head.

Highside: "Well, he's a damn liar. I'm telling you, he's a damn liar. If I'm lying, I'm dying. He's not worth believing. Since you found his criminal record and found out he did time in Raiford, well, there you go. A lying criminal. Ain't that a shocker? Who on earth would believe a lying criminal? I would say it's his word against mine. My word is just as good as his. My word might be better because I'm rehabilitated and he's not. I don't know what kind of case you think you got on me, but you got nothing. Now, you just go ahead and let me go 'cause you are interfering with my evening."

Josh: "We ain't going anywhere Highside. We got a pistol on you and we called ATF. The agent is probably drawing up the warrant right now. We're going to be turning you over to him on a federal charge."

Highside: "Oh, that's different. Now I'm scared to death! I ain't gonna get life on a gun charge. I might get a little something even if you win the case. Like I said, it ain't my gun anyway. My lawyer will have a say about that. So, are you gonna keep me in this crackerjack jail?"

Josh: "Looks like we are. We are going to book you into the county jail tonight. I'm sure ATF will be picking you up in the morning and taking you to the Federal Courthouse in Mobile to answer the gun charge."

Highside: "Well, I'm going to be wanting to call my lawyer and tell him you guys are trying to screw me over on some fake frame-up on a murder job with some guy I never met. Trying to stick me with a gun that ain't mine and I ain't never seen before. Some sleazeball at the bank probably slipped it in the pouch when I was getting my money."

Josh: "OK, well the bank pouch right there says SunTrust Bank. That must be your branch in Tampa. We'll go check that out for you and interview that sleazeball that you say slipped that gun inside your bag."

Highside: "You go right ahead. You go interview that guy. It was one of them down there that done it. He's probably in league with some of your other lying witnesses you got. You got nothing on me, Clouseau: you got nothin. You need to stop bugging me. Why don't you go on and get back to investigating stolen beach balls and umbrellas? This is way out of your league."

Josh: "We are through here, Highside, for now. Here's my card. Pass it along to your lawyer. Just give us a call when you decide you want to cooperate."

Highside: "I just cooperated with you. There ain't nothing else I need to cooperate on. I just gave you the whole story. You're trying to pin some murder on me. I know it. You know I know it. But hey, I'm used to it. I ain't scared. Good luck, Lieutenant, with your murder case."

Josh and Detective Larry Hooper walk out of the interview room with Highside leaning back in the chair laughing. The two Lieutenants walk back to Josh's office and confer.

Josh: "Well, we aren't going to be able to put that murder on Highside if this is all we have. It's Shovelhead's testimony against Highside. One criminal testifies against another criminal. It's not much. We have the money, but I can't see the DA charging a homicide just on that. We have to have something else turn up."

Detective Larry Hooper: "Let's wait and see what the bank records come up with. Let's pass this on to Joyce. It might be the same bank that's on the zippered bag—SunTrust in Tampa. Let's check to see if there are any large amounts of cash coming and going there. We'll check his credit cards and calls—all that stuff. Maybe we will be able to turn up something else."

Josh: "Yeah, that's right. I'll get his complete file from Joyce. I want to read it over the weekend. There might be something in there I might have missed."

Detective Larry Hooper: " That sounds good. If you don't need anything else, I'm going to head out."

Josh: "Nothing at the moment. See you."

49

UNDER PRESSURE

The next two days are busy for Josh. He was trying to run down the leads regarding the murders of Randi Reynolds and Preston Rodrigues. He wanted to make sure they had a tight case on Dempsey. They still had the open murder of Lauren Scavone. On Friday morning at about 8:15 am, Lieutenant Myers gets a call from the 911 dispatcher.

Dispatcher: "Lieutenant, I have a call from the Patrol Sergeant. He wants to speak to you. I'll connect you."

Josh: "OK, thanks."

Patrol Sergeant Steve Dawson: "Hey Josh."

Josh: "Hi, Steve, what have you got?"

Dawson: "I'm out here at Alabama Point. We got a body washed up on the beach."

Alabama Point is a white sandy beach at the tip of Perdido Pass on the east side of the water. It's right at the entrance to the pass through the bay. It overlooks the bridge. It's a beautiful beach setting.

Josh: "A body washed up on the beach? Is it a drowning?

Dawson: "Well, he's all wet."

Josh: "They usually are."

Dawson: "This particular one is fully dressed."

Josh: "A fully dressed drowning? OK, anything else, Dawson?"

Dawson: "He has on a life jacket."

Josh: "A fully dressed body with a life jacket. Maybe he fell off a boat out there and drowned."

Dawson: "I guess it could be, but he has a hole in the back of his head and a lot of blood around his mouth."

Josh: "So you are saying he was either hit by a meteor or there could be foul play?"

Dawson: "I'm not sure Josh, that is why I'm calling you. In the Patrol Division we don't do meteors"

Josh: "I think you enjoy feeding me the facts very slowly, Dawson, just like you did this morning."

Dawson: "It's more dramatic that way, Josh. You know, kinda like Law and Order. All I need is that big sound "Boom, boom.""

Josh: "Yeah, boom, boom, that's exactly what we need. A sound machine that makes the noise every time we get a case. Maybe then we can solve the case in an hour. Wouldn't that be great?"

Dawson: "So what am I going to do with this drowning man with a life jacket with a hole in the back of his head?"

Josh: "I'll be down there right away with a couple of my detectives."

Dawson: "Thanks, Josh."

Josh arrives at the Alabama Point with two of his detectives. The Orange Beach Police Marine Unit is already in the water along with a small Coast Guard boat. They both responded to the call. Tourists are starting to gather and stare at the beach. The patrol division has pushed them back up by the dune. But the beach is wide open and they can still see the activity. The body is a male Caucasian, face down in the sand, right at the water's edge. He has a large hole in the back of his head and he is wearing a life jacket. Josh turns the body over and looks at his mouth, which has a lot of blood on it. Josh opens his jaw and looks inside with a flashlight. He sees a hole in the roof of his mouth.

Josh to the other detectives: "There is a bullet hole in the roof of his mouth. The hole in the back of his head will be the exit wound. Any vessels in the area connected to this Dawson?"

Dawson: "So far, we haven't found any Josh. We don't have any witnesses. A couple walking on the beach early this morning came along the body just out in the surf and called the Marine Unit. They were quick here out of the Pass. With one of the Patrol Units, they fished him out and drug him through the surf and put him where you see him now."

Josh: "Do you have any ID yet?"

Dawson: "There is no ID on him. We've put out a broadcast of his description with the clothes he's wearing to Gulf Shores PD and, Escambia County Deputies, Baldwin County Deputies. Everyone on the coast to see if anyone is reported missing. So far, we don't have anything."

Josh: "Is forensics on their way?"

Dawson: "Yes, they are on their way. We've also called the Medical Examiner as well since we saw the hole in the back of his head."

Josh: "The Medical Examiner just needs to get a beach chair and an umbrella and park it over here for as busy as we've been in the last few weeks."

Dawson: "She'd probably enjoy that. Give her a change from the usual."

Josh: "I suppose. I'd like to go back to the usual. These bodies are piling up around here. We got a whole lot of work to do."

The forensics team arrives and starts their process: photographing the body and the scene, documenting the evidence. Dr. Terri O'Leary arrives, does a cursory exam, and steps over to Josh.

Terri: "Well, Josh, just as you described. What you see is what you get. Likely the cause of death is going to be that bullet wound. With that life vest, it probably wouldn't have been a drowning. We'll still have to examine the lungs to make sure. If they're clear, I'd say that the gunshot is the obvious cause of death."

Josh: "Could be a suicide, could be a homicide. We don't know what it is yet."

Terri: "Could be an accident too. Stranger things have happened to people."

Josh: "Yeah, ain't that the truth. Getting shot in the mouth when you are out somewhere in the water wearing a life vest and fully clothed. We just have to figure it out."

Terri: "That's why they pay you that Lieutenant money Josh."

Josh: "Thanks, Doc: I can always count on you to be uplifting. See you later."

Just then, Steve walks over to Josh and his two detectives.

Dawson: "We just got a call from Gulf Shores PD. They have a Mrs. Lunde in their department and she is reporting her husband missing since last night. When she woke up this morning, there was a suicide note lying on the kitchen table. In a frantic call, she calls the Gulf Shores PD. She gave them a full description. Tan shirt, blue jeans, white shoes, thinning brown hair. Five foot eight inches. Weighs about 165. Said his name is Jerry Lunde."

Josh: "I think we just found Mr. Jerry Lunde. If he left a suicide note at home, it looks like he was determined to go through with it."

Josh: "Steve, why don't you get with the Gulf Shores PD and get with Mrs. Lunde to coordinate with the medical examiner to see if she can make an identification that this is her husband?

Josh turns to one of his detectives: "Asterino, this is your case. Why don't you go over and interview Mrs. Lunde? See if he had a firearm. If it's missing or still at the house. Maybe we can account for the weapon that caused the death as well. Let's see if we can get this mystery unraveled pretty quick."

Asterino: "We'll do Lieutenant. I'll head over to Gulf Shores PD and get on this right away. I'll talk to Mrs. Lunde about any gun and help with the medical examiner. I'll bring the police chaplain as well."

Josh: 'Thanks, Mike."

Mike: "You got it."

During the interview with Mrs. Lunde, she informs Mike that her husband does have a gun. She's not sure where he keeps it. He kept it hidden for safety reasons. She produces the suicide note that she grabbed from the kitchen table and hands it to Mike Asterino. It reads: My Dearest Joann,

> "I am so sorry for leaving you like this, but I had no choice.
> I have developed a gambling habit and have lost all of
> our money. In my attempt to get it back, I started stealing
> money from work. It was easy to hide at first. But I knew
> that after embezzling close to half a million dollars, I would
> not be able to hide it much longer. When Ms. Scavone was
> murdered, I was able to use that as a cover and told Mr.

Campbell that it was Ms. Scavone who was stealing the money. Mr. Campbell decided to have an audit done to get to the bottom of things. I knew I would be found out. Being fired and going to prison is something I could never do. I know this is a coward's way out, but I feel it's the only way. Forgive me, my darling. I never meant to hurt you."

Love, Jerry

Mike escorts Mrs. Lunde back to her home and searches for a gun. After about an hour, he can find the case but not the gun.

Mike calls Josh: "Hey Boss, I am at the Lunde residence. I found a gun case but no gun. I also read the suicide note he left."

Josh: "Thanks, Mike: what did the note say?"

Mike: "He admitted he was the one embezzling money from D Campbell Landscape. Almost half a million dollars. When Campbell decided to get an audit done to find out what was going on, Lunde knew he would be found out and didn't want to face the consequences. The sad thing is he spent all their money before he started stealing from work. I feel so bad for Mrs. Lunde. She is left with nothing. Of course, if he had a life insurance policy, it probably won't pay out for suicide."

Josh: "Well, that ties up one loose end. If you would head over to D Campbell Landscape and fill in Doctor Campbell what we found out about Lunde we can close that avenue."

Mike: "Sure thing, I'll head over right now."

Mike heads to Doctor Campbell's office. The receptionist greets him, and he asks to speak with Mr. Campbell. Mike is escorted to Doctor's meeting room.

Doctor enters the room and says, "Detective, what are you here to hassle me about now? At this point, I'm going to have to refer to my attorney and you can run all things through him. I have a business to run, and this constantly coming to my office confronting me about all these deaths that I have nothing to do with is getting old."

Mike: "Relax, Mr. Campbell. This meeting is for information purposes only."

Campbell: "Information? What information?"

Mike: "We found the body of your accountant Jerry Lunde early this morning washed up at Alabama Point with a bullet in his head."

Campbell: "What?"

Mike: "Didn't you wonder where he was when he didn't show up for work?"

Campbell: "He's on vacation. He isn't supposed to be back for another week, so nothing was amiss here. You said he had a bullet in his head?" What the Hell?"

Mike: "He left a suicide note for his wife. He developed a severe gambling habit. He admitted to being the one who was embezzling money from you. He knew when you got the results from the audit, you would know it was him, and he didn't want to go to prison. The sad thing is he went through all his money first. His poor wife, Joann, is now left with nothing. She'll probably have to sell the house just to get by."

Campbell: "What a low-life piece of shit. Gambles away their money and mine. Tries to shift the blame to Lauren for stealing the money, leaves his wife with nothing, and takes the chicken shit way out."

Doctor picks up a large envelope that is sitting on the conference table.

Campbell: " This is the audit results right here. I was sitting down and going through them. I guess there is no urgency at this point."

Mike stands up: "I won't take any more of your time."

Doctor stands up as well and shakes Mike's hand: "I want to apologize for my outburst. This summer has been the summer from hell and I have been under a lot of stress."

Mike: "Don't worry about it. It comes with the territory."

Doctor: "I feel so bad for Mrs. Lunde. She didn't deserve any of this."

Mike: "We gave her the name and number of a grief counselor and the police chaplain was with her when I left. It will be tough on her."

Campbell: "Yeah, she was dealt a rotten hand today."

Mike leaves the office and heads back to work.

Doctor Campbell sits back in his chair and thinks about Mrs. Lunde. He tries to imagine her situation. In the scheme of things and his wealth, the money her husband stole from him was a lot, but it wasn't going to break the bank by any means. He gets on the phone with his banker. He instructs him to get a cashier's check made out to Joann Lunde for $300,000.00. He had it sent special delivery with a note.

> Mrs. Lunde,
>
> I am sorry for everything that has happened.
>
> You should not have to bear the brunt of what your husband did.
>
> I hope this check will help ease your burden.
>
> Sincerely,
>
> Doctor Campbell

After Joann Lunde reads the note and sees the check, she can hardly breathe. Never in a million years would she have expected such generosity from the man her husband stole money from. She makes her way to her bedroom, lays down on the bed, and starts to cry. A gut-wrenching howl. How could Jerry do this to her? *"WHY? WHY?"* She screams at the top of her lungs. *" I HATE WHAT YOU DID TO ME! I HATE YOU! YOU COWARD! YOU FUCKING COWARD!!!*

She cries for what seems like hours. When she has nothing left and is completely drained. She gets up and jumps in the shower. Every person in Gulf Shores and Orange Beach knows what her husband did. It's been all over the news. Joann is afraid to go out in public to suffer the stares, pointing, and whispers. In the weeks ahead, she sells her house, packs her things, and heads to Oklahoma, where her sister lives. On her way out of town, she stops at D Campbell Land Development and thanks Doctor for the generous gift. Doctor hugs her and wishes her well. A sad ending to what Joann thought was a beautiful life.

50

THE PAST ARRIVES

It has been long several days for Lieutenant Myers. They had served a search warrant on Shovelhead Dempsey's house: they recovered key evidence. They got a confession from Shovelhead. They searched Highside's car and got the money he was going to give to Shovelhead. They interviewed Highside as well. They dealt with the suicide of Doctor Campbell's bookkeeper Jerry Lunde. Doctor Campbell was still a suspect in the case involving Randi Reynolds and Lauren Scavone. Lieutenant Myers still did not know who hired Highside. Who was Highside's contact in Orange Beach or someplace else? Who and why did someone hire Highside who hired Shovelhead to kill Randi Reynolds and or Lauren Scavone? There were so many things Josh did not have answers to. Now Doctor Campbell's bookkeeper washed up on the shore. The same bookkeeper who accused Lauren Scavone of embezzlement. Josh just does not have a connection to any of these except Doctor

Campbell. Josh thinks to himself. *Was the bookkeeper stealing the money and Doctor Campbell found out about it? That would be an easy motive for his suicide. His plot had been uncovered. That does not connect with the other two murders. Does Doctor Campbell have anything to do with them?*

Josh had taken some of the files home that night and he decided he was going to do a little Friday night investigation by himself and go through them piece by piece. After he made himself a quick sandwich, he sat down at his kitchen table and laid out the files. He poured himself a glass of George Dickel Tennessee Whiskey over some ice. A taste he acquired when he was stationed at Fort Campbell, Kentucky. Just an hour or so from Nashville. He has some soft music playing quietly in the background. He picked up the files and started going through them. First, the crime scene diagram. Then Lauren Scavone, the reports and interviews of her friends. He read page upon page of witness statements about what Lauren had been doing that day. He read about her background. Josh slowly sipped the whiskey as he read the documents. He found it exceedingly difficult to read the reports about Randi's life and murder since he had been in an intimate relationship with her and had been deeply in love with her. As he tried to slog through all the documents, he couldn't help but cry. It started as a quiet silent weep. Just tears streaming down his face with every report he read. Every detail of Randi's murder, the devastation of her body. The ruthless brutal attack on the most beautiful woman he had ever met. His life, his love, his future. He could no longer hold in his emotions. He let loose, put his head in his arm, and sobbed. Sobbed for Randi, for her loving family, for the love he lost. It was several minutes before he was able to compose himself enough to continue. He finally got up and went into the bathroom and washed his face. He looked at himself in the mirror and realized how haggard he looked after the long hours he had been putting in.

He went back to the table and sat down. Took another sip of his whiskey and continued. He needed to see if there was something there, something he had missed. Something that might help him unravel the whole conspiracy behind the murders.

Josh says out loud to nobody but himself: "I will get them Randi: I will get the bastards who did this!"

Wiping his tears again, he took a big gulp of George Dickel and kept reading. Next, he got to Shovelhead's criminal history file, his records for arrests from the Mobile PD, and his packet from the Florida State Penitentiary, where he had been incarcerated with Highside Manthe. He saw Dempsey's prison mugshot. Read about his duties in making license plates. Working in the tobacco fields. Inside the prison, his disciplinary record seemed like he was always involved in some sort of minor infraction with the corrections officers. He didn't want to follow the rules, was always involved in something, and somehow was always in some kind of trouble, albeit minor. Dempsey was a mess: his life was a mess. Constantly in and out of prison. Reading all about Dempsey cemented what Lieutenant Myers already knew. Dempsey was not a pro in murder. Far from it. He did some things not to get caught, His leaving the gun at the scene, and his attempts to cover up. Acquiring the signs and the gun. His easy getaway. An attempt at being a semi-pro, but murder was a complicated business. It took a keen mind to get away with it all. Dempsey certainly wasn't that. That's why they had him solid on both of the murders. After reading his file, Lieutenant Myers felt that the assessments during the interview were correct. They matched his whole life history. He felt he had read Dempsey right. But where will that lead him? He needed more. He needed to get more. He was on to Highside, but he didn't have him solid yet. Just had a federal gun charge. He needed more to make this murder and find out why and what was behind it.

Josh moved onto Highside's file. His criminal rap sheet from Tallahassee Florida. His records from the Tampa PD. Then Hillsboro County Sheriff's Department and the Pasco County Sheriff's Department. Every department in that region where Highside lived had records of his activities. There were intelligence reports on him, and mugshots when he was young. The report of the homicide where he killed another biker and did twenty-five years at Raiford State Prison. Josh then started to read the prison file from Raiford about Highside's time being incarcerated. Unlike Dempsey, Highside was a model prisoner. A trustee even. Given special privileges because of his good behavior. Josh could not find any disciplinary records in his file. He was given jobs that were considered prime jobs in prison for his model behavior and likable demeanor. The writeups from the corrections officers were all positive. No, Highside was a cagey smooth operator. He knew how to work every system he ended up being in. He was not going to be brash and argumentative. He was smart. He wanted out and he wanted to shorten that twenty-five-year sentence. He knew that his way out was to do easy time and not add to his problem. There were some notations from the corrections officers saying they felt he was still running some criminal activities with the biker gang in Tampa while he was in prison. They reported those findings to outside law enforcement in Tampa. There was no record that they were able to ever prove anything.

Josh then picked up the psychiatric report of Highside Manthe that came from Raiford State Prison. He started reading the routine assessment from the psychiatrist after the evaluation he had done on Manthe. It's typical for these evaluations to be done on all prisoners. The psychiatrist had stated that Manthe was a sociopath who could operate at an extremely high level. He could turn his violence on or off when it suited him. His goal was always him and him alone. The biker gang was just a means to get him everything he wanted. According to the psychiatrist, it fits into his need for violence, control, and doing things his way. Josh read about the original murder that Highside committed on another biker. Josh turned the page and started reading about his history. His place of birth is Tampa, Florida: what was the high school he went to? Places he had lived. His father was a construction worker in Tampa. He did not come from a family of large means. He had one brother who had died young in a car accident. Then there was a notation that he had been married. Josh looked at the date he was married and the name of his spouse. Chelsea Manthe. Josh stopped. *Chelsea? Chelsea?* He says to himself. He then went back and frantically started digging through the file furiously, looking for records of his spouse. Josh found an arrest report for Highside for aggravated battery at a strip club in Pasco County, Florida. Manthe had hit another patron at the bar with a beer bottle. Arrested along with him was his spouse, Chelsea Manthe. She was charged with disorderly intoxication. They were both booked into the Pasco County Jail. Josh saw her description, a white female, five foot six inches. Brown eyes and dark brown hair. One hundred ten pounds. Josh looked feverishly for the booking mugshot. He finally finds it. A brunette female dressed in biker garb. Josh looked at the photograph. It was more than thirty years ago. He looked again at it very closely. *Could it be? Is it?! It can't be.* Josh kept looking at the photograph. He could not take his eyes off it. He just sat and stared at the face in the picture. He put the picture down. He

TAMI RYAN & JIM CAVANAUGH

got up out of his chair, he started pacing around his table. He ran his fingers through his hair. He shook his head. He leaned back against the counter. He picked the picture up again and looked at it. He threw it down on the kitchen table, he paced some more. Furiously tried to put the facts together. He grabbed the bottle of George Dickel and poured it until his glass was full. He took a big, long swig. Sat back down and stared at the photograph. Held it up and said out loud. "Well, hello Mayor!"

51

THE PARTING OF THE CLOUDS

Josh had a stressful weekend. Rolling around in his head what he has uncovered Friday night, he now believes that Mayor Higgins is somehow involved in the murders in Orange Beach. His mind was a stadium of screaming thoughts. He wanted to do this right, he had to do this right. If his facts were wrong it would be a terrible outcome. But if his facts were right, then this had to be done with extreme care. On Sunday afternoon, Josh took a long walk on the beach. Snaking through the tourist families and sunbathers. He walked through the water from the Perdido Pass to Gulf Shores State Park, almost the length of the city of Orange Beach, and back again. If anyone saw him, they would think he was a man just enjoying the beach. Fit and tan as he strolled like many others but in fact, he was a man hard at work. A man deep in thought playing a chess game inside his head trying to anticipate not only every move he must make but every move that the killer will make.

There were no easy answers. The choices felt like you either fight the bear or jump into the raging waters of the gorge. Josh went home and made himself a sandwich. Watched the news and went to bed early. It was going to be a long week. On Monday morning he was in the office early and called his team together at 9:00 a.m. for a strategy session. Before that, he had gone up to see the chief of police. He trusted the chief completely: he worked with him his whole career: he was a solid and honest officer. Josh told the chief what he had uncovered with the interrogation of shovelhead Dempsey. The uncovering of Highside, a convicted killer who had hired Shovelhead. Now the discovery that Highside's ex-wife is none other than Mayor Higgins.

The chief took a deep breath and said: "Josh, of course, you have my total support. But what exactly does this mean? The fact that she is the ex-wife of Highside Manthe does that necessarily mean that she is involved in this murder conspiracy."

Josh: "Chief, I'm not sure, I have to follow the facts. But I can't find any reason why this Highside character would want to kill Randi Reynolds. I can understand why Shovelhead Dempsey killed her: He was paid to do it. I can also understand why he killed the gun trafficker. Because he wanted no loose ends. He told us so. But Highside Manthe lives in Tampa, and there has got to be some reason why he is involved in wanting Randi Reynolds killed."

Chief: "But what about Doctor Campbell? Lauren Scavone? He was dating Randi Reynolds, and now his bookkeeper has washed up like a dead crab. He is directly connected to all three of these people. The last you told me, he has lawyered up."

Josh: "Chief, I am not ruling him out. Initially, he did seem to be cooperative, but lately, he seems like someone put ben-gay on his balls. We'll just have to see. So far, I just don't have a motive for him. He is very rich: he can get any woman he wants."

Chief: "Sometimes you don't find a motive. It's not required for a murder charge."

Josh: "That's true, chief. But there is always a motive and if you can uncover it, it somehow unlocks the vault of the mind. So, I want to press on this new lead now with the mayor and see if there is a motive I can uncover. I am going to swear my team to complete secrecy. We are all trustworthy. So, if you hear that we are rattling the bushes around the mayor, you will know what's going on."

Chief: "OK, Josh, you shake the bushes, you shake the forest, and we'll deal with whatever comes. Mayor, governor, judge, senator, I don't care who it is. If they are part of the murder conspiracy, we want them charged."

Josh: "Thanks, Chief: I will keep you advised. He walks back down to his office. At the meeting with the team, he advises them of the delicate situation where the mayor has arisen as a possible suspect in the murder conspiracy of Randi Reynolds. Josh starts to give out assignments for the team."

Josh: "I want the bank, credit card, and telephone records for Highside Manthe. We know he was paying Dempsey fifteen thousand for the murder. Maybe we can find out where that fifteen thousand came into Highside's bank. We might be able to track it back. Also, I want you to pull anything on his credit cards, Venmo, or anything that might show us a cash transaction."

Mike Conover: "Josh, you know the US Treasury Department has a currency transaction reporting requirement."

Josh: "Only you, Mike, would spit out something like that. What does that mean?"

Conover: "Anytime a bank or financial institution handles a cash transaction, it must report that movement to the US Treasury Department. Treasury keeps a computerized record of all those reports. Now, this does not include checks, ACH, or wire transfers, which is what most banking involves. This requirement only takes hold when cash is received or dispensed more than 10K. We can get that checked for you under Highside Manthe's name."

Josh: "Thanks, Mike. That is great. There are a few efforts to see where Highside might have received some money. I want the same thing for Mayor Chelsea Higgins: bank records, credit card, Venmo, and Mike. You could also check on those treasury records."

Conover: "We'll do Josh."

Josh: "Sergeant Miller, work up an investigative package of the Mayor's vehicles, home, phone, and any known close friends and associates. Let's have a deeper picture of her than what we generally know." Also, we still have the outstanding that her assistant Maria is missing. Has there been any updated information on that?"

Sergeant: "Nothing new on that, Lieutenant. We did call Sarasota PD and sent someone to her family's house, but she has not turned up, and they are extremely worried about her. They have our contact info as well. They assured us they would call if Maria happened to show up. We still have the BOLO out on her car."

Josh: "Somehow, somewhere, that's part of this whole thing. Detective Hooper and I are going to travel to Huntsville to interview Chelsea Higgins's family members. We'll try to be discreet, but of course, she might get wind of it. But we have to start somewhere." Tuesday morning Josh and Detective Hooper head north to Huntsville. About 6 ½ hours from Orange Beach. They made an appointment to talk to Chelsea's sister Meredith, who is the CEO of The Higgins Corporation, for Wednesday at 9:00 a.m.

They arrive at 9:00 a.m. at the office of Higgins Corporation and introduce themselves to Meredith Higgins. They immediately ask for her confidential assistance in a delicate matter that involves homicide in Orange Beach. Ms. Higgins agrees to speak with the detectives in confidence.

Josh outlines the framework of the murder of Randi Reynolds, The apprehension of shovelhead Dempsey, and the uncovering of Highside Manthe in the plot and his arrest on a related federal gun charge.

Meredith: "Highside Manthe? That's the loser ex-husband of Chelsea. He's a walking pocket of puss."

Josh: "So, you can see the reason why we are here. It's pretty obvious on its face since Highside Manthe is involved in the murder conspiracy. We don't have any reason as to why he would want Miss Reynolds killed. We are looking to see if Mayor Higgins is involved."

Meredith was shocked: "Mayor? Mayor? Chelsea Higgins is the mayor of Orange Beach. Really?"

Josh: "Does that surprise you?"

Meredith: "That bitch should not be the mayor of any place. The only place she should be is in prison for the murder of our father."

Josh: "What? By all means, please continue."

Meredith begins, "One fall weekend in late October several years ago, our trail cameras had shown a lot of deer activity. Dad, Chelsea, and I had decided to do a family hunting day. We got everything loaded up on our ATVs and headed out. We went out to the farthest back corner of the property. We have ATV trails everywhere so it was an easy drive to that area of dense woods. We were shocked at how many deer were there. We had our normal procedures for hunting as a family. The same procedure

we had followed for ten years. We all knew our role. As we got
started and moved out quietly on foot. Through the fields, along a
tree line, and found our positions in the woods. You have to wait
and be still or the deer will see or smell your presence. Dad saw
a huge buck just standing there at the same time Chelsea and I
did. It was a 16-pointer. Head up, listening to all the sounds of
the woods. His ears twitched at every noise deciding if he was
safe or needed to bolt at any particular sound. We were all star-
struck by this massive, beautiful creature. I know my dad was a
whirlpool of emotions, having a tug-of-war inside. Does he kill this
behemoth or let it live? He raised his gun and looked through the
scope. His finger is on the trigger. A shot rang out in the quiet of
the woods. Chelsea and I move towards the sound. We had both
seen the huge buck through our scopes as well but knew our dad
had the better shot. When we got to our dad to check out his new
kill, we were stunned to see our dad lying in a pool of blood. Dad
had been shot right through the back. I immediately get on the
phone and call 911. Screaming into the phone. "This is Meredith
Higgins. My father, Walter Higgins, has been shot in the back
corner of our property! Please send an ambulance immediately!"
We both knew that it would be difficult for the sheriff's deputies
to find us. Chelsea agreed to ATV back to the house and guided
the sheriff's deputies and paramedics to where we were. It didn't
take long for the Deputies to get to the property. As they get there,
they see I am crying and hugging my dad with his head on my
lap. I am covered in blood. Dad is sprawled out on his back, dead.
There was nothing the paramedics could do. The shot had killed
him instantly. The sheriff's deputy starts asking us what happened.
As we describe our morning and our adventure to the woods. We
saw the same buck that Dad saw. Our routine is dad gets first shot

always." The sheriff's deputy then turned to Chelsea and got her story. Chelsea told them that when she looked through her scope, it was the biggest buck any of us had ever seen. She wanted it so badly: her mind went blank and she forgot about the routine. She wanted to be the one to shoot it. She didn't have a clear view of either our father or me. Since she didn't see either of us through her scope. She figured we were safe and out of the way when she took the shot." I screamed at her: "What the hell is wrong with you? You "forgot" the hunting routine and just started shooting? Chelsea, YOU KNOW THE ROUTINE! Look at what your selfishness has caused! All for a trophy buck?" Meredith continues, Chelsea appeared to be horrified and distraught that she is the one who shot our father. As the paramedics tried to calm her, Chelsea continued to be inconsolable. They had no choice but to give her a sedative to calm her down. I could not believe what was happening. This can't be real. Our dad is gone. Our DAD is gone. The family pillar of strength is gone. The Higgins family as we know it, is no more. What was Chelsea thinking? How could she be so selfish? Oh wait, the one thing Chelsea is, is selfish. She has single-handedly destroyed the Higgins family. I will never forgive her for this. Accident or not."

Josh: "So she is a crack shot with a rifle?"

Meredith: "She was better than me and dad, She took to it like a bee to honey. She never missed."

Josh: 'What kind of rifle did she hunt with?"

Meredith: "A bolt action .308 Remington with a scope."

Josh: "Do you think she still has it.?

Meredith: "She got it back from the sheriff's office after Dad was killed and she took it when she left for Orange Beach. That's all I know."

Josh: "Do you think your sister would be capable of murder?"

Meredith: "She would kill anybody who got in her way. If you think she harmed someone then look to see if somehow that person is obstructing her. If that is the case, she would do it without compunction or remorse. She is a cold-blooded reptile when anything or anyone impedes her goals. Other than that, she is as sweet as cotton candy."

Josh: "Thank you, Meredith. As we stated this morning, we want to confirm our need for confidentiality. We do not know how this is going to play out."

Meredith: "Of course, Lieutenant, You have my word. We operate here every day in the aerospace industry with the US government. We must hold top clearances and understand the need that things can be a remarkably close hold. I would just ask that you would let me know if there are any major developments that you can share before we are made public."

Josh: "Of course, Meredith. You have my word."

Josh and Detective Hooper thank Meredith for her time and head over to the Madison County, Alabama, Sheriff's Department. They talk to a Detective Lieutenant about Walter Higgins, pick up a copy of the entire file regarding his death, and head back to Orange Beach.

Once back in Orange Beach with his team assembled Josh asks for what information has been uncovered.

Mike: "We received a Suspicious Activity Report Statistic (SAR Stats) from the US Treasury's Financial Crimes Enforcement Network (FINCEN), which is the report I was describing, where banks must report cash transactions over 10K."

Josh: 'That was fast."

Mike: "Yes, well, it's a record held by the Treasury Department, so we can get it very quickly."

Josh: "What's in it, Mike?"

Mike: "Mayor Higgins withdrew 50K in cash on June the first. That is all it's going to tell us regarding the mayor. However, FinCEN also reported that Lennie Manthe deposited 35K in cash on June the third."

Josh: "I was never good at math, but 50-35, is that still 15K?"

Mike: "I'm in ATF you might need to talk to the IRS if you want to get all technical."

Joyce: "We've expedited our subpoena request with SunTrust Bank in Tampa, Florida. The head of security is a retired chief from Florida, and he helped us get the records immediately. SunTrust bank records show that Lennie Manthe wrote a check for $35k towards a new Audi convertible on June fifth."

Josh: "Good work Joyce. In Huntsville, we found out that the Mayor's sister, Meredith Higgins, believes Chelsea murdered their father years ago with a .308 rifle. She was never charged and it was ruled an accidental death. Her sister told us Chelsea was a crack shot with a rifle and a scope and never missed. We have implication here that she may be involved with Randi's murder by paying Highside, but we also have reason to suspect she is involved in Lauren Scavone's murder. As you all know, we think that the shot that killed Ms. Scavone came from Bird Island. Likely from a vessel there since there would be nowhere for a killer to hide. What about the workup you did on the mayor? Does she own a boat?"

Detective Asterino: "No, sir, she does not own a boat. She does own a red Porche Carrera. She has a house on Ono Island with a dock where you could easily park a boat, but she does not own one. She probably has lots of friends who own boats, but she doesn't."

Josh: "Let's send some teams out to all the local marinas in Orange Beach and Gulf Shores to see if the mayor rented a boat for the Fourth of July weekend. That's a pretty popular thing to do. Let's see where that leads us. Can we get a subpoena for the mayor's cell phone records?"

Sergeant Miller: "Yes, sir, we will right away. We can get the phone records from her desk phone in her office. That is a work phone, and we have immediate access to it."

Josh: "OK! Get them both and get back as quick as you can."

52

DAVEY JONES LOCKER

Josh is rolling now. Hard facts are coming together to give him a clear picture of the puzzle. He hasn't worked out in his mind the exact motive, but he can see several strong leads pointing directly at the mayor for the murders of Randi Reynolds and Lauren Scavone. *Why would the mayor want to kill these two women? What could she gain from that? What could be her motive?*

He rolls around in his mind the facts as he knows them. *Both Lauren and Randi had ties to D Campbell Development. Lauren worked there and Randi had an intimate relationship with Doctor Campbell. The mayor knows Doctor Campbell. She has worked with him to get land purchases done properly. Was the mayor involved in a conspiracy with Doctor Campbell to murder these women? Does that make any sense? Is this entirely unrelated? Are these some consequential facts that aren't going to amount to anything?* Josh feels like he is pointing in a direction now, but he has to be careful. Once again, confirmation bias is a dangerous thing. He doesn't want that to cloud his judgment. Josh prides himself on never charging the wrong person.

I need hard facts. Not supposition and conjecture. Not things that look like things. Hard provable facts. I got those on Shovelhead. I got him solid. The partial print, the DNA on the murder weapon. The sign, the van, his confession. I've got him locked down. I've got him all the way. Highside hired him. I don't have Highside yet. Just a statement from Shovelhead but he is a convicted felon, liar, and biker. I've got to have more than that. I've got some cash transactions, but that's hardly proof. It's just things that fit together if you have other solid evidence. There is still a long way to go here.

Sergeant Miller walks into Josh's office.

Josh: "Yes, Sergeant, do you have something for me?"

Miller: "Lieutenant, we went down to the IT phone tech and swore them to secrecy. We've pulled all the phone records from the mayor's desk phone. We called the DA to get a subpoena for her cell phone records, but we haven't gotten that back yet. We are trying to expedite that."

Josh: "Thank you, Sergeant Miller: I appreciate you getting on that so fast."

Miller: "Yes sir, I think you are going to like what we found."

Josh: "Let's have it. Give it to me slowly so I can enjoy it more."

Miller: "First, we found a call to the Sunshine Marina—the one over on the back bay. It was July 1st from the mayor's phone to that particular marina."

Josh: "That could be very helpful."

Miller: "We also have a phone call from her desk phone on May 28th to Highside Manthe's cell phone in Tampa Florida."

Josh: "Well now, that's very interesting. Any other calls to Manthe?"

Miller: "No sir, from her desk phone, we only found one."

Josh: "One call to Manthe and one call to the marina. What was the date again on the marina call?"

Miller: "July 1st sir."

Josh: "Thank you, Sergeant."

Josh walks out of his office and goes over to Detective Hooper's office which the Orange Beach PD made available to him to work on the case.

Josh: "Larry, come on, we've got to go to a marina. But first, I need to call Lieutenant Kevin Murphy over at the Alabama Marine Patrol. I want him to meet us at the marina. He knows everything about the water and boats. He will be very helpful to us for something like this."

Hooper: "Let's go."

The two lieutenants head out to the Sunshine Marina after making the call to Lieutenant Murphy. Murphy agrees to meet them there. He's on his patrol boat in the back bay anyway. He would be there when they arrived. Within a few minutes, the three Lieutenants huddle up outside the Sunshine Marina. Josh fills Murphy in on what he has and what he has learned about the mayor.

Josh: "I believe the rifle shot that killed Lauren Scavone came from Bird Island probably from a boat. Now the mayor is a suspect in her murder. She made a call to the Sunshine Marina on July 1st, three days before the murder. I want to talk to the marina operator to see if they can glean some information. I want Kevin along so he can help us with any boating issues or information."

The three lieutenants walk into the marina and ask for the manager Cliff Sunday, an affable South Alabama character who is always laughing and smiling. He has a busy marina business. He rents charter boats, fishing boats, and pleasure boats. He's got saltwater in his veins. Sunday greets the three lieutenants with a big wave and a smile.

Sunday: "Good Morning gentlemen. How can I help you on such a beautiful day? Do you want to go out and catch some Blue Marlin? Do you want to charter a boat? I can fix you all up."

Just then Cliff notices Lieutenant Murphy from the Marine Patrol.

Sunday: "Hey Lieutenant, excuse me, I didn't see you right away. What are you doing here? I thought you already had a boat. I hope I'm not in trouble. The Marine Patrol don't come around here unless there's trouble."

Kevin just smiles at Cliff: "No, Mr. Sunday, everything is fine. We just have some questions we'd like to ask. This is Lieutenant Josh Myers from the Orange Beach PD and this is Detective Larry Hooper from the Baldwin County Sheriff's Department."

Sunday: "Well, a cornucopia of cops from everywhere. I like cops, come on in boys, and step into my office and have a seat. Ask away. Whatever you need I am willing to provide."

Josh begins, "This inquiry is very delicate, and I cannot let all of the information out just now, but I want to ask if Chelsea Higgins rented a boat from your Marnia sometime in July."

Sunday: "Chelsea Higgins? Do you mean the mayor? That Chelsea Higgins?"

Josh: "Yes, that's right, Chelsea Higgins the mayor."

Sunday: "Yes, I remember the mayor coming in here in early July and she did rent a boat. We rent a lot of boats for the 4th of July. People love to party and they love being on the water during the fireworks. Mayor Higgins came in and rented a boat. Let me look in the records."

Cliff Sunday turns to his computer, hits some keys, and up pops the screen.

Sunday: "Yep, I got it right here, first of July. She rented a twenty-three-foot with a cabin. It is a nice boat."

Murphy: "What kind of boat was it exactly?"

Sunday: "Well it was one of our nicer rentals called a Ranger Tug. It's got a very strong sea-going hull. Has a nice cabin. It's got a small deck on the back. It's for people who want to take a cruise along the coast. Maybe do a little fishing. Very good visibility from the front. Just a nice vessel. They cost a lot of money as well. She rented it for a week and she picked it up July 1st. She returned it early. She brought it back on the fifth. She left it at the dock, and put the keys in the box. Everything was in order as far as we could tell. She paid her bill promptly."

Murphy: "Cliff, do you have that boat here now?"

Sunday: "Yes sir, I got it right here. It's at the end of the marina. It's a burgundy one. Do you want to go take a look?"

Murphy: "Yes, we would, Cliff: we would like to go on board if that's alright."

Sunday: "Of course, anything for Lieutenant Murphy. Let me get the key. I can go with you if you need me to, but I suspect Lieutenant Murphy knows his way around these boats better than I do."

Murphy: "Thanks, Cliff: there's no need for you to come along. We might be there for a while. We just want to take a look around."

Sunday: "Of course, here's the key. Take all the time you need. You can take it out for a spin if you'd like to. That is a great vessel."

Murphy: "Thanks, Cliff."

The three Lieutenants walk down the dock towards the end and they spot the Ranger Tug along with numerous other fishing and pleasure boats. Lieutenant Murphy steps aboard.

Josh: "You state troopers are pretty nimble. You hopped up on that boat like you were a twenty-year-old."

Murphy laughed: "I've been jumping on and off boats my whole life. My Colonel recognized that and put me on Marine patrol. It's just part of who I am."

Josh: "I'm pretty much a landlubber. I love the beach but I'm not much for boats. Let's take a look around."

As the three lieutenants walk around the boat, they open up some of the cabinets inside the pilot house. They see it has a small cooking area. A fold-up seat where you could eat a meal. It has a set of stairs inside the cabin that leads down to the bunk area.

Josh: "Wow, this is a nice boat. The mayor didn't skimp when she got this thing."

Murphy: "This gem would cost you about one hundred fifty thousand dollars. If you get all the bells and whistles, it would cost even more. These are great boats."

The lieutenants continue to go through the cabin, opening all the doors. Check all compartments, look under the bunks, they look through everything. They are looking for any obvious signs of evidence. So far none of them have noticed anything of use. Of course, it's been a couple of months since the mayor rented this thing. No telling how many other people have been on this boat since then. Josh takes a deep breath.

Josh: "It's OK. It's important evidence that she rented this boat. We found the boat, and looking at the configuration of this thing, do you think a person could sit down in the well of this bunk area and fire a rifle up through this open door of the pilot house out the stern? Could that be a clear shot and be hidden from view from either side?"

Detective Hooper: "Clearly, you could. You would just have to affix a seat and maybe a prop for your rifle to rest it on. Of course, shooting from a moving boat isn't easy."

Murphy: "Even when resting on a beach, a boat will continue to move as the water moves. It won't move as much as if it was in the water completely but still, shooting would be very difficult. We do a lot of training shooting from a moving vessel. But it can be done. It depends on how calm the water is. Any boats passing by may cause a wake. What matters also is how good the shooter is, how good the weapon is, and, of course, the distance. There are certainly a lot of factors involved. Do you remember a few years back when the pirates off the coast of Africa had taken over a commercial vessel? The US Navy responded and three Navy Seals shot from the deck of a U.S. Navy destroyer to take out the Somalian pirates. The difficulty of those shots when you are on a vessel at sea, shooting at another vessel at sea is extremely difficult. Of course, Navy Seals are highly trained, they constantly practice and they have the ultimate weapons. So, it can be done, it just adds another layer of complexity to the shot."

Josh: "Our killer fired two shots. The first shot missed. The second was right in the X-ring. The rifle we think Chelsea owns is a .308 Remington bolt action. That would mean the killer would fire one shot, work the bolt to eject the empty casing to fire the second shot. They would only have to pick up one casing and remove their stand and their seat along with whatever case they carried their rifle in and any other equipment they had. It would be easy to do for someone who has experience shooting."

Murphy: "For sure. There wouldn't be a lot of equipment and if only two shots were fired, the rifle could be stowed in a duffle bag or rifle case. It could easily be carried on a boat without anyone paying any attention."

Josh: "I guess that's all we are going to get right now. I wish I had a crystal ball so I would know where this boat was on the 4th of July at 10:00 p.m. If I knew that, things would be a lot different."

Murphy: "Hold on just a second Josh."

Murphy turns and walks over to the pilot house and looks at the controls around the steering wheel at the equipment.

Murphy: "This vessel has a plotter."

Josh: "Plotter? What do you mean a plotter?"

Murphy: "A plotter is a tracker, a GPS tracker. It's used for many things in nautical operations. Fishermen want to know the locations of certain fishing spots. Vessels can be located by GPS for emergency reasons. In often-used routes, the Captain can guide his vessel safely along those routes. There are many reasons Captains use these plotters."

Josh: "You mean it tracks the GPS location of the boat?"

Murphy: "That's exactly what it does. It stores the information in the computer database on the boat. In case you ever have to go back and check a trip you took, and you want to use the same route to a certain island, you can track it: you want to go back to a prosperous fishing hole, you can track it."

Josh: "All that is stored in the boat's computer?"

Murphy: "It's in the plotter's computer and since this boat is equipped with one, then yes."

Josh: "Can we access it?"

Murphy: "I'm sure we can. We just have to get Cliff over here and have him pull the screen up for us."

Detective Hooper: "You guys wait here: I'll go get Cliff."

Within a few minutes, Detective Hooper returns with Cliff. They tell Cliff that they want to look at the plotter and they want to see where that vessel went on the 4th of July. Cliff sits down in the Captain's seat, gets on the computer, and pulls up the screen.

Cliff: "The vessel was on Ono Island on the morning of the 4th of July. You can see here that it left Ono Island, sailed down in the bay, and crossed over to Bird Island. It looks like about 7:00 p.m. The boat was there for a few hours, until around 9:45 p.m."

Josh: "This boat was on Bird Island from 7:00 p.m. to 9:45 p.m.?"

Cliff: "Yep, that's right."

Josh: "What happens after 9:45 p.m.?"

Cliff: "This is odd. At about 9:45 p.m. it went out Perdido Pass. Remember, by this time, it's pitch black out in the Gulf."

Murphy: "No doubt. You can't see your hand in front of your face."

Cliff continues, "It went out of the Perdido Pass straight as an arrow three nautical miles out from the Pass."

Murphy: "That is unusual."

Josh: "Why is that?"

Murphy: "Most vessels will turn either right or left down the coast. That way, they can still see the lights of the shore. They don't have to go out three miles. They can go out just a few hundred yards and cruise up and down the coast. Why would they want to go straight out three miles in the middle of the night unless they were destined for somewhere? A fishing boat maybe, but most fishing trips don't start at 10:00 p.m. on the 4th of July evening."

Josh: "Go on Cliff, what happens next."

Cliff: "It stops after the three nautical miles and doesn't move. It looks like it might have anchored for about twenty minutes or so."

Josh: "So, it doesn't move for about twenty minutes?"

Lieutenant Murphy looks at the screen and the data: "Yes, I agree. That looks like an anchored vessel."

Josh: "OK, keep going."

Cliff: "The boat then comes back on the same route. Straight as an arrow back into the Perdido Pass and then on up into Ono Island and docks at this location."

Josh: "Can it give you an address?"

Cliff: "No, it can't give an address, but it can give the GPS coordinates."

Josh: "Let's get all this written down."

Lieutenant Murphy writes down all of the information from the plotter. They tell Cliff that they will need to get the data from the plotter permanently.

Cliff: "That's no problem. I can download it for you on a thumb drive and you can have it."

Josh: "Can you also preserve it on the computer?"

Cliff: "Yes I can save it as well."

Cliff walks back to the shop to grab a thumb drive and the three lieutenants talk.

Josh: "Kevin, that was a big help. I had no idea or knew anything about boat plotters. I am sure glad we had you here."

Kevin: "I'm always glad to help in any way I can. It looks like you are going to need a little more help. Cause if you're thinking what I'm thinking. What's at the end of those three nautical miles?"

Josh: "Exactly, Now all we need are some divers. I know the state troopers have a dive team."

Murphy: "We sure do. I will get a call into them immediately."

Josh: "The fire department has a dive team as well. So does Gulf Shores PD. Let me call some of the local guys. Get the state troopers and the fire department. The more the merrier. We can use the Orange Beach marine police unit, your vessel. What else will we need Kevin?"

Murphy: "I want to call in the Coast Guard. I'll call the Chief Petty Officer down at the station, Tim Caven. Tim's first-rate. He'll bring his 41-foot Coast Guard Vessel up along with his crew. They are always a tremendous help. That'll give us enough boats to launch divers and we will go see what we can find. We will need a day to arrange all this. Let's get all these calls in now and give everybody the time to get their gear together and get their vessels ready. Then we can start the day after tomorrow. The weather is supposed to be good this week. We can strike while the iron is hot."

Two days later the dive teams assembled along with police officers from the assembled agencies and the Coast Guard. They moved out three miles out from the Perdido Pass. The divers go down and, in no time, recover a metal box and a rifle case. They're immediately brought to the surface and placed on the Coast Guard boat. Inside is a .308 Remington bolt action rifle with a scope. They also recover binoculars, shooting gloves, coveralls, and eye and ear protection. The whole process didn't take more than a few hours. Quick easy work that day.

Lieutenant Myers calls Special Agent Mike Conover at ATF and provides him with the serial number of the .308 Remington rifle. He asks for an urgent trace.

Lieutenant Myers then has the rifle taken to the Alabama State Forensics Laboratory. The rifle is compared to the two bullet fragments that were recovered from Lauren Scavone and her condo. It's an exact match.

Special Agent Conover calls back the next day. The rifle was purchased years ago in Huntsville, Alabama at Harry's Gun Shop. The purchaser was Chelsea Higgins.

Josh leans back in his chair, puts his feet up on his desk, and crosses them at the ankles. He starts to think about all the information that he has uncovered with solid proof and facts. He tries to discern the motive behind why Mayor Higgins would want to kill Lauren Scavone and Randi Reynolds. He remembers the wisdom he got from Meredith Higgins in Huntsville. *If you find somebody in Chelsea's way, she would be more than willing to kill them without compunction.*

If you find somebody in Chelsea's way. Josh repeats this phrase a few times. *How was Lauren and Randi in Chelsea's way?* Somehow this must be related to Doctor Campbell and or his company. Josh thinks back to when he had his liaison with the mayor in Birmingham. Josh thinks to himself. *She had been very sexually aggressive that night. If she was like that with me, she would easily be the same with Doctor Campbell. After all, he is handsome and uber-rich. Why wouldn't she be? Maybe Lauren and Randi were in the way of her getting her claws into Campbell.*

Whatever the motive, hard facts are pointing to the mayor. Josh now had to obtain a warrant for her arrest.

53

BEYOND A DOUBT

Detective Lieutenant Josh Myers has a warrant for Mayor Chelsea Higgins. The warrant is for the Capital Murder of Lauren Scavone and the conspiracy to murder Randi Reynolds. Josh is feeling good, as this is a culmination of solid detective work and a few good breaks. Team work really, with all the investigators involved. The time for talk is over. The time for action has begun.

Josh calls the mayor's office and gets her on the phone.

Josh: "Mayor, I need to come and see you. I'll be there in twenty minutes."

Chelsea: "I'm very busy, Lieutenant. Can't it wait? I don't know if I can see you in twenty minutes."

Josh: "Respectfully, Mayor, you cannot put this off. I'm on my way."

Chelsea: "Am I being followed, Lieutenant?"

Josh: "Should you be followed, Mayor?"

Chelsea: "I know your detectives have been following me. I've seen them for the last couple of days. Although I haven't seen them this morning, I am going to assume you have pulled them off my tail. Also, there is a rumor that you've been asking questions about me at one of the local marinas."

Josh: "We can discuss all this when I get there. I am on the way."

Josh arrives at the Mayor's Office twenty minutes later.

Receptionist: "Good Morning, Lieutenant. Can I help you?"

Josh: "I'm here to see the Mayor."

Receptionist: "I am sorry. She left a few minutes ago in quite a hurry. She didn't say where she was going."

Josh turns and quickly leaves the office.

Josh: "Sergeant Miller, I need to find the mayor. She has left her office. You guys know her car. Check some of the known places she frequents. I need to find her as soon as possible."

Joyce: "You got it, Lieutenant."

Within thirty minutes, one of the police radio cars radios Josh.

Patrolman: "We've found the mayor's car. It's at the Turquoise Towers Condominiums. It's in the parking garage."

Josh thinks to himself. *Doctor Campbell's residence.*

Minutes later, Chelsea arrived at Doctor's residence. She told the doorman that she needed to see Doctor immediately.

The doorman gets on the phone with Doctor: "Hello Mr. Campbell. Mayor Higgins is here and she says she needs to see you immediately. It's very important."

Doctor: "What? Really? Ok, send her up." Within minutes there is a knock on the door. Doctor opens it immediately.

Doctor: "Chelsea, what are you doing here? I don't conduct business at my home. You know that. You could have had me come to your office or we could have met at mine. What is so damned important that you felt the need to come here?"

Chelsea: "I had this great idea. It just came to me and I wanted to tell you immediately. Let's go on a trip. We've talked about it. Life has been busy and with everything that has been going on, I think we should get away. Let's go someplace exotic. Like Fiji!"

Doctor: "Fiji? When did you plan on us going?"

Chelsea: "How about right now?"

Doctor: "Today? You want to leave today?"

Chelsea: "Why not, you can arrange it. I know you've got people on standby."

Doctor: "Chelsea, come in and sit down. Let's talk logistics. Do you want a drink?"

Chelsea: "Sure, wine please."

The phone rings and Doctor picks it up: it's the doorman again.

Doorman: "I am so sorry to bother you again, Mr. Campbell, but Lieutenant Josh Myers is here to see you."

Doctor: "Lieutenant Myers? Ok, send him up." Doctor thinks. *What the hell is going on today?*

Chelsea: "What's the matter Doctor? You have a weird look on your face."

Doctor: "I don't know what's going on. Suddenly Lieutenant Myers is here to see me."

Chelsea: "Lieutenant Myers? Oh, maybe he's got more info on the death of your accountant. He can call you with that kind of info. I'll tell him to stop bothering you. We can slip out the back and leave Orange Beach behind."

Doctor: "This makes no sense. It has been confirmed that Jerry Lunde committed suicide. There must be something else going on that he feels the need to show up at my private home and not just call me or ask to come to the police department?"

Just then the doorbell rings. Chelsea is standing in the middle of the living room with her glass of wine. The front door is a distance from the living room. Doctor goes to the foyer and answers the door.

Doctor: "Hello Lieutenant, what the hell is going on? Isn't this something that we could have discussed at your office? Or mine?"

Josh: "Is the mayor here?"

Doctor: "Yes, she's in the living room."

Josh: "Let's go see her. I'll explain everything."

They walk to the living room together and the mayor is nowhere to be found.

Doctor: "She's here. Maybe she is off trying to find the restroom."

    Both Josh and Doctor walk around the penthouse looking for Chelsea. At the same time, they spot her on the balcony but on the other side of the railing. Doctor's penthouse is on the fifteenth floor overlooking the Gulf. Below, there is a large swath of sandy beach filled with beach chairs. There is a warm Gulf breeze on a beautiful clear day.

Josh: "Mayor, come in off the balcony. It's dangerous. Come in and we can discuss everything."

Chelsea: "What's there to discuss Lieutenant? I've come here to talk to Doctor about taking an exotic trip and getting married while we were gone."

Doctor: "Married? What are you talking about Chelsea? We are not getting married. We have never once talked about getting married. What is going on? Someone better start filling me in."

Josh: "I have a warrant for the arrest of Mayor Chelsea Higgins for the murder of Lauren Scavone and conspiracy to murder Randi Reynolds."

Doctor just stands there with his mouth open, trying to absorb what he was just told. His mind is all over the place. The police have been to his office numerous times asking about Lauren and Randi. Making assumptions that he could somehow be responsible for both murders. Now Lieutenant Myers is in his home with a warrant for Mayor Higgins.

Doctor to Chelsea: "Oh My God. Is this true Chelsea? Did you kill Lauren and Randi? What the hell for?"

Chelsea: "Both those bitches deserved it. That little snot Lauren was trying to keep me from you. Telling me that you were sleeping with her, Randi, and ME. Telling me I was nothing special to you. I was nothing more than a washed-up urinal cake. Always trying to block me when I came to your office. Acting like some guard at the gate! And Randi! She was no good for you. A realtor? Doctor, a realtor? She sells houses for God's sake. Ok, so big houses but that does not put her on the same level as you and me."

Doctor: "Really Chelsea? What level is that?"

Chelsea: "You know, the upper crust of society. My family is very wealthy and well-known all over Alabama. So is yours. Our families have come from money. Our families are well respected. Randi comes from county bumpkin FarmVille in Wisconsin. She comes from cows and manure. That is not a person who will ever be the upper crust."

Doctor: "You killed two people. Just to get what you think you deserve?"

Josh: "Three people Doctor. We believe she also murdered her father several years ago to get her share of her inheritance early.

Her motives for killing Lauren and Randi were the same. Greed. She wanted you, Doctor. She wanted to be Mrs. Campbell and everything that comes with the title."

Chelsea: "I deserve it. I deserve the best life. Doctor can give me that lifestyle. We can do so many great things together. Doctor, don't you see, we can build an empire together. We would be unstoppable."

Doctor: "Chelsea! That was never going to happen. I would never marry you. We had sex. Nothing more. Lauren and I had sex. Nothing more. My only plan was to marry Randi and I was working on that. You took that possibility away from me!"

Josh thinks, "*And Doctor, you took that away from me.*"

Josh: "Mayor, did you harm your assistant Maria Fletcher?"

Doctor just stares at Chelsea and thinks, "*Can this get any worse?*"

Chelsea: "That little skank tried to blackmail me. She had a video of us, you and I having sex on my desk. She was going to show everybody. I had to protect you Doctor from that embarrassment."

Doctor: "Protect me or protect yourself?"

Chelsea: "What difference does it make? I outsmarted her. I had her in my office for drinks while we discussed her "payment." I gave her a drink that had roofies in it. When she started to get groggy. I helped her to her car: I snagged her phone and sent her on her merry way. I have no idea what happened to her. She didn't show up for work the next day so I figured she skipped town. I took her phone and put it in the safe in my office."

Josh: "OK, Chelsea, we've cleared the air. We got it all out and you told us everything we need to know. Doctor here will be my witness to your confession. You can deal with this in a court of law."

Chelsea: "I'll deal with this my way. My decision is now easy."

Josh: "Chelsea! That's the wrong decision! Please listen to me, Chelsea. I'll help you in any way I can. Just come back in off the balcony!"

Chelsea: "Help me, Josh? You can't help me. There is nothing you can do to help me. We all know that. There is nothing anyone can do. So, I think I'll go down to the beach."

Josh observes Chelsea sucking in a deep breath. He knows, with all his training, that is the clear sign of imminent suicide. Josh tries to close the gap between them by taking a few steps. As he starts towards Chelsea, she takes her second deep breath and let's go of the railing. Josh and Doctor rush to the railing and watch as Chelsea plummets to the ground. She falls like a ship's anchor and a dull thud is the last sound she makes on Earth.

Josh immediately calls fire and paramedics. Doctor is in shock. He slumps onto the floor of his balcony. Everything is spinning. After a few minutes, he manages to get on his hands and knees. Before he can stand up, he vomits violently.

Josh: "Doctor, are you alright?" Josh calls for a second paramedic to come and attend Doctor Campbell. Josh rushes out of the penthouse down to the beach below. He gets there at the same time that fire and paramedics get there. A crowd has already gathered. There were a few people on the beach that afternoon who witnessed the fall. Several people were screaming and crying at the gruesome sight. Josh's detectives cordon off the area and get to work on the scene. A couple of his detectives go up to the penthouse and get a statement from Doctor Campbell.

After Josh knows the scene is secure, he hurries over to the mayor's office and searches her desk and personal belongings. He asks her assistant if she has the code for the safe. She does and gives it to Josh. He finds the safe and opens it. Inside, he finds a bag of roofies and Maria's cell phone. He turns on the phone and finds there is no security code. He looks through the pictures and comes across a video of Chelsea and Doctor having sex on her desk. Just like she said. Josh goes back to his office, calls Meredith Higgins, and fills her in on his final conversation with Chelsea.

The next morning Josh goes to his office and thinks, *"What a fucking nightmare!"* He sits with his investigative team. They go over everything they discovered when he gets a call from the DA saying Shovelhead Dempsey wants to meet. He has some new evidence he wants to share.

Josh to his team: "We have Shovelhead for the murder of Randi Reynolds and Preston Rodrigues solid. Mayor Higgins confessed to killing Lauren Scavone and conspiracy to murder Randi Reynolds. The only one who slipped through was Lennie "Highside" Manthe. Maybe this new evidence Dempsey has will answer some questions."

That same afternoon Josh meets with the DA and Shovelhead's defense attorney. Josh is presented with some new evidence from Dempsey. It seems that Shovelhead not only wants to avoid the death penalty, but he also wants to serve his time in the Federal Penitentiary instead of the harsher state prison environment. Dempsey's attorney explains that during the initial meeting between Shovelhead and Highside at The Barrel Tavern. Shovelhead had cut a small hole in his biker vest. Inside he had affixed his cell phone's video camera. It seems Shovelhead had learned a few things while inside the penitentiary. Make sure you have something left to deal with, and he did. Shovelhead videotaped the whole murder conspiracy that Highside hired him for. It's absolute concrete proof against Highside Manthe for conspiracy to commit murder.

Once they all viewed the tape, the DA said he was agreeable to the terms as long as Shovelhead would appear as a witness against Lennie "Highside" Manthe. The DA stepped out and called the US Attorney to arrange that Shovelhead's sentence could be served in the Federal Pen. On the ride back from the DA's office, Josh gets a call from Sergeant Miller.

Joyce: "Lieutenant, we need you to come by the canal road, right at the Gulf Shores city limits. Some fishermen discovered a car in the water. We are pulling it out now. We've run the plate, and it comes back to a Maria Fletcher."

Josh: "That's the Mayor's assistant who has been missing. I'll be there in fifteen minutes."

As Josh gets to the scene, the car is pulled from the water and Maria's body is still inside. The Medical Examiner shows up.

Josh: "Hi Terri. Please check her blood for roofies. Let me know if her death is from drowning."

Terri O'Leary: "No problem, Josh."

Subsequently, Shovelhead Dempsey will never see the light of day with his confession of two murders. Highside Manthe will be charged with conspiracy to murder Randi Reynolds. The added videotape sealed his fate. Chances are he will never get out either.

Josh heads back to his office and assumes his heavy responsibilities of notifying Lauren and Randi's families of the outcome of the case. They are shocked at the reason for their daughters' murders but also thankful they don't have to sit through a trial.

As Josh gets in his car, he thinks *This has been the summer from Hell. Now it's time for me to take a few days off and try to get my head clear. I need some strategic forgetting to erase this summer from my mind.*

The pain and agony of the summer weighs him down like a steel trench coat. The only thing he will never forget is Randi.

On Josh's third day off, it was a beautiful coastal day. After a few light chores and dinner, Josh drives to the beach. He walks out near the water and sits down. A lonely shadow alone with his thoughts. Trying to make sense of how to take chaos out of his life. As he sits there with the sun setting off to the west, the sound of the gulf waves is hypnotic in their rhythmic movement, almost lulling Josh into a trance. A small boy about six years old is running nearby in the shallow water. He runs up to Josh.

Boy: "Hey Mister, what are you doing? Did you see any sharks?"

Josh: "Mostly land sharks."

Boy: "I've never seen a land shark, what is it?"

Josh: "Well son, I hope you never do."

Boy: "Are you here by yourself?"

Josh: "I'm waiting for someone."

Boy: "Who?"

Josh: "My girl."

The little boy looks up and down the beach. It's very sparse at this time of day.

Boy: "I don't see anyone, mister. Where is she?"

Josh: "She's there."

Boy: "Where?"

Josh raises his hand and points out to the Gulf of Mexico.

Josh: "She's there watching for me."

Again, the little boy looks and says, "Where?"

As a tear rolls down Josh's cheek, he whispers, "Somewhere.... Beyond the Sea!"

Made in United States
North Haven, CT
06 September 2024

56990198R00212